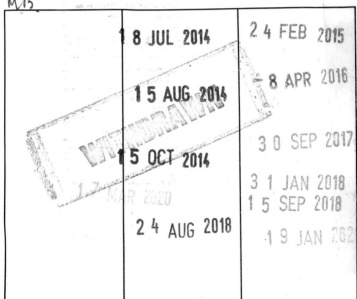
Glasgow Life and its service brands, including Glasgow Libraries, (found at www.glasgowlife.org.uk) are operating names for Culture and Sport Glasgow

Published in Great Britain 2014
by Mills & Boon, an imprint of Harlequin (UK) Limited,
Eton House, 18-24 Paradise Road, Richmond, Surrey, TW9 1SR

WEDDING WISHES © 2014 Harlequin Books S.A.

A Wedding at Leopard Tree Lodge, Runaway Bride Returns! and Rodeo Bride were first published in Great Britain by Harlequin (UK) Limited.

A Wedding at Leopard Tree Lodge © 2010 Liz Fielding
Runaway Bride Returns! © 2009 Christie Ridgway
Rodeo Bride © 2009 Myrna Topol

ISBN: 978-0-263-91190-9
eBook ISBN: 978-1-472 -04485-3

05-0614

Harlequin (UK) Limited's policy is to use papers that are natural, renewable and recyclable products and made from wood grown in sustainable forests. The logging and manufacturing processes conform to the legal environmental regulations of the country of origin.

Printed and bound in Spain
by Blackprint CPI, Barcelona

A WEDDING AT LEOPARD TREE LODGE

BY
LIZ FIELDING

CHAPTER ONE

Destination weddings offer up a host of opportunities for
a ceremony with a difference…
— *The Perfect Wedding* by Serafina March

'WHERE?'

Josie Fowler wasn't sure which stunned her most. The
location of the wedding which, despite endless media speculation, had been the best kept secret of the year, or the fact that
Marji Hayes, editor of *Celebrity* magazine, was sharing it with
her.

'Botswana,' Marji repeated, practically whispering, as if
afraid that her line might be bugged. If it was, whispering
wouldn't help. 'I called Sylvie. I had hoped…' Her voice trailed
off.

'Yes?' Josie prompted as she used one finger to tap
'Botswana' into the search engine of her computer. Silly
question. She knew exactly what Marji had hoped. That the
aristocratic Sylvie Duchamps Smith would rush to pick up the
pieces of the most talked about wedding of the year. Sylvie,
however, was too busy enjoying her new baby daughter to pull
Marji's wedding irons out of the fire.

'I realise that she's still officially on maternity leave, but I
had hoped that for something this big…'

Josie waited, well aware that not even a royal wedding

would have tempted Sylvie away from her new husband, her new baby. Trying to contain a frisson of excitement as she realised what this call actually meant.

'When I called, she explained that she's made you her partner. That weddings are now solely your responsibility.' She couldn't quite keep the disbelief out of her voice.

Marji was not alone in that. There had been an absolute forest of raised eyebrows in the business when Sylvie had employed a girl she'd found working in a hotel scullery as her assistant.

They'd got over it. After all, she was just a gofer. Someone to run around, do the dirty work. And she'd proved herself, become accepted as a capable coordinator, someone who could be relied on, who didn't flap in a crisis. A couple of bigger events organisers had even tried to tempt her away from Sylvie with more money, a fancy title.

But clearly the idea of her delivering a design from start to finish was going to take some swallowing.

She'd warned Sylvie how it would be and she'd been right. She'd been a partner for three months now and while they had plenty of work to keep them busy, all of it pre-dated her partnership.

'You're very young for such responsibility, Josie,' Marji suggested, with just enough suggestion of laughter to let her know that she wasn't supposed to take offence. 'So very … eccentric in your appearance.'

She didn't deny it. She was twenty-five. Young in years to be a partner in an events company but as old as the hills in other ways. And if her clothes, the purple streaks in her lion's mane hair, were not conventional, they were as much a part of her image as Sylvie's classic suits and pearls.

'Sylvie was nineteen when she launched SDS Events,' she reminded Marji. Alone, with no money, nowhere to live. All she'd known was how to throw a damn good party.

Despite their very different backgrounds, they'd had that

nothingness in common and Sylvie had given her a chance when most people would have taken one look and taken a step back. Two steps if they'd known what Sylvie knew about her.

But they had worked well together. Sylvie had wooed clients with her aristocratic background, her elegance, while she was the tough working class girl who knew how to get things done on the ground. An asset who could cope with difficult locations, drunken guests—and staff; capable of stopping a potential fight with a look. And in the process she'd absorbed Sylvie's sense of style almost by osmosis. On the outside she might still look like the girl Sylvie had, against all the odds, given a chance. But she'd grabbed that opportunity with all her heart, studied design, business, marketing, and on the inside she was a different woman.

'And if I changed my appearance no one would recognise me,' she added, and earned herself another of those patronising little laughs.

'Well, yes.' Then, 'Of course there's no design involved in this job. All that was done weeks ago and at this late stage…'

In other words it was a skivvy job and no one with a 'name' was prepared to take it on. The wretched woman couldn't have tried any harder to make her feel like the scrapings at the bottom of the barrel and Josie had to fight the urge to tell her to take her wedding and stick it.

Catching her lower lip between her teeth, she took a deep breath; she still had quite a way to go to attain Sylvie's style and grace, but this was too important to mess up.

With this wedding under her belt—even in the skivvy role—she could paint herself purple to match her hair and clients would still be scrambling to book her to plan their weddings.

Not as a stand-in for Sylvie, but for herself.

But she'd had enough with the I-really-wish-I-didn't-have-to-do-this delaying tactics.

'Can we get on, Marji? I have a client appointment in ten minutes,' she said and Emma, her newly appointed assistant, who was busy filling in details on one of the event plans that lined the walls of her small office, glanced up in surprise, as well she might since her diary was empty.

'Of course.' Then, 'I'm sure I don't have to impress upon you the need for the utmost confidentiality,' she said, making it absolutely clear in her lemon-sucking voice that she did.

Not true.

Josie had seen the build-up to the wedding of Tal Newman, one of the world's most highly paid footballers, to Crystal Blaize. The ferocious bidding war against all-comers had cost *Celebrity* a fortune—money that the couple were using to set up a charitable trust—and the magazine was milking it for all it was worth. Hyping up the secrecy of the location was all part of that. It also helped keep rival publications from planting someone on the inside to deliver the skinny on who behaved badly and grab illicit photos so that they could run spoilers.

If she let slip the location, SDS might as well shut up shop.

'My lips are sealed,' she said. 'I'm not even sure where Botswana is,' she lied. According to the screen in front of her, it was a 'tranquil' and 'peaceful' landlocked country in southern Africa.

Marji clucked at her ignorance. 'It's a very now destination, Josie.'

'Is it? That information seems to have passed me by.' But then she didn't spend her life obsessing over the latest fads of celebrities.

'And Crystal is such an animal-lover.'

Animals? In Africa?

'So that would be… Elephants? Lions?' No, smaller… 'Monkeys?'

'All of those, of course. But the real stars will be the leopards.'

Even with his underdeveloped human sense of smell, Gideon McGrath knew Leopard Tree Lodge was close long before the four-by-four pulled into the compound. There was a sweet, fresh green scent from the grass that reached out across the sparse bush that drew the animals from across the Kalahari, especially now as they neared the end of the dry season.

Once his pace had quickened too, his heart beating with excitement as he came to the riverbank that he had claimed as his own.

The driver who'd picked him up from the airstrip pulled into the shaded yard and he sat for a moment, gathering himself for the effort of moving.

'*Dumela, Rra!* It is good to see you!'

'Francis!'

He clasped the hand of the man who emerged from the shadows to greet him with a broad smile of welcome.

'It has been a very long time, *Rra*, but we always hoped you'd come…' His smile quickly became concern. 'You are hurt?'

'It's nothing,' he said, catching his breath as he climbed down. 'I'm a bit stiff, that's all. Too many days travelling. How is your family?' he asked, not wanting to think about the tight, agonising pain in his lower back. Or its cause.

'They are good. If you have time, they will be pleased to see you.'

'I have some books for your children,' Gideon said, turning to take his bag from the back seat. He spent half his life on the move and travelled light but, as he tried to lift it, it felt like lead.

'Leopards?' Josie repeated. 'Aren't they incredibly dangerous?'

'Oh, these are just cubs. A local man has raised a couple of orphans and he's bringing them along on the day. All you'll have to do is tie ribbons around their necks.'

'Oh, well, that's all right then.' Maybe. She had a cat and even when Cleo was a kitten her claws were needle-sharp…

'The wedding is going to be held at Leopard Tree Lodge, you see?' Marji told her. 'It's a fabulous game-viewing lodge.

Utter luxury in the wilderness. To be honest, I totally envy you the opportunity to spend time there.'

'Well, golly,' she said, as if she, too, couldn't believe her luck.

'You won't even have to leave your private deck to view the big game. None of that racketing about in a four-wheel drive getting covered in dust. You can simply sit in your own private plunge pool and watch elephants cavorting below you in an oxbow lake while you sip a glass of chilled bubbly.'

'Well, that's a relief,' Josie replied wryly, recognising a quote from a tourist brochure when she heard one. Marji might believe that she was offering her a luxury, all expenses paid holiday; she knew that once on site she wouldn't have a minute to spare to draw breath, let alone dally in a plunge pool admiring the view.

Relaxation in the run-up to a wedding was the sole privilege of the bride and good luck to her. Although, with half a dozen issues of *Celebrity* to fill with pictures, even she wasn't going to have a lot of down time before, or during, the big day.

For the person charged with the responsibility of ensuring that everything ran smoothly it was going to be a very hard day at the office, although in this instance it wouldn't be her own calm, ordered space, where everything she needed was no more than a phone call away.

As she knew from experience, even the best organised weddings had the potential for last minute disasters and in the wilds of Botswana there would be none of the backup services she was usually able to call on in an emergency.

And it would take more than a look to stop a leopard disturbing the party. Even a baby leopard.

'There's nothing like being covered in dust to put a crimp in your day,' she added as, with the 'where' dealt with, she confronted a rather more pressing problem.

Unless the word 'wilderness' was simply travel brochure

hyperbole—and the reference to elephants sloshing about in the river at her feet suggested otherwise—there wasn't going to be an international airport handy.

'How is everyone going to get there?'

'We've booked an air charter company to handle all the local transport,' Marji assured her. 'You don't have to worry about that—'

'I worry about everything, Marji.' Including the proximity of elephants. And the damage potential of a pair of overexcited leopard cubs. 'It's why SDS weddings run so smoothly.'

'Well, quite. If Sylvie's company wasn't so highly thought of we wouldn't be having this conversation.' She paused, her train of thought disrupted. 'Where was I?'

'Transport?' Josie prompted, doing her best to keep a lid on her rising irritation.

'Oh, yes. Serafina was due to fly out first thing tomorrow. You heard what happened?'

The official version was that Serafina March, society wedding 'designer'—nothing as common as 'planner' for her—and self-proclaimed 'wedding queen' who had been given the awesome responsibility of planning this event, had been struck down by a virus.

Insider gossip had it that Crystal had thrown a strop, declaring that she'd rather get married in a sack at the local register office than put up with another moment with 'that snooty cow' looking down her nose at her.

Having been looked down on by Serafina herself on more than one occasion, Josie knew exactly how she felt.

'How is Serafina?'

'Recovering. It's just a shame she can't be there, especially when she's put her heart and soul into this wedding.' Then, having got that off her chest, she proceeded briskly, 'The bride's party will be flying out the following day but Tal has a number of official engagements in the capital so he and Crystal won't arrive until the next evening. Plenty of time for you to run through everything before they arrive so that you can iron out any last minute snags.'

'Since there's so little to do, maybe I could leave it until the day after tomorrow?' Josie suggested, unable to help herself.

'Better safe than sorry. This is going to be a fairly intimate wedding. Leopard Tree Lodge is a small and exclusive safari camp, however, so we've chartered a river boat to accommodate the overflow.'

Wilderness, water and wild animals—three things guaranteed to send shivers down the spine of the average event planner. And there was also the word 'camp'—not exactly reassuring.

No matter how 'luxurious' the brochure declared it to be, a tent was still a tent.

When she didn't rush to exclaim with excitement, gush at the honour being bestowed on her, Marji said, 'All the hard work has been done, Josie.'

All the interesting work.

The planning. The design. Choosing food, music, clothes, colour scheme, flowers. The shopping trips with a bride whose credit never ran out.

'You just need me to ensure that everything runs smoothly,' Josie said.

'Uh-oh!' Emma's eyebrows hit her hairline as she picked up on the edge she hadn't been able to keep out of her voice, but being patronised by Marji Hayes really was more than flesh and blood could stand.

'Absolutely. Serafina's organised everything down to the last detail.' The wretched woman had a skin as thick as a rhinoceros. It would take more than an 'edge'; it would take a damn great axe to make an impression. 'I just need someone to ensure her design is carried through. Check that all her wonderful detail is in place so that our photographers can get great shots for the series of features we have planned. Exactly what you'd do for Sylvie.'

'And ensure that the bride and groom have their perfect day?' she offered, unable to stop herself from reminding Marji that this was about more than a skirmish in her circulation war with the growing number of lifestyle magazines on the market.

'What? Oh, yes,' she said dismissively. Then, 'We're running out of time on this, Josie. I'll email the flight details and courier the files over to your office. You can read them on the plane.'

It was the opportunity of a lifetime but she'd been insulted, subtly and not so subtly, so many times in the last ten minutes that she refused to do what was expected and simply roll over.

'To be honest,' she said, her voice growing softer as her fingers did to her hair what she wanted to do to Marji, 'with so little to do, I don't understand why you need me at all. Surely one of your own staff could handle it?' She didn't wait for an answer but added, 'Better still, why don't you go yourself? Once you've dealt with all those little details you'll be able to chill out in that plunge pool.'

With luck, a leopard would mistake her for lunch.

'Oh, don't tempt me,' Marji replied with one of her trilling little laughs that never failed to set Josie's teeth on edge. 'I'd give my eye teeth to go, but I have a magazine to run. Besides, I believe these things are best left to the professionals.'

Professionals who didn't patronise the bride...

'I've promised Crystal the wedding of her dreams, Josie.'

Her dreams? Maybe.

It had no doubt started out that way, but Josie wondered how Crystal was feeling about it now. Giddy with excitement, thrilled to be marrying the man she loved in the biggest, most lavish ceremony she, or rather Serafina March, could imagine?

Or was she frazzled with nerves and desperately wishing she and Tal had run away to Las Vegas to say their vows in private?

Most brides went through that at some point in the run-up to their wedding, usually when they were driven to distraction by family interference. Few of them had to cope with the additional strain of a media circus on their back.

'We can't let her down,' Marji persisted, anxious as she sensed her lack of enthusiasm. 'To be honest, she's somewhat fragile. Last minute nerves. I don't have to tell you how important this is and I believe that Crystal would be comfortable with you.'

Oh, right. Now they were both being patronised. Tarred with the same 'not one of us' brush, and for a moment she was tempted to tell Marji exactly what she could do with her wedding and to hell with the consequences.

Instead, she said, 'You'll run a piece in the next issue of the magazine mentioning that I'm taking over?'

'It's Serafina's design,' she protested.

'Of course. Let's hope she's fit enough to travel tomorrow—'

'But we will be happy to add our thanks to you for stepping in at the last moment, Josie,' she added hurriedly.

It was a non-committal promise at best and she recognised as much, but everyone would know, which was all that mattered. And in the end this wasn't about her, or Marji, or even the wedding queen herself.

If Sylvie had taught her anything, it was that no bride, especially a bride whose wedding was going to be featured in full colour for all the world to see, should be left without someone who was totally, one hundred per cent, there for her on the big day. Josie let out a long, slow breath.

'Courier the files to my office, Marji. I'll email you a contract.'

Her hand was shaking as she replaced the receiver and looked up. 'Email a standard contract to Marji Hayes at *Celebrity*, Emma.'

'*Celebrity!*'

'Standard hourly rate, with a minimum of sixty hours, plus travel time,' she continued, with every outward appearance of calm. 'All expenses to their account. We've picked up the Tal Newman/Crystal Blaize wedding.'

As Emma tossed notebook and pen in the air, whooping with excitement, her irritation at Marji's attitude quite suddenly melted away.

'Where?' she demanded. 'Where is it?'

'I could tell you,' she replied, a broad grin spreading across her face. 'But then I'd have to kill you.'

'*Dumela, Rra. O tsogile?*'

'*Dumela*, Francis. *Ke tsogile.*'

Gideon McGrath replied to the greeting on automatic. He'd risen. Whether he'd risen well was another matter.

This visit to Leopard Tree Lodge had taken him well out of his way, a day and night stolen from a packed schedule that had already taken him to a Red Sea diving resort, then on down the Gulf to check on the progress of the new dhow he'd commissioned for coastal cruising from the traditional boat-builders in Ramal Hamrah.

While he was there, he'd joined one of the desert safaris he'd set up in partnership with Sheikh Zahir, spending the night with travellers who wanted a true desert experience rather than the belly-dancer-and-dune-surfing breaks on offer elsewhere.

He was usually renewed by the experience but when he'd woken on a cold desert morning, faced with yet another airport, the endless security checks and long waits, he'd wondered why anyone would do this for pleasure.

For a man whose life was totally invested in the travel business, who'd made a fortune from selling excitement, ad-venture, the dream of Shangri-La to people who wanted the real thing, it was a bad feeling.

A bad feeling that had seemed to settle low in his back with a non-specific ache that he couldn't seem to shake off. One that had been creeping up on him almost unnoticed for the best part of a year.

Ever since he'd decided to sell Leopard Tree Lodge.

Connie, his doctor, having X-rayed him up hill and down dale, had ruled out any physical reason.

'What's bothering you, Gideon?' she asked when he returned for the results.

'Nothing,' he lied. 'I'm on top of the world.'

It was true. He'd just closed the deal on a ranch in Patagonia that was going to be his next big venture. She shook her head as he told her about it, offered her a holiday riding with the gauchos.

'You're the one who needs a holiday, Gideon. You're running on empty.'

Empty?

'You need to slow down. Get a life.'

'I've got all the life I can handle. Just fix me up with another of those muscle relaxing injections for now,' he said. 'I've got a plane to catch.'

She sighed. 'It's a temporary measure, Gideon. Sooner or later you're going to have to stop running and face whatever is causing this or your back will make the decision for you. At least take a break.'

'I've got it sorted.'

Maybe a night spent wrapped in a cloak on the desert sand hadn't been his best idea, he'd decided as he'd set out for the airport and the pain had returned with a vengeance. Now, after half a dozen meetings and four more flights, the light aircraft had touched down on the dirt airstrip he'd carved out of the bush with such a light heart just over ten years ago.

It had been a struggle to climb out of the aircraft, almost as if his body was refusing to do what his brain was telling it.

His mistake had been to try.

The minute he'd realised he was in trouble, he should have told the pilot to fly him straight back to Gabarone, where a doctor who didn't know him would have patched him up without question so that he could fly on to South America.

Stupidly, he'd believed a handful of painkillers, a hot shower and a night in a good bed would sort him out. Now he was at the mercy of the medic he retained for his staff and guests and who, having conferred with his own doctor in London, had resolutely refused to give him the get-out-of-jail-free injection.

All he'd got was a load of New Age claptrap about his body demanding that he become still, that he needed to relax so that it could heal itself. That it would let him know when it was ready to move on.

With no estimate of how long that might be.

Connie had put it rather more bluntly with her '…stop running'.

Well, that was why he was here. To stop running. He'd had offers for the Lodge in the past—offers that his board had urged him to take so that they could invest in newer, growing markets. He'd resisted the pressure. It had been his first capital investment. A symbol. An everlasting ache…

'Are there any messages, Francis?' he asked.

'Just one, *Rra*.' He set down the breakfast tray on the low table beside him, took a folded sheet of paper from his pocket and, with his left hand supporting his right wrist, he offered it to him with traditional politeness. 'It is a reply from your office.' Before he could read it, he said, 'It says that Mr Matt Benson has flown to Argentina in your place so you have no need to worry. Just do exactly what the doctor has told you and rest.' He beamed happily. 'It says that you must take as long as you need.'

Gideon bit back an expletive. Francis didn't understand. No one understood.

Matt was a good man but he hadn't spent every minute of the last fifteen years building a global empire out of the untapped market for challenging, high risk adventure holidays for the active and daring of all ages.

Developing small, exclusive retreats off the beaten track that offered privacy, luxury, the unusual for those who could afford to pay for it.

Matt, like all his staff, was keen, dedicated, but at the end of the day he went home to his real life. His wife. His children. His dog.

There was nothing for him to go home for.

For him, this company, the empire he'd built from the ruins of the failing family business, was all he had. It was his life.

'Can I get you anything else, *Rra?*'

'Out of here?' he said as he followed the path of a small aircraft that was banking over the river, watched it turn and head south. It had been a mistake to come here and he wanted to be on board that plane. Moving.

The thought intensified the pain in his lower back.

After a second night, fuming at the inactivity, he'd swallowed enough painkillers to get him to the shower, determined to leave even if he had to crawl on his hands and knees to Reception and summon the local air taxi to pick him up.

He'd made it as far as the steps down to the tree bridge. Francis, arriving with an early morning tray, had found him hanging onto the guard rail, on his feet but unable to move up or down.

Given the choice of being taken by helicopter to the local hospital for bed rest, or remaining in the comfort and shade at Leopard Tree Lodge where he was at least notionally in control, had been a no-brainer.

Maybe the quack was right. He had been pushing it very hard for the last couple of years. He could spare a couple of days.

'Is that someone arriving or leaving?' he asked.

'Arriving,' Francis said, clearly relieved to change the subject. 'It is the wedding lady. She will be your neighbour. She is from London, too, *Rra*. Maybe you will know her?'

'Maybe,' he agreed. Francis came from a very small town where he knew everyone and Gideon had long ago learned that it was pointless trying to explain how many people lived in London. Then, 'Wedding lady?' He frowned. 'What wedding?'

'It is a great secret but Mr Tal Newman, the world's greatest footballer, is marrying his beautiful girlfriend, Miss Crystal Blaize, here at Leopard Tree Lodge, *Rra*. Many famous people are coming. The pictures are going to be in a magazine.'

As shock overcame inertia and he peeled himself off the

lounger, pain scythed through him, taking his breath away. Francis made an anxious move to help him but he waved him away as he fell back. That was a mistake too, but whether the word that finally escaped him as he collapsed against the backrest was in response to the pain or a comment on whoever had permitted this travesty of everything his company stood for was a moot point.

'Shall I pour your tea, *Rra?*' Francis asked anxiously.

'I wanted coffee,' he snapped.

'The doctor said that you must not have…'

'I know what he said!'

No caffeine, no stress.

Pity he wasn't here right now.

He encouraged his staff to think laterally when it came to promoting his resorts but the Lodge was supposed to be a haven of peace and tranquillity for those who could afford to enjoy the wilderness experience in comfort.

The very last thing his guests would expect, or want, was the jamboree of a celebrity wedding scaring away the wildlife.

The last thing he wanted. Not here…

If that damn quack could see just how much stress even the thought of a wedding was causing him he'd ban that too, but having prescribed total rest and restricted his diet to the bland and boring he'd retired to the safety of Maun.

'Tell David that I want to see him.'

'Yes, *Rra.*'

'And see if you can find me a newspaper.' He was going out of his mind with boredom.

'The latest edition of the *Mmegi* should have arrived on the plane. I will go and fetch it for you.'

He'd been hoping for an abandoned copy of the *Financial Times* brought by a visitor, but that had probably been banned too and while it was possible that by this evening he would be desperate enough for anything, he hadn't got to that point yet.

'There's no hurry.'

CHAPTER TWO

Luxurious surroundings will add to the bride and groom's enjoyment of their special day.
—*The Perfect Wedding* by Serafina March

JOSIE, despite her many misgivings, was impressed.

Leopard Tree Lodge had been all but invisible from the air as the small aircraft had circled over the river, skimming the trees to announce their arrival.

And the dirt runway on which they'd landed, leaving a plume of dust behind them, hadn't exactly inspired confidence either. By the time they'd taxied to a halt, however, a muscular four-wheel drive was waiting to pick up both her and the cartons of wedding paraphernalia she'd brought with her. 'Just a few extras…' Marji had assured her. All the linens and paper goods had been sent on by Serafina before she had been taken ill.

The manager was waiting to greet her at the impressive main building. Circular, thatched, open-sided, it contained a lounge with a central fireplace that overlooked the river on one side. On the other, a lavish buffet where guests—kitted uniformly in safari gear and hung with cameras—helped themselves to breakfast that they carried out onto a shady, flower-decked terrace set above a swimming pool.

'David Kebalakile, Miss Fowler. Welcome to Leopard Tree Lodge. I hope you had a good journey.'

'Yes, thank you, Mr Kebalakile.'

It had felt endless, and she was exhausted, but she'd arrived in one piece. In her book that was as good as twenty-four hours and three planes, the last with only four seats and one engine, was going to get.

'David, please. Let's get these boxes into the office,' he said, summoning a couple of staff members to deal with all the excess baggage that Marji had dumped on her, 'and then I'll show you to your tree house.'

Tree house?

Was that better than a tent? Or worse?

If you fell out of a tent at least you were at ground level, she thought, trying not to look down as she followed him across a sturdy timber walkway that wound through the trees a good ten feet from the ground.

Worse…

'We've never held a wedding at the Lodge before,' he said, 'so this is a very special new venture for us. And we're all very excited at the prospect of meeting Tal Newman. We love our football in Botswana.'

Oh, terrific.

This wasn't the slick and well practised routine for the staff that it would have been in most places and, as if that wasn't bad enough, it was the groom, rather than the bride, who was going to be the centre of attention.

The fact that the colour scheme for the wedding had been taken from the orange and pale blue strip of his football club should have warned her.

Presumably Crystal was used to it, but this was her big day and Josie vowed she'd be the star of this particular show even if it killed her.

'Here we are,' David said, stopping at a set of steps that led to a deck built among the tree tops, inviting her to go ahead of him.

Wow.

Double wow.

The deck was perched high above the promised oxbow lake but the only thing her substantial tree house—with its thatched roof and wide double doors—had in common with the tent she'd been dreading were canvas sidings which, as David enthusiastically demonstrated, could be looped up so that you could lie in the huge, romantically gauze-draped four-poster bed and watch the sun rising. If you were into that sort of thing.

'Early mornings and evenings are the best times to watch the animals,' he said. 'They come to drink then, although there's usually something to see whatever time of day or night it is.' He crossed the deck and looked down. 'There are still a few elephants, a family of warthogs.'

He turned, clearly expecting her to join him and exclaim with delight.

'How lovely,' she said, doing her best to be enthusiastic when all she really wanted to look at was the plumbing.

'There are always birds. They are…' He stopped. 'I'm sorry. You've had a long journey and you must be very tired.'

It seemed that she was going to have to work on that one.

'I'll be fine when I've had a wake-up shower,' she assured him. 'Something to eat.'

'Of course. I do hope you will find time to go out in a canoe, though. Or on one of our guided bush walks?' He just couldn't keep his enthusiasm in check.

'I hope so, too,' she said politely. Not.

She was a city girl. Dressing up in a silly hat and a jacket with every spare inch covered with pockets to go toddling off into the bush, where goodness knew what creepy-crawlies were lurking held absolutely no appeal.

'Right, well, breakfast is being served in the dining area at the moment, or I can have something brought to you on a tray if you prefer? Our visitors usually choose to relax, soak up the peace, after such a long journey.'

'A tray would be perfect, thank you.'

The peace would have to wait. She needed to take a close look at the facilities, see how they measured up to the plans in the file and check that everything on Serafina's very long list of linens and accessories of every kind had arrived safely. But not before she'd sluiced twenty-four hours of travel out of her hair.

'Just coffee and toast,' she said, 'and then, if you could spare me some time, I'd like to take a look around. Familiarise myself with the layout.'

'Of course. I'm at your command. Come to the desk when you're ready and if I'm not in my office someone will find me. In the meantime, just ring if you need anything.'

The minute he was gone, she took a closer look at her surroundings.

So far, they'd done more than live up to Marji's billing. The bed was a huge wooden-framed super king with two individual mattresses, presumably for comfort in the heat. It still left plenty of room for a sofa, coffee tables and the desk on which she laid her briefcase beside a folder that no doubt contained all the details of what was on offer.

Those bush walks and canoe trips.

No, thanks.

Outside, there was the promised plunge pool with a couple of sturdy wooden deck loungers and a small thatched gazebo shading a day bed big enough for two. Somewhere to lie down when the excitement got too much? Or maybe make your own excitement when the peace needed shaking up—that was if you had someone to get excited with.

The final touch was a second shower that was open to the sky.

'Oh, very "you Tarzan, me Jane",' she muttered.

To the front there were a couple of director's chairs where you could sit and gaze across the oxbow lagoon where the family of elephants had the same idea about taking a shower.

All she needed now was the bubbly, she thought, smiling as a very small elephant rolled in the mud, while the adults used their trunks to fling water over their backs. Kids. They were all the same…

Looking around, she could see why *Celebrity* was so keen. People were crazy about animals and the photographs were going to be amazing. But, while the place had 'honeymoon' stamped all over it, she wasn't so sure about the wedding.

It had required three aircraft to get her here and the possibilities for disaster were legion.

She shook her head, stretched out cramped limbs in the early morning sunshine. She'd worry about that when it happened and, after one last look around, took herself inside to shower away the effects of the endless journey, choosing the exquisitely fitted bathroom over the temptations of the louche outdoor shower.

She was here to work, not play.

Ten minutes later, having pampered herself with the delicious toiletries that matched the 'luxury' label, she wrapped herself in a snowy bathrobe and went in search of a hairdryer.

Searching through cupboards and drawers, all she found was a small torch. Not much use. But, while she had been in the bathroom, her breakfast tray had arrived and she gave up the search in favour of a caffeine fix. Not that David had taken her 'just coffee and toast' seriously.

In an effort to impress, or maybe understanding what she needed better than she did herself, he had added freshly squeezed orange juice, a dish of sliced fresh fruit, most of which she didn't recognise, and a blueberry muffin, still warm from the oven.

She carried the tray out onto the deck, drank the juice, buttered a piece of toast, then poured a cup of coffee and stood it on the rail while she ruffled her fingers through her hair, enjoying the rare pleasure of drying it in the sun.

It was her short punk hairstyle as much as her background that had so scandalised people like Marji Hayes when Sylvie had first given her a job.

Young, unsure of herself, she'd used her hair, the eighteen-hole Doc Martens, scary make-up and nose stud as armour. A 'don't mess with me' message when she was faced with the kind of hotels and wedding locations where she'd normally be only allowed in the back door.

As she'd gained confidence and people had got to know her, she'd learned that a smile got her further than a scowl, but by then the look had become part of her image. As Sylvie had pointed out, it was original. People knew her and if she'd switched to something more conventional she'd have had to start all over again.

Admittedly the hair was a little longer these days, an expensively maintained mane rather than sharp spikes, the nose stud a tiny amethyst, and her safety pin earrings bore the name Zandra Rhodes, who was to punk style what Coco Chanel had been to business chic. And her make-up, while still individual, still her, was no longer applied in a manner to scare the horses.

But while she could manage with a brush and some gel to kill the natural curl and hold up her hair, the bride, bridesmaids and any number of celebrities, male and female, would be up the oxbow lagoon without a paddle unless they had the full complement of driers, straighteners and every other gadget dear to the crimper's heart.

Something to check with David, because if it wasn't just an oversight in her room they'd have to be flown in and she fetched her laptop from her briefcase and added it to her 'to do' list.

She'd barely started before she got a 'battery low' warning.

Her search for a point into which she could plug it to recharge proved equally fruitless and that sent her in search of a telephone so that she could ring the desk and enquire how on earth she was supposed to work without an electrical connection.

But, while David had urged her to 'ring', she couldn't find a telephone either. And, ominously, when she took out her mobile to try that, there was no signal.

Which was when she took a closer look at her room and finally got it. Fooled by the efficient plumbing and hot water, she had assumed that the fat white candles sitting in glass holders were all part of the romance of the wilderness. On closer inspection, she realised that they were the only light source and that the torch might prove very useful after all.

Wilderness. Animals. Peace. Silence. Back to nature.

This was hubris, she thought.

She had taken considerable pleasure in the fact that Marji Hayes had, through gritted teeth, been forced to come to her for help.

This was her punishment.

There had been no warning about the lack of these basic facilities in the planning notes and she had no doubt that Marji was equally in the dark, but she wasn't about to gloat about the great Serafina March having overlooked something so basic. She, after all, was the poor sap who'd have to deal with it and, digging out the pre-computer age backup—a notebook and pen—she settled herself in the sun and began to make a list of problems.

Candlelight was the very least of them. Communication was going to be her biggest nightmare, she decided as she reached for the second slice of toast—there was nothing like anxiety to induce an attack of the munchies. As she groped for it there was a swish, a shriek and, before she could react, the plate had crashed to the deck.

She responded with the kind of girly shriek that she'd have mocked in anyone else before she saw the small black-faced monkey swing onto the branch above her.

'Damn cheek!' she declared as it sat there stuffing pieces of toast into its mouth. Then, as her heart returned to something like its normal rate, she reached for a sustaining swig of coffee. Which was when she discovered that it wasn't just the monkey who had designs on her breakfast.

'Is that coffee you're drinking?'

Letting out the second startled expletive in as many minutes as she spilled hot coffee on her foot, she spun to her left, where the neighbouring tree house was half hidden in the thickly cloaked branches.

'It was,' she muttered, mopping her foot with the edge of her robe.

'Sorry. I didn't mean to startle you.'

The man's voice was low, gravelly and rippled over her skin like a draught, setting up goose bumps.

'Who are you?' she demanded, peering through the leaves. 'Where are you?'

'Lower.'

She'd been peering across the gap between them at head height, expecting to see him leaning against the rail, looking out across the water to the reed-filled river beyond, doing his David Attenborough thing.

Dropping her gaze, she could just make out the body belonging to the voice stretched out on one of those low deck loungers.

She could only see tantalising bits of him. A long, sinewy bare foot, the edge of khaki shorts where they lay against a powerful thigh, thick dark hair, long enough to be stirred by a breeze coming off the river. And then, as the leaves stirred, parted for a moment, a pair of eyes that were focused on her so intently that for a moment she was thrown on the defensive. Ambushed by the fear waiting just beneath the surface to catch her off guard. The dread that one day someone would see through the carefully constructed shell of punk chic and recognise her for what she really was.

Not just a skivvy masquerading as a wedding planner but someone no one would let inside their fancy hotel, anywhere near their wedding, if they could see inside her head.

'Coffee?' he prompted.

She swallowed. Let out a slow careful breath.

Stupid…

No one knew, only Sylvie, and she would never tell. It was simply lack of sleep doing things to her head and, gathering herself, she managed to raise her cup in an ironic salute.

'Yes, thanks.'

Without warning, his mouth widened in a smile that provoked an altogether different sensation. One which overrode the panicky fear that one day she'd be found out and sent a delicious ripple of warmth seeping through her limbs. A lust at first sight recognition that even at this distance set alarm bells ringing.

Definitely her cue to go inside, get dressed, get to work. She had no time to waste talking to a man who thought that all he had to do was smile to get her attention.

Even if it was true.

She didn't do holiday flirtations. Didn't do flirtations of any description.

'Hold on,' he called as she turned away, completely oblivious to, or maybe choosing to ignore her 'not interested' response to whatever he was offering. Which was about the same as any man with time on his hands and nothing but birds to look at. 'Won't you spare a cup for a man in distress?'

'Distress?'

He didn't sound distressed. Or look it. On the contrary, he had the appearance of a man totally in control of his world. Used to getting what he wanted. She met them every day. Wealthy, powerful men who paid for the weddings and parties that SDS Events organised. The kind of men who were used to the very best and demanded nothing less.

She groaned at falling for such an obvious ploy. It wouldn't have happened if she'd had more than catnaps for the last twenty-four hours. But who could sleep on a plane?

'The kitchen sent me some kind of ghastly herbal tea,' he said, taking full advantage of her fatal hesitation.

'There's nothing wrong with herbal tea,' she replied. 'On the contrary. Camomile is excellent for the nerves. I thoroughly recommend it.'

She kept a supply in the office for distraught brides and their mothers. For herself when faced with the likes of Marji Hayes. Men who got under her skin with nothing more than a smile.

There was a pack in the bridal emergency kit she carried with her whenever she was working and she'd have one now but for the fact that if she were any calmer, she'd be asleep.

'I'd be happy to swap,' he offered.

Despite her determination not to be drawn into conversation, she laughed, as no doubt she was meant to.

'No, you're all right,' she said. 'I'm good.'

Then, refusing to allow a man to unsettle her with no more than a look—she was, she reminded herself, now a partner in a prestigious event company—she surrendered.

After all, she had a pot full of good coffee that she wasn't going to drink. And unless he was part of the wedding party—and, as far as she knew, no one was arriving until tomorrow—he'd be gone by morning.

'But if you're desperate you're welcome to come over and help yourself.'

'Ah, there's the rub,' he said before she could take another step towards the safety of the interior, leaving him to take it or leave it while she got on with the job she'd come here to do. 'The mind is willing enough, but the back just isn't listening. I'd crawl over there on hot coals for a decent cup of coffee if it were physically possible, but as it is I'm at your mercy.'

'You're hurt?' Stupid question. If he couldn't make the short distance from his deck to hers there had to something seriously wrong. She would have rung for room service if there had been a bell. Since that option was denied her, she stuck her notebook in the pocket of her robe, picked up the coffee pot and said, 'Hang on, I'll be right there.'

His tree house was at the end of the bridge, the furthest from the main building. The one which, according to the plan she'd been given, had been allocated to Crystal and Tal as their bridal suite.

Definitely leaving tomorrow, then.

There was a handbell at the foot of the steps and she jangled it, called, 'Hello,' as she stepped up onto his deck.

Then, as she turned the corner and took the full impact of the man stretched out on the lounger—with not the slightest sign of injury to keep him there—she came to an abrupt halt.

Even from a distance it had been obvious that he was dangerously good-looking. Up close, he looked simply dangerous.

He had a weathered tan, the kind that couldn't be replicated in a salon and never entirely faded, even in the dead of winter. And the strength of his chin was emphasized by a 'shadow' that had passed the designer stubble stage and was heading into beard territory.

She'd already experienced the smile from twenty metres but he wasn't smiling now. On the contrary, his was a blatantly calculating look that took in every inch of her. From her damp hair, purple-streaked and standing on end where she'd been finger-drying it, her face bereft of anything but a hefty dose of moisturiser, to her bare feet, with a knowingness that warned her he was aware that she was naked beneath the robe.

Worse, the seductive curve of his lower lip sparked a heat deep within her and she knew that he was far more deadly than any of the wild animals that were the main attraction at Leopard Tree Lodge.

At least to any woman who didn't have her heart firmly padlocked to her chest.

Resisting the urge to pull the robe closer about her and tighten the belt, betraying the effect he had on her, she walked swiftly across the deck and placed the coffee pot on the table beside him.

'Emergency coffee delivery,' she said, with every intention of turning around and leaving him to it.

Gideon had watched her walk towards him.

Until ten minutes ago, he would have sworn he wasn't in the mood for company, particularly not the company of a woman high on getting her man to sign up for life—or at least until she was ready to settle for half his worldly goods. But then the tantalising scent of coffee had wafted towards him.

Even then he might have resisted if he hadn't seen this extraordinary woman sitting on the deck, raking her fingers through her hair in the early morning sun.

If he had given the matter a second's thought, he would have assumed anyone called Crystal to be one of those pneumatic blondes cloned to decorate the arms of men who were more interested in shape than substance when it came to women.

Not that he was immune. Shape did it for him every time.

But she wasn't blonde. There was nothing obvious or predictable about her. Her hair was dramatically black and tipped with purple and her strong features were only prevented from overwhelming her face by a pair of large dark eyes. And while her shape was blurred by the bulky robe she was wearing, she was certainly on the skinny side; there were no artificially enhanced curves hidden even in that abundance of white towelling.

In fact she was so very far from what he would have expected that his interest had been unexpectedly aroused. Rather more than his interest if he was honest; a sure sign that his brain was under-occupied but it certainly took his mind off his back.

An effect that was amplified as she stepped up onto his deck and paused there for a moment.

Straight from the shower, her face bare of make-up, her hair a damp halo that hadn't seen a comb, without sexy clothes or high heels, it had to be the fact that she was naked under that robe that momentarily squeezed the breath from his chest as she'd walked towards him.

'You're an angel, Miss Blaize,' he said, collecting himself.

'Not even close,' she replied.

She'd worked hard to scrub the inner city from her voice, he judged, but it was still just discernible to someone with an ear for it.

'On either count,' she added. 'I'm sorry to disappoint, but I'm plain Josie Fowler.'

She wasn't the bride?

Nor was she exactly plain but what his mother would have described as 'striking'. And up close he could see that those dark eyes were a deep shade of violet that exactly matched the highlights in her hair, the colour she'd painted both finger and toenails.

'Who said I was disappointed, plain Josie Fowler?' he said, ignoring the little leap of gratification that she wasn't Crystal Blaize. It was her coffee he wanted, not her. 'I asked if you'd share your coffee and here you are. That makes you an angel in my eyes.'

'You're easily satisfied…?'

On the contrary. According to more than one woman of his acquaintance, he was impossible to please—or maybe just impossible—but right now any company would be welcome. Even a big-eyed scarecrow with purple hair.

'Gideon McGrath,' he said in answer to the unvoiced question. Offering her his hand.

She hesitated for the barest moment before she stepped close enough to take it, but her hand matched her features. It was slightly too large for true femininity, leaving him with the feeling that her body hadn't quite grown to match her extremities. But her grip was firm enough to convince him that, apart from the contact lenses—no one had eyes that colour— its owner was the real thing.

'Forgive me for not getting up, but if I tried you'd have to pick me up off the deck.'

'In that case, please don't bother. One of us with a bad back is quite enough. Enjoy your coffee,' she said, taking a clear step back.

'Would you mind pouring it for me? It's a bit of a stretch,' he lied. But he didn't want her to go.

'Bad luck,' she said, turning to the tray and bending to fill his cup. 'Especially when you're on holiday.' Then, glancing back at him, 'What on earth made you think I was Crystal Blaize?'

Her hair, drying quickly as the sun rose, began to settle in soft tendrils around her face. And he caught the gleam of a tiny purple stud in her nose.

Who was she? What was she? Part of the media circus surrounding the coming wedding?

'One of the staff called you the "the wedding lady"?' he replied, pitching his answer as a question.

'Oh, right. Milk, sugar?' she asked, but not bothering to explain. Then, looking over the tray, 'Actually, that would be just milk or milk. There doesn't appear to be any sugar.' She sighed as she straightened. 'I was assured that this place was the last word in luxury and to be sure it looks beautiful...'

'But?'

'There's no power point or hairdryer in my room, no sugar on your tray and no telephone to call the desk and tell them about it, despite the fact that David told me to ring for anything I needed. I can't even get a signal on my mobile phone.'

'You won't. The whole point of Leopard Tree Lodge is to get away from the intrusion of modern life, not bring it with you,' he said, totally ignoring the fact that he'd been fuming about the same thing just minutes before.

Well, obviously not the hairdryer. But he could surely do with a phone signal right now, if only to reassure himself that this was a one-off. That someone in marketing hadn't decided that weddings were the way to go.

Since he was the one who'd laid out the ground rules before a single stone had been laid or piece of timber cut, however, he could hardly complain.

But it occurred to him that if 'plain Josie Fowler' was with the wedding party, she would be given free run of the communications facilities and, if he played his cards right, she'd be good for a lot more than coffee.

'The electricity to heat the water is supplied by solar energy,' he explained, 'but it doesn't run to electrical appliances.'

'Once I'd clocked the candles, I managed to work that out for myself,' she replied. 'The escape from reality thing. Unfortunately, I'm here to work. If I was mad enough to come here for a holiday I'd probably feel quite differently.'

Clearly that prospect was as unlikely as a cold day in hell.

'You don't like it?'

'I'd like it better if it was beside a quiet bay, with a soft white beach and the kind of sea rich people pay to swim in.'

'This is supposed to be a work-free zone,' he pointed out, more than a touch irritated by her lack of enthusiasm. He put all his heart and a lot more into building his hotels, his resorts, some of them in exactly the kind of location she described.

But this had been his first. He loved it and hated it in equal measure, but he had the right.

'For others, maybe,' she retaliated, putting her hand to the small of her back and stretching out her spine, 'but for the next few days it's going to be twenty-four/seven for me.'

'Sore back?' he asked.

'Just a bit. Is it catching?' she asked with a wry smile.

'Not as far as I know.'

Maybe.

Her back hadn't seized up—yet—but just how many of his guests arrived feeling as if they were screwed up into knots? Zahir had built a very profitable spa on the coast at Nadira, where most of his travellers chose to spend a couple of days after the rigours of the desert. Would that work here, too? Massage, pampering treatments, something totally back to nature…

There was plenty to keep the dedicated naturalist happy. Canoe trips, bush walks, birdwatching, but big game viewing was the big attraction and that was primarily a dawn and dusk event.

Not that he was interested, but it would be useful to mention the possibilities for expansion when it came to negotiations with potential buyers.

'So, tell me, what's the deal with the herbal tea and no sugar?' she asked.

'It's a mystery,' he lied. 'Unless the ants have got into the stores.'

'Ants?'

'Big ones.' He held thumb and forefinger apart to demonstrate just how big.

Her eyes widened a fraction. 'You're kidding?'

He said nothing. There were ants that big but the storeroom had been designed and constructed to keep them out.

She had, however, been rather dismissive of Leopard Tree Lodge. Worse, she was on a mission to disrupt it.

Protecting the unspoilt places where he built his resorts from pollution of every kind—including noise—had been high on his agenda from the outset. And, in his admittedly limited experience, weddings tended to be very noisy affairs.

Unfortunately, *Celebrity* would have a contract and wouldn't hesitate to sue him and his company for every lost penny if he messed with their big day. And that would be small beer compared to compensation for distress to the bride, the groom, their families, the bridesmaids…

He was stuck with the wedding, so tormenting the woman he now realised was the wedding planner was about as good as it was going to get.

CHAPTER THREE

A wedding is a day to spend with friends…
                    —*The Perfect Wedding* by Serafina March

THE WEDDING PLANNER, however, refused to fulfil the role assigned.

There was no girly squeal at the thought of giant ants munching their way through the sugar supply. No repeat of the shriek provoked by the raid on her breakfast by a thieving monkey.

She merely shook her head, as if he'd done no more than confirm her worst fears, took a small black notebook out of her robe pocket, wrote something in it and then returned it to her pocket before turning back to the tray.

'There's a little pot of honey, here,' she said, picking it up and showing it to him. 'According to my partner, it actually tastes better in coffee as well as being healthier than refined sugar.'

'That'll be fine. I don't want milk.' He watched her open the pot, then said, 'Partner?'

From the way Francis had spoken, he'd assumed she was on her own. He hadn't noticed anyone with her, but he hadn't been interested enough to look until the scent of coffee had reached him.

'Is he with you?'

'She.' She stirred a spoonful of honey into his coffee. Then, realising what kind of partner he meant, she added, 'Sylvie's my business partner. And no. She's got a project of her own keeping her busy right now.'

The thought widened her mouth into a smile that momentarily lit up her face, transforming the 'striking' into something else. Not beauty—her features were not classically proportioned. It was nothing he could put a name to. He only knew that he wanted to see it again.

'Not that she'd have come with me even if she was free. Weddings are my department.' Then, as if aware that she hadn't made it clear, 'I'm an events planner.'

'I'd just about worked that out. It was just that when Francis said you were the "wedding lady" I assumed that you were the bride.'

'Not in this life,' she said matter-of-factly as she handed him the cup. 'My role is simply to deliver the wedding on time, on budget, with no hitches. Will that do?' she asked as he sipped it and, when he smiled, made another move to go.

'Stay. Sit down,' he said with a gesture at the lounger beside him.

'Do you always issue invitations as an order?' she asked, ignoring the invitation.

'On the contrary, I always issue orders as an invitation.' Then, before she could walk away—he couldn't remember the last time he'd had to work this hard to keep a woman's attention; when he'd wanted to—he said, 'Simply?'

'Sorry?'

'You think delivering a wedding here will be simple?'

That earned him a smile of his own. A slightly wry one, admittedly, with one corner of her mouth doing all the work and drawing attention to soft, full lips.

'Weddings are never simple,' she said, perching on the edge of the lounger rather than stretching out beside him as he'd hoped. Keen to be off and conquering worlds. No prizes for guessing who that reminded him of. 'Certainly not this one.'

'But you're the wedding lady,' he reminded her. 'It was your bright idea to have the wedding here.'

'You don't approve the choice of location?' she asked, her head tilting to one side. Interested rather than offended.

He shrugged without thinking and as he caught his breath she moved swiftly to steady the cup with one hand, placing her other on his shoulder.

'Are you all right?' she said.

No. Actually, far from all right.

As she'd leaned forward her robe had gaped to offer him a tantalising glimpse of the delights it was supposed to conceal. Her breasts were not large, but they were smooth, invitingly creamy and, without doubt, all her own and he was getting an overload of stimulation. Pain and pleasure in equal measure.

'A noisy celebrity wedding doesn't seem to fit the setting,' he said and, doing his best to ignore both, especially the warmth of her palm spreading through him, he looked up.

Her face was close enough to see the fine down that covered her fair, smooth skin. Genuine concern in those extraordinary eyes. But what held his attention was a faint white scar that ran along the edge of her jaw. It would, under normal circumstances, have been covered by make-up, but Josie had come on her errand of mercy without stopping to apply the mask that women used to conceal their true selves from the outside world.

No make-up. No designer clothes.

It left her more naked than if she'd stripped off her robe and he had to clench his hand to stop himself from reaching out, tracing the line of it from just beneath her ear to her chin as if he could somehow erase it, erase the memory of the pain it must have caused her, with his thumb.

'What about the other guests who are here to watch the wildlife?' he demanded, rather more sharply than he'd intended as he sought to distance himself. 'Don't they get any consideration?'

'There won't be any,' she said, removing her hand as she sat back, distancing herself. Leaving a cold spot where it had been.

'Exactly my point.'

'No, I meant that there won't be any other guests, Gideon. We've taken over the entire resort for the wedding so we won't be disturbing anyone.'

'Apart from the animals. Every room?'

'And the rest. We've got a river boat coming to take the overflow.'

'Well, I hate to be the one to say "I told you so", but here comes your first complication. I'm not going anywhere.'

'Then you're going to have to bivouac in the bush because you're certainly not staying here,' she replied.

He didn't bother to argue with her. She'd find out just how immovable he could be soon enough.

'Did you get a good discount for block booking?' he asked.

'What?' She shook her head. 'There's nothing discount about this wedding but, since I wasn't part of the negotiations, I couldn't say what financial arrangements were made with the owners. I was brought in at the last minute when the original wedding planner had to pull out. Not that it's any of your business,' she added.

'If it had been your call?' he pressed. 'Would you have chosen Leopard Tree Lodge?'

'The venue is the bride's decision,' she replied. Then, with the smallest of shrugs, 'I might have tried to talk her out of it. Not that the location isn't breathtaking,' she assured him. 'The drama of flying in over the desert and then suddenly seeing the green of the Okavango delta spread out below you, the gleam of water amongst the reeds. The river…'

She was going through the motions, he realised. Talking to him, but her brain was somewhere else. No doubt working out the implications of a cuckoo in the nest.

'The photographs are going to be breathtaking,' she said,

making an effort. 'Any special deal that *Celebrity* managed to hammer out of the company that owns this place is going to be cheap in return for the PR hit. Six weeks of wall-to-wall coverage in the biggest lifestyle magazine in the UK. Well, five. The first week is devoted to the hen weekend.'

Undoubtedly. A full house as well as a ton of publicity. Whoever it was on his staff who'd negotiated this deal had done a very good job. The fact that he or she hadn't brought it to his attention in the hope of earning a bonus suggested that they knew what his reaction would have been.

Not that they had to. His role was research and development, not the day-to-day running of things. No doubt they were simply waiting for the jump in demand to prove their point for him. And earn them a bonus.

Smart thinking. It was just what he'd have done in their position.

'If the setting is so great, what's your problem with it?' he asked.

It was one thing for him to hate the idea. Quite another for someone to tell him that it was all wrong for her big fancy media event.

'In my experience there's more than enough capacity for disaster when it comes to something in which such strong emotions are invested, without transporting bride, groom, a hundred plus guests, photographers, a journalist, hair and make-up artists, not to mention all their kit and caboodle six thousand miles via three separate aircraft. One of them so small that it'll need a separate trip just for the wedding dress.'

'You're exaggerating.'

'Probably,' she admitted. 'But not by much.'

'No. And that's another problem,' he said, seizing the opening she'd given him. 'It's a gift to the green lobby. They'll use the high profile of the event to get their own free PR ride over the carbon footprint involved in transporting everyone halfway round the world just so that two people can say "I do".'

'You think they should have chosen the village church?'

'Why not?'

'Good question,' she said. 'So, tell me, Gideon McGrath, how did you get here? By hot-air balloon?'

For a man who probably flew more miles in a year than most people did in a lifetime that sounded very appealing and he told her so.

'Unfortunately, there is no way of making a balloon take you where you want to go.'

'Maybe the trick is to want to go where the balloon takes you,' she replied.

'That's a bit too philosophical for me.'

'Really? Well, you can stop worrying. Tal Newman's PR people have anticipated the negative reaction and he's going to offset the air travel involved by planting a sizeable forest.'

'Where?' he asked, his interest instantly piqued. A lot of his clients offset their travel, but maybe he could make it easy for them by offering it as part of the package. Do more. Put something back, perhaps. Something meaningful…

'The forest?' She shook her head. 'Sorry, that information is embargoed until the day before the wedding.'

'In other words, you don't know.'

'No idea,' she admitted. 'Everything about this wedding is on a "need to know" basis. Not that you could call anyone and tell them.' She thought about that and added, 'You know it's possible that the lack of communication may be one of the reasons *Celebrity* seized on this location. Without a signal, there's no chance of the guests, or staff, sending illicit photographs to rival magazines and newspapers via their mobile phones so that they can run spoilers.'

'I thought you said the location was the bride's call?'

'It is for my brides but this isn't just a wedding, it's a media event. Of course Crystal apparently loves animals so it fits the image.'

He snorted derisively.

'Any animals she sees here are going to be wild and dangerous—especially the furry ones. She'd have done better getting married in a petting zoo.'

'You might say that,' she replied with a dead-straight face. 'I couldn't possibly comment.' Then she took out her notebook and jotted something down. 'But thanks for the idea.'

He laughed, jerking the pain in his back into life.

Josie's hand twitched as if to reach out again, but she closed it tight about her pen and he told himself that he was glad. He preferred his relationships physical, uncomplicated. That way, everyone knew where they were. The minute emotions, caring got involved, they became dangerous. Impossible to control. With limitless possibilities for pain.

'You don't believe in any of this, do you?' he said, guarding himself against regret. 'You provide the flowers and frills and fireworks but underneath you're a cynic.'

'The flowers and frills,' she replied, 'but it was stipulated by the resort that there should be no fireworks.'

'Well, that's a relief. You never know which way a startled elephant will run.'

'That's an image I could have done without,' she said. 'But, since you won't be here, there's no need to concern yourself. How was the coffee?'

Gideon looked at his empty cup. 'Do you know, I was so absorbed by all this wedding talk that I scarcely noticed.' Holding it out for a refill, he said, 'I'll concentrate this time.'

Josie replenished it without a word, then leaned forward to stir in another spoonful of honey.

'Enough?' she asked, raising long, naturally dark lashes to look questioningly at him.

'Perfect,' he said as he was offered a second glimpse of her entrancing cleavage. A second close-up of that faint scar.

Was it a childhood fall? A car accident? He tried to imagine what might have caused such an injury.

'So, what have you actually done to your back?' she asked, distracting him. 'Did you get into a tussle with a runaway elephant? Wrestle an alligator? Total a four-by-four chasing a rhino?'

'Actually, since we're in Africa, that would be a crocodile,' he pointed out, sipping more slowly at the second cup. Savouring it. Making it last. He didn't want her to rush off. 'The creatures you should never smile at.'

'Sorry?'

'It's a song. *Never smile at a crocodile…*' As he sang the words, he felt the tug of the past. Where the hell had that come from?

'*Peter Pan*,' she said. 'Forgive me, but I wouldn't have taken you for a fan.'

He shrugged without thinking, but this time it didn't catch him so viciously. Maybe the doc was right. He just needed to relax. Spend some time talking about nothing much, to someone who didn't want something from him.

Apart from his room.

Obviously a woman at the top of her field in the events industry—and she had to be good or she wouldn't be in charge of Tal Newman's high profile wedding—would have that kind of easy ability to talk to anyone, put them at their ease. He'd only been talking to her for a few minutes and already he'd had two good ideas.

Even so.

Most women he met had an agenda. Hers was to evict him and while, just an hour ago, he would have been her willing accomplice, just the thought of getting on a plane tightened the pain.

She might not be a babe, nothing like the women he dated when he could spare the time. Who never lasted more than a month or two, because he never could spare the time, refused to take the risk…

What mattered was that she had access to coffee, the little pleasures that made the wheels of life turn without squeaking, and she would have that vital contact with the outside world.

The fact that she was capable of stringing an intelligent

sentence together and making him laugh—well, smile, anyway; laughing, as he'd discovered, was a very bad idea—was pure bonus.

'My father was into amateur dramatics,' he told her. 'He put on a show for the local kids every Christmas.'

'Oh, right.' For just a moment she seemed to freeze, then she pasted on a smile that even on so short an acquaintance he knew wasn't the real thing. 'Well, that must have been fun. Were you Peter?' She paused. 'Or were you Captain Hook?'

Something about the way she said that suggested she thought Hook was more his thing.

'My father played Hook. I didn't get involved.' One fantasist in the family was more than enough.

She lifted her eyebrows a fraction, but kept whatever she was thinking to herself and said, 'So? Despite the paternal advice, did you smile at one?'

'Nothing that exciting. Damn thing just seized up on me. I was planning to leave yesterday, but apparently I'm stuck here until it unseizes itself,' he said, firing a shot across her assumption that he would be leaving any time soon.

'That must hurt,' she said, her forehead puckering in a little frown. 'Have you seen a doctor?'

Good question.

She was going to be responsible for the health and safety of a hundred plus people. If anyone hurt themselves—and weddings were notoriously rowdy affairs—she needed to know there was help at hand.

Or maybe she was finally getting it. What his immovability meant in terms of her 'block booking'.

'There's a doctor in Maun. He flew up yesterday, spoke to my doctor in London and then ordered complete rest. According to him, this little episode is my body telling me to be still.' He made little quote marks with his fingers around the 'be still'. He wouldn't want her, or anyone else, thinking he said things like that.

'It's psychological?'

Something about the way she said that, no particular shock or surprise, suggested that it wasn't the first time she'd encountered the condition.

'That's what they're implying.'

'My stepfather suffered from the same thing,' she said. 'His back seized up every time someone suggested he get a job.'

She said it with a brisk, throwaway carelessness that declared to the world that having a layabout for a stepfather mattered not one jot. But her words betrayed a world of hurt. And went a long way to explaining that very firm assertion—strange for a woman whose life revolved around it—that marriage wasn't for her.

'I didn't mean to imply that that's your problem,' she added with a sudden rush that—however unlikely that seemed—might have been embarrassment.

'I promise you that it's not,' he assured her. 'On the contrary. It's made worse by the fact that I'm out of touch with my office. That I'm stuck here when I should be several thousand miles away negotiating a vital contract.'

Discovering that the marketing team he'd entrusted with selling his hard won dream appeared to have lost the plot and being unable to do a damn thing about it.

'I'm beginning to understand how that feels.' She was still leaning forward, an elbow on her knee, chin propped on her hand, regarding him with that steady violet gaze. 'The being out of touch thing. I usually spend the twenty-four hours before a big event with my phone glued to my ear, although who I'd call if I had a last minute emergency here heaven alone knows.'

'Necessity does tend to be the mother of invention when you're this far from civilisation,' he agreed.

'Even in the middle of civilisation when you're in the events business. Clearly, this is going to be an interesting few days.' Then, looking at him as if he was number one on her list of problems, 'Would a massage help?'

'Are you offering?' he asked.

Josie had thought it was quiet here, but she was wrong.

There was no traffic, no shouting or sirens—the constant background to daily life in London—but it wasn't silent. The air was positively vibrating with energy; the high-pitched hum of insects, bird calls, odd sounds she couldn't identify, and she was suddenly overwhelmed with a longing to lie back, soak it all up, let the sun heat her to the bone.

The shriek of a bird, or maybe a monkey, snapped her out of her reverie and she realised, somewhat belatedly, that Gideon McGrath's dark eyes were focused not on her face, but lower down.

Typical man...

'All I'm offering is coffee,' she said crisply, rising to her feet, tightening her belt.

'Pity,' he replied with a slow, mesmerising smile. It was like watching a car roll towards you in slow motion; one minute you were safe, the next...

'Shall I leave the pot?' she asked.

'Better take it with you, or the room service staff will get their knickers in a twist hunting for it.'

'It's not a problem,' she said abruptly. Calling herself all kinds of a fool for allowing herself to be drawn in by a smile, a pair of dark eyes. He might be confined to a deck lounger, but he was still capable of inflicting terminal damage and she wished she'd stuck with her initial response which had been to ignore him. 'I'll let them know where it is.'

'Don't bother about it. Really. You've got more than enough on your plate.'

'It's no trouble,' she assured him, backing towards the exit. 'I'll be visiting the kitchen anyway.' She had to talk through the catering arrangements for the pre-wedding dinner with the chef. 'I can mention the mistake with the herbal tea while I'm there if you like.'

'No. Don't do that, Josie.'

Something about his persistence warned her that she was missing something and she stopped.

'It wasn't a mistake,' he said. 'The tea.'

'I'm sorry, I don't understand…' Then, quite suddenly, she did. 'Oh, right. I get it.' She stepped forward and snatched up the coffee pot, brandishing it at him accusingly. 'This is a banned substance, isn't it?'

'You've got me,' he admitted, his smile turning to a wince as he shrugged without thinking and she had to fight the urge to go to him yet again, do something to ease the pain.

'I believe I'm the one who's been had.' And, before he could deny it, she said, 'You've made me an accessory to caffeine abuse in direct contravention of doctor's orders and—' as he opened his mouth to protest '—don't even think about apologising. I can tell that you're not in the least bit sorry.'

'Actually, I wasn't going to apologise. I was going to thank you. Everyone keeps telling me that I should listen to my body. Its demands for caffeine were getting so loud that I'm surprised the entire camp couldn't hear it.'

'Not the entire camp,' she replied. 'Just me.'

'You were very kind and I took shameless advantage of you,' he said with every appearance of sincerity. She wasn't taken in.

'I was an idiot,' she said, holding up her hand, palm towards him as if holding him off, despite the fact that moving was clearly the last thing on his mind.

'Not an idiot.'

'No? So tell me about the sugar?'

'You didn't give me sugar,' he pointed out.

'I would have done if you'd…' She stopped, furious with herself.

'The honey was inspired,' he assured her. 'Tell your partner that I'm converted.'

'So what else is banned?' she demanded, refusing to be placated.

'White bread, red meat, salt, animal fats.'

Gideon knew the list by heart. His doctor had been trotting it out for years at the annual check-ups provided for all staff. Annual check-ups which the firm's insurance company insisted should include him, despite his protestations that it was totally unnecessary. Now she'd got him captive, she was taking full advantage of the situation.

'All the usual suspects, in other words.'

'Along with the advice to walk to work…' as if he had time '…and take regular holidays.'

He spent half his life at holiday resorts, for heaven's sake; why would he want to go to one for fun?

And of course there was the big one. Get married.

According to actuarial statistics, married men lived longer. But then that doctor was a woman, so she would say that. He wasn't going to.

'The holiday part doesn't appear to be working,' Josie pointed out.

'Nor does the diet. My life has been reduced to steamed fish, nut cutlets and oatmeal,' he complained. And there wasn't a damn thing he could do about it. Unless, of course, he could convince Josie to take pity on him.

She'd been quick with a tender hand and he was sure that if he'd asked she'd have gone and fetched sugar for him from her own tray. If he'd done that she'd be really mad at him.

She might even have indulged his massage fantasy if she hadn't caught him with his eyes rather lower than they should have been.

'I take it that I can cross ants off the list of things I have to worry about,' she said without the least sign of sympathy.

Okay, so she was too mad to indulge him now, but it wouldn't last. She laughed too easily to hold a grudge.

'If I say yes, will you have lunch with me?' he asked.

'So that you can help yourself to forbidden treats from my tray?'

'Me? I'm helpless. Of course, if you forced them on me there isn't a thing I could do to stop you.'

'You can relax,' she replied, but her lusciously wide mouth tightened at the corners as she fought to stop it responding to his outrageous cheek with a grin. 'I wouldn't dream of it.'

'I'd make it worth your while,' he promised.

'Give it up, Gideon. I can't be bribed.'

Of course she could. Everyone could be bribed. You just had to find out what they wanted most in the world. Preferably before they knew they wanted it.

'You're going to need a friendly ear in which to pour your frustrations before this wedding is over.' That he would be the major cause of those frustrations didn't preclude him from offering comfort. 'A shoulder to cry on when everything falls apart.'

'All I need from you is your room,' she replied. 'Besides, you're supposed to be on a low stress regime.'

'It would be your stress, not mine,' he pointed out.

'Yes, well, thanks for the offer,' she said, losing the battle with the smile and trying very hard not to laugh. 'I appreciate your concern, but SDS Events do not plan weddings that fall apart—'

'You didn't plan this one.'

'—and you won't be here long enough to provide the necessary shoulder for tears or any other purpose.'

'I'll be here until my back says otherwise.' And, quite unexpectedly, he didn't find that nearly as infuriating as he had just half an hour earlier.

'Your back doesn't have a say in the matter. I hate to add to your stress, but unless you intend playing gooseberry to the bride and groom you would be well advised to make other arrangements.'

'Are you telling me that this is going to be the bridal suite?'

'Twenty-four hours from now, you won't be able to move in here for flowers,' she assured him, so seriously that he laughed.

It hurt like hell but he didn't care. He was throwing a spanner in the wedding works and he didn't have to lift a finger—let alone a telephone—to do it.

'I'm glad that amuses you, Mr McGrath. They do say that laughter is very healing, which, since you have to be out of here by first thing tomorrow, is just as well. Maybe you should try the plunge pool,' she suggested. 'It will take the weight off your muscles. Ease the pain.'

'I'm willing to give it go,' he assured her. 'But I'll need a hand.'

'No problem. I'd be happy to give you a push.'

'But will you stick around to help me out?'

'Sorry, I have a full day ahead of me. Enjoy the herbal tea and nut cutlets.'

'You're full of excellent ideas, Josie. You just don't follow through.'

'Don't test me,' she warned.

She turned with a splendid swish of her robe, giving him an unintentional glimpse of thigh.

'I'll give you one thing,' he called after her.

'Your bed?'

'Communication.'

She stopped and, when she turned back to face him, he said, 'If you'll make a call for me.'

'You want me to call your wife and tell her you're catching the next plane home?'

'There's no one waiting for that call, Josie.' No one to rush back to. 'I want you to ring my office. Give me your notebook and I'll write down the number.'

She came closer, drawn by the temptation, took the notebook from her pocket and handed it to him with her pen. It was the kind of notebook he favoured himself, with a pocket at the back for receipts and an elastic band to hold it together. He slipped the band and it fell open at the bookmarked page where she'd started writing a list.

Hairdryers?
Ring???
Phone?
Florist
Caterer
Confectioner

He smiled and beside 'Ring' he jotted down a number.

'Call Cara,' he said, handing it back to her. 'She's my PA.'

'And say what?'

'Just ask her what the hell is going on in Marketing.'

'What the hell is going on in Marketing,' she repeated, then shook her head. 'I can see why you're stressed. You're on holiday. Let it go, Gideon.'

'Holidays are my work, which is why I know that David has a satellite telephone and Internet access. He keeps it a dark secret from the guests, but I'm sure he'll make an exception in your case.'

'You—' She let slip a word that was surely banned from the wedding planners' handbook. 'Had again.'

'You're going to need me on your side, Josie.'

'I need you gone!'

He left her with the last word and his reward was a view of an unexpectedly sexy rear as she walked away. A pair of slender ankles. He was already looking forward to making his acquaintance with the legs that connected them.

'I don't suppose you've got a London newspaper to spare for a man dying of boredom?' he called after her.

'Never touch them,' her disembodied voice replied from the bridge. 'Far too stressful.'

'Liar,' he called back as he tugged on the bell pull that Francis had extended from its place by the bed so that it was within reach of the lounger.

He really should have explained what David had meant

when he'd told her to 'ring'. Actually, David should have told her himself, but maybe he'd been distracted.

She was a seriously distracting woman.

'Don't forget lunch.'

CHAPTER FOUR

A stylish wedding often owes more to natural elements than the designer's art…

—The Perfect Wedding by Serafina March

JOSIE was trying very hard not to grin as she walked back through the trees to her own deck and, once safely out of reach of those dangerous eyes, a mouth that teased without conscience, she swiftly recovered her senses.

Gideon McGrath might be in pain but it hadn't stopped him flirting outrageously with her. Not that she was fooled into thinking it was personal, despite the way he'd peered down her robe until she'd realised what he was doing and moved.

All he was interested in was her coffee. In having her run his errands.

'One o'clock…' His voice reached her through the branches.

And her lunch, damn it!

She was sorely tempted to stand by the rail and eat that luscious blueberry muffin, very slowly, just to torment him.

Perhaps it was just as well that the monkeys had taken advantage of her absence to clear her tray. Upsetting the milk, scattering the little packets of sugar, leaving nothing but crumbs that were being cleaned up by a bird with dark, glossy green plumage who gave her a look with its beady eyes as if daring her to do anything about it.

She wouldn't want the man to get the impression that she gave that much of a damn and, quite deliberately turning her back towards him, she looked up at a monkey chittering at her from a nearby branch. He turned on the charm with a smile, an outstretched hand, the moment he'd snagged her attention, hoping for more little treats.

It had to be a male.

'You've cleaned me out,' she said. 'Try next door.'

She was treated to a bare-toothed grin before the little monkey swung effortlessly away into the trees, putting on a dazzling acrobatic show just for her.

'Show off,' she called after him. But the fact that she was smiling served as a reminder, should she need it, of just how dangerous that kind of self-serving charm could be. How easy it was to be fooled, sucked in.

She took a slow breath, then turned her face up to the sun, absorbing for a moment the heat, the scent of warm earth, the exotic high-pitched hum of the cicadas.

Five years ago she had been peeling vegetables and washing up in a hotel kitchen; the only job she could get.

Today, *Celebrity* magazine was paying for her to stay in one of the most exclusive safari lodges in Africa. Paying her to ensure that the year's most expensive wedding went without a hitch. And, with her name attached to this event, she would be one of the 'chosen', accepted in her own right; finally able to justify Sylvie's faith in her.

Gideon McGrath could flirt all he wanted. It would take more than his devastating smile to distract her from her purpose.

She swiftly unpacked, hung up her clothes, then waxed up her hair before dressing for work. At home she would have worn layers of black net, Lycra and jersey; the black tights, T-shirt, a sleeveless belted slipover that came to her thighs, the purple DMs that had become her trademark uniform.

On her first foray into a 'destination' wedding, on the island of St Lucia, she'd shed the neck-to-toe cover-up in favour of black shorts, tank top and a pair of strappy purple sandals.

The misery of sunburn, and ploughing through soft sand in open-toes, had taught her a sharp, painful lesson and she hadn't made the same mistake again. Instead, she'd invested in a hot weather uniform consisting of a black long-sleeved linen shirt and a short skirt pulled together with a purple leather belt. Despite the heat, she'd stuck with black tights, which she'd also learned from experience, protected her legs from the nasty biting, stinging things that seemed to thrive in hot climates. As did her boots.

She took a folder from her briefcase that contained the overall plan for the wedding as envisaged by her predecessor, the latest guest list Marji had emailed to her—she'd need to check it against the rooms allocated by David—and her own lists of everything that needed to be double and triple-checked on site.

Marji had also sent her the latest edition of *Celebrity* with Crystal's sweetheart face and baby-blue eyes smiling out of the cover. The first of half a dozen issues that would be dedicated to the wedding.

She glanced in the direction of Gideon's tree house. It wasn't the requested newspaper—far from it—but it did contain a dozen pages of the bride on her hen party weekend at a luxury spa. Impossibly glamorous girls poolside in barely-there swimsuits, partying till all hours in gowns cut to reveal more than they concealed would do a lot more to take his mind off his back than the latest FTSE index.

It was just the thing for a man suffering from stress overload.

Then she felt guilty for mocking him. Okay, so he'd taken shameless advantage of her, but it had to be miserable having your back seize up when you were on holiday in a place that had been designed to wipe out all traces of the twenty-first century. No television or radio to distract you. No way to phone home.

If he was as incapable of moving as he said he was. He looked fit enough—more than fit. Not bulky gym muscle, but the lean, sinewy lifestyle fitness of a walker, a climber even.

That first sight of him had practically taken her breath away. Not just his buff body and powerful legs, but the thick dark hair and sexy stubble. Eyes from which lines fanned out in a way that suggested he spent a lot of time in the sun.

Eyes that unnerved her. Seemed to rob her of self-will. She'd been on the point of leaving him more than once and yet she'd stayed.

She dismissed the thought. It had been a long trip and she never had been able to sleep on a plane. She was simply tired.

The only thing that bothered her about Gideon McGrath was that he was here. Immovably so, according to him, and she could see how impossible it would be for him to climb aboard the tiny four-seater plane that had brought her here.

But there had to be a way. If it had been a life-threatening illness, a broken leg, they would have to get him out somehow. She'd ask David about that.

The entire complex would very shortly be full to bursting with the wedding party, photographers, hairdressers and make-up artists for the feature on the build-up to the wedding, the setting, and no one was immune from an accident, falling ill.

She needed to know what the emergency arrangements were.

Meanwhile, whatever he came up with, they were going to need Gideon McGrath's goodwill and co-operation and she regretted dropping yesterday's newspaper in the rubbish bag before she'd left the flight from London. Getting him out of Tal and Crystal's bridal suite was her number one priority and, for that, she needed to keep him sweet. Even if it did mean hand-feeding him from her lunch tray.

She put on her sunglasses and, shouldering her bag, she headed back across the bridge. Trying very hard not to think about slipping morsels of tempting food into his mouth. Giving him a massage. Helping him into the plunge pool.

She jangled the bell to warn him of her arrival, then stepped up onto his deck.

He hadn't moved, but was lying back, eyes closed and, not eager to disturb him, she tiptoed across to the table.

'Admit it, Josie, you just can't keep away,' he said as she put the magazine down.

She jumped, her heart jolting against her breast as if she'd been caught doing something wrong and that made her mad.

'I'm on an errand of mercy,' she said, then jumped again when he opened his eyes. He did a good job of hiding his reaction to her changed appearance. Was doubtless a good poker player.

But, for a woman who knew what to look for, the mental flinch that was usually accompanied by a short scatological four-letter word was unmistakable.

He had enough control to keep that to himself, too—which was impressive; there was simply a pause so brief as to be almost unnoticeable unless you were waiting for it, before he said, 'So? Have you changed your mind about the massage?'

And it was her turn to catch her breath, catch the word that very nearly slipped loose. Was it that obvious what she'd been thinking? Had he been able to read her mind as easily as she'd read his?

It wasn't such a stretch, she realised.

He must know how important it was to her that he move and she let it out again, very slowly.

'Sorry. It was your mental well-being I was concerned about. I didn't have a newspaper,' she said, 'but I did have this in my bag.'

He took one glance at the magazine she was offering him and then looked up at her. 'You've got to be kidding?'

'It's the latest issue.' She angled it so that he could see Crystal on the cover. 'At least you won't mistake me for the bride again.'

'I always did think you were an unlikely candidate,' he admitted, taking it from her and glancing at the photograph of the bikini-clad Crystal. 'She is exactly what I expected, whereas you are…'

He paused, whether out of concern for her feelings or because he was lost for words she didn't know. Unlikely on both counts, she'd have thought.

'Whereas I am what?' she enquired.

'I'm not sure,' he replied. 'Give me time and I'll work it out.'

'There's no rush,' she said, taking a step back. 'You've got until ten o'clock tomorrow morning. And in the meantime you can get to know Crystal.'

'Why would I want to do that?'

She shrugged. 'You tell me. You're the one who wants to share her room.'

Deciding that now might be a good moment to depart, she took another step back.

'Wait!'

And, even after all these years, her survival instinct was so deeply ingrained to respond instantly to an order and she stopped and turned without thinking.

'Josie?'

It had taken no more than a heartbeat for her to realise what she'd done, spin on her heel and walk away.

'I'm busy,' she said and kept going.

'I know, but I was hoping, since you're so concerned about my mental welfare, that you might fetch a notebook and pen from my laptop bag?'

Gideon had framed it as a question, not an order and she put out her hand to grasp the handrail as the black thoughts swirling in her brain began to subside and she realised that his 'wait!' had been an urgent appeal rather than the leap-to-it order barked at someone who had no choice but obey.

She took a moment while her heart rate slowed to catch her breath, gather herself, before turning slowly to face him.

'Do correct me if I'm mistaken,' she said, 'but I'd have said they were on the doctor's forbidden list.'

'At the top,' he admitted, the slight frown at her strange reaction softening into a rerun of that car-crash smile.

'Well, there you are. I've done more than enough damage for one day—'

'No. It's important. I've had a couple of ideas and if I don't make some notes while they're fresh in my mind, I'm just going to lie here and…well…stress. You wouldn't want that on your conscience, would you?'

'You are a shameless piece of work, Gideon McGrath,' she told him, the irresistible smile doing nothing good for her pulse rate.

'In my place, you'd do the same.'

Undoubtedly.

And, since they both knew that right now her prime motivation was keeping him stress-free, he had her. Again.

It took a moment for her eyes to adjust to the dim interior, but at first glance his room appeared to be identical to her own. It certainly wasn't any larger or fancier, so presumably Serafina had chosen it as the bridal suite purely because of its isolation at the furthest point from the main building.

Tomorrow it would be decked with flowers. There would be fresh fruit, champagne, everything laid on for the stars of the show.

For the moment, however, it was bare of anything that would give a clue to the character of its occupant. There was nothing lying on the bedside table. No book. No photograph. Nothing to offer any clues as to who he was. What he was. He'd said travel was his business, but that could mean anything. He could work for one of the travel companies, checking out hotels. A travel writer, even.

No laptop bag, either.

'I can't see it,' she called.

'Try the wardrobe.'

She opened a door. A well-worn carry-on leather grip was his only luggage and, apart from a cream linen suit, his clothes

were the comfortable basics of a man who had his life pared
to the bone and travelled light.

His laptop bag was on a high shelf—put there out of reach
of temptation by his doctor?

'Got it!'

She took it down, unzipped the side pocket, but there were
no files, no loose paperwork. Obviously it wasn't just his
wardrobe that was pared to the bone. The man didn't believe
in clutter. Not that she'd been planning to snoop, but a letter-
head would have given her a clue about what he did.

'Forget the notebook, just bring the bag,' he called impatiently.

All he carried was a small plain black notebook held
together by an elastic band, an array of pens and the same state-
of-the-art iPhone that she used and a small but seriously expensive digital camera.

She extracted the notebook, selected a pen, then zipped the
bag shut and lifted it back into place.

'I thought I asked you to bring the bag,' he said when she
handed them to him.

'You did, but I thought I'd give you an incentive to get back
on your feet.'

His eyes narrowed and he took them on a slow, thoughtful
tour of her body. It was as if he were going through an empty
house switching on the lights. Thighs, abdomen, breasts
leaping to life as his eyes lighted on each in turn. Lingered.

Switching on the heating.

Then he met her eyes head-on with a gaze that was direct,
unambiguous and said, 'If you're in the incentive business,
Josie, you could do a lot better than that.'

She'd had her share of utterly outrageous propositions from
men since she'd been in the events business, most of which had,
admittedly, been fuelled by alcohol and, as such, not to be taken
seriously, even if the men involved had been capable of
carrying them through.

They were all part of the job and she'd never had any problem dealing with them so the heat searing her cheeks now had to be caused by the sun. It was rising by the minute and the temperature was going up with it.

'Lunch?' he prompted.

'What?'

'As an incentive?'

Another wave of heat swept over her cheeks as he laughed at her confusion. Furious with herself—she did not blush—she replaced her dark glasses and managed a brisk, 'Enjoy the magazine, Mr McGrath.'

'I don't think so,' he said, holding it out to her. 'Give it to Alesia.'

'Alesia?'

'The receptionist. The girls on the staff will get a lot more enjoyment than I will, catching up with the inside gossip on the wedding.'

'Are you quite sure?' Something about him just brought out the worst in her. The reckless… 'You have no idea what you're missing.'

'You can tell me all about it over lunch.'

The man was incorrigible, a shocking tease, but undoubtedly right. And thoughtful, too. Who would have imagined it?

Taking the magazine from him, she said, 'So, what would you like?' His slate-grey eyes flickered dangerously, but she didn't fall for it again.

'For lunch? Why don't you surprise me?' he said after the briefest hesitation.

'I thought I already had,' she replied, mentally chalking one up to herself. 'Don't overdo it with that heavy pen,' she warned. 'I need you fit and on your feet, ready to fly out of here tomorrow.'

'Don't hold your breath,' he advised.

'So that would be a light chicken soup for lunch…' she murmured as she walked away. 'Or a little lightly poached white fish.'

'Chilli.'

Nothing wrong with his hearing, then.

'Or a very rare steak.'

'Maybe just a nourishing posset…'

A posset? Gideon frowned. What the heck was a posset? It sounded like something you'd give a sick kid…

Oh, right.

Very funny.

And she'd also managed to get in the last word again, he realised as the sound of her humming a familiar tune faded into the distance.

Never smile at a crocodile…

He grinned. Any crocodile who came face to face with her would turn tail and run, but plain Josie Fowler didn't frighten him. She could strut all she wanted in those boots but she'd made the fatal error of letting him see beneath the mask.

He knew that without wax her spiky purple-tipped hair curled softly against her neck, her cheeks. That her eyes needed no enhancement and, beneath the unnatural pallor of her make-up, her complexion had a translucent glow.

But, more important than the surface image, he'd recognised an odd defensiveness, a vulnerability that no one who saw her now, head high, ready with a snappy retort, would begin to suspect.

She'd had the last word, but he had the advantage.

Josie hummed the silly song as she walked along the bridge to the central building, well pleased to have got in the last word. It would serve Gideon McGrath right if she delivered up some bland invalid dish.

Probably not a posset, though.

She didn't want to risk the cream and eggs giving him a heart attack, although actually, come to think of it…

'Behave yourself, Josie,' she muttered as she stepped out of the sun and into the cool reception area and got an odd look from a sensibly dressed middle-aged woman who was wearing a wide-brimmed hat and carrying binoculars.

Although, on consideration, that probably had less to do with the fact that she was talking to herself than the way she looked.

In London she didn't seem that out of place. Here…

'Hello, Miss Fowler.' The receptionist greeted her with a wide smile. 'Have you settled in?'

'Yes, thanks. You're Alesia?'

'Yes?'

'Then this is for you,' she said, handing over the magazine.

The woman's eyes lit up as she saw the cover. 'It's Crystal Blaize,' she breathed. 'She is so beautiful. Thank you so much.'

'Don't thank me, thank Mr McGrath. He said you would like it.'

'Gideon? He thought of me, even when he is in so much pain? He is always so kind.'

Gideon? If she was on first name terms with him, he must be a regular visitor, which went some way towards explaining his almost proprietorial attitude to the place. The fact that he seemed almost… well… at home here, despite the lack of any personal touches in his room.

'Have you met her?' Alesia asked.

'Who? Oh, Crystal. Yes.' Briefly. She'd insisted on a meeting before she'd left, wanting to be sure that Crystal was happy with the arrangements. Happy with her. 'She's very sweet.'

And so desperately grateful to have someone who didn't terrify the wits out of her to hold her hand on her big day that Josie had dismissed the gossips' version of Serafina's departure as utter nonsense.

Apparently Marji, with more of a heart than she'd given her credit for, had taken pity on her.

Or maybe she just wanted to be sure that the bride didn't turn tail and run.

'Is Mr Kebalakile in his office?' she asked.

'Yes, Miss Fowler. He said to go straight through.'

'Come in, come in, Miss Fowler,' David said, rising to his feet as she tapped on the open door. 'Are you settled in? You've had breakfast?'

'It's Josie,' she said. 'And yes, thank you. It was perfect.' What she'd had of it. But it had gone down well with the monkey. 'I do, however, have a few problems with the accommodation. Only,' she hastened to add when his face fell, 'because I'm here on business rather than attempting to get away from it all.'

'You mean the lack of communications?'

'Since you bring it up, yes. How, for instance, am I expected to ring for service without a telephone?'

'You don't need a telephone, there's a bell pull by the bed.' He mimed the tugging action. 'It's all explained in the information folder left in the room.'

That would be the one she hadn't got around to reading.

'It's low-tech, but it's low maintenance too. It's just a question of renewing the cords when some creature decides to chew through them. And it works even when it rains.'

'It doesn't reach to the *Celebrity* offices, though.'

He grinned, presumably thinking she was joking.

'David, I'm serious. I understand you have a satellite link for the telephone and Internet?'

'Sorry. I was just imagining how much cord...' He shook his head. 'You're quite right. We have excellent communication links which are reliable for almost one hundred per cent of the time.'

Almost? She didn't ask. She had enough to worry about without going to meet trouble halfway.

'They are, of course, yours to command.'

Of course they were. She wasn't a guest. She was a collaborator on a wedding that was going to make this the most talked about place in the world by next week. Gideon must have realised that, even if she was too slow-witted to work it out for herself. She'd have to take it slowly today so that her brain could keep up, or she was going to do something really stupid.

'I've had a desk brought in here for you,' he said, indicating the small table in the corner. 'I'm out and about a lot so you'll have the office to yourself most of the time but just say if you need some privacy.' He produced a key. 'The office is locked when I'm not here, so you'll need this.'

She'd have willingly sat on his lap if it gave her access to the Net, but it was clear that this wedding was a very big deal for Leopard Tree Lodge.

It might be a venue for the seriously rich—who might, like Gideon, disapprove of their retreat being contaminated by mere celebrities—but everyone was feeling the pinch right now.

'Thank you, David. We'll be working together on this so it makes perfect sense to share an office.' With that sorted, she moved on. 'Next problem. Can you tell with what the situation is with Mr McGrath?'

'You've met Gideon?' He seemed surprised.

'Briefly,' she admitted.

'Well, that's excellent. I'm sure the company did him good.'

'I sincerely hope so. Since he's occupying the bridal suite?' she added.

'Ah. Yes. I was going to—'

'As you know, the photographer will be arriving first thing tomorrow in order to set everything up for a photo shoot and then cover Crystal and Tal's arrival,' she continued, firmly cutting off what she suspected would be an attempt to persuade her to switch rooms. Gideon might be a valued guest but, while she was sympathetic, her responsibility was to her client. 'Presumably you have some way of evacuating casualties?'

'There is a helicopter ambulance,' he admitted, 'and Gideon has been offered a bed in the local hospital.' She let out the metaphorical breath she'd been holding ever since she'd realised she had a problem. 'However, as his condition requires rest and relaxation rather than medical intervention, he chose to remain where he is.'

'Who wouldn't? But—'

'Our own doctor consulted with his doctor in London and they both agreed that would be much the best thing.'

'But not essential?' she pressed.

'Not essential,' he admitted. 'But, since Gideon owns Leopard Tree Lodge—' He raised his hands in a gesture that suggested there wasn't a thing he could do.

Josie stared at him.

He owned Leopard Tree Lodge?

'I didn't know,' she said faintly. 'He didn't mention it.'

'He probably thought you knew. He owns many hotels and resorts these days, but this was his first and he oversaw every phase of the building.'

Oh…sugar. Proprietorial was right. But surely…

'If he owns this place,' she persisted, grasping at the positive in that, 'he must know that the room is taken. That every room is taken. Why it's absolutely essential that he moves.'

Except that he hadn't.

On the contrary, he had maintained that a noisy celebrity wedding was utterly out of place in this setting, which suggested that not only didn't he understand, he didn't approve.

'He didn't know about the wedding, did he?' she demanded.

'I couldn't say, but obviously Gideon doesn't have anything to do with the day-to-day running of the business. Hotel bookings are handled by a separate agency. Gideon's primary role is looking for new sites, developing new resorts, new experiences.'

'So why is he here?' she asked. A reasonable question. This was an established resort.

'His spirit needs healing. Where else would he go?'

His spirit?

Obviously he meant the man was stressed…

'Would you like to get in touch with your office now?' he asked, making it clear that he had nothing more to say on the matter.

She considered challenging him, but what would be the point? David wasn't going to load his boss onto a helicopter and ship him out.

She'd have to talk to Gideon herself over lunch, make him see reason.

He might not like the idea of a celebrity wedding disturbing the wildlife, but as a successful businessman he had to realise how much he had to gain from the publicity.

So that would be chilli…

'I'm sure you would like to let them know you've arrived safely,' David urged, doing his best to make up for his lack of help over the cuckoo sitting in her bridal nest. 'My computer is at your disposal.'

'Yes. Thank you.'

'If I could just ask you not to mention the facility to any of the wedding guests? If word gets out, neither of us will be able to move for people wanting to "just check their email". People think they want to get away from it all, but…' He shrugged.

'Point taken,' she said. 'And I'll try not to get under your feet more than I have to. In fact, if you could point me in the direction of a socket where I could recharge my net book I'll be able to do some work in my room.' Then, as he took it from her, 'What do you do when the sun isn't shining? You do have some kind of backup?' she asked, suddenly envisaging a whole new crop of problems. 'For fridges, freezers?'

'We use gas for those.'

'Sorry?'

'It's old technology. Gideon considered using paraffin but gas meets all our needs.'

'So do you use gas for cooking too?'

'In the kitchen. We also have traditional wood-fired stoves in the compound which we use for bread and roasts.'

'Fascinating. Well, I'll try not to be too much of a burden on your system, but I would like to check my email for any updates from *Celebrity*. The guest list seems to change on the hour.' She might get lucky and discover someone had cancelled. 'And I need to telephone my office to warn them that I don't have a signal here.'

'Please, help yourself,' David replied, leaving her to it. 'I'll be outside when you're ready to be shown around.'

CHAPTER FIVE

From the original and chic to quirky and fun, add a highly individual touch to your reception. Use your imagination and follow the theme of the wedding for your inspiration...

—*The Perfect Wedding* by Serafina March

JOSIE downloaded the latest changes to the guest list from Marji onto a memory stick and sent it to print while she called her office.

'No mobile signal? Ohmigod, how will the celebs survive?' Emma giggled. 'Better watch out for texting withdrawal symptoms—the twitching fingers, that desperate blank stare of the message deprived— and be ready to provide counselling.'

'Very funny. Just get in touch with Marji and warn her that there are no power points in the rooms, will you. The hairdresser and guests will need to bring battery or gas operated dryers and straighteners.'

While she had the phone in her hand, she double-checked delivery details with the florists, caterers, confectioners. That left Cara, Gideon's PA, and she dialled the number with crossed fingers. With luck, the answer would be sufficiently compelling to get him on her side...

'Cara March...'

March? As in Serafina...

'Miss March, Josie Fowler. Gideon McGrath asked me to call you.'

'Gideon? Oh, poor guy. How is he?'

In pain. Irritable. About to fire your sorry ass…

'Concerned. He wants to know—and I'm quoting here—what the hell is going on in Marketing.'

'Marketing?'

'I get the feeling that he's not entirely happy about having the Tal Newman wedding at Leopard Tree Lodge.'

'Oh, good grief, is that this week?' she squeaked.

'I'm afraid so.'

'Damn! And bother Gideon for taking a sentimental side trip down memory lane this week. If he'd just stuck to his schedule, gone straight to Patagonia as he was supposed to, he'd never have known about it.'

Sentimental? Gideon?

'You don't think he would have noticed six weeks of articles in *Celebrity*?' Josie enquired, wondering why his staff had conspired to keep this from him.

'Oh, please. Can you imagine Gideon reading *Celebrity*? Besides, he's far too busy hunting down the next challenge to notice things like that. He never changes his schedule, takes a day off…'

'No?'

'Look, tell him it's nothing to do with Marketing, will you. Aunt Serafina called in at the office to drop something off for my mother absolutely yonks ago. She asked me for a brochure and, like an idiot, I gave her one. I had no idea she was looking for somewhere unusual, somewhere off the beaten track for the Newman wedding. And I'm here to testify that she doesn't understand the word "no".'

'Oh.'

'You're the woman who *Celebrity* sent in my aunt's place, aren't you?' she asked.

'Yes. How is she?'

'Spitting pips, to be honest, but that's not your fault. She can be a little overwhelming if you're not used to her.'

'So I've heard. Her design is amazing, though. Tell her I'll do my best to deliver.'

'Actually, I won't, if you don't mind. Just the sound of your name is likely to send her off on one. But you can tell Gideon that I'm entirely to blame and he can fire me the minute he gets back if it will make him feel any better.'

'He won't, will he?'

Anyone with Serafina March for an aunt deserved all the sympathy they could get.

'Probably not. Josie…about Gideon. Since he's there, see if you can persuade him to stay for a while. We've all been concerned about him. He really does need a break.'

'You just wish he'd chosen somewhere else.'

'I have the feeling that Leopard Tree Lodge might have chosen him,' she said.

Terrific. Now she was involved in the conspiracy to keep him here. She picked up the printout of the latest guest list, praying for an outbreak of something contagious amongst the guests.

'All sorted?' David asked as she joined him in the lounge.

'Not exactly,' she said, skimming through Marji's updates. No one had cried off. On the contrary. 'We're going to have to find another room.'

'How's it going?'

Gideon McGrath, cool and relaxed as he lay in the shade, removed his sunglasses as Francis set down the lunch tray beside him, giving Josie the kind of glance that made her feel even more hot and frazzled than she already was.

'How's your back?' she shot right back at him. She was in no mood to take prisoners.

'It's early days.' Then, once Francis had gone, 'The coffee helped, though.'

'I'm glad to hear it,' she replied, helping herself to a glass of water from a Thermos jug. 'And what's on that tray had better finish the job.'

'You're just teasing me with false hope.'

'It's chilli,' she said, in no mood for teasing him or anyone else. 'Why didn't you tell me you own this place?'

'Does it matter?'

He said it lightly enough, but there was a challenge in those dark eyes that suggested it did.

'It does when the manager feels he can't ask you to leave, despite the fact that the room has been bought and paid for by a bona fide guest,' she replied.

'None of my resort managers would expect a sick guest to leave. You, I take it,' he said, 'have no such inhibitions.'

'Too right. Although, since we both now know that you're not a guest, you'd better enjoy that chilli while you can.'

'That sounds like a threat.'

'I don't make threats. I make promises. Unless you make your own arrangements to leave, I'll be ordering up an air ambulance to take you out of here first thing in the morning. You'd better decide where you want it to take you.'

'Ambulances only have one destination,' he pointed out. 'They're not a taxi service.'

'Right. Well, that's an additional incentive because I'm betting they don't have an la carte menu at the local hospital,' she replied, refusing to think what that would be like.

He was successful, wealthy. Hospital would be a very different experience for him, she told herself, blocking out the memory of her mother shrinking away to nothing in a bare room.

Gideon McGrath would be in a private suite with the best of everything. Maybe. Would the local hospital have private suites?

'Is that really chilli?' he asked gently, as if he genuinely sympathised with her dilemma. And, just like that, all the hardfaced determination leached out of her and she knew that she couldn't do it.

'I wanted you in a good mood,' she admitted. 'I even phoned your PA and gave her your message.'

'What did she say?'

'The exact word was unrepeatable,' she replied. 'Have you never heard of Serafina March?'

'March? That's Cara's name. Is she a relative?'

'Her aunt. She's the queen of the designer wedding. She wrote *The Perfect Wedding*, the definitive book on the subject.'

'I take it there is some reason for you telling me this.'

'You can relax, Gideon. This hasn't got anything to do with your marketing department thinking up new ways to drum up business. Serafina visited her niece in the office and saw some photographs of this place. Quiet, off the beaten track, just what she was looking for.'

'Why didn't someone just say no?'

'Apparently she is unfamiliar with the word. Cara offered to take the blame, fall on her sword if it will help.'

'Only because she knows she's indispensable.'

She'd said that too, but Josie didn't tell him that. Instead, she swallowed a mouthful of water, then, hot, tired, she pushed her glasses onto the top of her head, tilted it back and poured the rest of it over her face, shivering as the icy water trickled down her throat, between her breasts. Then she poured herself another glass before turning to find Gideon staring at her.

'Did you want some water?' she offered.

'Er… I'll pass, thanks.'

She glanced at the glass in her hand and then at him. 'No…' Then, despite everything, she laughed. 'You really shouldn't put ideas like that into my head. Not after the morning I've had.'

'Pass me the chilli and take the weight off your feet,' he said. 'My shoulder is at your disposal.'

It was a very fine shoulder. More than broad enough for a woman to lay her head against while she sobbed her heart out. Not that she was about to do that.

'You already said,' she reminded him, uncovering the chilli and passing it to him, along with a fork. 'But if your shoulder was truly mine I'd have it shipped out of here so fast your feet wouldn't touch the ground. The wise decision would be to go with it.'

Gideon grinned as he tucked into the first decent food he'd had for two days. She was a feisty female and if they'd been anywhere else he'd have put his money on her. But it was going to take more than tough talk to shift him. This was his home turf and all the muscle was on his payroll.

She poured herself another glass of water, this time to drink, and needed no encouragement from him to sink onto the lounger beside him.

'Damn, this is good,' he said. Then, glancing at her, 'Aren't you hungry?'

Her only response was to lift her hand an inch or two in a gesture that suggested eating was too much effort. Maybe it was. Now she was lying down, her eyes closed, the I'm-in-charge mask had slipped.

He'd seen it happen a dozen times. Visitors arrived hyped up on excitement, running on adrenalin and kept going for an hour or two, but it didn't take long for the journey, the heat, to catch up with them. It had happened to him once or twice and it was like walking into a brick wall.

'Okay, give,' he said. 'Maybe I can help.'

'You can, but you won't.' She caught a yawn. 'You'll just lie there, eating your illicit chilli and gloating.'

No… Well, maybe, just a little. He was in a win-win situation. He could make things as difficult for her as possible but, no matter what horrors occurred at this wedding, he knew the pain wouldn't show on the pages of *Celebrity*.

Short of the kind of disaster that would make news headlines, the photographs would show smiling celebrities attending a stunningly original wedding, even if they had to fake the pictures digitally.

In the meantime, he had the pleasure of the wedding planner doing everything she could to make him happy.

He smiled as he lifted another forkful of his chef's excellent chilli. Then lowered it again untasted as he glanced at her untouched lunch.

Was she really not hungry? Or was the food…?

He eased himself forward far enough to lift the cover on her plate.

Steamed fish. Beautifully cooked, no doubt, and with a delicate fan of very pretty vegetables, but not exactly exciting. Clearly, she'd taken the ultimate culinary sacrifice to give him what he wanted.

'I won't gloat,' he promised.

'Of course you will,' she replied without moving. Without opening her eyes. 'You're hating this. If you could wave a magic wand and make me, Crystal, Tal and the whole wedding disappear you'd do it in a heartbeat.'

'My mistake,' he said. 'I left the magic wand in my other bag.'

Her lips moved into an appreciative smile. 'Pity. You could have used it to conjure up another couple of rooms and solved all our problems.'

'Two? I thought you were just one room short?'

She rolled her head an inch or two, looking at him from beneath dark-rimmed lids. Assessing him. Deciding whether she could take him at his word.

'Don't fight it,' he said. 'You know you want to tell me.'

'You're the enemy,' she reminded him. Then, apparently deciding that it didn't matter one way or the other, she let her head fall back and, with a tiny sigh, said, 'My problem is the chief bridesmaid.'

'Oh, that's always a tricky one. Has she fallen out with the bride over her dress?' he hazarded. 'I understand the plan is to make them as unflattering as possible in order to show off the bride to best advantage.'

Her mouth twitched. 'Wrong. I promise you the bridesmaids' dresses are show-stoppers.'

'Oh, right. The bride has fallen out with the bridesmaid for looking too glamorous?'

'Not that either.'

'The bride caught her flirting with the groom?' Nothing. 'Kissing the groom?' A shake of her head. 'In bed with the groom?'

'That would mean the wedding was off.' Her voice was slowing as she had to think harder to find the words. 'This is worse. Much worse.'

'What on earth could be worse than that?'

'The chief bridesmaid has dumped her partner.'

'Oh.' He frowned, trying to see why that would be a cause for wailing and gnashing of teeth. 'Surely that means you've got an extra bed? You could share her room and the happy couple could have yours. Problem solved.'

'Problem doubled,' she replied. 'The reason she dumped him is because she has a new man in her life and she's not going anywhere without him.'

'Okaaay,' he said, still not getting it. 'One man out, one man in. No gain, but we're just back to square one.'

'If only life were that simple. Unfortunately, her ex is the best man and while I'd love to suggest that you move in with him, solving one of my problems,' she said, still awake enough to wield her tongue with sarcastic precision, 'it seems that he wants to show the world just how much he isn't hurting. To that end, he's bringing his brand new girlfriend with him.'

'You're not convinced that it's true love?'

'Anything is possible,' she admitted, 'but it would have made my life a whole lot easier if he'd declared himself too broken-hearted to come to the wedding…'

All the tension had left her body now. Her hand, beside her, was perfectly still. Her breathing was slowing. For a moment he thought she'd gone, but an insect buzzed noisily across the deck just above her and she jerked her eyes open, flapped at it.

'*Celebrity* would have loved a tragic broken-heart cover story, a nice little tear-jerker to wrap around the wedding,' she said, easing herself up the lounger, battling her body's need for sleep, 'and bump up the emotional headline count. And a new best man would have been easier to find than another room.'

'You're all heart, Josie Fowler.'

'I'm a realist, Gideon McGrath. I've left David juggling the accommodation in an attempt to find some space somewhere—anywhere. Hopefully with sufficient distance between the best man and the bridesmaid to avoid fingernails at dawn.'

'And if he can't?'

'If the worst comes to the worst I'll let them have my room.'

'And where will you sleep?' he persisted as she began to slip away again.

'I can crash in the office,' she mumbled. 'I've slept in worse places…'

And that was it. She was gone. Out like a light.

He took his time about finishing the chilli, wondering where Josie had slept that was worse than David's office floor. Who she was. Where she came from, because she certainly wasn't one of those finishing school girls with cut-glass accents who regularly descended on his office to organise the launch parties for his new ventures.

It wasn't just her street smart, in-your-face image that set her apart. There was an edginess about her, a desperate need to succeed that made her vulnerable in a way those other girls could never be.

It was a need he recognised, understood and, replacing his plate on the tray, he eased himself off the lounger, straightened slowly, held his breath while the pain bit deep. After a moment it settled to a dull ache and he wound out the shade so that when the sun moved around Josie would be protected from its rays.

That done, he tugged on the bell to summon Francis, then he made it, without mishap, to the bathroom.

Maybe he should make Josie's day and keep going while he had sufficient movement to enable him to get onto a plane. Perhaps catch up with Matt in Patagonia.

Just the thought was enough to bring the pain flooding back and he had to grab hold of the door to stop himself from falling.

Josie opened her eyes. Glanced at Gideon.

He was lying back, hands linked behind his head, totally relaxed, and for a moment her breath caught in her throat. She met good-looking men all the time in her job. Rich, powerful, good-looking men, but that was just work and while they, occasionally, suggested continuing a business meeting over a drink or dinner, she was never tempted to mix business with pleasure.

It had to be because she was out of her comfort zone here, out on a limb and on her own, that made her more vulnerable to a smile. He had, despite the bickering, touched something deep inside her, a need that she had spent a long time denying.

While there was no doubt that he was causing her all kinds of bother, it was as if he was, in some way that she couldn't quite fathom, her collaborator. A partner. Not a shoulder to cry on—she did not weep—but someone to turn to.

She wanted him gone. But she wanted him to stay too and, as if he could hear the jumble of confused thoughts turning over in her brain, he turned and smiled across at her.

The effect was almost physical. Like a jolt of electricity that fizzed through her.

'Okay?' he asked, quirking up a brow.

'Y-yes…' Then, 'No.'

Her mouth was gluey; she felt dried out. Not surprising. It had been a manic forty-eight hours. A long evening at the office making sure that everything was covered while she was away. A quick meeting with the bride, a scramble to pack and get to the airport. And she'd spent most of her time on the plane getting to grips with 'the design', making sure she was on top of everything that had to be done.

'There's water if you need it,' he said, nodding towards a bottle, dewed with moisture, that was standing on the table between them.

'Thanks.'

She took a long drink, then found the stick of her favourite strawberry-flavoured lip balm she always kept in her pocket.

'What was I saying?' she asked.

'That you'd slept in worse places than David's office.'

She paused in the act of uncapping the stick, suddenly chilled despite the hot sun filtering through the trees as she re-membered those places. The remand cell. The six long months while she was locked up. The hostel…

She slowly wound up the balm, taking her time about applying it to her lips. Taking another long pull on the water while she tried to recall the conversation that had led up to that.

The shortage of rooms. The wretched bridesmaid and the equally annoying best man. That was it. She'd been telling him about the need for yet another room. And she had told him that she'd sleep in the office if necessary…

After that she didn't remember anything.

Weird…

She stopped worrying about it—it would all come back to her—and, in an attempt to make a joke of it, she said, 'You won't tell David I said that, will you? About sleeping on his office floor. I don't want to give him an excuse to give up trying to find somewhere.'

'I won't,' Gideon assured her. 'Not that it matters. David won't let you sleep in his office. Not if he values his job.'

'His job?' She frowned. 'Are you saying that you'd fire him? When you're one of the reasons we're in this mess?'

'There are health, safety, insurance considerations,' he said. 'You're a guest. If anything were to happen to you while you were bedded down on the office floor, you'd sue the pants off me.'

'Too right.' She'd considered denying it, but clearly it

wasn't going to make any difference what she said. 'The pants, the shirt and everything else. Better leave now,' she urged him. Then, just to remind him that he owed her a favour, 'Did you enjoy your lunch?'

'Yes, thanks. Your sacrifice was appreciated.'

Sacrifice? Didn't he know that city girls lived on steamed fish and a mouthful of salad if they wanted to keep their figures? At least when they were being good. She could eat a pizza right now, but the fish would do and she turned to the tray. It wasn't there. There was nothing but the bottle of water.

'What happened to my lunch?' she asked.

'Room service cleared it hours ago.'

'Excuse me?' She glanced at her watch, frowned. It showed a quarter past four. Had she made a mistake when she'd moved it forward?

'You've been asleep for nearly three hours, Josie.'

'Pull the other one…I just closed my eyes,' she protested.

'At about half past one,' he agreed. 'And now you've opened them.'

At quarter past four? No… She looked around, desperately hoping for some way to deny his claim.

The sun had been high overhead when she'd joined Gideon for lunch. The light seemed softer, mellower now and, looking up to check how far it had moved, she realised that someone had placed a shade over her.

'Where did that come from?' she asked, startled. Then, still not quite able to believe it, 'I've really been asleep?' She could have sworn she'd simply closed her eyes and then opened them a moment later. It had felt like no more than a blink. 'Why didn't you wake me?'

'Why would I do that?' he asked. 'You obviously needed a nap.'

'Three hours isn't a nap!' she said, telling leaden limbs to move, limbs that appeared to be glued to the lounger. 'There'll be emails. Messages. I have to talk to the chef.

Unpack the linen and check that everything's there. That it's the right colour,' she continued in a rush of panic, forcing her legs over the edge. 'I've got a hundred favour boxes to put together.'

'Relax, Josie. No one rushes around in the afternoon heat. Take your cue from the animals.'

'And do what?' she demanded. 'Slosh about in the river?'

'Not in the afternoon. That's when they find a cool corner in the shade, lie down and go to sleep.'

'Check,' she said. 'Done that.'

'So has everyone else with any sense. Including the chef.' He grinned. 'Now is the time to take a dip.'

She glanced towards the wide oxbow lake that had been formed by the erosion of the bank where the river had once formed a great loop. Animals had begun to gather at the water's edge. Small deer, a couple of zebras and then, as she watched, a giraffe moved majestically towards the water and a lump caught in her throat.

This was real. Not a zoo or a safari park or David Attenborough on the telly and she watched transfixed for a moment before remembering that she had work to do and, turning back to Gideon, said, 'Actually, bearing in mind your advice about crocodiles, I think I might give that one a miss.'

'What do you think the plunge pool is for?'

'Oh, I know that one... "You can simply sit in your own private plunge pool and watch elephants cavorting below you in an oxbow lake while you sip a glass of chilled bubbly,"' she quoted, trying not to think about how good that sounded right now. 'I've read the guidebook.' Or, rather, had it read to her.

'Sounds good to me.' He began to unbutton his shirt to reveal a broad tanned chest with a delicious sprinkling of dark chest hair. 'Get your kit off and I'll ring for room service.'

Jolted from her distracted gaze, she said, 'Excuse me?'

'You're the one who suggested water therapy. I wasn't convinced but the champagne sold it to me.'

Josie was hot, dehydrated and a little water therapy—the delicious combination of cool water, hot skin and the best-looking man she'd met in a very long time—was much too tempting for a woman who hadn't had a date in a very long time.

It was in the nature of the job that events planners were working when other people were partying.

And part of the appeal.

She didn't have to think about why she didn't have a social life when she was too busy arranging other people's to have one of her own.

'You're not interested in water therapy,' she told him. 'You just want a drink.'

'If I wanted a drink,' he said, 'champagne wouldn't be my first choice. But, as a sundowner, a glass or two would help relax the muscles.'

'That sounds like a plan,' she said, well aware that he was simply amusing himself at her expense. Using her desperation to be rid of him to get what he wanted. It was the coffee, the chilli all over again but, even if she had been foolish enough to fall for it, she had far too much to do. And three fewer hours in which to do it. 'I'll smuggle a bottle past the guards for you.'

'I can't tempt you?'

Oh, she was tempted—no question about that—but a splash of water on her face and a reviving pot of tea was as good as it was going to get this evening.

'I'll take a rain check,' she said, forcing herself to her feet. 'The guests will start arriving tomorrow, including a bride and groom who'll be expecting this suite to be waiting for them.'

'Ah…'

'Ah?' She didn't like the sound of that 'ah'.

'I knew there was something I had to tell you.'

'Please let it be that you're leaving.'

'Sorry…' His regretful shrug was so elegantly done that she found herself wondering what he would be like on his feet. How he would move. Imagined the graceful ripple of those thigh muscles…

'No, Gideon,' she snapped, dragging herself back from the edge of drool. She'd tried the placatory approach, been Miss Sugar and Spice. Now she was going to have to get tough. 'You're not in the least bit sorry so don't pretend you are.'

'I am sorry that my presence is causing you difficulties. Why don't you email *Celebrity* and tell them that someone has to stay at home? Couldn't the bride manage with one less attendant? Or maybe just do her own make-up?'

'Was that it?' she enquired. 'What you had to tell me? It's a great idea, but far too late. Most of the guests are already on their way so, if that's it, I've got things to do.'

'No, there's something else. You'd better sit down,' he advised.

'I'm liking this less and less,' she said, but she was still feeling a bit light-headed. Maybe she needed another minute or two to fully wake up and she sank back down. 'You'd better tell me.'

'Tal Newman arrived in Gabarone today. He's got dinner with the Botswana national team tonight and tomorrow he's giving some youngsters a football master class before taking part in a parade giving him the freedom of Gabarone.'

'Yes. I've got the programme. It's just an average day in the life of the world's most famous football player,' she said. 'So?'

'It seems that no one thought to organise something to keep Cryssie occupied so she decided that, rather than hang around in the hotel all day, she'd fly on here and have a quiet day recuperating from the journey and hanging out with you instead.'

'Fly on here? Fly. On. Here.' She repeated the three words slowly, while her brain attempted to translate them into something meaningful. 'You're telling me that Crystal…' and when did he get so familiar with Crystal Blaize that he was calling her Cryssie? '…is on her way here? Right now?' Then, with dawning horror, 'You knew that and you just let me lie there and sleep!'

'No–'

Josie almost collapsed with relief.

'—she arrived just after lunch. She came looking for you, but when she saw how exhausted you were she wouldn't let me wake you.'

'What?' Then, leaping to her feet, 'Ohmigod! Where is she?'

Gideon was too busy making a wild grab for her as the blood rushed from her head to offer a suggestion. Or maybe too short of breath.

It had rushed from her in a little 'Ooooph' as his hands circled her ribs.

Rushed from him in a deeper 'Umph' as she made a grab for his shoulders, sank against him.

For a moment she was too winded to move. And even when she managed to suck in some air she couldn't quite manage to lift her cheek from the warm skin of Gideon's neck, her breasts from where they were cosied against his ribs. Disentangle her legs. And the two of them remained that way for a moment, locked together in immovability.

'Are you okay?'

His voice wasn't just sound, it was vibration that rumbled through her, became part of her.

'No.' In the stillness, as they caught at their breath, everything became pure sensation and she was a lot more than all right.

His pulse was pounding in her ear, she could almost taste the scent of his sun-baked skin and, beneath her hands, his strength seemed to pour into her through the hard-packed muscle of his shoulders.

'You?'

'No.'

She lifted her head, afraid that she might have done some irreparable damage to his back, but the visual impact of his stubbled chin, parted lips up so close was like falling a second time.

His 'no' had been the same as hers and the heat that came off him had nothing to do with the temperature but from some fire raging within him, a fire that sparked an answering inferno deep within her. A raw, painful need that burned deep within her belly, sparking at the tips of her breasts, burning her skin.

They had been verbally fencing with one another since he'd teased a cup of coffee out of her. Holding one another off with words while their eyes, their bodies, had been communicating in another language. One that did not need words.

Now there was nothing between them, only the ragged snatch of her breath.

Not a creature moved. Even the cicadas seemed to pause their endless stridulating so that the air was thick with the silence, as if the world was holding its breath. Waiting.

She was so close to him now that all she could see were a scatter of tiny scars high on his forehead, glints of molten silver glowing in the depths of his slate-grey eyes.

His breath was hers, her lips were his but which of them had closed the infinitesimal gap between them was unknowable.

In the still, quiet world that existed only for them, his kiss was slow, thorough, tormenting her with the promise of his power to quench the fire.

His hands softened as he drew her down to him, intensified his kiss and her body moulded naturally to his. But even that was not enough. She wanted to be closer, wanted to be naked, wanted him in the way that a woman yearned for a man, drawn by the atavistic need to surrender to the illusion of safety within his arms.

Wanted to be held, touched…

As if he could read her mind, his hands abandoned her shoulders and began to move tantalisingly, tormentingly slowly down her body, lingering agonisingly at her waist before descending to her thighs while his tongue plundered her mouth so that in her head she was screaming for more.

He responded to her urgent moan, sliding his hand beneath

her short skirt and pulling her into him so that she could feel the sudden hard urgency of his need, counterpoint to the melting softness of her desire.

She wanted to be touched, possessed, loved…

Even as she sank deeper into his embrace and his arms enfolded her, that 'loved' word, that dreadful word, the tool of mendacious men, betrayer of gullible women, splintered through her mind like a shaft of ice and she broke free, slithering from his grasp to the floor before he could stop her.

'Josie—' He followed, crashing onto the deck beside her, his hands reaching for her.

'Don't…'

She flinched, digging her heels into the deck, scooting away from him. Putting herself out of reach. Dragging the back of her hand over her mouth in an attempt to wipe away all trace of the touch, the taste of his seductive lips, the delicious temptation…

'What have I done?' he asked, but this time making no effort to follow her, hold her. And why would he? She wasn't blaming Gideon. Nothing had happened that she hadn't participated in eagerly, willingly and for a moment, one blissful moment in the warmth of his arms, she had managed to forget, shut out reality. Not this brilliant, sun-filled world, but the darkness within her.

'Nothing… It's not you. It's me. Just…' She shook her head, incapable of explaining. Finding the words to apologise for behaving so badly.

'Don't?' he offered, a great deal more gently than she deserved.

She nodded once. Then, forcing herself to behave normally, like an adult. 'Are you hurt?' He'd come down off the lounger with a hell of a crash.

'Only my pride. I don't normally get that reaction when I kiss a woman.'

That she could believe. It had been the most perfect kiss. So bewitchingly sensuous that for a moment she had been utterly seduced. Nothing less would have stolen away her wits, her determined self-control, even for a moment.

'There was nothing wrong with the kiss, Gideon.' She could still feel the heat of it singing in her blood, telling her that she was strong, could do anything. Tempting her to reach out to him, test her power. 'I just…'

She lifted her hands in a helpless gesture. She'd turned her life around. Was in control. She would never allow anything, anyone to take that from her again.

His eyes narrowed.

'Can't?' he offered helpfully, completing her unfinished sentence for the second time.

She knew that look, recognised the speculation as he wondered what had happened to her. Who had hurt her. Whatever he was thinking, he was wrong. Nothing he was imagining could be as bad as the truth.

CHAPTER SIX

The dress. Individual, unique, it is a statement of everything the bride feels about herself. A matter for secrecy,
intrigue and speculation…
—*The Perfect Wedding* by Serafina March

JOSIE steeled herself for the usual prurient inquisition—was it
rape or abuse? No man had ever asked her if he'd done something to turn her off. Not that Gideon had. For a moment she
had so utterly forgotten herself that she was still shaking with
a surge of need unlike anything she'd ever experienced.

But the question never came.

'Don't worry about it, Josie,' he said, so casually that if
she hadn't been so relieved she might have felt insulted. 'It
was nothing.'

Nothing?

'You don't have to apologise. Or explain.'

'No?'

Easy for him to say. He probably had women throwing themselves at him all the time. Not that she had. Thrown herself. She'd
had a giddy spell, had been off balance physically and mentally
or she would never have reacted so wantonly to his closeness.

The kiss had not been forced upon her. It had been inevitable from the first moment she'd set eyes on him. She'd recognised the danger, thought she could control it…

'No,' she said, turning the word from a question to a statement as she eased herself carefully to her feet—she didn't want a repeat of that giddy spell… 'Nothing at all.' Then, because he hadn't moved, 'Do you need a hand up?'

He looked up at her for a moment as if considering the physics of the skinny girl/big bloke leverage situation.

'Not a good idea.'

No. It would be too easy to repeat that tumble and it was obvious that he didn't want to risk that.

Nor did she, she told herself hurriedly.

'Shall I call someone?'

'Forget about me,' he said, apparently content to sit on the deck, his back against the hard frame. 'You've got a bride to worry about.'

'Yes…' She backed slowly away—any injudicious move was likely to stir up all those hormones swirling about her body, desperate for action. 'Did she say where she'd be?'

'Her room, I imagine.'

'Her room?' She finally snapped out of the semi-inert state where her brain was focused entirely on Gideon. 'This is her room!' she declared.

'Yes, well, that was the other thing I was about to tell you. Before you threw yourself on me.'

'What a pity I didn't do more damage.'

'Is that any way to speak to a man who, while you were snoring your head off, has single-handedly sorted out your accommodation problems?'

She was fairly sure that the snoring slur was simply his attempt to put up a wall between them and who could blame him?

Ignoring it, she said, 'What did you do? Rub a magic lamp and produce another tree house out of thin air?'

'Is that what you do when, on the morning of the wedding, the bride tells you that a long lost cousin from New Zealand has arrived with all his family and you have to find room for half a dozen extra people at a reception?'

'I don't need magic to produce an extra table,' she snapped back. 'It's my job.' Then, because this was no way to cool things down, she extended a hand, palm out like a traffic cop. 'Stop.' She took a deep breath. 'Back up.' He waited, a questioning tilt to one of those devilish brows while she took another breath. Started again. 'Thank you so much for involving yourself with my accommodation problem, Gideon. Would you care to update me?' she enquired politely.

She got an appreciative grin for her efforts and all those escaped hormones stampeded in his direction and she took a step forward as she almost overbalanced.

Maybe he noticed because he said, 'Sit down and I'll fill you in.'

She did but only, she told herself, because he was having to peer awkwardly up at her in a way that must be hurting his back. Not that he'd been feeling pain a few minutes ago…

Stop. Oh, stop…

Ignoring the low lounger—she wasn't risking a second close encounter with all those free roaming pheromones—she crossed to a canvas director's chair that David had fetched so that they could have a cosy chat over her supine body.

Tempted as she was to pitch in with yet another sarcastic comment, she suspected he was waiting for it and, since she hated being predictable, said, 'When you're ready?'

'The best man and his new girlfriend have been allocated the captain's cabin aboard the river boat. It's not like this, but they'll have the deck for game viewing and the pool if they want to cool off.'

'What about the captain?' she asked.

'He can use the first mate's cabin.'

'And the first mate?' She held up a hand. 'No, I don't want to know.' She swallowed. He was in pain, he didn't want the wedding here, but he'd still gone out of his way to help her. 'Just… well, thank you. That's an enormous help.'

Gideon, the dull ache of unfulfilled lust competing with the hard frame of the sun-lounger digging into his back for attention, was concentrating so hard on Josie that they didn't stand a chance.

A woman had every right to change her mind and she didn't have to apologise. It was obvious, from the moment he'd set eyes on her, that there had been something between them, that rare arc of sexual energy that could leap across a room on a glance. An exchange between two people destined to be naked together in the very near future. For a night, or a lifetime. Or not.

You were with someone else, or she was and there would be a shrug, an acknowledgement of what might have been.

On this occasion it had not just arced, there had been lightning and it was going to take a lot more than a shrug, a regretful look to make him forget how she'd felt in his arms. That look on her face as she'd scrambled to distance herself from him. Dismay, desperation…

It wasn't what he'd done that had sent her running. It was what she'd come close to doing.

'You've been very kind, Gideon,' she said, her words, like her body, as stiff as a board.

'Well, you know what they say. There's no such thing as a free lunch.' He lifted a brow, hoping to provoke her, get her to loosen up, let go. Get back the Josie who said exactly what she thought instead of what she thought she should say. 'I imagine that surrendering your lunch wasn't an entirely altruistic gesture?'

'Not in the least,' she admitted without a blush.

Better…

'Which brings us to the larger problem of the bridal suite. What'll it take to fix that?' Then she did blush, possibly remembering his earlier comment about incentives.

Much better…

'Nothing. It's sorted.'

'Really?' She brightened.

'We're going to be room mates.'

Gideon saw the blush fade from her cheeks as she rose slowly to her feet.

'Well, you and David have had a busy afternoon,' she said.

He'd known that she wasn't going to be happy about it and, under the circumstances, it didn't take a genius to see what she must be thinking.

'I'm sorry, but David and I went through the guest list to see if there was any way either of us could double up. But, like the Ark, everyone is coming to this wedding two-by-two. We are the only singles.'

'You could leave,' she pointed out.

'I did consider it,' he admitted. 'I even made it as far as the bathroom, but it seems that the very thought of getting on a plane was enough to make my back seize up again.'

'How convenient.'

'You think I'm enjoying this?'

'Oh, God, no,' she said, her face instantly softening, full of compassion, and that made him feel like a heel because right at this moment he was enjoying the situation rather a lot. 'I'm sorry. That was a horrible thing to say…'

He could have told her that she had an instant cure, but under the circumstances he thought it unwise and instead watched as, for the second time in ten minutes Josie struggled to come to terms with a situation she couldn't quite get her head around.

'Is flying a problem for you?' she asked.

He laughed. He knew he shouldn't but he couldn't help himself. 'Are you asking me if I'm afraid of flying?'

'It's nothing to be ashamed of,' she assured him.

'Have you any idea how many miles I fly each year?'

'Well, no, but it's a fact that the more miles you fly the shorter the odds become…'

'Stop. Stop right there. I have a pilot's licence, Josie. I own my own light aircraft. I stunt fly for fun.'

'Stunt fly?'

'It's one of the extreme holidays my company offers.'

'Oh. Right. It's just that if the problem is psychological…' She stopped. 'No. Right.' Then, 'But if you can't move, how are you going to move rooms?' she asked.

'I'm not moving anywhere. You're moving in here.'

Josie frowned. 'Say that again?' she said, hoping that she'd misheard him, misunderstood.

'You're moving in here.'

'Dammit, Gideon, you are not listening to me,' she exclaimed, throwing her arms up in the air, walking around the deck in an attempt to expel all that pent-up emotion she'd been keeping battened down. Refusing to look at him. 'This is Tal and Cryssie's room. It's all been planned.'

'Yes, well, the first casualty of battle is always the plan,' he said. 'You—or rather Cara's aunt—looked at the layout and saw privacy. Cryssie took one look and saw herself isolated about as far from civilisation as it was possible to be and her response was a firm thanks, but no thanks.'

'What?' Josie came to a halt. In front of her, at the water's edge, a line of zebras raised their heads, looking for all the world like a row of startled dowagers at a wedding who'd just heard the vicar swear… 'But she had already approved everything,' she said, turning back to face Gideon.

'Maybe it looked different on paper. Whatever, she flatly refused to be "stuck out here where anything could eat me".'

He put on a high-pitched girly voice and, despite the fact that she was already furious with him on a number of counts, would have happily throttled him at that moment, she snorted with laughter.

'She didn't say that.'

'No? Ask her.' Then he smiled too. 'I really do think you'd have been better off with the petting zoo.'

'It would have been my choice too, but it's too late for that,' she replied. 'So where have you put her?'

'She's in the tree house nearest to the central lodge, which

was, fortunately, vacated this morning. David has put the photographer and make-up artist who flew in with her next door.'

'In my room? I close my eyes for ten minutes—'

'Three hours.'

'—and you move someone else into my room.'

'You'd already accepted that you would have to surrender
your room, Josie—'

True, but she didn't have to like it.

'—and the rest of the guests won't have gone until the
morning. You might believe that we're in need of a major PR
hit, but Leopard Tree Lodge is always full at this time of year.
Cryssie did turn up a day early with her entourage and she's
lucky to have any kind of room.'

'I know and I'm sorry about that, but you should have
woken me up.'

'I'm too soft-hearted for my own good.'

'You're too chicken. You knew you'd get an argument and
hoped that if I was faced with a fait accompli I'd just roll over.'

'That too,' he admitted, with just enough of a grin to suggest
he believed he'd got away with it.

'I'd better go and shift my things,' she said. 'But this isn't over.'

'No need. Alesia did it for you.'

'Alesia…'

Not only her client, but half the staff had apparently walked
through here this afternoon. Seen her "snoring her head off".
Discussed what was best without reference to her.

He'd been right about one thing. She'd needed the sleep. But
that was all he was right about.

This was her job, her responsibility, but she didn't bother
to say what she was thinking. Instead, she turned on her heel
and went inside.

Her toothbrush was sitting in a glass beside his on the
bathroom shelf. Her clothes were hanging beside his cream
suit. Her purple wheel-on suitcase was snuggled up cosily
alongside his battered soft leather grip.

Even her briefcase had been brought in from the deck and placed tidily on the desk. And she knew exactly what he had done.

He hadn't discussed this with David. Employee or not, as the manager of this hotel he would never have agreed to something like this without consulting her. It was Gideon. Determined not to leave either Leopard Tree Lodge or surrender his own precious tree house to the unwanted bride and groom, he'd told David that this was her idea.

No doubt he'd shrugged, brushed aside the inconvenience, done a good job of presenting himself as the nice guy who was putting himself out to do everyone a favour.

And why wouldn't David have believed him? After all, there she was, fast asleep, totally at home in Gideon's tree house. Jane to his Tarzan.

It was all as neat and nice as the vast bed that Gideon seemed to believe she would share with him.

'Is everything there?' he asked when she emerged, blinking, into the late sunshine. Looking up at her from the deck, where he was looking more comfortable that he had any right to be.

'Oh, yes. They haven't missed a thing,' she said, sliding her dark glasses over her eyes.

'Well, good.' She noted that he sounded a little less certain now. 'I know how busy you are and I thought it would save you some time.'

'You thought that, did you?'

He shook his head. 'Okay. Tell me what's wrong.'

'Wrong?' she repeated, keeping it light, casual as if she had absolutely no idea what he was talking about, all the while holding in the urge to laugh hysterically. 'What could possibly be wrong?'

'I don't know. I've sorted out your accommodation problem. Your bride has got the room she wants. And that bed is big enough for both of us to sleep in without ever finding one another.'

There wasn't a bed big enough in the entire world…

'You were prepared to take the office floor, Josie. This has got to be better than that.'

'Maybe so, but it should have been my decision.'

'I made it easy for you.'

'No, you made it easy for yourself. No argument. Decision made. Everyone happy. Job done.'

He didn't bother to deny it but, with a shrug that could have meant anything, he said, 'I get the feeling you're about to prove to me how wrong I was about that.'

'It's just as well that sleeping on a hard surface is good for the back, or that since you're not going to sue yourself, there can be no objection to you sleeping on the office floor. You are so out of here.'

Josie didn't wait for his response, but went in search of Crystal, muttering a furious 'damn' with every step.

What was really galling was that she knew Gideon was right. She should be grateful to him for taking the time and trouble to summon David and sort everything out, relieving her of at least one worry.

He owned this place and he didn't have to share one inch of his precious space with her. It wasn't even the fact that he was a man that bothered her. She would have moved in with one of the *Celebrity* staff, male or female, without a second thought if they weren't already doubled up.

It was the obvious answer, the grown-up answer, one she might even have got around to suggesting herself, given enough time and a lack of any other option—although she'd still have taken the office floor, given the choice.

But, while he'd no doubt acted from the best of motives, Gideon couldn't possibly know how it made her feel to have control over what she did, where she slept, taken out of her hands.

How helpless, powerless that made her feel.

Or that it was something she'd vowed long ago would never happen to her again.

Stupid, stupid, stupid, she thought, slowing as she approached the last set of steps.

There were two rules.

One—never make a threat you aren't prepared to carry out or, worse, make one that you're powerless to deliver on.

Two—if you can't control the things around you, you can at least control yourself.

She'd just broken them both.

She stopped as she reached the steps to Crystal's tree house. Took a moment to regain control over her breathing, wipe Gideon McGrath from her mind.

Crystal appeared, swathed in a gorgeous silk kimono wrap, before she'd managed either.

'Josie! I was just going for a swim. Want to join me?'

'I haven't got time for a swim, but I'll walk down with you. I'm sorry I was asleep when you arrived. You should have woken me and I'd have sorted out your room for you.'

'No need. Gideon was so sweet; he sorted it all out in a minute. You must have been totally wiped to have slept through all that coming and going.'

'Even so. It's my job, Crystal—'

'Cryssie, please.'

'It's my job, Cryssie. Come to me if you have any problems, okay? Day or night.' Then, 'How's your tree house?'

'Great. Really cute, although I have to admit that when we flew in I thought I'd arrived at the end of the earth. Then, when David took me right out there into the woods…'

'Serafina thought, I imagine, that you and Tal would welcome the privacy.'

'Oh, please. This is a media wedding; there is no such thing as privacy.'

'So why did you do it? It's not as if you're keeping the money.'

She shrugged. The boldly coloured silk wrap shimmered in the sunlight and as they walked through the boma a couple of middle-aged men, showing off their day's 'bag' of photographs over a sundowner, nearly broke their necks as they did a double take.

'People think I'm just another dumb underwear model who's bagged herself an equally dumb footballer,' Cryssie, said, apparently unaware of the stir she was creating. Or maybe she was so used to it that she no longer noticed.

They were much of a height, but that was all they had in common. Cryssie was absolutely stunning and Josie, who'd never worried about her lack of curves or the fact that the only heads that turned in her direction were in disbelief, felt a pang of something very like envy as she realised why Gideon had suddenly become Mr Helpful instead of Mr Obstructive.

Who wouldn't fall under the spell of such beauty?

'We were going to have the press all over us anyway, so we decided to make it mean something.' Cryssie stopped by the edge of the pool, oblivious to the sudden stillness as she slipped off her wrap to reveal a matching strapless swimsuit and a perfectly even tan. 'We're using the money to set up sports holiday camps for special needs kids.'

Not only beautiful, but caring too. Who could compete with that?

'That's a wonderful thing to do.'

'We've been lucky and it's worth the circus to put something back. But this is the last. We're not going to be living our lives, having our babies on the front pages of the gossip mags. So,' she said, turning a hundred watt smile on Josie, 'we're going to have to give them their money's worth.'

'I'll certainly do my best.'

As she settled on a chair and stretched out, a white-jacketed waiter appeared.

'Sparkling water, please. No ice. Josie?'

Josie glanced longingly at the pool, but shook her head. 'Thanks, but I have to get on.'

'Maybe we could have dinner together later? Talk things through. About seven?'

'Of course. Is there anything you need before then?'

'No. Oh…'

'Yes?'

'There is my dress. I've unpacked it and hung it over the wardrobe door.' She did something with her shoulders that was far too pretty to be called a shrug. 'It's not very big, is it? There's no room inside and we've got a photo shoot tomorrow.'

'You want me to look after it?'

'Please. I don't want Tal to see it before the big day.'

'No problem. I'll pick it up on my way back.'

'Thanks. Oh, and I expect he's told you, but I invited Gideon to the wedding'

'Gideon?' Josie managed to keep the smile pinned to her face but the wretched man had been a problem since the moment she'd first set eyes on him and she'd thought she would be safe at the wedding.

'One extra won't be a problem, will it? You'll have to redo the seating plan anyway because of Darren and Susie's bust-up,' Cryssie said, blissfully unaware of the turmoil in her breast. 'I'll be happy to give you a hand. I've got nothing to do after dinner.'

'That'll be fun,' Josie managed. Rearranging the seating plan was the least of her worries. It happened at every wedding, although, as she'd told Gideon, normally it was simply a matter of a few extra dining chairs. Beds was a new one. 'You can tell me about all the guests at the same time. That way, I'll be prepared for every eventuality. In the meantime, just ask someone to find me if you need me for anything.'

'Great.' Then, 'Oh…'

She waited, wondering what other bombshell Cryssie was about to explode.

'I think Darren's new girlfriend is a vegan.'

She let out a sigh of relief. 'She won't be the only one. I'll make sure that the chef knows about it.'

Her cue to visit the kitchens.

* * *

Gideon stayed where he was for a while, lost in thought. It wasn't that he didn't know what he'd done wrong. Josie had left him in no doubt.

She'd got it all wrong, of course. He hadn't for a moment imagined that she'd throw a virginal strop if he suggested she move in with him. Although maybe kissing her hadn't been such a great idea under the circumstances. If he'd been thinking with his head, it would never have happened. And she'd made it perfectly clear that if she'd been thinking at all, it wouldn't have happened.

But that wasn't what was bugging her.

She wasn't concerned that he'd make an unwelcome move on her. The way that kiss had ended had left him in no doubt that, spontaneous, passionate, urgent as it had been, she had problems. Despite a very natural urge to hold her, reassure her, kiss her again, taking his time about it, he'd taken his cue from her and backed off, acted as if it had been nothing. Made a joke of it, even though the heat of her strawberry-flavoured lips had been burning a hole through his brain and he'd been feeling no pain.

He knew he'd convinced her; she wouldn't have offered him her hand to help him up if she'd been in any doubt. It would have been too easy to simply pull her down into his lap.

No. It was the fact that he'd taken the decision without consulting her, choosing to let her sleep on rather than disturbing her, that had made her so mad.

'It should have been my decision.'

And she was right. He should have waited until she'd woken up but he was so used to taking decisions, leaving everyone else in his wake, that he'd forgotten that this was her show, not his.

He hauled himself to his feet. Steadied himself. The back was in a co-operative mood despite the row, or maybe because of it. If it was psychological, stress-related, it wasn't this kind of adrenalin rush that triggered it. But he'd known all along what the problem was.

It had begun on the day he'd decided to offload Leopard

Tree Lodge, rid himself of the one resort in his portfolio that he couldn't bear to visit. Couldn't stop thinking about.

He moved carefully across the deck to the tree house; the pain had definitely eased, but he wasn't about to take any chances. Once inside, it took a moment for his eyes to adjust to the different light level, but then he opened the wardrobe door and saw exactly what Josie had seen.

A stunning piece of feminine kit made from purple chiffon hanging next to his suit. A pair of high heeled shoes that appeared to consist solely of straps beside his loafers. His grip, her suitcase.

Alesia had only done what he'd asked her, but the result did not give the impression of two strangers sharing a room out of convenience—her stuff at one end, his at the other. It had the intimacy of the wardrobe of two people sharing a room, sharing a bed because they were together, an item. Because they wanted to.

He could have asked Francis to pack for him, but it was time to go, get out of here. If he called an air taxi now he'd be in time to get away tonight and, without waiting, he bent to pick up his grip.

The chef had been able to spare her an hour to go through the menu for the pre-wedding dinner.

After she'd gone through the menu, including special dietary needs, she'd checked the linen, then she and the head waiter had laid out a table so that they both knew what they'd be doing on the day of the wedding.

She had thought that the colours might be a bit overpowering, but strong light needed rich colours and the orange cloths and pale blue draw sheets looked stunning against the evening sun. The table flowers would be marigolds and forget-me-nots. To her intense relief, there were no balloons; the chance of small pieces of latex being ingested by animals was too great to risk.

It was almost dark by the time she headed back through the trees, but there were solar lamps along the bridge, on the steps and decks, threaded through the trees. It gave everything an ethereal fairyland quality.

'Are you okay on your own?' she asked Cryssie when she stopped to pick up the wedding dress. Now it was dark she could understand why she might not want to be alone out at the far end of the lodge. Might have felt a little nervous herself...

'Absolutely. It's been mad for the last few weeks. It's great to get a bit of peace, to be honest. I'm looking forward to an early night.'

'Well, you know where I am if you need anything. I'll see you later.'

That done, she straightened her shoulders and headed back to face Gideon. Eat a little humble pie.

The deck was bathed in cool, low level light, but there was no sign of Gideon and no candles had been lit inside.

He couldn't have surrendered, surely? Taken her at her word. He could barely move...

'Gideon?' she called, assailed by a sudden rush of alarm.

'I'm on the floor. Please try not to fall on top of me.'

'Where are you? What happened?'

'I'm in front of the wardrobe.'

She felt her way cautiously in the direction of his voice and collided with the edge of the open wardrobe door.

'Ouch!'

'Sorry. I should have warned you about that.'

'I'm okay.' Apart from the crack on her forehead and the odd whirling star.

She felt for the top of the door, carefully hung the dress over it, then got down on her knees and felt around until she'd found his leg. Warm, strong...

'Careful where you're putting your hand,' he warned as she edged forward and she jerked it away.

'What happened?' she repeated. 'Did you fall? Have you hurt your head?'

'No and no. I bent to pick up my bag so that I could pack and my back seized again.'

'You are such an idiot.'

'I've been lying here for hours just waiting for you to tell me that. Where the hell have you been?'

'Doing my job. Talking to the chef, discussing arrangements with David, counting tablecloths.'

Putting off the moment when she'd have to face him, apologise.

'Vital work, obviously,' he replied.

'It's what *Celebrity* is paying me for. Nursemaiding you isn't part of the deal,' she snapped. Then, not sure whether she was more furious with herself or with him, 'Damn it, Gideon, I came back ready to apologise, play nice and you've set me off again.'

'Play nice?' he repeated, with a soft rising inflection that suggested all manner of pleasurable games. 'Well, that's more like it.'

In the darkness, with no visual stimulus, his low, gravelly voice was enough to send a sensuous curl of heat winding through that hidden central core that she kept locked away. Just as his eyes had lit up her body when she'd come face to face with him that morning. As his touch had seduced her into a reckless kiss.

Every part of him seemed to touch her with an intimacy that effortlessly undermined her defences.

Control… Control…

'Are you in pain?' she asked, summoning up her best 'nanny' voice, the one she kept for panicking brides, weeping mothers-of-the-groom and pageboys intent on mayhem. Determinedly ignoring the seductive power of his voice. Blocking out feelings that she couldn't handle.

'It's getting better. Isn't lying on a hard surface supposed to be therapeutic? Maybe bringing me down was my back's way of telling me what it needs.'

'Smart back. Maybe you should sleep down here,' she suggested.

'Is that your best offer?'

'Oh, shut up. I'll light the candles,' she said, shuffling back the way she'd come so that she could move around him. She misjudged his length, caught his foot with her knee.

'Ouch!'

'Sorry…'

She backed off carefully, crawled towards the bed, banged her head against the wooden frame. 'Ouch!'

Gideon began to laugh.

'It's not funny!'

'No. Sorry…'

That was enough to set her off and, as he peppered his laughter with short scatological expletives each time he jarred his back, she broke down and, helpless with laughter, collapsed beside him, provoking another, 'Ouch!'

For a moment the two of them lay, side by side in the dark, trying to recover. It took an age for her to smother the outbreaks of giggles, but every time she said 'Sorry' it set them both off again. Then his hand found hers in the dark and all desire to laugh left her.

CHAPTER SEVEN

Some brides want to include a much-loved dog, pony or
other animal as part of their big day. This can be a challenge…

—*The Perfect Wedding* by Serafina March

'THAT's better. Are you okay?' Gideon asked as she hiccupped
and gasped as she tried to get her breath back.

'I th-think s-so.' No question. Infinitely better. She'd had
no idea that a man holding your hand could make you feel so
safe. 'You?'

'A lot better than I was ten minutes ago.' She felt, rather than
saw, him move his head and she knew that he was looking at
her. 'They do say laughter is the best medicine.'

'That would be why you were swearing so much.'

'Sorry…'

'Don't!' she warned and Gideon's hand tightened as, for a
moment, neither of them dared to breathe. When, finally, Josie
was certain that she was safe from another fit of the giggles,
she said, 'I'd better light the candles.'

'No hurry. This is good.'

Before she could react, the bell rang at the foot of the steps,
and then a dark figure appeared in the open doorway.

'*Rra*?'

'We're here, Francis. Give us some light, will you?'

'Are you hurt, *Rra*?' he asked as he lit the candles and the room filled with soft light. 'Oh, madam, you are here too. Can I help you?'

'Just see to the nets, Francis,' Gideon said. 'We're fine where we are.'

Nets?

Josie watched Francis unfasten them from the bedposts and spread them out so that they turned the bed into a gauzy cloister. Her turn to let slip an expletive. She'd thought they looked romantic, but they were mosquito nets.

'Is there anything I can bring you? *Rra*, madam?'

'A large single malt whisky for Miss Fowler and a bottle of mineral water for me, Francis. And I'm sure Miss Fowler would welcome something to nibble on. It's a long time since she had lunch.'

'Yes, *Rra*.'

'A long time since lunch?' she challenged, the minute he'd gone. 'I didn't have any lunch. And the monkey ate my breakfast. It's no wonder I nearly passed out on you.'

'Don't worry, I'll share.'

'I won't. I hope you enjoy your mineral water.' Then, 'Why didn't you let Francis help you up?'

'No rush. It's therapeutic, remember? Just lie there quietly until he comes back.'

'I haven't got a bad back,' she reminded him. Not because she didn't want to stay where she was, her hand feeling small and feminine tucked in his. But it wasn't wise, not when just being close to him was jump-starting emotions that she'd successfully held in stasis for so long that she'd become complacent, assuming herself to be immune.

'Maybe not, but you don't want to risk another dizzy spell. It being so long since you've eaten.'

'You are soooo thoughtful.'

'That's me. A man you can count on in a crisis.'

'A man you can count on to cause a crisis,' she retaliated.

Then, before they started in on one another again, she said, 'Oh, for goodness' sake. I have something to say so will you just lie there and be quiet for a moment so that I can get it off my chest?'

'An apology? They're worse than a trip to the dentist,' he said sympathetically.

She was forced to bite her lip, take a breath. He really, really didn't deserve one, but she would apologise if it killed her. 'The thing is, Gideon… What I have to say is…'

'I'm not sure that there's time for this before Francis comes back.'

'You're not making this easy.'

'Sorry…'

It was a deliberate attempt to set her off again, she knew, but she held her breath, stared straight up at the ceiling, refusing to be distracted.

'What I want to say is that I might… just…be a little bit of a control freak—'

'What a coincidence. I'd have said that too,' he broke in, so that she lost the momentum of the apology she'd been rehearsing as she'd counted tablecloths.

Just from his voice, she knew that he was smiling, undoubtedly with smug self-satisfaction. That was his problem, not hers, however, and, before he could say something that would make her forget every one of her good intentions, she pressed on.

'As I was saying, I have a very real problem with people taking over my life, leaving me without a choice…'

This was where he was supposed to interrupt, say that he understood, that he had been heavy-handed and was sorry. Instead, there was a long pause, then Gideon said, 'Is that it?'

'…and, as I was saying before I was rudely interrupted, I apologise for my overreaction to your high-handed actions,' she spat out through gritted teeth. Then, when he still didn't leap in to agree that he had been high-handed in the extreme, she added, 'Although, to be honest, I believe I would have been perfectly justified in dumping you over the railing and leaving you to the mercy of the crocodiles.' She allowed herself a smile. 'Okay, that's it. I'm done.'

'Well, that's a relief. I was beginning to think I was the one who should be feeling guilty.'

She didn't say a word.

'I see. Right, well, here's my version of the take it or leave it non-apology. In my company I make the decisions and I expect everyone to do what I tell them—'

'You must be such fun to work for.'

'I'm a generous and caring employer—'

'And maybe just a little bit of a control freak?'

'On the contrary. I welcome the involvement of my staff, I leave them to run their own departments—which is why I didn't know about the wedding—and people stay with me because I'm successful.'

'Yes?' she prompted, since he seemed to have forgotten the apology bit.

'But in the future I'll do my best to remember that you don't work for me.'

'In other words, you'll have a full and frank discussion with me before you start rearranging my life? Even if it means waking me up.'

'I wouldn't go so far as to say that.'

'No? I can see why you're so at home here, Gideon.'

'Go on,' he said, 'give me all you've got.'

She shrugged. 'It's obvious. A leopard can never change his spots.'

She'd expected him to come back with a smart answer, but he didn't say anything.

'Gideon?' she prompted after what seemed like an age.

'Yes,' he said, obviously coming back from somewhere deep inside his head. 'I have no doubt that you've hit the nail firmly on the head.'

What? She turned to look at him. He too was staring up at the ceiling but, sensing her move, he turned to look at her. Smiled. Not the slow killer smile that melted her inside. It was superficial, lying on the surface, a mask…

'Now we've got all that out of the way, are we going to be room mates?' he asked. 'Or, since it's too late to fly out of here tonight, am I to be banished to the office floor?'

She sighed dramatically. 'I thought my apology covered that, but here's how it is. One,' she said—she would have ticked it off on her finger, but he still had her hand firmly in his—'since I've been informed by Cryssie that you accepted her invitation to the wedding, it's clear that you have no intention of going anywhere until after the weekend.'

'We were both just being polite,' he assured her.

'Cryssie is a sincere and charming woman. She certainly meant it, even if you didn't so you'd better start thinking about a wedding present.'

'Done. And two?' he said.

'What?'

'You said one. I'm assuming there was a two, possibly a three.'

'Oh, yes. I just couldn't get past how quickly you could sort out a wedding present.'

'I'm making a donation to their new charity.'

'She told you about that? You two did have a nice chat.'

'Such a sincere and charming woman,' he agreed. 'And there's no such thing as free PR. Two?'

'Two,' she said, playing for time while she recalled her train of thought. Oh, yes… 'Since Health and Safety rules cover everyone—even the boss—it seems that, like it or not, we're stuck with one another. Control freaks united.'

'And three?' he enquired hopefully.

'There's no three.'

'Pity. I liked the way that was going.'

'Okay, here's three,' she said, finally breaking the connection, letting go of his hand and sitting up. 'You've got a reprieve from the office floor, but I haven't yet decided whether or not you're going to sleep on this one.' Then, as he pushed himself up so that he was leaning against the timber wall, 'Well,' she said, 'didn't you make a fast recovery once you got your own way.'

'I didn't say I couldn't move. I just didn't want to take a chance on it going again and knocking myself out on the wardrobe door.'

'Just left it for me to walk into,' she said, getting up and crossing to the wardrobe, picking out a change of clothes. 'So you really will be leaving in the morning? I'll be happy to pack for you,' she offered quickly, afraid her voice might have betrayed the little flicker of disappointment that had shimmered through her at the thought of him leaving. 'Just in case your back decides it would rather stay here.'

'What about the wedding?'

She glanced back at him. He had that delicious rumpled look that only men could pull off without having to spend hours in front of a mirror getting it just right. Too tempting.

'If the donation was big enough, I'm sure Cryssie would forgive you. Didn't you say something about having to be in Patagonia?'

'Did I?' He shook his head. 'My deputy has gone in my place.'

'But you're a control freak. Won't leaving something that important to a deputy cause you serious stress?'

Gideon hadn't given Patagonia a thought since Josie Fowler had waltzed onto his deck wearing nothing but a bathrobe that morning. He'd been having far too much fun teasing her, enjoying the fact that she gave as good as she got, but as she closed the wardrobe door he saw the white full length dress cover hanging over the wardrobe door.

'What the hell is that?' he demanded, all desire to tease draining away at the shock of seeing it here, in his room.

'It's Cryssie's dress.'

'Obviously. What's it doing here?'

'We've got a photo shoot in the bridal suite tomorrow,' she reminded him. 'Exquisite gossamer-draped bed, candles, rose petals, fabulous PR for Leopard Tree Lodge and—'

'I don't want it in here,' he said, on his feet before he had even thought about it.

'Gideon!' She put out a hand as if to support him.

'I'm fine!' he said, brushing her away.

She didn't back off, but stayed where she was for a long moment. Only when she was sure that he wasn't going to collapse did she finally let her hand drop, take a step back.

'It's not only the photo shoot,' she said, shaken by his reaction, anxious to make him understand. 'Tal will be arriving tomorrow afternoon.'

'So?'

'Well, it's obvious. He can't see it before the big day. It would be unlucky.'

Unlucky…

The word shivered through him and he put his hand flat on the wall, not because of his back but because his legs, having taken him up like a rocket, were now regretting it.

'It's not staying in here,' he said stubbornly.

'This is my room, Gideon,' she returned with equal determination. 'Your decision, remember? And that dress is my responsibility. It's not leaving here until I take it to Cryssie on her wedding day, along with a needle and thread to put the last stitch in the hem, just as I do for all my brides.'

'Tradition, superstition, it's a load of damned nonsense,' he said furiously. 'What about the tradition that he doesn't see her before the wedding? They're sleeping together, for heaven's sake.'

'That's on the day of the wedding, Gideon. And he won't. Her chief bridesmaid will spend the night before the wedding with Cryssie and Tal is going to bunk down with his best man…' Her voice trailed off and she groaned as she realised that plan had flown out of the window when the number one bridesmaid had switched partners.

'Problem?' he asked.

'Just another challenge for Mr Fix-it,' she replied sharply. Then, her face softening in concern, 'Maybe you should sit down before you try, though. You look a bit shaky.'

'I'm okay,' he said and, pushing himself off, he made it unaided as far as the sofa before the bell rang again. He remained on his feet, helping himself to the whisky from the tray Francis was carrying, downing it in one.

'*Rra!*'

'Sorry,' he said, replacing it on the tray. 'Wrong glass. You'd better bring another one.'

'That won't be necessary,' Josie said quickly.

'Bring one,' he repeated angrily. He wasn't used to having his orders countermanded. 'What's special on the menu tonight? Something tasty for Miss Fowler, I hope?' he continued, not because he was hungry, but because he wanted to annoy her. Wanted her gone…

'Chef is recommending a tagine of lamb, *Rra*.'

'What do you say, Josie?' he said, turning to look at her. 'Do you fancy that?'

'Don't worry about me, Francis,' she said, ignoring him. 'I'll get a drink in the bar if I want one. And I'll be eating in the dining room, too. Just bring Mr McGrath whatever Chef's prepared for him.'

'You can tell Chef that—'

'Gideon!'

He lowered himself carefully onto the sofa and said, 'You can tell Chef that I am sorry he's been put to such inconvenience, Francis.'

'He is happy to do it for you, Mr Gideon. We all want you to be better. My wife is hoping that she can welcome you to our home very soon. She wishes to thank you for the books.'

'I won't go without visiting her,' he promised.

'You bring his wife books?' Josie asked when Francis had gone.

'For their children.' Then, before she could make something of that, 'So, you're abandoning me for the delights of the dining room?'

'You don't want my company, you just want my lamb,' she replied. 'I'm sure whatever the chef makes for you will be delicious.'

'Low-fat girl food,' he retaliated. 'The chilli didn't do me any harm. Quite the reverse. I was on the mend until you decided to kick me out.'

Until she'd turned up with a wedding dress.

'I'm not keeping you here,' she reminded him. 'And, since you seem to be mobile, there's no reason for you to stay.'

'Who's your date?' he asked, ignoring her blatant invitation to remove himself.

'Now you're on your feet you can come to the dining room and find out,' she said sharply, taking her tone from him. 'Now, if you'll excuse me, since I've been working, I'm going to take a shower.'

'Don't forget the matches. You'll need to light the candles,' he said as she opened the door. 'Although, personally, I prefer to shower under starlight.'

'Have you ever tried to put on make-up by starlight?' She shook her head. 'Don't answer that.'

'What's the matter?' he asked as she hesitated in the doorway.

'Something…scuttled.'

'What sort of something?'

'How the heck would I know? It's dark.'

'You're not scared of spiders, are you?'

'I can handle the average bathroom spider,' she said, 'but this is Africa, where the spiders come larger, hairier. And they have teeth.'

'Fangs.'

'Fangs. Great. That makes me feel so much better.'

'The thing to remember, Josie, is that they're more frightened of you than you are of them.'

'You know that for a fact, do you?' she asked as she returned for the matches.

'Any creature with two brain cells to rub together is more frightened of us than we are of them. From hippos to ants. They only lash out in panic.'

'Well, that's reassuring,' she said. 'I'll do my best not to panic it, whatever it is.'

'Do you want me to come and guard your back while you're in the shower?'

She glanced at him and for a moment he thought she was going to say yes. Then, with a determined little shake of the head, 'I don't need a guard, I need a light.'

As she looked quickly away, the nets, glowing in the candlelight, moved in the light breeze coming in off the river and she was held, apparently entranced.

'You don't get that kind of magic with electricity,' he said as her face softened.

'No…' Then, abruptly, 'I'll make sure to mention it to the photographer. *Celebrity* will like that nineteenth century effect.'

'I'd be happier if you liked it.'

The words slipped out before he'd considered what they might mean. But then unconsidered words, actions had marked the day. He hadn't been entirely himself since he'd smelled the tantalising aroma of coffee, caught a glimpse of Josie through the branches.

Or maybe he was being himself for the first time in a decade.

'It's a mosquito net,' she pointed out. 'What's to be happy about?'

'Of course. You're absolutely right.'

She looked at him as if she wasn't sure whether he was being serious. That made two of them…

'So what am I likely to find in the bathroom?' she demanded. 'I'm assuming not hippos.'

'Not great climbers, hippos,' he agreed. 'It's probably just a gecko. A small lizard that eats mosquitoes and, as such, to be welcomed.'

'Well, great. But will it take a bite out of me?' she asked.

'Not if you're polite,' he said, wondering if perhaps he might, after all, have hit his head. He didn't appear to be making much sense. 'Step on it and all bets are off.'

'Oh, yuck…'

'I'm kidding, Josie. They live high on the walls and the ceiling and, anyway, you'll be safe enough in those boots. Just make sure you shake them out before you put them on in the morning.'

She glared at him.

'Basic bush-craft.'

Her response to that was alliterative and to the point as she struck a match and, braving the dark, advanced to where a row of tea lights were set in glass holders on a shelf. The flames grew, steadied and were reflected endlessly in mirrors that had been carefully placed to reflect and amplify the light.

'Okay?' he called.

'I can't see anything that looks as if it's about to leap out and devour me,' she replied. 'But, while this is all very pretty, I want lamps available for every bathroom. Big, bright gas lamps that will shine a light into every corner.'

'Where's the excitement, the adventure in that?' he asked.

'Believe me, Gideon, I've had all the excitement I can handle for one day.'

'It's not over yet,' he reminded her. 'Better leave the door open, just in case. All you have to do is scream…'

There was a sharp click as Josie responded by shutting the bathroom door with a firmness that suggested he was more trouble than an entire bath full of spiders.

Maybe she was right.

Gideon set down the glass, his grin fading as he leaned his head against the back of the sofa and closed his eyes to avoid looking at the wedding dress.

He'd get up, move it in a minute. For now he was content just to sit there, listening to the shower running in the bathroom, the comforting sound of another person sharing his space. Even if she was getting ready for a 'date'.

Obviously, she was having dinner with Cryssie but the fact that she'd chosen to tease him a little about it brought the smile back to his face. That she'd made the effort to provoke him, maybe make him jealous was a result and he could use that.

Even as the thought slid into his mind he recoiled from it.

He'd been using her all day, having her make phone calls, fetch and carry for him—admittedly with mixed results; she was no pushover. And she hadn't handed her lunch over without an ulterior motive.

He refused to accept that he was a control freak as she'd suggested, but he was single-minded, totally focused on growing his business.

He'd sorted out her bed shortage simply to prove that he could do it when no one else could.

That was what he did. New challenges, more exciting resorts, ever more extreme adventure breaks—the kind that his father had dismissed as ludicrous.

Who on earth would want to travel across the world to bungee jump? Go dog-sledding in the far north of Canada? Trekking through the Kalahari?

Nothing had mattered more than proving himself better than the adults who, stuck in the past, had been too stupid to listen to a teenage boy who'd seen the future.

Not his family.

Not even Lissa, the woman whose genius for design had turned this place from a basic boy's own safari lodge, much like any other, into a place of beauty. Who'd taken the utilitarian and made it magic with candles, mirrors, nets.

The wedding dress taunted him and, unable to bear it a moment longer, he hauled himself off the sofa, lifted it down and stuffed it inside the wardrobe so that it was out of sight.

He used his arm to wipe the cold sweat from his face, then leaned against the door, forcing himself to let go of the tension that had snapped through him like a wire the minute he'd seen it hanging there, like a ghostly accusation.

He'd come here to draw a line under the past but, instead of closure, it seemed to be pursuing him, hunting him down.

What was it his doctor, Connie, had said? '…sooner or later you're going to have to stop running…'

The water was still running in the shower, tantalising him with its promise of soothing, reviving heat. With the image of being crammed in there with Josie, her hands on his shoulders, sliding down his back, easing away the pain with those capable hands. Just the thought of it warmed the muscles, eased the ache, sent a hot flood of desire coursing through his veins as he imagined her small breasts against his wet skin as she kneaded away the aches, dug into the hollow at the base of his spine. In his heart…

He recoiled from the thought. Dammit, he was still using her, even inside his head.

Not good. Forget hot— what he needed was a cold shower and he opened the bathroom door just wide enough to grab a towel from the rack. As the candles flickered in the draught something moved, catching his eye, and he opened the door a little wider. It wasn't a gecko that had lost its grip sitting in the middle of the floor, but a hunting spider on the prowl for supper.

Suddenly everything went quiet as the water was turned off. He had one, maybe two seconds before Josie stepped out of the shower, saw the spider and screamed.

His chance to be a hero.

His reward, a naked woman in his arms.

As the shower door clicked, he dropped the towel on the spider, scooped it up, shut the door quietly behind him.

He steadied himself, then carried it outside, shook it carefully over the rail.

CHAPTER EIGHT

Wedding favours were traditionally five almonds to represent health, wealth, long life, fertility and happiness; the modern wedding planner will add something that memorably reflects the couple's interests.
—*The Perfect Wedding* by Serafina March

JOSIE pulled down a towel, wrapped it around her, opened the shower door, paused to take a careful look around.

The bathroom was a myriad of reflected lights, stunningly beautiful, and there wasn't a creepy-crawly, or even a friendly lizard, in sight.

'You are such a wuss, Josie Fowler,' she said as she dried off. Then she brushed her teeth, applied fresh make-up, used some wax on hair that had wilted in the steam and finally emerged, wearing the fishnet T-shirt she kept for evenings beneath a simple slipover, ready for the next round with her nemesis.

'It's all yours,' she said to an empty room.

Gideon was nowhere to be seen. Neither was Cryssie's wedding dress.

'Gideon!' she yelled, surging out onto the deck.

He emerged from the outdoor shower, dark hair clinging wetly to his neck, his forehead, wearing only a pitifully small towel—stark white against his slick sun-drenched skin—wrapped around his waist.

Standing straight, he was so utterly beautiful that for a moment she struggled for words.

'You shrieked?' he prompted.

She made an attempt to gather herself. 'The dress…' She swallowed. 'What have you done with Cryssie's dress?'

'I put it out of harm's way,' he said. 'In the wardrobe.'

'Oh…'

'What did you think I'd done with it? Tossed it into the trees for the monkeys to play with?'

'No. Sorry. It's just—'

'Your responsibility. I heard you, Josie. This is your room and you've every right to keep whatever you want in it.'

'It was just that you were so obviously disturbed by its appearance, angry even—'

'Forget it,' he said, so fiercely that she drew back a little. 'Let it go, Josie,' he said, rather more gently. 'It's not important.'

Clearly it was. His dislike of weddings was obviously rooted in something rather deeper than an aversion to long white dresses. But it was equally obvious that he didn't want to talk about it.

'I realise that all this is nothing but a huge pain in the backside for you, Gideon—'

'A little higher than that,' he suggested, doing his best to make light of it by making fun of her.

'Dammit, Gideon!' she snapped. 'This is really important to me. Sylvie has taken a huge gamble making me a partner and so far I haven't been exactly trampled in the stampede of women desperate for me to plan their weddings. I have to get this right…'

'Why?'

'Why?' she repeated, confused. 'Surely that's obvious?'

'Why was it a gamble?'

She sucked in her breath. He wasn't supposed to ask that. She shouldn't have said it, wouldn't have let it slip if she hadn't been so wound up. So desperate that everything should go without a hitch.

'You're motivated, enthusiastic and you care deeply that Cryssie's big day is special,' he pressed. 'In her shoes, I'd rather have you than Cara's scary Aunt Serafina holding my hand on my big day.'

If Sylvie had been here, it was exactly what she would have said and she was forced to blink hard to stop a tear from spilling over.

Not good. Determined not to lose it completely and blub, she took her eyes on a slow ride down that luscious body until she reached his feet. Then she shook her head.

'Sorry, Tarzan, they wouldn't fit.' And, just to prove to herself that she was firmly back in control, she made herself look up, meet his gaze. Nothing had changed. He knew what she was doing and he wasn't diverted. The question was still there…

Why was it a gamble?

'And, to be honest, embroidered, beaded satin slingbacks really wouldn't be a good look for you,' she added a little desperately.

For a moment he continued to look at her, challenge her and she thought he wasn't going to let it go, but finally he shrugged. 'You think the beads would be pushing it?'

'The bigger the feet, the less you want to draw attention to them,' she replied.

He looked down at her boots, lifted an eyebrow, said nothing.

'Cryssie will be waiting,' she said, desperate to escape. 'I'll… um… just get my briefcase.'

Gideon followed her inside. 'It's a working dinner?'

'We've got to rearrange the table layouts. Then we're going to start on the favour boxes.'

'Favour boxes?'

'Little table gifts for the guests. The boxes have been specially created to look like Tal's football strip. We have to slot them together, then fill them with all the bits and pieces,' she explained. As if he'd be interested.

'Could you do with an extra pair of hands?'

'Excuse me?' A tiny laugh, pure disbelief, exploded from her. 'Are you offering to help?'

'Now I ask you, is that likely?' he replied. 'I was going to suggest that you ask Alesia and some of the other girls to give you a hand. I've no doubt they'd love to be involved.' He shrugged. 'Just a thought.'

Just a thought. A crazy, foolish thought. The very idea of him sitting around with a bunch of women making wedding favour boxes was so ridiculous that anyone would laugh.

Everyone knew that he didn't do weddings. The engraved invitations arrived once in a while, *Gideon McGrath and Partner* inscribed in copperplate—he was never with anyone long enough for his family, friends or colleagues to be sure who it would be. Not that it mattered that much. The invitations were a formality. They knew he wouldn't attend.

The excuse would be solid. The gift generous.

Yet here he was, stuck in the middle of the biggest wedding of the year, a wedding he wanted nothing to do with, and, like an idiot, he'd volunteered to help and even Josie Fowler, who'd known him for less than a day, had understood how ridiculous it was. Assumed that he had to be kidding.

And why wouldn't she?

He could scarcely believe it himself.

'Josie!'

'Sorry,' she said as Cryssie claimed her wandering attention. All through dinner, while Cryssie had been chattering away, telling her how she'd met Tal, about the country estate they'd bought, her mind had kept drifting back to Gideon on his own back there in the trees.

His casual, 'Could you do with an extra pair of hands…?'
Not him. He couldn't have meant him.

He was so anti-weddings that he'd ordered Cryssie's dress out of his room. Her room. Their room!

And yet, even as he'd dismissed the idea out of hand, suggested asking Alesia, waved her away, urging her not to keep the blushing bride waiting, she'd felt a little sink of uncertainty. The feeling that she'd thoughtlessly spurned something rare.

That she'd hurt him…

'Where are you sitting?' Cryssie asked. 'I can't find you.'

'I'll be running things behind the scenes,' she said absently.

'That's just rubbish. I'm going to put you on this table,' she said, carefully pencilling her in. 'Right here, next to Gideon.'

'No, really,' she protested. The fact that she cared whether she'd hurt him was the biggest warning yet. Far bigger than drooling over his gorgeous body. Much more dangerous than losing her senses and kissing him. Fantasising about dribbling oil over his back and soothing the pain away. That was physical.

Caring about his feelings was on a whole different level.

But Cryssie wasn't listening.

'I want you both at the pre-wedding dinner too.'

Falling back on the need for professionalism, she summoned up the book of rules to support her. 'Serafina March would not approve.'

'Really?' Then, with a burst of giggles that attracted indulgent smiles from other late diners, 'Well, to be honest, I wouldn't have asked her.'

Josie glanced at the bottle of champagne Cryssie had insisted on ordering and sighed.

'Why don't you leave the rest of this to me, Cryssie?' she said, gathering everything up. 'It's going to be a long day tomorrow and you'll want to look your best for your photo shoot.'

'But I was going to help you with the favours,' she protested.

'Better not risk it,' she said. 'You might damage your nails.'

Cryssie extended a hand to display her exquisite extensions and giggled again. 'They are great, aren't they?'

'Gorgeous,' she said. Definitely time to get her up the wooden hill… 'Come on. I'll put this stuff in the office and then walk you back to your room.'

The champagne had made Cryssie talkative and more than a little weepie as she cleaned off her make-up. Josie just held her for a while as she babbled on about her mother, her dad.

'You will be there, Josie?' she sniffed, a long way from the poised young woman who, a few hours earlier, had dismissed this whole wedding as a media event.

'Every step of the way,' she promised, fighting back tears of her own. She did a good 'hard' act in the office, tried to remain detached, professional, throughout even the most touching event. Weddings, though, were an emotional quagmire, with a trap for the unwary at every turn. 'Come on. Into bed. Tal will be here tomorrow.'

Cryssie was asleep by the time Josie had hung up her discarded clothes. She blew out the candles, leaving her like Sleeping Beauty, enclosed within the gauzy nets, the little torch within hand's reach in case she woke in the night, while she returned to the dining room.

It was empty now. Everyone had moved on to the open fire pit in the boma, the candles had been extinguished and there was only the low level glow of the safety lighting.

As she fetched her boxes from the storeroom she could hear bursts of laughter as they drank their nightcaps and told tall stories in a wide range of accents. People had come from all over the world to stay here, experience this. By the morning they'd all have moved on to other camps, other sights. Crossing the desert, taking in the Victoria Falls, going into the mist to find the gorillas.

She, meanwhile, had more than a hundred favour boxes to deal with. She'd normally have the girls in the office doing this in spare moments, but she couldn't even call on Alesia to give her a hand. The reception desk was closed with only an emergency bell.

She found a box of matches on the service trolley, moved three candles to one of the larger tables, lit them, then spread herself out and set to work, tucking in the flaps of the flat-packed little boxes. Losing all sense of time as people gradually drifted away to their rooms, the fire died down and, within the small world of the candlelight, everything became quiet.

This wasn't a resort where people stayed up late.

They would all be up before light to grab a cup of coffee and a muffin before heading off at first light to get in another game drive, guided walk, or to glide through the reeds in a canoe in the hope of catching one of the rarer beasts on an early morning hunt or drinking at the water's edge.

'Josie?'

She started, looked up. 'Gideon…' He looked ashen in the candlelight. 'How did you get here?'

'Slowly,' he said.

'Oh, God… Sit down,' she said, leaping up, pulling out a chair. 'Do you need someone? Can I get you anything?'

'No. I'm fine. Don't fuss…' Then, as he sank carefully on the chair, 'What the hell do you think you're doing? Have you any idea what time it is? I thought you must have fallen off the bridge…'

'You were waiting up for me?' she asked, astonished.

'I've been lying down all day. I'm not tired.' Then, 'Yes, I was waiting up for you.' He didn't wait for her to laugh at him again, but looked around. 'So much for everyone pitching in to help. Where's Cryssie?'

'I put her to bed. She had a glass or two of champagne and got a bit emotional.'

'Nerves?'

'No. She was missing her mum,' she said, sitting back down, reaching for another box, concentrating hard on putting it together.

'Oh, right. When's she arriving?'

'She's not. She died when she was a teenager. Hence the tears.'

'I didn't know. That's tough.'

'Especially at moments like this. You go through the day-to-day stuff, managing, but…'

And, without warning, it got her, just as it had caught Cryssie. One minute she had been giggling with excitement, full of the joys, the next there had been tears pouring down her face at the prospect of facing the biggest, most important day of her life without her mother to support her.

It would have been so easy to break down and weep with Cryssie, but she'd held back the tears, knowing that to join in would have dragged them both down into a black pit. But it had got to her and now Gideon had provided the emotional catalyst. A stranger, a man she barely knew, staying up to make sure she got home safe. It was years since anyone had done that and, without warning, the box in her hand crumpled and, just as she'd known the moment to reach for Cryssie, he was there, solid as a brick wall, to prop her up as the memories flooded back.

The times when she'd been frightened, angry, in despair. The times when something amazing had happened. That day when, just before Sylvie had gone into church to be married herself, Sylvie had hugged her and told her that she wanted her to be her partner.

She'd been so happy, thought she might burst with pride and the only person she'd wanted to tell was her mother. Just to let her know she was all right. That everything had worked out, that she was okay…

'Sorry,' she said as her tears seeped into his shirt. 'It's been years since anyone waited up to see me home safe.'

'How many years?'

'Nearly eight.'

She let her head lie against his chest, letting the scent of freshly washed linen fill her head. That was a good memory too. Being tucked into clean pyjamas, feeling safe, protected…

'I was seventeen, almost eighteen. There'd been a party at college. It was late when I got home but Mum was sitting up for me as she always did. Pretending to be engrossed in some old movie. She made us hot chocolate and we sat in the kitchen while I told her about the party. About some boy I'd met who'd walked me home. Just talked, you know, the way you do in the middle of the night when it's quiet and there's no one to butt in.' Her throat closed with the ache of that last night of pure happiness. 'Being still like that, with no distractions, no radio…' without her mother's second husband yelling for a beer or a sandwich or his cigarettes '…I suddenly saw how tired she looked. That her clothes were hanging on her. And I knew then. Knew she was sick.' A little shiver ran through her as she recalled the fear. 'I said that maybe she should make an appointment for one of those well-woman clinics. Just for a check-up…'

But she'd already seen the doctor.

She sniffed and, as she pulled away, hunted in her pockets for a tissue, looked helplessly at the crushed mess of blue and orange card in her hand.

He made no attempt to hold her, just took the useless box from her and replaced it with a handkerchief. A proper one. White. Folded. Perfectly ironed. And that nearly set her off again but Gideon, playing the calm, unemotional role, said, 'I hope there are spares.'

'Loads,' she said, mopping up the dampness on her cheeks, grateful for the fact that she never used anything but waterproof mascara—panda eyes was such a bad look at a wedding. 'They had to be printed specially and you never know the exact number until the last minute.'

He picked one up, turning it over to examine it, before fitting it together as if he'd been doing it all his life.

'Maybe you should save some. I bet they'll go for a fortune on eBay after the wedding.'

'They'd go for a lot more if they were complete.'

'That's the next job? Filling them?'

She nodded.

'Better not waste time then.'

She watched for a moment as he placed the box he'd finished with the others, then picked up another and handed it to her before carrying on. Folding, tucking, lining them up in serried ranks of little football shirts on the table.

'Are they all the same?' he said when it was obvious they had a lot more than fifty. 'Don't the women get a Cryssie lookalike in a blue dress with orange ribbons?'

'That is such a sexist remark,' she replied, doing her best not to grin, but failing. 'This is an equal opportunities wedding.'

'I know, but it made you smile.'

'Yes, it did. Thanks.'

'Any time.'

Probably… Then, because that wasn't a wildly sensible thought, 'I'm sorry about weeping all over you.'

'I'll dry out. I'm sorry about your mother.' She fumbled with another box, dropped it, but as she bent to pick it up he stopped her.

She gave a little shake of her head and, not wanting to think about that terrible year, she began to quickly count the boxes off in tens.

'Okay, we've got enough,' she said, stacking them carefully in a couple of collapsible plastic crates that David had provided. 'Would you like a cup of tea? Coffee?'

'There won't be anyone in the kitchen at this time of night.'

She rolled her eyes at him. 'You might need a fully quali-fied chef to boil a kettle but I'm not that useless.'

'Throw in a sandwich and you've got me,' he said.

'I've already got you. It's getting rid of you that's defeating me.'

'You're right. I've been pushing myself into your business all day,' Gideon said, much too gently. 'I'll get out of your way.' He eased himself carefully to his feet, touched her arm in a small, tender I'm-here-if-you-need-me gesture. 'I'll leave a light on.'

'Don't…'

Josie didn't want him to go. He'd been driving her crazy all day, but only because she wanted to show the world that she didn't need anyone. That she could do this on her own. That she was worthy…

'You start a job, you finish it,' she said, concentrating very hard on ripping open a box containing the little nets of sugared almonds. 'You can make a start on those while I get us both a sandwich.'

He didn't say anything, but he didn't move either. She risked a glance. His expression was giving nothing away, but there was a damp patch on his shirt, right above his heart, where she'd cried on him and that told her pretty much everything she needed to know about Gideon McGrath.

He might be a little high-handed, inclined to take over, want to run things, but he wasn't afraid of emotion, wouldn't quit when something mattered to him. He wasn't her enemy, he was her ally.

'A good employer understands that feeding the workforce is vital,' she told him, growing in confidence as he stayed put. 'Especially if they're working unsociable hours.'

Gideon watched Josie battle with herself, wanting him to stay, asking in the only way she knew how. Unable to bring herself to say the simple words. Please stay… Please help… Wondered what had happened to her that had made her so afraid of opening up.

He was seized by an overwhelming urge to grab her, shake her, tell her that life was a one-off deal and she should live it to the full, not waste a minute of it.

He fought it.

'I don't work for cottage cheese,' he said, responding in kind, making it easy for her. Making it easy on himself.

'Oh?' One of her brows kicked up. 'So what will it take?'

'That's for me to know and you to find out. Let's go and take a look in the fridge.' He caught his breath as he turned awkwardly and his hand landed on her shoulder as he steadied himself.

'Sit down. I can manage,' she said anxiously.

'It's not a domestic kitchen. You'll need help.'

'I spent a year working as a hotel scullery assistant,' she replied. 'Believe me, there's nothing you can tell me about hotel kitchens.'

'Great, I'll direct, you do the work,' he said, putting the obvious question on hold.

Accepting that he wasn't going to take no for an answer, she took his hand, eased beneath it so that his arm was lying across her shoulders, then tucked her arm around his waist. 'Okay, let's go.'

There was nowhere to sit in the kitchen, so she propped him against a handy wall while she filled the kettle from the drinking water container, lit the gas, then opened one of the large fridges.

'Right. Let's see. There's cheese, cold meat, cold fish…' She peered at him around the door, all violet eyes and hair. 'What can I tempt you with?'

Not food…

'How about something hot?' he replied.

'Hot?'

Josie could still feel the heat where she'd been pressed up against Gideon as they'd walked to the kitchen and now her cheeks followed suit, warming in response to something in his voice that suggested he wasn't talking about food.

'Chilli hot or temperature hot?' she said, glad of the cool air tumbling out of the fridge.

'You're doing the tempting. You decide.'

'Okaaay…'

He wanted tempting, she could do tempting…

'I'm thinking white bread,' she said. 'Butter, crispy bacon, eggs fried so that the yolks are still running and…'

'And?'

Was he a ketchup man or a brown sauce man?

'A great big dollop of brown sauce,' she said, going for the spice.

'With a sandwich like that you could tempt a saint, Josie Fowler.'

'I think we both know that you're no saint, Gideon McGrath,' she replied, taking out a catering pack of bacon, piling on the eggs and butter before closing the fridge door.

She expected him to be grinning, but he was looking at her with an unsettling intensity and for a minute she forgot everything. What she was doing, what she'd been thinking…

Before she could collect herself, he'd pushed away from the wall and relieved her of her burden.

She still hadn't moved when he took down a pan from the overhead rail, set it on a burner and began to load it with slices of bacon.

'You've done that before,' she said, sounding like an idiot, but she had to say something, anything to break the silence, restore her balance. It had been out of kilter all day. An endless journey, her body clock bent out of shape, Cryssie's tears… She scrambled for all the reasons why she should be reacting so oddly. Any reason that didn't include Gideon McGrath.

'Once or twice,' he admitted as he lit the gas. 'And, this way, I'll be the one in the firing line if the chef decides to throw a tantrum in the morning.'

'He won't. He's a sweetheart,' she said, seizing on the chance to focus on something else. 'I was worried about his reaction to Serafina choosing an outside caterer for the wedding breakfast, but he was really sweet about it.'

Gideon shook the pan to stop the bacon from sticking, then glanced at her. 'The wedding is on Sunday, isn't it?'

'Yes. Is that important?'

'Paul belongs to a church that doesn't permit its members to work on Sunday.'

'Oh?' She reached up for a spatula. 'Shall I take over?'

'I'm good,' he said, taking it from her, adjusting the heat. 'You could butter the bread,' he suggested.

'Gee, thanks,' she said. 'My natural place in the kitchen. Taking orders from a man who thinks he knows best.'

'This is my kitchen,' he reminded her. 'When we're in your kitchen you can give the orders.'

'Don't hold your breath.'

'I never do.' He pointed with the spatula. 'You'll find the bread through there.'

She fetched the bread from a temperature-controlled storeroom, cut four slices, then tested the butter. It was too hard to spread and she ran some cold water, stood the butter in it. Waited.

Apart from the sizzle of the bacon, the faint hum of the refrigerator, the kitchen was unnaturally silent. Her fault. She'd chopped the conversation off at the knees. It was a protective device. Her automatic response to anyone who said or did anything that suggested more than a superficial acquaintance. Not just men. She did it to women, too. You couldn't lie to friends.

'How're you doing there?' he asked.

She half turned. 'Give me a minute.' Then, desperate to resume communication but on a less risky level, she said, 'How do you know all that? About Paul. I thought you don't involve yourself with the day-to-day running of your hotels and resorts.'

'I don't. I can't. But Leopard Tree Lodge was my first permanent site and Paul has been with me since it opened. I interviewed him myself. He'd been working in a big hotel in South Africa but they couldn't accommodate his religious observances within their schedule.'

'But you could.'

'I told you,' he said, 'I'm a generous and caring employer.'

'Oh, right. You brought books for his children, too?'

He glanced across at her, a small smile creasing the corners of his mouth, sparking something warm and enticing in his eyes. 'They're all grown up now. His youngest is studying medicine in London.'

And he was still buying the books, she'd bet any amount of money, she thought, doing her best to resist an answering heat that skittered dangerously around her abdomen. Just bigger and more expensive ones.

'The butter should be soft enough by now,' he said, flipping the bacon. Then, as she tested it with the knife, then carried it across the work surface, 'Tell me about being a scullery assistant.'

'What's to tell?' she replied, concentrating very hard on buttering the bread. 'I scrubbed, I washed, I peeled. End of story.'

'What about college? Even if you were going into catering, starting at the bottom, a year seems like a very long apprenticeship.'

She carried on spreading. She sensed that he was looking at her, but dared not risk looking across at him.

'I didn't finish my course,' she said, bending down for plates. 'My mother was dying. Someone had to nurse her.'

'She had a husband.'

'Yes. Did we decide on coffee or tea?'

'This late? I think we should stick to tea, don't you?'

'We should probably be having cocoa,' she said, but she was happy to go along with whatever he said, as long as he was thinking about something other than her career path. Her stepfather.

She took one of the teapots lined up for the morning trays, spooned tea into the cage, poured on boiling water.

'His back prevented him from doing very much, I imagine,' Gideon said, picking up the bacon and laying it across the bread.

Mugs, milk…

'Without my mother's salary, one of us had to work but I'd have rather starved than left her to his neglect,' she finally replied as he cracked the eggs on the side of the pan, dropped them in the hot bacon fat so that the whites bubbled up. 'The prospect of spending time with his dying wife effected a miraculous cure and he found himself a job pulling pints of beer in The Queen's Head.' She shrugged. 'Well, it was, in many ways, his second home.'

CHAPTER NINE

The wedding breakfast, great food, is at the heart of the celebration.
—*The Perfect Wedding* by Serafina March

GIDEON could feel the deeply buried anger that was coming off Josie in waves. She was covering it with the sharp sarcasm she used whenever she felt threatened, but there was a brittle tension about her, a jerkiness about her movements that was at odds with her natural grace.

That she despised the man her mother had married was obvious, but there was more to it than that. There was also a *don't go there* rigidity to her posture that warned him not to push it.

'Couldn't you have returned to your course after your mother died?' he asked, taking a different tack. Coming at her sideways. Wanting to know what was driving her. What emotional trauma was keeping her prisoner.

'No.' She poured the tea into two mugs, everything about her stance screaming, *Don't ask...* 'Milk? Sugar?' she asked calmly, her voice a complete contradiction to the tension in her body.

'Just a splash of milk,' he said, compassion compelling him to let it go.

She added the milk, returned it and everything else to the

fridge while he turned the eggs, then lifted them onto the bacon. Began to clean down the surfaces while he fetched the brown sauce, moved onto the stove. Then dealt with the pan in the swift, no-nonsense manner of an experienced kitchen hand.

'I'll bet they missed you when you left the kitchen,' he said, picking up the plates, heading back to the dining room.

Josie picked up the mugs of tea and followed him.

'Maybe they did. I certainly didn't miss them,' she said, not looking back.

Not one of them.

They'd treated the youth who'd been locked up for snatching some old lady's handbag better than they'd treated her.

It was as if there had been a fence around her hung with warning signs.

She'd been given all the worst jobs. Had to work twice as hard as anyone else, do it before she was asked. Do it better than anyone else. Never answer back, no matter what the provocation. Never give Chef—who'd treated her like a leper—the slightest excuse to fire her.

Gideon bypassed the table where they'd been working on the favours, crossing to one at the far side of the dining room where it overlooked the river far below them.

There were animals near the water, creatures taking advantage of the darkness, tiny deer no bigger than a dog, animals she didn't recognise.

'Your back seems easier,' she said as Gideon pulled out a chair for her.

'It's amazing what interesting company, the prospect of good food will do.'

'Interesting? Mmm…' she said. 'Let me think.' Glad to escape the dark thoughts that had crowded in while she was in the kitchen, she put a finger to her lips as if she was considering what he'd said. '"I had supper with an *interesting* woman." Is that something a girl wants to hear?'

He smiled, but dutifully rather than with amusement, she thought, and said, 'If I was offered a choice between spending time with a beautiful woman or an interesting one, I'd choose interesting every time.'

'Oh, please,' she said. 'Give me a break.'

And then he did laugh, which was a result and, content that she'd finally distracted him, she gathered the sandwich, now oozing egg yolk, and groaned with pleasure as she bit into it.

'What I said about holding your breath, Gideon,' she mumbled, catching a drip of egg yolk and licking her finger, 'forget it. You can do this for me any time, anywhere.' Then, 'If I was given a choice between spending time with a good-looking man or one who could cook, I'd go for the cook every time.'

Gideon hadn't bothered to light a candle; the moon had risen, almost full, silvering the river, the trees on the far bank, the creatures gathered by the water's edge, offering enough light to see him smile.

Encouraged, she said, 'Where did you learn to do this?'

'I spent a lot of time camping out by myself in the early days,' he said, sucking egg from his thumb. 'Trekking, walking, canoeing. Trying out ideas to see if they worked before I sent paying customers out into the wild.'

'Is that how you started in the business? Adventure holidays?'

'Not exactly. My family have been in travel since Thomas Cook started it all in the mid nineteenth century. It's in my blood.'

'And here I was thinking that you were some kind of go-getting entrepreneur blazing the trail for adventurous souls who like to risk their necks for fun.'

'Yes, well, that's the problem with family businesses. They get top-heavy with generations of nephews and cousins, most of whom are little more than names on the payroll. Everyone is too polite, no one is prepared to take charge, innovate, shake things up. And while the same people come back year after year, followed by their children and their children's children, it survives. A family business for family holidays. That was the selling slogan.'

'A bit nineteen-fifties. I did a design course,' she explained when he threw her a questioning look. 'I guess the Internet changed all that with cheap online flights.'

'They sleepwalked into it. I saw the danger, tried to convince my father that he had to do something to counter the threat. But fifteen years ago he was too busy playing Captain Hook in the local panto to listen to a kid babbling on about how computers were going to change everything, let alone some newfangled thing called the Internet.'

'It's so much a part of our lives now that we forget how fast it happened. Cheap flights, online booking. Who needs a travel agent these days?'

'People who are looking for something different. When I was at university there were all these students keen to go off somewhere after taking their finals and do something crazy before they settled for the pinstriped suit. One of them was moaning about it in the bar. How endlessly time-consuming it was if you wanted to do anything except book two weeks on the Costa del Sol. I asked him what he wanted to do and sorted it for him. He told all his mates and, when the lecturers started to come to me for advice, I realised I had a business.'

'And the family firm?'

'It staggers on. They've closed a dozen or so branches and when staff retire they're not replaced. The cousins have discovered that if they want to draw a salary they have to put in a day's work.'

'You're not interested in turning it around?'

'I tried. I went to my father, showed him what I was doing. His business, he told me, was family holidays, not daft jaunts for youngsters. His customers didn't go bungee jumping in New Zealand, dog sledding, white water rafting. Except, of course, they do. People of all ages want to feel their hearts beat faster. Feel the fear and do it anyway. Leap out of an aeroplane, walk across the desert, take a balloon ride over Victoria Falls…'

'Go on a walking safari in Botswana,' she prompted when he stopped. Because that was where all this was leading. Here. To this riverbank.

'A walking safari in Africa,' he agreed. 'I'd met someone at university whose father worked here for the diamond people. She'd raved about the Okavango delta, the birds, the wildlife and when I called her, asked for her advice, she invited me to visit, offered to be my guide.'

She?

'She brought me to the places she knew. We walked, camped, made notes. Made love.'

Yes. Of course they had. She'd known it from the minute he'd said 'she'.

'On our last night, we pitched camp here. Cooked over an open fire, sat out beneath the stars and, as the moon rose, just like this, I caught the glint of a pair of eyes in a tree on the far side of the river. A leopard lying up, waiting for dawn to bring its prey to the water's edge. We thought we were the watchers, but it must have been there all evening, watching us.'

Josie felt the hairs on the back of her neck rise. She shivered, glanced nervously across the river as she remembered Marji saying that the area was famous for leopards.

'Will it be there now?'

'Not that one but a descendant will certainly be out there, somewhere close. It seemed like an omen. The walkers love the birds, the insects, everything, but everyone wants to see the cats.'

'Do they?' She gave a little shiver. 'I love my little tabby, Cleo but I'm not sure about the big, man-eating kind.'

'I'll show you, tomorrow,' he said.

She didn't bother to argue. Tell him that a London sparrow was about as exciting as she wanted the wildlife to get. She knew that this had nothing to do with her; she was just a conduit for his thoughts.

'That's why you built this lodge?' she prompted. 'Because of the leopard?'

'Lissa…Lissa immediately spotted the potential for a permanent camp. A destination. Somewhere to mark the end of the journey, to relax after the walking, the hard camping in the wild.'

Lissa.

Beautiful? It was a name that fitted a beautiful woman. Elegant, sophisticated, unlike her own solid, workmanlike name.

Interesting?

And clever too, she thought with a pang of envy that tore at her heart. Not jealousy. She had no right to be jealous. But something in his voice invoked a longing to claim that special tenderness in his voice as he'd said Lissa's name for herself.

'I was thinking about something fairly basic. Tents with plumbing similar to those I'd seen at smaller campsites in Kenya,' he said. 'Lissa was dreaming up this.'

He lifted a hand, no more than that, but it encompassed her vision.

Beautiful, interesting, clever and he loved her…

'She sounds like a very special woman,' Josie said, doing her best to hold herself together. Trying not to think of the way his mouth had tasted, the way his body had fitted hers or how he'd told her there was no one waiting for him. That he was no different—

'She was an extraordinary woman,' he said. 'She knew so much. When she was out here she seemed to feel things, notice things that I would have missed.'

Was?

No…

He wasn't looking at her now, but at the riverbank below them.

'We opened a bottle of champagne on the day we drove in the first deck supports. Drank a glass, poured one on the hot earth in gratitude for letting us be here. Then I asked her to marry me.'

Everything was beginning to fall into place and she didn't want to hear it, hear his heart breaking. But it was equally obvious that this was why he was here. And why he was in such pain.

He needed to talk and she had always known how to listen.

'What happened, Gideon?'

He turned from the river, looked directly at her.

'I was here, overseeing the final work on the lodge. Bedding in the systems, testing everything, getting to know the staff. Lissa was at home, organising the wedding.'

He turned away, looking across the water, but she doubted if he was seeing anything.

'We were going to come here afterwards for our honeymoon. Just us, with the whole place to ourselves for a few days before the first guests arrived.'

They'd have spent their honeymoon in the last tree house, she thought. As far as they could get from civilisation. Making love. Making a life. Watching the leopards watching them.

'The communications systems had finally been installed and my first call was to let her know what flight I'd be on. She wanted to come and meet me but I told her to stay home in the warm, that I'd make my own way from the airport.'

No…

'I let myself in, called her name. When I didn't get an answer I went upstairs. Checked all the rooms. She'd picked up her wedding dress and it was hanging up in the spare room in a white cover—'

Her hand flew to her mouth as she tried to stifle the groan, but he didn't hear her. It was clear that he was somewhere else, in another world, another life…

'— and I was just thinking that she wouldn't want me even that close before the big day when the doorbell rang. It was a policeman. Apparently, Lissa had decided to surprise me, meet my plane.'

No, no, no… She didn't want to hear this.

'She must have been lying there on the freezing road, dying while I was travelling warm and dry on the train. If I hadn't called… If I'd just got on the damn plane…' Something snagged in his throat.

'You've never been back here, have you?' she asked.

He shook his head.

'Why now?' she asked, not for her—she understood the need for closure—but for him. Because anyone with half a brain cell could see that this was the stress, the cause of all his pain. He'd locked up all that grief, blaming himself and it was breaking him apart. He needed to say the words, open up.

'I had an offer for the Lodge from a hotel group a while ago and I thought well, obviously, that's the answer. Cut it away, set myself free.'

'It's not that easy.'

'No,' he said, 'it wasn't easy at all. There were just so many things that kept cropping up. The security of tenure for the staff. Paul's Sundays. And Francis had been here, taking care of us from the start. He was the first person to congratulate us on our engagement. Lissa was godmother to one of his children…'

'You take care of them.' Not a question.

'I send them things. Pay school fees,' he said. 'I don't give them what matters. What they deserve. But when it came to selling this place cold…' He shook his head. 'I couldn't do it. Not until I'd been here, told them face to face. Told Lissa…'

'I'm so sorry, Gideon.'

'Me too,' he said, doing his best to make light of it. 'It was a damn good offer.'

'Good enough?' she prompted.

And the attempt at a smile faded. 'No. Now I've been here I know that I can never let it go,' he said. 'It's part of her. Part of me. I was wrong to stay away.'

'Yes,' she said. 'You were.'

Because he wasn't looking for sympathy, only truth.

'It's a very hard thing to acknowledge, but I'm a lot more like my father than I ever wanted to believe,' he said, reaching out, taking the hand that had been aching to reach out to offer some human comfort. Afraid that if she touched him it would shatter the moment. Now he took it, held it, as if he was the one comforting her. 'Avoiding painful reality is, apparently, a family failing.'

'That's a little harsh.'

'Is it? His displacement activity is dressing up and raising money for charity. Mine is to discover ever more exotic holiday destinations. We are both very good at ignoring what we don't want to face.'

'Most people do that,' she said. Her mother had blanked out the blindingly obvious until she couldn't ignore it any longer.

Her own tragedy was that she couldn't. But this wasn't about her.

'What would Lissa have done?' she asked.

'If she'd been the one left behind?' He didn't have to think about it. 'She wouldn't have run away from Leopard Tree Lodge. She'd lived close to nature all her life and understood that death is part of life. Something to be accepted.'

Thinking about that did something to his face. He wasn't smiling exactly, but it was as if all the underlying tension had drained away.

'She'd have come here,' he said. 'She'd have lit a fire, cooked something special, opened a bottle of good wine. She'd have scattered my ashes on the river, poured a glass of the wine into the water to see me on my way. One into the earth to thank it for what it gave us. One for herself. Then she'd have eaten well and got on with her life.'

Josie thought that the wine would have been watered with tears, but he surely knew that. It was being here, making a fitting end that was important.

'We all deal with loss in our own way, Gideon. You've built an empire on her vision,' she reminded him. 'She lives in that.'

'I wish that were so, Josie, but the truth is that I was so busy making new places that I forgot this one. Running,' he said. 'That's what my doctor told me before I left London. That I was running on empty…'

'You're not running now,' she said. 'You could have left at any time. A private air ambulance would have taken you anywhere you wanted to go. You fought me to stay here.'

'That isn't why I fought you.' His hand tightened imperceptibly over hers and she caught her breath. 'You know it's not. It's been ten years, Josie. I haven't been celibate in all those years, but you are the first woman in all that time that I've…' he paused, searching for the right word '…that I've seen.'

'Yes…'

That was the word. She had seen him, too. From that first glimpse of him through the leaves, it was as if a light had come on in her brain.

A red light. Danger…

'It's the purple hair,' she said quickly. 'And now I understand why you were so angry about the wedding.' She'd never forget the look on his face when he'd looked up and seen Cryssie's dress hanging over the wardrobe door. She'd have to find another home for it… 'It must have been like coming face to face with your worst nightmare.'

He shook his head. 'I've already been there, Josie. This is just a wedding. Speaking of which, we still have work to do,' he said, releasing her hand, easing back his chair so that he could stand up. Then, as she joined him, he caught her arm. 'There!' he said. 'Do you see him?'

She didn't want to take her eyes off Gideon, but his urgency was telegraphing itself from his hand to her brain and she turned to look across the river. It took her a moment, but then she saw the cat's eyes reflected back from the safety lights.

'What is it?' she whispered. But she already knew and he didn't answer, only his hand tightened in warning as the big cat streaked to the ground, struck some hapless creature near the water's edge. It happened so fast that before she could react, think, it was over; cat and prey were back in the tree.

'What was it?' she asked, turning instinctively to bury her face in his sleeve.

'A small deer. A dik-dik probably. It's nature's way,' he said, putting his arm around her as, sickened by the savagery of it, she shuddered. 'It's the food chain in action. When a leopard kills, everything feeds. Jackals, birds, insects lay their eggs, the earth is enriched.'

She looked up into his face. 'Life goes on?'

He hesitated but, after a moment, he nodded. 'Life goes on. It's a circle. Birth, marriage, death… This weekend it's marriage. Something to celebrate. Come on. Let's finish those favours.'

'It's very late.'

'That's okay.' He picked up the mugs and, taking her arm, he said, 'You can keep me awake by telling me a fairy story.'

'Sorry?'

'Who waved the magic wand and transformed you from scullery assistant Cinderella to partner princess?'

The teasing note was back in his voice, a little gentler than before, maybe, but the black moment had, apparently, passed.

'Oh, I see,' she said, grabbing for that and responding in kind. 'You've shown me yours, now I'm supposed to show you mine?'

'We could do that instead, if you prefer,' he replied with a questioning tilt of the head, that break-your-heart grin that assured her he was kidding.

'Let's stick with Plan A,' she said, glad that there was only the flickering candlelight as the heat rushed to her cheeks anyway. Betraying a need that he had touched within her to be a whole person. Not in the physical sense, although that was undoubtedly part of it; she was attracted to him in ways that she'd never dreamed possible.

It was the emotional vacuum within her that ached tonight.

A longing to reach out to someone you could trust, love with your whole heart and know that he would be there, no matter what.

Not the role for a man eaten with guilt because he wasn't there. For a man still in love with his dead fiancée.

'But if you've got that much energy, you can make a start on the sugared almonds while I wash up,' she said, taking the mugs from him. 'One net in each box. Don't miss any.'

She didn't wait for the comeback. She needed a back-to-earth moment on her own, her hands in hot dishwater while she composed herself.

She didn't get it.

'Well, you were quick,' she said as he followed her into the kitchen, turned on the tap at the handwash sink.

'I didn't think you'd want bacon fat all over your pretty boxes,' he said, soaping his hands, drying them on a paper towel.

She swilled the plates, rinsed them, put them to drain, accepted the paper towel he pulled from the dispenser and offered her.

'Thanks.'

He was looking at her quizzically, as if wondering what on earth was so bad about a Cinderella rags-to-riches success story that she wouldn't talk about it. And obviously, if that was all it had been, there wouldn't have been a thing.

But that wasn't the story. Beloved daughter to rags was the story and the only person she'd shared that with was Sylvie.

'Do you want to help me get the rest of the stuff from the office?' she asked, hoping that the more he had to think about, the less he'd bother about her. 'Since I've got an extra pair of hands, we might as well do it all at the same time.'

'The guests don't just get the sugared almonds?'

'Oh, right—' she laughed '—that would go down well. No. Five sugared almonds to represent health, wealth, long life, fertility and happiness. And, to reinforce the wishes, we have five favours. The almonds, a packet of seeds—love-in-the-mist is popular—a mint silver coin with this year's date, something individual to mark the day and the box itself to keep them all in.'

She picked up a paperknife and ripped open a box that was packed with dozens of small turquoise chamois leather pouches.

'Tiffany?' Gideon said, taking one and tipping the contents into the palm of his hand. It was a stunning sterling silver key ring with a fob in the shape of a football, enamelled with Tal's colours and engraved with both their names and the date. 'Very pretty.'

'Everything done in the best possible taste,' she agreed as he replaced it. Then, as he made a move to pick up the box, 'No!'

'What?'

'Your back. Here, take these,' she said, thrusting the feather-light box of seed packets at him before he could argue. 'I'll bring these last two.'

Arguing over that did the trick. By the time she'd conceded, allowed him to carry the heavier boxes, they were off the dangerous subject of her past and for the next hour conversation was minimal as they concentrated on filling the boxes as quickly as possible before stowing them safely away under lock and key in the office.

By the time she'd staggered back to the tree house, Gideon at her elbow, she was too tired to worry about sharing a bed with him.

It was all she could do to remove her make-up, brush her teeth, pull a nightie over her head. She didn't even bother to ask him which side of the bed he preferred. Just staggered out of the bathroom and fell into it.

Gideon waited on the deck until he heard Josie's bare feet patter from the bathroom to the bed. He'd asked Francis to have it—and Cryssie's bathroom—checked thoroughly for anything that might have fallen onto the deck and crawled in there, although she was so exhausted she probably wouldn't have noticed an elephant hiding in the corner.

He stayed for another moment, looking out across the river, remembering the past. Remembering that it was the past, that nothing he could do would change it. That he could only change the future.

Then he went inside, closed the doors, rolled up the sidings, fastening them in place so that the air could circulate, leaving only the screens between them and nature to keep out flying insects.

For the first time in years, he wanted nothing to come between him and the sounds of the earth coming to life at the beginning of a new day.

The rooms would all have been sprayed while the guests were at dinner, but he lit a coil to discourage any mosquito that had escaped. Straightened the nets where Josie had collapsed through them and crawled beneath the sheet.

She was lying on her stomach, her arm thrown up defensively, her shoulders, her cheeks, her eyelids luminous in the candlelight.

Why hadn't he thought her beautiful when he'd first seen her? he wondered. Was the perception of beauty changed by knowing someone? Cryssie was stunning, sweet too, but twenty minutes had been enough for him to know that an hour of her company would be too long.

Josie, on the other hand, kept him on his toes. Challenged him every step of the way. Never gave an inch. Had the toughness of tensile steel. A natural tenderness. A fragility that called to every protective instinct.

She also cried messily and somewhere in her past had got so screwed up that she couldn't talk about it, not even when he'd opened up to her about Lissa. He understood that. It had taken him ten years to find the right moment, the right person, someone who knew how to listen.

He bent over her, touched his lips to her shoulder, murmured, 'Sleep safe…' before he tucked the nets around her, doused the candles.

He normally slept naked and, since she'd clearly gone out like a light the minute she'd hit the pillow, Josie wasn't about to have a fit of the vapours. But he'd been ribbing her all day about getting some action, had come closer to it than he had done in a long while. Now it was too important to risk her waking up and getting the wrong idea so he kept his shorts on as he climbed into the vast emptiness of the far side of the bed.

And did not feel alone.

CHAPTER TEN

A well planned wedding should run like clockwork, but
always be prepared for things to go wrong.
—*The Perfect Wedding* by Serafina March

'JOSIE…'

She brushed away the sound, the tickle of breath against her
ear, burrowed deeper into the pillow.

'Wake up.'

Who was that? Where was she? Who cared? It was dark,
definitely not time to get up.

'Go 'way…'

'It's important,' the voice insisted and, finally, the urgency
of the summons began to seep through to her brain.

'What is it? What's wrong?' she said, blinking to unglue her
eyelids. Yawning. Stretching… Oh, shoot! 'Gideon!'

He was fully dressed, shaved, while she was… She was
wearing a nightdress that had twisted around and would undoubtedly be missing some of the important bits.

She didn't look, just grabbed the sheet, glared at him.

'What?'

'I thought you'd like to see an African dawn.'

'You are so wrong about that.'

'Trust me, you'll love it. Francis has brought coffee, muffins warm from the oven…' He waved one under her nose so that she leaned forward, following it like an eager puppy.

Certain that he'd finally got her attention, he whisked it out of reach. 'On the deck. Fully dressed. You've got ten minutes.'

'Or what?' she demanded.

'Or you'll regret it for the rest of your life.'

Not a chance, she thought, staggering to the bathroom, peering at herself from beneath lids that needed matchsticks to keep them open.

Coffee, yes. Muffin, yes. Then she was going back to bed until morning.

She pulled a shirt, the first pair of trousers that came to hand, to cover her modesty. Emerged to the scent of warm earth, coffee and muffins, the air filled with the sounds of insects tuning up for the day.

Gideon handed her a cup of coffee. 'Sit down.'

She needed no second bidding, but he wasn't concerned that she was going to fall down. The minute she had collapsed into a chair, he produced a pair of socks from his pocket and said, 'Give me your foot.'

Then, as she responded without thinking, 'What are you doing? Are they my socks?'

'They were in your boots,' he said, sliding them onto her feet. 'You can change them when you come back.'

'Come back from where?' she asked as he picked up one of her boots and continued dressing her as if she were a three-year-old.

'I've made sure nothing's crawled into them in the night,' he said, sliding it over her foot, lacing it up.

'The only place I'm going is back to bed,' she declared.

'If that's an invitation, you're on,' he said, the second boot in his hand. 'If not, let's go.'

'Where?' she demanded as he laced up boot number two.

'To feel the fear and do it anyway. You can bring the muffin.'

'I remember you,' she grumbled, grabbing the muffin and

following him down the steps. 'You're the guy who issues an invitation as if it's an order.'

The dining room was already buzzing with visitors gathering for dawn walks and drives, but Gideon turned aside before they reached it, heading for the jetty she'd been shown on her tour. It was where the river boat, due in later that morning, would tie up.

By the time they'd reached a boatman, waiting beside a boat that looked a little like a cross between a punt and a canoe, the sky had begun to pale.

'*Dumela, Rra. Dumela, Mma*,' he said.

'*Dumela, Moretse. O tsogile?*'

'*Ke tsogile, Rra*,' he replied with a full-beam smile. Then he turned to Josie, repeated the greeting. She looked at Gideon.

'He asked if you rose well,' he said. 'You say "*ke tsogile*".'

She obediently repeated the phrase, then said, 'And what's the response if I was hauled out of a deep sleep by a man who refused to take no for an answer?'

'It's like "How d'you do?", Josie. There is only one answer.' Then, 'He's waiting for you to get into his boat.'

'I was afraid of that,' she said, looking at the very small craft. 'Here goes the last of the Fowlers,' she said as she stepped in, choosing the rear of two front-facing seats.

'Don't you want to sit in front?' Gideon asked.

'No. I'm good,' she assured him. 'I'll hide behind you and, if we meet anything on the prowl for breakfast, it'll see you first.'

He grinned.

'I'm serious,' she said as he took the seat in front of her, said something to the boatman. 'Don't, whatever you do, smile at any passing crocodiles.'

And then they were off, moving silently, smoothly through water turning pink to reflect the sky where tiny bubbles of cloud were threaded like gold sequins against the red dawn.

Gideon said something to the boatman and he nodded.

'What?' Josie asked.

'He thinks the rain will come early this year.'

'Not before Sunday,' she begged. 'Tell me that it won't be before Sunday.'

'Probably not for another week or so.' Then, 'There's a heron.'

A tall white bird looked up as they passed, but didn't move. Deer of all shapes and sizes, zebra, giraffe had come to the water to drink.

Gideon named them all for her. Shaggy waterbuck, tiny dik dik, skittish gazelles. Pointed out birds that she would never have seen. Identified a vivid flash of green as a Malachite Kingfisher.

Before she knew it, Josie was leaning forward, her hand on his shoulder, eager to catch everything. The zebra lined up as if waiting to be photographed, as if you could capture this in a picture. It wasn't just the sight of animals in the wild; it was the scent of the river, the strident song of the cicadas, the grunts and snorts, the screams of monkeys overhead in the trees. The splash of an elephant family having an early morning bathe. The sun bursting above the horizon like the first dawn.

And Gideon.

He'd given her this and, as they drifted back towards the jetty, she laid her cheek against his back. Said, 'Thank you.'

He turned, smiled, responding almost absently to her thanks with a touch to the cheek, before crossing to the majestic river boat which was in the process of docking alongside the jetty.

By the time she had showered, turned herself back into the 'wedding lady', the florist had arrived with a planeload of flowers. The photographer, with the hair and make-up girl in attendance, grabbed Cryssie and bore her away, taking the chance to get some pictures of her around the lodge, while she and the florist worked to create the fantasy bridal suite.

By lunchtime, all the main players had arrived, apart from the groom and, as anticipated, she was soon fielding complaints about the lack of a phone signal from both men and women.

'Problems?' Gideon asked, joining her as she was being berated by one particularly irate young man.

'This is ridiculous. I've got to talk to my agent today—'

'And you think that shouting at Miss Fowler is going to make that happen?'

'What?' Gideon had spoken quietly but, even with the buzz in the room, the man's attention was instantly engaged. 'Who are you?' he demanded.

'Gideon McGrath,' he said, not offering his hand. 'I own Leopard Tree Lodge so if you have a complaint, bring it to me.'

Accepting that as an invitation, he forgot all about her, turning to someone with the power to help him. 'I can't get a signal on my mobile and I have to talk to my agent—'

'After you've apologised to Miss Fowler.'

The man blinked, clearly not used to being interrupted.

'Or you could call your agent from Gabarone. There's a plane leaving in the next five minutes.'

'Gideon,' Josie said, stepping in quickly to avert disaster, 'may I introduce Darren Buck? He's one of Tal's teammates. And his best man.'

'Really?' Gideon said, without a flicker to suggest that he was in the least bit impressed, either by his iconic status as a football star or the fact that he was an important player in the forthcoming event. 'That explains a lot.' Then, 'Which is it to be, Mr Buck?'

Darren Buck, the hottest thing on two legs, apart from the groom, was no taller than Gideon and had an angelic smile that made him a *Celebrity* favourite, but he was built like a brick outhouse and had a famously short fuse. Josie held her breath as the reality of the choices he was being offered sank in. Gideon clearly had no idea of the danger but, as the two men faced off, it was Darren Buck who backed down, favoured her with that famous smile.

'I'm sorry, Miss Fowler. My agent is negotiating a TV deal for me but that's no excuse for shouting at you. If I can help in any way, please don't hesitate to ask. My apologies, Mr McGrath.'

Gideon nodded once and, as if released, the man turned and walked away.

Josie's breath escaped like steam from a pressure cooker. 'Have you any idea what you just did?' she demanded, not sure whether to slap him or hug him.

'Darren Buck is a bully, but this isn't a football field,' he replied, as calm as he'd been throughout the confrontation. 'I have no doubt that you could have handled him with one hand tied behind your back, but I won't have my staff subjected to that kind of behaviour.'

'I'm sure he'll be on his best behaviour from now on,' she said. It wasn't her that Gideon had stepped in to protect, but his staff. People he cared about. 'But thank you, anyway.'

'How is everything going?'

'Fine. Cryssie has her bridesmaids to gossip with. The bridal suite looks stunning.' She looked up as another plane circled overhead. 'And guests are pouring in. All we need now is the groom.'

'Does that mean you're free for lunch?'

'Theoretically,' she said. 'I'll even share forbidden treats, but you'll have to put up with non-stop pleading for email and phone access. Hiding out in the tree house isn't likely to save us.'

'I'll get David to send round a notice,' he said, 'but in the meantime I thought you might like to escape this madness for two or three hours. Have lunch out.'

'Lunch out?'

No! The way her heart had picked up a beat warned her that she was already too deeply involved with this man. Cared too much. Was looking for him whenever she turned a corner, entered a room. Missed him when he wasn't there. How had that happened?

No, no, no...

Then, as the incongruity of what he was asking struck her, 'Where do you go out for lunch around here?'

'There's a place just along the river I'd like to show you.'

'Oh…' Of course. There had to be other places like this. Well, maybe not quite like this, but success bred competition.

'I thought it would give you a break while everyone settles in. It's our job to handle any queries.' His eyes creased in that slow smile that reached her toes. 'We're quite good at it.'

'Yes. I noticed,' she said, fighting off an ear to ear grin.

'Ten minutes? I'll be waiting outside in the compound. Bring a camera if you have one. And your passport.'

'My passport?'

'We're right on the border here. It's always best to be prepared.'

'Oh. Right,' she said. It was only when he'd disappeared into the office that she realised that she seemed to have accepted his invitation, despite her determination not to.

'I feel as if I'm playing hooky,' she said as Gideon drove through the compound gates, raising a plume of dust in their wake. A touch light-headed, as if mind and body weren't quite connected.

'Is there anything you have to do in the next three hours?' he asked.

'No, but…'

'You worked half the night.'

'That's par for the course.'

'No doubt. But the next two days are going to be non-stop. You need down time. Am I right?'

'Absolutely right,' she said, laughing.

'Hold that thought.'

'Yes, sir!' Then, as she saw a twin-engine plane parked in the shade, 'Oh, this is the airstrip.'

'Full marks for observation. Let's see what else you notice,' he said as he pulled up alongside, came round to offer her a steadying hand as she jumped down.

'Er… When you said "just along the river" what exactly did you have in mind as a scale of reference?' she asked.

Gideon shrugged. 'At home you drive out into the country for lunch at some village inn. Africa's bigger. Here you hop in a plane.'

'I've done all the checks, Gideon. Filed your flight plan,' the pilot said. 'She's all ready to go.'

'Thanks, Pete. Enjoy your lunch.'

Josie watched as the pilot climbed into the four-by-four and, before she could gather her wits, drive off with the only transport back to the Lodge.

She turned to Gideon, who was walking slowly around the plane, visually checking that everything was there, despite the pilot having assured him that he'd already done it.

It should have filled her with confidence, but she was too angry to think about that.

'Do you recall me saying to you that I have a very real problem with people taking over my life, leaving me without a choice?' she said.

Gideon looked up, frowned. 'I invited you to lunch, Josie.'

'And my passport? Where are we going? I want to know.'

'You won't trust me?'

The way he'd trusted her last night, when he'd laid his broken heart out in little pieces for her. Talked about things he'd kept bottled up for years. That was what he was asking.

'It's not a question of trust,' she protested.

'Isn't it? You didn't ask where we were going when you thought it was just a ride along the river in a Land Rover. What's the difference between getting in a canoe with me on a river swarming with crocs and hippos, taking off into the bush on four wheels, or climbing aboard an aircraft so that we can do in an hour what would take all day to do by road?'

'I gave you an argument this morning, if you remember, despite the fact that I was half asleep. Even though you didn't bother to mention the crocs and hippos.'

She'd started to give him an argument about lunch, but he'd deflected her, just as he'd deflected Darren Buck.

'I didn't want you to be worrying about anything this morning. I just wanted you to feel the wonder so that when you thought of Leopard Tree Lodge you wouldn't remember it filled with people like Darren Buck. Only the quiet, the peace, the beauty of it.'

Josie knew she was making a fool of herself. That Gideon McGrath was offering her something rare. His time. A part of himself.

'Do you believe I'd do anything to hurt you?' he asked when she didn't respond.

'No.' It was a sincere question and she answered it honestly. 'Not intentionally.'

He couldn't help it if she lost her head, her heart... Because she was very much afraid that the only thing she'd remember when she thought about Leopard Tree Lodge would be Gideon McGrath. That first heart-stopping smile. Standing over the kitchen range as he'd cooked supper for them both. Spilling his heart out in the moonlight.

'That's the best anyone can promise, Josie,' he said. 'You can walk around all your life trussed up in emotional armour plating in case someone gets its wrong. Or you can take the risk.'

Feel the fear and do it anyway...

'So?' he prompted. 'Do you want to climb aboard? Or shall we walk back to the Lodge?'

As she drew in a long breath of the warm, earthy air she looked back along the track to the Lodge. She could scurry back there, hide away in her emotional burrow. But it no longer felt like a safe retreat. It felt dark, stifling, suffocating...

When she'd been locked up, shut away, she'd had no choice but to endure. Learn to control her feelings so that she could be free. This prison, she realised, was of her own making and the only thing keeping her there was her own fear.

She turned back to Gideon, waiting patiently for her decision. 'Let's go,' she said stiffly, afraid that if she didn't hold herself tightly together, she might betray just how big a deal this was.

He was too busy buckling himself into the seat beside her, calling up air traffic control as he taxied out onto the airstrip, concentrating on take-off to notice one way or the other.

He banked over the Lodge and headed east, keeping conversation to pointing out the sights as they flew over them. A family of elephants at the water's edge, giraffe and zebra grazing together. A herd of antelope.

She'd been too tired to take much notice when she'd flown up from Gabarone. Now she took in everything. The dark green snake of vegetation that marked the river. The endless dry bush spread beyond it. The occasional village. The astonishing sight of a town set in what appeared to be the middle of nowhere.

And then, off in the distance, she saw a mist rising from the earth. 'What's that?'

'It's what I've brought you to see. *Mosi O Tunya.*'

'Oh?'

'The smoke that thunders,' he prompted, clearly expecting some response. 'You haven't heard of it?'

She shook her head.

'The first European to see it was Dr David Livingstone. He did what all good explorers do and named it after the reigning monarch.'

She frowned. 'Livingstone? Nineteenth century? Queen Victoria…' Then, as she caught up, 'The Victoria Falls?' She looked from him to the mist, closer now. 'I had no idea it was so near. Is that the spray?'

'That's the spray,' he confirmed, picking up the radio and calling air traffic control. Then, 'Make the most of it if you want pictures; I can only go round once.'

Josie had her cellphone with her, but she left that in her bag. She didn't want to look at one of the natural wonders of the world through a viewfinder; she wanted to see it, feel it at first hand.

As he circled she could see that it wasn't an open waterfall like Niagara, but dropped, over a mile wide, into a deep gorge. The size, the scale of it was awesome, breathtaking and she didn't say a word until, a few minutes later, they had landed on the Zambian side of the Falls.

'That was incredible, Gideon. Thank you so much.' Then, 'I'm sorry for being such a—'

'Don't,' he said, pressing his fingers to her lips to stop the word. 'Don't apologise for saying what you thought, felt. You were honest.' Then, letting his hand drop, 'Do you want to take a closer look?'

At that moment the only thing she wanted to get closer to was him, but he had already turned to a waiting car.

'Gideon, man! Good to see you,' the driver said.

They did that man-hug thing and then Gideon turned to her. 'Josie, this is Rupe. Rupe, Josie.'

'Let me guess,' she said, a little overwhelmed that he'd not only thought to bring her here, but had arranged a car to pick them up. But then that was his business… 'You've been here before.'

'One of my earliest ventures was organising trips for the bungee jumping nuts. From that,' he said as they passed a great wrought iron bridge laced with a rainbow where the mist was lit up by the sun. 'It's still a favourite.'

'Have you ever tried it?'

He just grinned. Of course he had.

'Before you suggest it,' she said, hurriedly, 'no. Definitely, absolutely, a thousand times no.'

'Smart woman,' he replied. Then, 'Here we are.'

He got out first, offered her his hand as if she were visiting royalty, walked her across to a point where there was a clear view of the mighty Zambezi pouring into the gorge in a dizzying rush.

'Words are inadequate,' she said after a while.

'Did you bring a camera?' he asked. 'I'll take your photograph.'

'Just this,' she said, handing him her phone.

'You should be looking at the Falls, not me,' he said. She turned obediently.

'Do you want me to take one of the two of you?' Rupe said.

Before she could rescue him from the embarrassment, Gideon had handed the cellphone to Rupe, put his arm around her and, looking down at her, said, 'Say, cheese, Josie.'

'Cheese, Josie.'

'Okay. Let's eat,' he said, retrieving her phone, checking the picture before handing it back to her, glancing at his watch. 'Pick us up in half an hour, Rupe,' he said, taking a cold bag the man was holding. 'Come on, this way. Take care; the steps are wet. Better hold my hand.'

He went first, leading her down steps cut from the rock that led down into the depths of the gorge. He didn't go far before he placed the cold box on a large flat rock.

'Help yourself to a step,' he said. 'It's not the Ritz but the service is quick,' he said. 'Soda or water?'

'Water, please,' she said, and held the bottle to the pulse throbbing in her neck, before opening it and taking a mouthful.

'This is amazing,' she said. Everywhere was overgrown with ferns and tropical plants dripping with moisture in the steamy atmosphere. It reminded her of the tropical hothouse at Kew, except this was the real thing. 'A bit Garden of Edenish.'

And they were the only people in it.

He looked in the box. 'Sorry, no apples. There's a naartje, will that do?'

'Tell me what it is and I'll let you know.'

'A small orange—a bit like a tangerine,' he said, showing her.

'It's green.'

'It's ripe, I promise.'

'Okay, hand it over. What else have you got in there?'

'Nothing exciting. Sandwiches. A Scotch egg. I'll do better next time.'

Next time? He was saying that there would be a next time? No… But she couldn't believe how much she wanted there to be a next time.

'Cheese, egg, salad?' he said, looking up, catching her staring.

'Salad. Thanks,' she said quickly.

'Are you okay, Josie?'

'Yes,' she said quickly. Then, because he was still looking at her, 'No…'

Next time meant a future and that meant telling him everything, just as she'd told Sylvie when she'd offered her a job. Because she had a right to know and if she hadn't been honest someone else would have told her. Warned her…

And she had to do it now, before there was the possibility of any next time. Before they went back to Leopard Tree Lodge. Now…

CHAPTER ELEVEN

Create a fragrant memory for your guests by choosing
wedding flowers with beautiful and distinctive scents.
—*The Perfect Wedding* by Serafina March

JOSIE put down the sandwich, rubbed the back of her hand over
her forehead.

'You asked me if I trusted you,' she said.

He handed her a sandwich, leaned back against the rock.
'You answered that by getting into a plane with me, even
though you didn't know where I was taking you.'

'That was a physical thing. The trust that you wouldn't hurt
me.'

'Not intentionally,' he said. 'I understood the qualification.
The vulnerability we all feel when we open ourselves up to
someone. Expose our weaknesses, our fears.'

'You said it was the most we could hope for,' she said,
looking up at him, trying to see behind those dark eyes. Find
something in them to reassure her that he would understand
what she was about to tell him. 'Will you kiss me, Gideon?'

Gideon felt the plastic pack collapse beneath his fingers,
crushing the sandwich inside.

Would he kiss her?

Did she have any idea what she was asking?

Last night, as they'd worked together, knowing that she

was doing everything she could to distract him from asking her about her past, all he'd wanted to do was hold her, tell her it would be all right. Instead, he'd concentrated on the job in hand, showing her how he felt by doing what he could to help.

He'd lain propped on his elbow half the night just watching her sleep, memorising her face. The shape of her ear, the little crease that appeared by her mouth from time to time as if she were smiling in her dreams, the long inviting curve of her neck.

She had no way of knowing that when she'd leaned her head against his back this morning in the canoe, a wordless gesture that was more speaking than a thousand thanks, he'd had to force himself to walk away before he did something stupid. He'd seen how she'd reacted to a kiss that she hadn't seen coming. The fear…

When he'd seen that idiot Darren Buck shouting at her, it had taken every atom of self-control to stop himself from grabbing the man and pitching him bodily out of the Lodge.

Now, because of something he'd just said, she'd decided this was the moment to share whatever horror lurked in her past. What? What had he said? He reran the last few moments in his head.

Next time…

The words dropped into the waiting slot with an almost audible clunk. He'd said them without thinking, because he hadn't needed to think about it. This was different from his earlier attempts to move on, date. That had taken effort. This was—had been from the moment he'd first set eyes on Josie— effortless.

Next time. The possibility of a future…

But first she had to lay the ghosts of her past. And she was asking him to kiss her now, before she told him, because she was afraid that afterwards, when he knew, he might not want to.

Would he kiss her? In a heartbeat.

Should he?

Suppose, afterwards, he was so repelled by what she told him that he couldn't bring himself to kiss her again? How much worse would she feel then? How could he live with himself if he confirmed everything that she most feared?

Not intentionally…

She was looking up at him with those huge, impossibly violet eyes. The same eyes that had wept for her mother last night, had looked at him with such compassion as he'd spilled out his heartache, guilt. Could he do any less for her?

He dropped the sandwich back into the cold box, squeezed himself onto the step beside her.

'Sure?' he asked, hoping that she wouldn't pick up on the uncertainty in his voice.

'No.' She shook her head. 'Sorry. I shouldn't have asked…'

'Be still,' he said. Then again as, startled, she looked up at him and he captured her face between his hands, lowered his lips to hers, 'Be still…'

Her lips were soft, strawberry-flavoured, sweet and he was trembling as he fought to keep his kiss light, tender, when everything was telling him to go for broke, take her over the edge so that she would forget whatever nightmare she was about to reveal. To make her his, there in a steamy grotto as old as time.

Or was it Josie who was trembling?

He leaned back, looked down at her. 'Okay?'

She nodded and he put an arm around her shoulder so that she could lean into him, so that she wouldn't have to look at him. So that she couldn't see his face.

She didn't speak for a while, and when she did it was about those last months with her mother. 'She was terrified of hospitals, Gideon, wanted to die at home.'

'You nursed her? How long?' he prompted when the pause had gone on too long.

'Months. Six, seven, maybe. Alec didn't help much.'

'Alec? He was your stepfather? What happened to your father?'

'He was killed in the first Gulf war. It was really hard for her and Alec was funny, charming, had all the moves and Mum must have been desperately lonely. She also had the house that her parents had left her, a war widow's pension and a nice little part-time job. He couldn't wait to move in. But Mum didn't do that. He had to marry her before he could get his feet under the table.'

'And you? Did he ever touch you?'

'No. He knew I could see right through him, would have leapt at the chance to get him out of the house. He was always very careful around me.' Then she drew back, looked at him. 'That's what you thought when I freaked out?'

'It crossed my mind.'

'No one hurt me like that, Gideon. It's just losing control. That's what sex is about, isn't it? Surrendering yourself totally?'

It was a question, not a statement, as if she was seeking confirmation. As if it was something she'd never done.

'It's an equal surrender, Josie. A mutual gift.'

'Equal?' It was as if some light had gone on inside her head. 'I never thought of it like that.'

It was true. He could scarcely believe it, but this feisty, modern, in-your-face woman didn't know. Had never experienced it for herself. Turned off, maybe, by the smooth operator who'd taken advantage of her mother. Seen it as a weapon...

'What happened, Josie?' he said, rather more urgently.

'The nurse who came in twice a day told me to go out, take a walk around the park, get some fresh air. That she'd sit with my mother. Alec was at work so I felt safe leaving her. It was a lovely day. I sat on a bench in the sun near the roses, sucking up the scent. I fell asleep, Gideon. I was gone for over an hour and when I got back the only person home was Alec. He said that my mother had started to fit just after the nurse left and he hadn't known what to do so he'd called an ambulance. He'd been waiting to tell me. By the time I got to the hospital they had her hooked up to all kinds of machines, exactly what she'd feared.'

'It wasn't your fault, Josie.'

'Of course it was.' She shook her head. 'I stayed with her for three days. He never once came near and when I went home to tell him that his wife, my mother, was dead, I found him sitting in her kitchen with the barmaid from the Red Lion. She was wearing one of my mother's dressing gowns, drinking tea from one of her cups...'

'Oh, love,' he said, but she shrugged off his attempt to comfort her.

'I went crazy, Gideon. Lost control. I smashed the cup from the woman's hands. Smashed everything from the table. The teapot went flying and she began to scream that she was scalded and, as Alec came for me, to grab me, I suppose, stop me from doing any more damage, I picked up a chair and hit him.'

The air was so still. Nothing stirred. And the only sound was the muffled roar of the Falls.

'The police came and took me away. But I was uncontrollable and a doctor had to be called to sedate me and, when he heard what had happened, he had me sectioned under the Mental Health Act. Locked up for twenty-eight days for my own safety.'

Josie swallowed hard, her throat tight with anger, even now. But it had been her fault her mother had died in hospital. Her fault she wasn't there to see her decently laid to rest.

'I was never charged with anything.'

'Well, that's something, I suppose. Hospital has to be better than prison.'

She turned on him. 'Do you think so? Do you really think so?' she demanded. 'Being banged up for assault would at least have given me some kind of street cred but there's a stigma to mental illness that you can never shake off. I was in there for six months, Gideon.'

'Six months? But you weren't sick; you were angry, grieving...'

'I hurt two people, Gideon. When I realised, understood what I'd done, I was appalled. But sorry is just a word. Anyone can say it. I was watched, monitored, drugged until I learned to control every emotion. Eventually, when I was good and obedient and stopped fighting them, they let me go.'

'What did you do?'

'I went home.' She could still remember exactly how she'd felt walking up to the door of her home. Having to knock. The door being opened by someone she didn't know. But even then she hadn't understood… 'He'd sold my mother's house. There were strangers living there. Other people's children playing on the swing my dad built for me.'

'But your life was there. How could he do that?'

'There was an old will leaving everything to me that she'd made after my dad died, but apparently they become invalid the minute you marry. My mother couldn't have known that and, as her husband, Alec automatically inherited everything. I went next door to a neighbour to find out where he'd gone. I didn't want to cause trouble,' she said quickly. 'The last thing I wanted was to go back into that hospital. But I didn't have any clothes. Nothing. Not even a photograph of my mum, my dad. His medals…'

She heard the crunch as the plastic sandwich carton she was still holding crushed between her hands and Gideon unhooked his arm from around her shoulder, took it from her, stood up to dump it in the box. He took out a bottle of water, opened it, took a long drink.

'The neighbour?' he asked when he finally turned back to face her. 'What did she do?'

She shook her head. It didn't matter. She'd seen his reaction. He couldn't wait to put some distance between them. Couldn't bear to look at her.

'Josie?'

'She told me to wait. Shut the door on me while she called Social Services to come and get me. She was afraid of me.'

She'd never forget that look. 'She'd known me all my life but she was terrified.'

She sighed.

'I was found a place in a hostel, a job in a hotel kitchen where the most important thing I was trusted to do was scrub pots. Obviously I couldn't be trusted to peel vegetables. That would have meant giving me a knife.'

'Wasn't there anyone you could turn to?'

'You think I'd have lived in that horrible place if there was?' she snapped. This was so not like telling Sylvie. She'd just listened. No questions. Just let it all come out. Then she'd made her a cup of tea and asked her if she wanted the job. End of story. Not this…anger.

'I'd gone berserk, Gideon. Scalded a woman for daring to drink out of one my mother's cups,' she said, cutting it short, wanting it over. 'Brought a chair down on my stepfather's head. Would you want me in your house?' She didn't wait for an answer. The Garden of Eden had lost its charm and she stood up. 'It's hot down here. I'm going back up—'

'Someone wanted you,' he reminded her before she'd taken a second step. 'Sylvie.'

Sylvie. Just the name was enough to bring her back from that dark place. 'You called her my fairy godmother and she was. Still is. She'd been let down by the agency supplying waiters for a reception at the hotel and the duty manager rounded up anyone he could find to fill in. You can tell how desperate he was…'

She'd done the work of five that night, bossing the chambermaids who hadn't got a clue—after all, no one in their right mind was going to argue with her—made sure the food and drink kept coming. Whisked away a very drunk actress who was about to make a fool of herself and found her a room where she could sleep it off. She'd seen an opportunity to impress and seized it with both hands.

'You must have been amazingly good for her to take you on without experience,' Gideon said.

'I just wanted it more. I was the only one who stayed to help her clear up when it was all over. Help her pack up her stuff. Sylvie comes from some really swanky aristocratic family but she'd had a rough time, lost her mother, her home, too. We bonded, I suppose.'

She took another step.

'How long has it been? Since the scullery.'

'Nearly five years.'

'And now you're here, taking charge of the most important wedding of the season.'

'Marji wanted Sylvie,' she said impatiently, taking another step. Wishing she'd never started this. Next time. There was never going to be a next time… 'But she's on maternity leave.'

'And there was no other wedding planner prepared to drop everything and grab the biggest job in town?'

She stopped, turned. 'What are you saying?'

'That maybe you're the one who needs to let go of the past, Josie. Stop worrying about what you think other people think about you. They really don't care as long as you do your job. What happened to you is shocking. This man stole everything from you. Your home, your memories, but unless you can let go you're handing him your future, too.'

'Well, thanks, Gideon. Like I haven't heard the pull yourself together, get laid and stop feeling sorry for yourself speech before.'

He shrugged. 'I couldn't have put it better myself. If you need any help with the second part of the plan, let me know.'

'If you have any ideas in that direction, the office floor is still vacant,' she said, and this time when she started up the steps he did nothing to stop her.

The car was waiting and she climbed into the back. She hoped Gideon might get into the front seat alongside his old friend Rupe, but he wasn't done.

'You were honest with me yesterday, Josie. I don't know what else I could have said.'

'Nothing,' she said. It wasn't what he'd said. It was the fact that he couldn't wait to get away from her.

'Did you ever look for him?'

She frowned. 'Alec? You're kidding? If I'd turned up on his doorstep he'd have called the police, told them I was harassing him.'

'I wondered if you'd made any attempt to get back your personal things. The photographs.'

'Oh, please. They would have gone into a skip with the rest of the rubbish when he moved.'

'Do you think so? Photographs are—'

Josie heard a bleep. 'Did you leave my phone on?' She took it from her bag. 'Well, what do you know?' she said, feigning enthusiasm. 'I've got a signal. Do you mind? I need to deal with this.'

She opened her messages and spent the next few minutes answering them, calling her office, using the time to block out the presence of the man beside her. Rediscover the Josie Fowler who'd left London. Tighten up the armour plating. Re-establish a safe boundary between her and her emotions.

He must have got the picture because he dropped the subject of her past while she kept her eyes on the scenery, straining to see the mist from the Falls for as long as it was visible. Then on the horizon. But she needed her sunglasses to keep her eyes from watering in the brilliant light.

The four-by-four was waiting for them when they landed and she didn't wait for him to help her down when they reached the compound.

'Thanks, Gideon. Great lunch,' she said, swinging herself down before he could help. He didn't follow her and at the door she glanced back, realised he was still sitting in the Land Rover. 'Are you all right?' she asked with a sudden pang of concern. 'Is it your back?'

'No,' he said. 'It's not my back. It's my foot. I appear to have got it firmly lodged in my mouth.'

'No.' He couldn't help his feelings. At least he hadn't tried to pretend. 'You were honest,' she said. 'And that is all any of us can hope for.'

Anything else was pie in the sky and she didn't hang around to embarrass him any longer.

She kept herself busy. Not looking for Gideon whenever she turned a corner, walked into a room. Not looking so hard, in fact, that she didn't see him even when she walked into the dining room. Not until he half rose, as if to invite her to the table he was sharing with some of the guests.

For a heartbeat there was nothing else. No sound, no movement, nothing but the two of them locked into some space where the world was in slow motion.

Then Cryssie grabbed her arm, wanting to tell her something and the noise rushed back and she turned away.

It was going to be a long day tomorrow and she ordered supper on a tray, then checked to see if there were any messages before heading for the tree house to obsessively check her lists.

She'd done it half a dozen times before she gave up waiting for him to return and went to bed. Lying in the dark, listening to the party going on until late. Pretending to be asleep when he did finally make it back.

There was no dawn call with coffee and muffins. Instead, she left him sleeping, grabbed a quick breakfast in the dining room with the photographer waiting for Cryssie and Tal, who were going out on a game drive to be photographed in the wilds.

Later, while the women took over the swimming pool and talked clothes non-stop as they had their nails done, Gideon took the men, needing an outlet for their pent-up energy, off to the nearest school to give the children a football master class.

Josie, meanwhile, kept an eye on the florists, back with even more flowers. Decorated the top deck of the river boat, laid up the tables for the dinner that night.

'You haven't laid a place for yourself,' Cryssie said when she came to see how it looked.

'Honestly, Cryssie…'

But Cryssie, it seemed, had an unexpectedly determined streak that belied her blonde bombshell image.

'There's an uneven number on that table,' she said. 'It looks untidy.'

And untidiness was, apparently, not to be tolerated.

Gideon had beaten her to the bathroom, changed and gone by the time she was finally satisfied that there wasn't another thing she could do and rushed back for her one minute shower, a quick pass with a pair of straighteners she'd borrowed to perk up her hair and the fastest make-up job in history.

She only had one posh frock with her and the vintage designer dress, midnight-purple chiffon, backless almost to her bottom, a handkerchief hem around her knees, was going to have to do double duty for tonight and the wedding.

Hair and make-up done, purple stockings so fine that they were practically non-existent clinging to her legs, she slipped it over her head. Fastened two velvet chokers studded with crystals around her neck. Pushed her feet into a pair of vertiginous Mary Janes. Checked her little black and purple velvet evening bag for the basic kit. Took a last deep breath.

'Game on,' she said, then she turned and came face to face with Gideon.

He was wearing the cream suit she'd seen hanging in the wardrobe, a dark open-necked shirt. Forget dinner. He looked good enough to eat.

'Cryssie sent me to look for you.'

'Why?' she asked. 'I wasn't lost.'

'No?' He extended a hand. 'Let's go.' And, when she hesitated, 'I'm not prepared to risk you stumbling on those heels.'

She hadn't seen him looking at her feet, but then she had no idea how long he'd been standing there before she'd turned around. She didn't argue but surrendered her elbow to his hand, allowed him to escort her along the bridge and down to the jetty.

What had been a plain wide wooden deck was now lined on either side with flowers, lit with lanterns that were reflected in the dark water. Small tables had been placed along its length where guests were being served pre-dinner drinks, canapés.

'It looks stunning, Josie. You've done a great job.'

'Let's get tomorrow over before you start congratulating me. Stay and have a drink,' she urged. 'I need to go up on deck, to be there, make sure everyone finds their seat.' She didn't wait for his answer, but broke away, walked quickly to the boat and climbed up onto the deck, took one final look around before nodding to the maitre d' to ring the ship's bell to summon everyone on deck.

'Penny for them?' Gideon asked.

The table with the odd number had been where Gideon was sitting and Cryssie had written her name on a place card and set it next to him. Josie had switched it so that he was at a table at the far end of the room, adjusted the table plan and reprinted it.

While she was directing people to their seats, someone had switched them back and, from the little grin that Cryssie had given her, she knew that she'd been rumbled.

'I was thinking about the food,' she replied. 'It's superb. I really wish that Paul and his team were catering the wedding tomorrow.'

'I'll tell him.'

'All your staff have been great, Gideon. You should be proud of them, proud of what you've made of Lissa's dream.'

Before he could answer, Tal rose, said a few words to welcome everyone to his and Cryssie's wedding. 'Make the most of it,' he urged them before he sat down. 'Neither of us will be doing this again.'

It got a laugh, a signal for the small band that had set up on the jetty to start playing.

'Are you free now?' Gideon asked. 'You don't have to rush off and do anything?'

'I'll have to restore order here…'

'Not until after the party.'

'Well, no…'

'It's just that I had the feeling you might have been avoiding me.'

'Me? Avoiding you?'

'You say that as if it was the other way around. I came looking for you last night but you'd disappeared. Then this morning you were up before dawn.'

'The one was linked to the other. Early to bed, early to rise. And you didn't appear to be lacking for company. An entire bouquet of bridesmaids hanging on your every word the last time I saw you.' That, at least appeared to amuse him and she was afraid she knew why. 'But thanks for taking the guys off our hands this afternoon,' she said quickly to cover her slip. 'Did you have fun?'

'The footballers were great with the kids. They had a whip-round for the school funds, too. Darren Buck was especially generous.'

'That'll go down well with the readers of *Celebrity*.'

'Do you dance, Miss Cynic?' Gideon asked as they joined the crowd drifting down the stairs, his hand to her back to steady her. Cool against her naked skin, raising gooseflesh even though the night was warm.

'No.'

'Never?'

Not when she wanted to keep her head.

'I don't think you'll be short of a partner,' she assured him. Then, as an altercation broke out between two of the women, 'Go and find Darren Buck, tell him to a get a grip on his women,' she said, hurrying to step between them just as the chief bridesmaid's replacement swung a left.

If she'd been wearing her boots she would have taken the full force of it, but the high heels gave her no purchase and she went down as if poleaxed.

'Josie!'

She blinked, slightly dazed by the speed of it as Gideon ran his fingers lightly over her cheek. 'That's going to be one hell of a bruise.'

'Just as long as the bridesmaid wasn't marked,' she said, wincing as she sat up, testing her jaw.

He grinned. 'You took the hit for the bridesmaid?'

'If she had to drop out it would make the numbers uneven,' she said. 'Is she okay?'

'Her mascara's run. Is that fatal?'

She snorted. 'Stop it. Help me up.'

'Put your arm on my shoulder.' She did as she was bid but, instead of helping her to her feet, he scooped her up and carried her inside.

'Gideon, put me down. Your back…'

'There's nothing wrong with my back.' He pushed open the swing door to the kitchen. 'It was a stress thing.' He stopped, looked down at her. 'Thanks to you, I'm not stressed any more.' Then, before she could say anything, 'Crushed ice here!'

It was Paul who made up the ice pack, but it was Gideon who applied it with the utmost gentleness to her jaw. Waved away Cryssie, who'd come running to make sure she was all right.

'I'm so sorry, Josie.'

'No problem,' she said. 'I just lost my balance. Gideon warned me about these heels. Could you make sure Darren's girlfriend is okay? She could probably do with some of this ice for her hand.'

'If you're sure there's nothing I can do?'

'I'll take care of her,' Gideon said. 'Go and enjoy your party.' Then, when she'd gone, 'Let's get you to your room.'

'You're not going to carry me!' she warned. 'I can walk.'

'Really? Well, that's a relief.'

'You have hurt your back!'

'No, but I very well might if I had to carry you all that way,' he said.

She jabbed him with her elbow but didn't object when he put his arm around her waist to support her as they walked slowly back along the bridge. He sat her on the bed, gave her a painkiller. By then her head was throbbing so badly that she didn't care that he was undressing her. She was just grateful to lie down and have someone tuck her in. Give her a kiss good-night.

Gideon watched her all through the night but Josie slept easily, only stirring as the sky turned pink.

'Hey…' he said. 'How do you feel?'

'Ouch?' she said with a rueful grin.

'Sorry…'

She laughed, then pulled a face as it hurt.

'Noooo…' She put her hand to the bruise along the edge of her jaw that threw the faint white scar into prominence. 'Does it look bad?'

'Nicely colour coordinated. I'll bet her knuckles are worse.'

'She was probably provoked.'

'No excuse.'

'No,' she said. 'There is never any excuse.'

Wanting to distract her, he ran a finger gently along the line of the scar. 'You seem to have a habit of leading with your jaw.'

'Oh, that. I was climbing on the back of the sofa, fell off and caught my chin on a table.' She looked up at him. 'Did you think it was the wicked stepfather, Gideon?'

'I couldn't have been more wrong about him, could I?'

'He used his good looks to take advantage of a lonely woman, but he was too lazy to be violent.' Then, 'Can you move? I need the bathroom.'

'Hold on,' he said. He climbed off the bed, fetched a robe, fed her arms into it as if she were a kid.

'I'm not an invalid.'

'No? How many fingers am I holding up?'

'One.'

'Do you feel dizzy? Sick?'

'No, I just need to –'

'Just checking.'

'I know,' she said. Touched his cheek, very gently. 'Thanks for taking care of me.'

Then she swung herself out of bed as if nothing had happened. An act? Or was she really that tough?

She emerged after the fastest shower in history, towelling her hair dry as she walked out onto the deck.

'Isn't there supposed to be coffee?' she asked hopefully.

'Any minute…' He stopped as the bell jangled on the steps but it wasn't Francis, it was David. 'Josie…' he said, coming to a halt when he saw her. 'How are you?'

'Fine. No real damage.'

'Right. Good.'

'What's up, David?' he asked.

'I'm afraid we've got a bit of a problem.'

'What kind of problem?' Josie asked, letting the towel fall.

'I've just had a call from Gabarone. The owner of the catering company is missing. The staff turned up early to prepare the wedding food this morning to find the premises locked and deserted.'

'But I spoke to him two days ago,' she said.

'Apparently there have been rumours that he was in financial difficulty. When someone eventually managed to get into the premises, there was nothing there.'

'Nothing?'

'Completely stripped. No equipment. No food.'

Gideon saw the colour drain from Josie's face and he turned to David. 'What have we got in the chill room?'

'Lamb, beef, poultry, but we haven't time to make an elaborate five-course wedding breakfast from scratch. Even with Paul…'

'No. It'll have to be something simple. A *braai*? The saffron rice salad you do with pine nuts. Tabbouleh. Salads. Get Pete on the phone. Tell him what you need. And fish, whatever he can grab off the early flight from the coast.'

'Excuse me?'

He turned to Josie.

'What's a *braai*?' she asked.

'A barbecue. I know it's not elegant, but I promise you'll have a feast that no one will ever forget.'

She swallowed. 'I'm sure it will be great. There's just one thing.'

'What?'

'The cake.'

He was brought to a juddering halt.

'The cake?'

'They were commissioned to make the cake. Three tiers of the finest fruit cake, almond paste, royal icing…'

He glanced at David, but he shook his head. 'We can't do that. With the best will in the world, Josie—'

'No,' she said. 'We're going to have to make those big cupcakes. Serafina doesn't approve of them—'

'Already I love them,' he said.

'We can use muffin cases. David?' she prompted.

'The cases aren't a problem, but we're running on skeleton staff today. Breakfast, cold lunch… I allowed everyone we didn't need to go home last night to leave the kitchen clear for the caterer.'

'I'll make them,' she said. 'The ingredients are basic enough. We can use white frosting but we need decorations.' She turned to him, totally focused on the wedding now. 'Can Pete find those on a Sunday morning?'

'He'll get them,' Gideon said. 'What do you want?'

'Whatever he can find in pale blue and orange. And we'll need cake stands. The three-tier kind.'

'Cake stands. Got it,' David said. 'I'll... um... go and get the ball rolling.'

'We'll be right behind you,' Gideon said.

Josie broke the news to Cryssie. Explained what they were going to do.

'Is there anything we can do to help?' she asked.

'No. You stay here, have your hair and make-up done. But, if I have your permission, I might round up one or two of your guests? Beating batter might keep them from beating each other. It'll make great copy for *Celebrity*.'

'Good plan. And tell Gideon that if he needs help with the barbecue, the lads will pitch in.'

'Thanks. I'll do that.'

Josie commandeered a corner of the kitchen and set up a cupcake production line. The bridesmaids all pitched in but none of them appeared to have ever made a cake before and the minute the photographer had got pictures of them, giggling and splattered with batter, she shooed them away as more trouble than they were worth.

Gideon scrubbed up and came to help the minute he'd got the barbecue pit set up. At least he only needed to be told once, although he wasn't above wiping a finger round the bowl like a kid. She caught him red-handed, slapped him with a spoon and, instead of licking it himself, he offered it to her.

'Come on,' he said, tempting her. 'Tell me you can resist.'

She looked up into hot liquid silver eyes and for a moment completely lost her head. She could not resist him. Not for a moment and, closing her lips around his finger, she surrendered to the dizzying tug of desire and, as the sweetness melted on her tongue, she thought she'd pass out.

'Good?' he asked. And when she struggled to speak,

'Maybe I should try.' He didn't wipe his finger around the bowl, but lowered his head, touched his tongue to her lips.

'Josie Fowler?'

She jumped, spun around. There was a man standing in the doorway.

'I've got two leopard cubs. Where do you want them?'

The wedding was perfect. The florists had done their thing again, this time surrounding the open air boma and poolside with huge swathes of bird of paradise flowers. Twining the posts of the thatched open-sided rondavel that had been constructed for the ceremony with roses and tiny fairy lights.

Josie was waiting at the steps to put the last stitch in the hem, then slipped into her seat beside Gideon at the back.

The bridesmaids came first, show-stopping in clinging dresses made from animal print silk with tiny ostrich feather fascinators. The lion, the zebra, the giraffe, and finally the leopard leading two tiny cubs on orange and blue ribbons.

Then it was Cryssie's turn. She was breathtaking in a strapless white gown cinched in with a basque that had been embroidered and beaded with the team's colours and, as she was led by the team's manager through the guests to take her place beneath the thatched canopy beside her groom, there was only a sigh.

This was always the moment that caught her out. The look of pure love on a groom's face as he saw his bride coming towards him.

Usually, she'd be sitting alone at this moment but today Gideon had been at her side from first light and, as the tears welled up, he reached for her hand. Startled, she turned to him and saw in his eyes that same look for her.

Afterwards, Cryssie hugged her. 'You are the best, Josie. And the cakes…' The tiny sparkly sprinkles that Pete had found had perfectly matched the beading on her dress. 'If they'd been designed for the wedding, they couldn't have been more perfect. You have been a star and I'll make sure everyone knows. Thank you both so much,' she said, looking past her to Gideon. 'And you two. Will you get married here?' she asked.

'No!'

'No,' Gideon said, beating her to it by a fraction of a second. 'We'll find a place of our own, Cryssie, and when we do, you'll be at the top of the guest list.'

She spun around to stare at him.

'Gideon, I…' She didn't say any more because he was kissing her.

It was the kind of kiss that Prince Charming would have given Cinderella. A sweet, true, for ever-and-ever kind of kiss.

And afterwards she couldn't think of a thing to say because whatever it was wouldn't be adequate. Would shatter the moment.

'Come on,' he said. 'You've been on your feet since dawn. Let's leave these people to enjoy themselves.'

'Gideon…'

'Three days.' He looked down at her. 'That's what you were going to say, isn't it? That we've only known one another for three days.'

'Yes.'

'That's a good sign, you know. Being able to read one another's minds. Do you want to have a guess at what I'm thinking?'

'I haven't a clue.'

He looked at her, grinned. 'That's not strictly true, is it?'

'No.'

He kissed her again. 'We're adults, not kids. I've wanted you from the moment I first saw you, fell in love with you, some-where between the coffee and the chilli.'

'No… It's not possible.'

'That's the nature of love. I wasn't supposed to be here. Neither were you. "There is a destiny that shapes our ends…", Josie. Trust me; I recognise the real thing when I feel it.'

She wanted to believe it so much…

'But when I told you about what I'd done, I saw the look on your face. You couldn't wait to get away from me.'

'That's what you thought?' He pulled her to him, holding her. 'Angel, when you asked me to kiss you, I knew it was going to be bad. I wanted to wrap you up in my arms, hold you, make it go away in the only way a dumb man knows how. But you needed me to hear it and I had to listen. If I looked horrified it was not because of what you'd done, but because so many people had let you down. Hurt you. I was so angry that I made a complete mess of it.'

'You could make all the hurt go away,' she said, leaning into him, feeling the steady, powerful beat of his heart against her cheek. 'Right now.'

'Maybe, but that's not you.' He pulled back to look at her. 'We're not a couple of kids, Josie. We're adults. I love you. I'm here for you and I always will be. Everything else can wait until we're married.'

The thought that such a man loved her enough to wait until she trusted him enough to marry him overwhelmed her.

'I don't know what to say.'

'We'll have a very short engagement?' he offered.

'The quickest in history,' she said. Then, 'So what do we do until then?'

'We'll date. I'll take you to the cinema, to dinner, for walks in the park, to meet my parents. You'll cook me supper. We'll have a really nice time and, when you are really, really sure, we'll set a date and get married.'

I'm sure, she thought. Never more sure of anything in my life…

'And tonight?' she whispered.

'Tonight…' He looked up to a velvet African sky. 'Tonight we'll count the stars.'

The marriage of Josie Fowler and Gideon McGrath took place three months later on a tropical island that the tourist world had not yet discovered. It was a simple affair. No bridesmaids, just Sylvie at her side. No hothouse flowers, only the orchids growing wild and, the only creatures, the birds, crickets, tree frogs. The guest list didn't trouble *Celebrity*. This was not a public occasion, but something precious for the two of them and those who were closest to them. Gideon's family, close colleagues. Sylvie, her husband and her baby girl. And friends, including Cryssie and Tal. And Josie's staff, who were, for once, simply there to enjoy the day.

Josie's dress was a simple white column of silk, over which she wore a little bolero, scattered with tiny amethyst beads.

Her hair had been restrained into a short bob with only one vivid splash of purple that echoed the colour of her eyes. As they stood beneath the trees, the air scented with vanilla orchids, hand in hand as they said the vows that made them one, Gideon felt such an overwhelming sense of peace, love, joy.

They ate simple food served in the open and then, as the sun set, they left the party to walk along the beach to the cottage that Gideon had found for their honeymoon.

They started sedately enough, but the minute they were out of sight they began to run, arriving laughing and breathless at the open French windows where Gideon picked her up and carried her inside, not stopping until they reached the bedroom.

Sitting in the centre of a bed scattered with flower petals, there was a large white beribboned box.

'More presents?'

'This one is special.'

'Gideon, I don't need presents, I've got you…'

'For ever,' he said, 'but I think you'll want this.'

'It's heavy. Not diamonds, then…' she said, pulling on the ribbons.

'More precious than that.'

'Really?' She looked up at him but there were no clues to be found in his beloved face. 'What?' she asked, laughing.

Then, as if she could see into his mind, she knew.

'Gideon?'

He said nothing and she turned back to it. She hadn't thought her heart could beat any faster than it had today, but this was different and she could hardly breathe as she lifted off the lid.

The first thing she saw was the box containing her father's medals. She picked it up, opened it, touched them. Laid them aside. Opened an album of photographs.

Her mother as a girl.

'Oh,' she said as she saw her father, unbelievably young, in his uniform. Their wedding. She sat down, turning the pages. Groaning over school photographs. Remembering trips. 'That's me on my first bike.'

'And guess what,' he said. 'You're wearing a purple jumper.'

'My mother knitted it for me…'

She leaned against him and gasped, exclaimed, laughed, cried as she turned each page. 'It's my life. My history.' Then, turning to him, 'Did I ever tell you how much I love you?'

'Not more than twenty times a day.'

'It's not enough. I don't know how you got this…' She put her hand over his mouth before he could tell her. 'I don't want to know. I only know that you could not have given me anything more precious, more perfect. But this is my past,' she said. 'You are my future.' And she cradled his face in her hands, kissed him. 'From this day forward, Gideon…'

RUNAWAY BRIDE RETURNS!

BY
CHRISTIE RIDGWAY

Christie Ridgway started reading and writing romances in middle school. It wasn't until she was the wife of her college sweetheart and the mother of two small sons that she submitted her work for publication. Many contemporary romances later, she is happiest when telling her stories despite the splash of kids in the pool, the mass of cups and plates in the kitchen and the many commitments she makes in the world beyond her desk.

Besides loving the men in her life and her dream-come-true job, she continues her longtime love affair with reading and is never without a stack of books. You can find out more about Christie or contact her at her website, www.christieridgway.com.

To firefighters and all first responders
who dedicate their lives to saving ours.

Chapter One

If Owen Marston hadn't already been flat on his back in a hospital bed, he might have been tempted to knock himself out so he didn't have to deal with the family members gathered around him. Less than twenty-four hours had passed since he'd been admitted, and already he couldn't wait to get out of this place with its pink plastic pitchers and beeping machinery. He craved time alone, but he was managing to keep it together okay, mostly by pretending he wasn't here and by pretending that what actually had happened had not.

To that end, he tuned out his mother's conversation and thought of his spacious condo, his big bed, his large-screen TV. Solitude. God, he needed it.

"And your hair still smells like smoke," his mother said, the anxious edge of her voice breaking into his reverie. Her fingers worried the pearls at her throat. "Caro, don't you think your brother's hair still smells like smoke?"

"Mom," Caro replied, her voice patient. "It doesn't matter that Owen's hair smells like smoke. It's no big deal that the thread count on the sheets isn't up to snuff, and that the pattern of the curtains is an offense to anyone with taste. This is a hospital, not a hotel, a resort or a spa. We're interested in Owen getting good health care, not concierge service."

Their mother ignored his sister's points to appeal to Owen's younger brother. "Bryce, don't you think your brother's hair still smells like smoke?"

The woman was seriously losing it. Bryce didn't seem bothered by the fact, though. Sprawled in a nearby chair, he kept his attention focused on his iPhone. Maybe he was checking the latest sports scores, though more likely he was poring over some financials e-mailed to him by his assistant.

Their mother huffed out a sigh. "Bryce, are you listening—"

"Call for you, Owen," his brother said. "Granddad on speaker phone." He slid the device onto the fake woodgrain surface of the plastic table pulled up to Owen's bed.

Owen glared at Bryce, who just shrugged as their grandfather's used-to-smoke-a-pack-a-day voice carried into the room. "Boy, I just heard you're in the hospital. How come nobody told me this yesterday?"

Owen looked around. His father, who had a minute ago been standing at the foot of his bed, was now gone, just another in his long string of well-practiced disappearing acts that he managed to make each time the elder Marston started in with his demands. His mother had her back turned now and was murmuring with Caro. In a convenient blink of an eye, Bryce was immersed in some paperwork he'd pulled from his briefcase.

Owen glanced toward the doorway again. A slim, feminine figure flitted past. His body jerked, his attention lasering on the fluttering ends of dark hair and the receding echo of stiletto heels.

Wait! Was that…? Could it be…?

His heart pounded and he shifted, struggling to lift up, but his ankle, his arm, his head and every muscle he had protested. Collapsing back to the pillow, he tried telling himself to take it easy. It couldn't have been her. Why would she show up now? And he wouldn't want her to, that was for damn sure, not when he felt as if he'd been rolled downhill in a barrelful of rocks.

His grandfather's voice sounded louder through the phone's speaker. "Why didn't anyone tell me yesterday?" Philip Marston demanded again.

Owen's gaze stayed focused on the empty doorway, and though tension still grabbed at his gut, he managed to keep his words even and calm. "Nobody told you yesterday, Granddad, because there was nothing definitive to tell until today. And today we knew you were locked in meetings with the governor all morning and afternoon."

"Well, I want a full report right now, young man. What the hell happened?"

"A little bump on the head, a little smoke inhalation and I broke my ulna." His sister had convinced him to go with royal blue for the cast that ran from hand to elbow, and it looked stupid to Owen now, but he felt even stupider for the way his heart had sped up when he imagined that feminine figure in the doorway. Especially since what he'd once thought he'd felt for that woman had been a figment of his imagination, too.

"And then I sprained my right ankle and broke my left foot." Thank God no cast on that one, just one of those big ugly boots.

"I warned you," Philip Marston said, his tone disapproving. "I warned you that this so-called career you've chosen was no good."

Owen's tension tightened, clamping on his lungs like a vise, but he didn't surrender a groan, much less a sigh. "Yes, Granddad, so you did."

"I'm glad you concede that," the old man grumbled.

Owen's chest squeezed tighter and acid burned in his belly.

"And I predicted—"

"You never once predicted this, damn it," Owen heard himself snap. Chest still painfully tight, he spoke right over his grandfather's raspy voice as a tirade he hadn't known was in him broke free. "You never predicted I'd fall through the roof of a two-story house."

"Owen—"

"You said I'd get bored, you said I was wasting my college education, you said I was turning my back on the family business. But admit you never once forecasted this, Granddad. You never once declared I'd find myself in a hospital bed, my body busted all to pieces, and—"

"Owen—"

"—and one of my best buddies dead."

On that last word—*dead*—Owen's outburst came to an abrupt halt. *Dead.*

Unable to draw a full breath, he ignored the sputter coming through the phone's speaker and thumbed off the gadget before tossing it to his brother, who was staring at him.

His mother was staring, too. His sister. His father had ventured into the room again and was looking at Owen with alarm, as well.

Of course they all looked alarmed. He knew why. It was because he was usually laid-back. Calm in a crisis. Impervious to pressure, and he'd withstood a hell of a lot of it to go his own way and become a firefighter instead of some dull suit in the Marston business empire. But crap, last night had been a disaster, and not only had his body betrayed him by breaking up in his fall, but now his imagination was playing tricks on him, too.

She was nowhere nearby.

"Ross," his mother said to his father. "Go out there and track down that doctor. It's time we get Owen released from this place. I think the atmosphere isn't doing him any good."

June Marston probably was certain it was the curtains that were making him surly, but what did he care? Getting out sounded terrific. His quiet, spacious condo sounded perfect.

"I want him home," his mother continued, "where I can keep an eye on him."

Now the alarmed one was Owen. His gaze shot toward his mom. "Home? Home, as in *your* home? No thanks, Mom."

"Owen—"

"Dad." He pinned his father with his gaze, though the older man appeared about a "hocus-pocus" away from going invisible again. "Just get me back to my condo. That's all I want." That and to turn back the clock twenty-four hours. Or, hell, if he was making wishes, there was a whole other day he'd like to undo, as well, just over a month ago, in Las Vegas, when a certain woman had high-heeled into his life.

His father cleared his throat. "Your mother may be right, Owen. How are you going to get around, hobbled like you are? Your condo's three stories, with the bedroom a flight of steps from the kitchen."

It didn't matter. He'd be dead before he—

Oh, God. There was that word again. *Dead.* Last night the world had turned to fiery hell, and when the flames finally subsided, Jerry Palmer was dead.

Jerry Palmer was dead.

From a dark place deep inside him, something cold welled up to wash over Owen's body. His stomach pitched and a clammy sweat broke over his flesh as tension tightened again around his chest.

How had this happened? Why had he lived when Jerry was dead? He closed his eyes, trying to get away from the question. Trying to get away, period.

"Ross." His mother's voice was distant. "I really think you need to find the doctor. Or maybe we just require some sort of administrator type to get the paperwork going to get Owen home."

Home. Hell, that's where he was going, no matter what noises his mother made. His home, here in Paxton, where he could hole up and lick his wounds and lock the door against the world, including his well-meaning but never-understood-him-anyway relatives.

His eyes were still closed when he heard a change in the pitch of his mother's voice. "Oh, wonderful. Young lady, are you here about my son Owen? I certainly hope so, as we'd like to expedite getting him out of here."

"Yes, I am here about Owen," a voice replied.

A voice he knew. A voice he'd been dreaming of since that weekend in Las Vegas. *Her* voice. His heart started pounding again and he felt the bruises riddling his body begin to throb.

She *was* here. Now. Why?

Why now, when it was five weeks ago that she'd stomped off following their argument in Vegas? Why now, when she hadn't contacted him since? But wasn't it just like her confounding, inconvenient self to show up today, as he was lying in a hospital bed wearing a ridiculous blue cast and feeling like a 0.5 on a scale of 1 to 10?

And with hair that still smelled of smoke. He lifted his hand to his bristly cheek before he forced himself to lift his eyelids and take in the woman who had the gall to appear so damn beautiful from her place in the doorway.

She was small and sleek, her black hair a shiny wing that curved to her throat. Her eyes were chocolate brown with lashes that were long and curled and that had brushed his throat when they danced—they'd been that close. Her skin was a flawless golden and her full lips the color of a plum. He'd kissed that mouth, nipped it, painted it with his tongue, lost himself in its sweet flavor.

He'd lost his head over those kisses. Over her.

"How are you, Izzy?" he asked, surprised to find that though his voice was roughened by the smoke inhalation, he wasn't growling like he wanted to.

"Better than you, I see," she said softly.

Her gaze trained on him, she took a step into the room and he crossed his arms over his chest, the stupid cast clunking against his breastbone. Izzy winced, her downturned mouth sympathetic. "Oh, Owen."

"'Oh, Owen,' what?" Damn, but he didn't want her feeling sorry for him. He wanted her…hell, he didn't want anything from her except one thing. And she was a flight risk, she'd proven that, so he knew what he had to do now that she'd ventured this close again.

Busted up or not, feeling about as weak as skim milk or not, he must do anything, say anything, agree to anything that would strong-arm her into sticking around long enough to solve the untenable situation they'd put themselves in five weeks before. He couldn't let her run away again.

It was Caro who reminded them both that there were other people in the room. She bounced up from her chair with a smile and held out her hand. "I'm Owen's sister, Caro."

Izzy returned a polite shake. "And I'm…" She glanced over at Owen, obviously asking for help.

He made a little gesture with his hand. "Caro, meet Isabella Cavaletti. Izzy, also meet my brother, Bryce, and my parents, June and Ross."

Handshakes were exchanged all around and then he gave his family one last piece of info to chew on. Might as well, since he now had this on his plate, too.

"Everybody," he said to the other Marstons in the room. "Meet my wife."

Izzy's plan hadn't been well formed. If forced to articulate it, she might have mumbled something about wanting a quick peek to reassure herself Owen was okay. As if a 3,000-mile flight for a single quick peek made any kind of sense.

And anyway, that quick peek had turned into a hover-in-the-doorway the instant she'd caught sight of the cast on his arm, the elastic bandages on his ankle, and the other foot in some sort of device that signaled an additional injury. She couldn't help but take in the dishevelment of his dark blond hair, the scrape high on his cheekbone, and the cut across the bridge of his nose. A man had never looked, she'd decided, so weary and so gorgeous at the same time.

His battered appearance had frozen her in place and then she'd been spotted by a tall, beautiful older woman wearing patrician pearls and a worried expression. Owen's mother, June Marston.

She'd looked much happier when she thought Izzy was a hospital employee rather than her son's wife. That apparently put a sour taste in her mouth, because now she was staring at Izzy, her lips pursed and her eyes wide in surprise. "Wife?" she echoed.

Owen seemed unwilling to offer more, so Izzy sucked in a breath and gathered together her charm. By now, it came naturally to her, being friendly with strangers, getting them to like her and feel comfortable with her right away. She'd developed the skill out of necessity as a child, and the practice now aided her in her career.

"I'm a library consultant," she told Owen's family. She tried out an engaging smile, one she hoped would distract them from noticing she wasn't answering the wife question, even as she stole another look at Owen, trying to better assess his condition. Her hands had gone cold and her stomach ached. Should it hurt so much that *he* was hurt?

"I travel around the country visiting public library systems," she continued, "to help them modernize their services and increase their ease of use and popularity."

Owen's brother had risen to his feet when they'd been introduced and his interest seemed to kindle at the words *modernize* and *increase*. A business type, she guessed, taking in his gray suit and starched white dress shirt. "What kind of suggestions do you generally make?"

"Often I propose redesigning to make the library feel and look more like a big-chain bookstore. Comfortable easy chairs, displays of the current bestsellers, coffee bars. That sort of thing."

"Coffee bars." Bryce appeared intrigued. "Really."

"Ask her about the Dewey decimal system," Owen put in.

Izzy sent him a surprised glance. Maybe he was better than he appeared. Even one hundred percent injury-free, she wouldn't have thought he'd remember that. They hadn't spent a lot of time together in Las Vegas, and little of it had been focused on their jobs. Instead, their hours had been dedicated to sweet and deep drugging kisses, to memorizing the lines of each other's bodies with sensuous touches that could turn urgent even when they were only swaying together on a dance floor.

"Okay, I'll bite," Bryce said, derailing the dangerous train of her thoughts. "What about the Dewey decimal system?"

She slid another look at Owen. "Well…"

"The day I met her, she was coming off a five-day librarians' convention wearing a round badge that read 'Dewey' with a red slash through it."

Bryce's face—less rugged than Owen's, but not less handsome—lit up with his boyish grin. "No Dewey decimal system?"

It was what labeled her a rebel in bibliophile circles. She was a heretic to some for her views on the archaic cataloging system. "I advocate shelving books in 'neighborhoods' based on subject matter. It makes more sense to patrons and is easier for them to use."

Bryce seemed to like the idea. "You must be a very persuasive and busy woman."

"Busy? Yeah," Owen confirmed, his voice dry. "So busy it's been impossible for her to call her—"

"Husband?" June Marston said, blinking as if

coming out of a coma. "Wife? The two of you are really married?"

Owen grimaced, looking to Izzy as if he were regretting spilling the secret. His mother rushed toward his bed, apparently interpreting his expression differently. "Owen, what's wrong? Are you in more pain? What do you need?"

Owen flicked another glance at Izzy, then directed his gaze back to his mother. "Look, Mom, I'll explain the married thing later. But right now what I really need is some peace and quiet." He shifted his shoulders on the pillow as if trying to get more comfortable. "Why don't you and everyone just go?"

That sounded perfect to Izzy. He could explain the married thing to his family at some later date and she'd come back when he was feeling better and they could be alone to discuss what she'd been avoiding the last five weeks. Maybe by then she'd have found some rational explanation for why she'd been AWOL all that time.

Ready to beat a hasty—if temporary—retreat, she went into an immediate backpedal, deciding she'd locate a nearby hotel. From there, she could call her best friend, Emily, the new librarian in this 'burg, and talk over the fastest way to fix this sticky predicament with the man she'd married on a whim in Las Vegas. Izzy's hip bumped into Owen's sister, Caro, who seemed to be guarding the door.

"'Everyone', Owen?" Caro asked.

"Everyone but—" he lifted his uninjured hand to point a forefinger at Izzy "—*you.*"

The Marstons were a clan of tall people. Strong. Possibly domineering. Because one minute Izzy was near the door and the next she'd been herded by a slender blond Amazon—aka Caro—to Owen's bedside. There, he caught her fingers with those of his that stuck out of his bright blue cast. They were long, hard fingers, and as she stared down at the tangle they made with hers, she felt a jolt in her chest. A sting at the corners of her eyes.

Because…it must be because she didn't like to see him harmed in any way. Not because he was her husband, of course—that wasn't really real. She didn't like seeing him hurt because she was a woman and he was a man—no, because she was a *human being* and he was a human being, and that's the way that good human beings felt toward each other.

His fingers tightened on hers. "You shouldn't have run out on me," he murmured. "Why did you?"

Heat rushed up her neck. She *shouldn't* have run out on him. That's not the way good human beings treated each other, it was true. She'd known she couldn't ignore their marriage forever, she'd known she'd been wrong even as she'd used their brief but blistering argument as the impetus to leave him behind in Las Vegas, but could coming back here and doing this face-to-face make it right? "I heard you were calling my name in the ambulance," she heard herself whisper, avoiding another awkward question by posing one of her own. "Why did you?"

Before he could answer—would he answer?—Ross Marston stepped up beside her. "Son, before we go we have to get a few details ironed out."

Owen rubbed his free hand against his whiskered chin. "What details, Dad?"

"I can get your mother to leave quietly now if you'll agree to come to the penthouse in San Francisco to recover once the hospital releases you."

His fingers twitched, squeezing Izzy's and then easing up. "I can't—"

"You can't stay at home alone, either," his mother said, folding her arms over the silk jacket of her expensive-looking pantsuit. "Owen Marston, you've always been stubborn, but you're going to need family around you."

"Mom—"

"Owen. You can't take care of yourself, not while you have only one working limb." She turned to Izzy. "Surely as his…his…good friend, or whatever you are, you can help me convince him that he can't go home to his condo by himself."

Looking at the banged-up and bandaged man, it certainly didn't seem like he should be trying to recuperate without some sort of full-time aid. With both legs like that, and one broken wrist, could he even make his way from the door to his bed? Izzy frowned. "What about Will?" she said, mentioning the friend who had been with him in Las Vegas the month before.

"He met with some trouble last night, too," Owen answered.

Her heart caught. *"What?"* Will had been the childhood summer love of her friend Emily, and it was the fault of the other couple, really, that she and Owen had said "I do" under the benevolent gaze of a very bad Elvis. "Is Will injured? Emily didn't tell me that when she called about you."

"Maybe she didn't want to worry you further," Owen said. "And he's going to be fine, but I'm not calling him to play nursemaid."

"That settles it then," June Marston put in, her voice brisk. "You're coming home to your father and me."

Owen's jaw tightened. "No. Remember, you're going on that cruise in a couple of days with Caro and her fiancé."

"We'll cancel. This is more important." One of his mother's hands wrapped around the rails surrounding her son's bed, and the other gripped her husband's forearm. "A young man lost his life last night. It could have been you."

This time Izzy's heart stopped. It was all deathly quiet in her chest as she stared at Owen. *A young man lost his life last night. It could have been you.*

Did that really happen? But the truth was there in Owen's face, in his eyes. Their summer-sky-blue went bleak and she couldn't believe that the man she'd laughed with and danced with and impulsively married could look so utterly sad.

His fingers, still entwined with hers, had gone cold. "Owen…" she whispered, as he closed his eyes. She didn't know if he was still aware she was in the room.

"Maybe I should go," she murmured as he continued to lie like a corpse—*God*—on the hospital bed.

"Yeah," he muttered. "Go away, Izzy. I've got enough to deal with right now."

It was permission to do what she wanted. A reprieve, from his own mouth, in his own words. But his fingers were still entwined with hers and she stared at them, the sight turning her insides to mush as a sudden decision tumbled out of her mouth. "I'll take care of him at his place," she offered, directing her words to Owen's parents.

Something about the man made her impetuous, and she'd yet to understand why or get control of it. "That's what he wants," she heard herself continue, "and if that's what he wants, he'll be more comfortable there and also recuperate faster."

Instead of looking at her, June and Ross Marston were gazing on Owen. So she looked at him, too. His eyes were open again and he was staring at her. She didn't have a clue as to what he was thinking. Though…was that a gleam of calculation in his eyes?

"What the hell are you saying, Izzy?" he asked.

She smiled, her extra-special charming one, because she figured she was going to need to be extra-special charming if she was going to help this man get back on his feet. The way she figured, her sub-conscious had come up with the idea as a way to atone for the sin of being such a craven coward five weeks before.

"I can rearrange my schedule to free up a few weeks. So I'm saying—" she told him, clasping his fingers in what she hoped was a reassuring grip "—I'm saying, 'Honey, I'm home,' for as long as you need me."

Chapter Two

Nice digs, Izzy thought, as she toured the middle level of Owen's condo while his brother settled him into the master bedroom upstairs. The bottom floor was a spacious garage. They'd parked Owen's SUV inside, but he hadn't allowed her to help maneuver him from the backseat where he'd been stretched out.

"Bryce can get me upstairs," he'd muttered, giving her a brief, hard look when she started to protest.

So he wasn't grateful to her, she acknowledged as she heard deep-voiced curses drift down the stairs. Or all that comfortable, either—with the pain from his injuries or her presence or perhaps both. But for her part, she thought she could be easy within the confines of his condo. There was a bedroom near his upstairs that he'd said she could use. She was used to making herself at home in strange hotel rooms, and Owen's abode—with its walls in contrasting shades of blue hung with groupings of framed, brightly colored primitive paintings—was several notches above any place she usually laid her head.

She ran her fingertips along the top of a manly yet soft-looking couch that had plump cushions and was set in front of an old trunk to serve as a coffee table. In the last five weeks when she'd thought of Owen, she'd never considered where and how he lived. Those few days they'd been together had been like a bubble in time. In her mind, after she'd left he'd still been in Las Vegas, standing in some casino somewhere like a slot machine with a better physique and all the flashy lights and tempting bells and whistles.

She crossed to a massive shelving unit built to surround a large-screen TV and that held DVDs, books and an interesting collection of firefighting memorabilia. Her finger slid along the rim of an old fireman's helmet.

"Where's the rest of your luggage?"

At the voice, she jumped and spun around, for a minute confusing the man coming into the room with the man she'd married. Their height was the same, and they had that same dark blond hair and square chin. But it was Bryce, not Owen, and she felt her tight stomach ease a little. She owed the man upstairs, and she hadn't been able to stop herself from offering to help him, but the idea of actually living with Owen did make her a bit nervous.

I can do this, though. I can dispense with the guilt I feel for running out on him by doing a good turn for the guy. She thought of the bandages, the cast, the cuts and bruises. *He needs me.*

"Where's the rest of your luggage?" Bryce asked again.

"I just have the one bag," she said, pointing to the small suitcase she'd set by the door. "I travel light."

Bryce's eyebrows rose. "I guess. I thought that was your makeup case."

Izzy shook her head. "I'm short. My feet are small. My clothes and shoes don't take up all that much room."

He was still looking at her one bag. "My brother, the lucky dog, marrying the only woman on planet Earth who can make do with less."

Make do with less? Izzy frowned. That wasn't how she saw herself. She was efficient. And capable of moving on in a moment—before she ever out-stayed her welcome.

"So…you really are married to him?" Bryce asked.

"Well…" She sighed. "It's a long story."

"I don't need to be anywhere anytime soon." He crossed to the couch and sprawled onto the cushions.

"At the moment, I'd rather talk about Owen. How's he doing?" Izzy glanced up at the ceiling.

"Down for the count for a while, I'd guess. The

meds and the trip home have done him in." He forked a hand through his hair. "I've been thinking. Maybe I should stay…."

"I thought you have a job more than an hour away in San Francisco."

He grimaced. "Yeah. The family biz. Granddad can't do it all by himself, though he wants to, and he and my dad are like oil and water. It's too far a commute, and in any case I would have trouble putting in my usual fourteen-hour days while taking care of Owen, too."

"But you see, I do have time." Then there was something else to consider—that chilling glimpse of Owen's desolate eyes that had scared her into volunteering for the gig as his personal home health aide. She was rebellious, yet not usually reckless, so it was still a surprise.

"And he seems willing to let you spend that time with him."

She held back a snort. "Only because it seemed the easiest way to put off your mother, I suspect."

Bryce laughed. "Yeah, I thought the same. She's a nice woman, really, but the prospect of having our mom hover could make a man desperate to settle for anyone else."

"Gee, thanks."

"Oops, sorry. It's not that you're not incredibly appealing in a chocolate-and-apricot-fairy kind of way—"

"Chocolate-and-apricot fairy?"

"Your hair. Your skin." He gestured to her and grinned. "Obviously, I'm the romantic brother in the family."

She'd thought marrying a woman after a three-days' acquaintance pretty darn romantic. Until she'd woken up the morning after the wedding and thought it was ridiculous and that both of them were certifiable. Owen had accused her of being a coward when he'd caught her checking out of the hotel, and she'd stalked off as if insulted—instead of showing her fear that he'd seen through her like no one else ever had.

"Why can't you imagine this might work?" he'd asked. She hadn't answered him, but she hadn't stuck around to end the marriage, either. Remembering the moment, her stomach jittered again with another attack of nerves and her gaze slid over to her one piece of luggage, conveniently resting beside the door. Maybe she should renege on her offer after all. Grab her little bag and get the heck out of town, just like she'd done in Las Vegas.

Leaving Owen behind again.

But this time hurt and needing...someone.

But he had family! Friends nearby! Roots in this town and also this nice home to call his own. She had none of those things, and she did just fine. Surely he would be okay—

"What happened?" she heard herself say, not taking her eyes off her suitcase, as if it were the governor's pardon that she could pick up if push came to shove. "I don't really know what happened the night of the fire."

She'd been avoiding finding out about it, too. Last evening she'd checked into one of those anonymous business hotels she was so familiar with—the ones that put a *USA TODAY* outside every door each morning, making it easy for her to avoid Paxton, California's, local headlines.

A glance at Bryce had her finding her way to an easy chair on the opposite side of the coffee table. She sank into it, eyeing him as he rubbed his face with his hands. "I don't like to think about it," he muttered.

Izzy had spent a lot of time alone as a child. Hence the interest in books. Hence the hyperactive imagination, and she realized that hers was cranking into overdrive without the benefit of facts to rein it in. She glanced with longing at her suitcase and the door just a few steps away. It would be so much easier…

"He and another guy were on top of a two-story house that was burning," Bryce said. "They were ventilating the roof. There was a collapse and Owen and the other man fell through—and through again, because fire had been eating at the guts of the place, too. They landed on the ground floor, banging up Owen. A beam also came down and…"

"And…?" she whispered.

"And crushed the other guy's chest. Jerry, his name was. Jerry Palmer."

Jerry Palmer. Izzy cursed her imagination, because she could picture a Jerry Palmer, see some man who was no longer in this world. And knowing the name made it so much more real about Owen, too—she could be a widow right now.

The man she'd married could have died.

Her gaze jumped to her suitcase again, but she dragged it away to focus on Owen's brother. "Bryce, I'm going to take care of him," she vowed. "I'm going to see him back on his feet. I promise."

He opened his mouth, but another voice sounded in the room. A little staticky, a lot grouchy. "What? You're going to leave me alone up here?"

"Intercom," Bryce explained, angling his head toward a device on the hallway wall that led to the kitchen.

"Oh." She rose at the same time as Bryce and saw him head toward the front door. "Wait. You're leaving already?"

"Is anyone there?" the surly voice sounded over the intercom again. "I'm bored. And starting to get cranky."

"'Starting'?" Izzy rolled her eyes and headed for the stairs, but then cast a last glance at Bryce, who already had his hand on the doorknob. "Words of wisdom, at least?"

"Just two." He gave her a bracing smile. "Good luck."

Owen breathed out a silent curse as the woman entered his bedroom, a tray in her hands. What had he been thinking to allow Isabella Cavaletti to play nurse to his patient? In a pair of jeans that clung to her petite but curvy frame, a V-necked T-shirt just hinting at those small breasts that had snuggled against his chest on the dance floor in Vegas, clearly she was going to cause new symptoms instead of helping to heal current injuries.

Just a breath of her fresh, sweet perfume and he was dizzy.

"Are you all right?" she asked, hurrying over to place the tray on his bedside table.

"I'm terrific," he said. No way was he going to let her know that her proximity made him woozy. He'd already spent way too much time at her mercy. Scowling, he admonished himself to hold tight to his righteous anger at her. "Five damn weeks, Izzy."

Hell. Had he said that out loud? It was all well and good to tell himself he was going to stay tough guy, but with those stupid meds in his system he was not in full control of himself. Five weeks. He hadn't meant to let her know he cared that much to keep count.

But for God's sake! Five damn weeks and not once had he heard from his wife.

She looked down, guilt stamped all over her face, so yeah, he'd definitely spoken his thoughts aloud. "I know how long it's been," she said, studying the carpet under her feet. "And I imagine you've spent the entire time trying to figure out the quickest, easiest way to undo what we did."

It took both people in the same place to do that, or at least knowing where both people were to do that. She could have been next door or in the Netherlands for all Owen had known. "More like I've been trying to figure out *why* we did what we did."

Without looking at him, she slid the tray from the bedside table and held it over his lap. "Scoot up a little bit. I made lunch."

Scooting up wasn't all the easy with three bum limbs, but he wasn't about to whine for help. And when she placed the food in front of him, he couldn't stop a half-smile from crossing his face. "You didn't forget."

She'd made him a grilled cheese sandwich that included sliced onions and tomato. His favorite. Sitting beside it was a glass of milk poured over ice.

"It wasn't that I had to remember. They're my favorite, too, right?"

"Right." That had been the craziest thing about those three days in Las Vegas. So much of it had felt so right. The way she fit against him, the way she liked her grilled cheese with onion and tomato, the way she took her milk over ice. But it was beyond preposterous to marry someone because their lunch choice mirrored your own. He'd realized that when she'd run away and not contacted him for five long weeks.

"I'll never hear an Elton John song and not remember—"

"Yeah." He shook his head. Somewhere into day two of their time together they'd made the mutual—and surreal—confession that they'd both misheard the chorus to the popular Elton John song "Tiny Dancer" as—

"Hold me closer, Tony Danza," she sang softly.

Owen winced. "Though it's nowhere close to being as dim as thinking Prince is singing 'Pay the rent, Collette,' in 'Little Red Corvette.'"

She frowned at him, her full lower lip pushing into a pout. He'd probably once considered that cute. "It wasn't me who thought Creedence Clearwater's song about a bad moon rising boasts that immortal line, 'There's a bathroom on the right.'"

Now he frowned. "It's a common mistake."

Even her snorts had a delicacy to them. "Says the guy who attended *way* too many fraternity beer bashes."

"Hey…" Well, there was a little truth in that, though how could she know? They hadn't spent time talking about their college years. He grimaced. "We're complete strangers to each other, aren't we?"

A flush rose up her neck and she looked away again. "Eat your lunch."

He picked up half the sandwich with his good hand. "What about you?"

"I'm not hungry."

She'd eaten like a bird those days in Las Vegas. And drank like a fish? But no, although they'd spent a fair amount of time in the bar at their hotel and also poolside with those froufrou, umbrella-topped drinks, he didn't think alcohol had played a major role in the tipsy feeling he'd felt in her company— and in the spur-of-the-moment decision they'd made to say "I do" to the strains of "Blue Suede Shoes."

"I blame Will and Emily," he muttered. "We were under the influence of their first-love vibes."

He heard a small, heartfelt sigh and shot Izzy a disgruntled look. That was the kind of thing that had gotten them into trouble five weeks ago. Those sweet little sighs, that soft look on her face, the dreamy expression in her eyes when she'd looked at her best friend, Emily, who had happened to run into Owen's best friend, Will, at the hotel. The other two had been childhood summer sweethearts and then lost touch after Will's parents had died, leaving him the sole support of his five brothers and sisters.

Their chance meeting had ended in Will and Emily making a date for drinks later, and they'd each dragged along their best friend. So there it was, Will and Emily, Owen and Izzy. They'd been witness to hours of amusing reminiscing, which included the long-ago vow the other two had once made to each other. "If only," Owen said now, "they'd not dreamed up that stupid promise to marry each other if they both weren't wed by thirty."

"Not so stupid now," Izzy said, perching on the

end of the mattress, beyond where his feet were propped on pillows. "They're moving in together."

Owen looked over. "Huh?" Last he remembered, right before they'd been called out to the fire, Will had been wondering how two such smart single guys like themselves had somehow got themselves hitched.

"I talked to Emily last night. Apparently what Will went through during the fire gave them both a clearer perspective on the promise they made in Las Vegas to love and cherish. They're a real couple now."

"Huh?" he said again. Will had come by his hospital room but had not a said a word about what he'd worked out with his wife. Maybe he hadn't wanted to rub it in. "Really?"

"She's packing boxes as we speak, and his ring is back on her finger."

Owen's gaze jumped from Izzy's face to her left hand. She'd had a ring, too. A simple gold circle that had come as part of the "Blue Suede and Gold Band" wedding package at the Elvis Luvs U Wedding Chapel. He remembered how her hand had trembled in his as he'd slid it down the short length of her slim finger. He remembered the tremulous smile on her lips and the glow in her eyes and how that dizziness he felt now he'd felt then, too, because she was so damn pretty and so...

His.

He'd liked the thought of that. He'd believed that what they'd had was real and could really work.

Before she'd left him and not bothered with a phone call or even an e-mail for thirty-seven days.

What was real was that he'd been an idiot. They'd both been idiots in that wedding chapel. "What the hell were we thinking?" he ground out again.

She shrugged, then studied the bedspread beside her. "I'd been having a pretty stressful time at the librarians' convention. Not everyone is onboard with doing away with Dewey."

"Yeah. I remember having to pull you from a debate with a couple of crazies wearing T-shirts reading 'Melvil Now and Forever.'"

"Melvil Dewey." Izzy nodded. "Outside of Emily, I'd been a pariah for the five days before I met you. It was refreshing to have someone who looked at me with such, um…um…"

"Lust?" he provided helpfully.

She gave him that pouting frown again. "I was going to say approval."

His snort wasn't nearly as elegant as hers. "If that's what you want to call it, Izzy."

"Huh." She narrowed her eyes at him. "Now I know why Bryce says he's the romantic brother in the family."

Owen wondered just what the hell his brother was doing talking himself up to Owen's wife. "Was he *flirting* with you?"

"You don't have to look like it's such a shock."

"No. I—"

"He called me a chocolate-and-apricot fairy."

Chocolate-and-apricot fairy? Owen blinked. "My brother Bryce said that? He *was* flirting with you."

Izzy crossed her arms over her chest. "What? I don't strike you as a tasty fairy?"

No. He looked at her full mouth, the sparks in her brown eyes, the warm flush along her cheekbones. She struck him as…she just struck him. Right in the gut.

And then lower.

He curled his right hand into a fist to keep from reaching out for her. Even then, and even in the left hand that was casted, he could remember the texture of her soft, warm skin against his palms. He could remember sliding his hand down her neck and the thrum of her heartbeat against the pad of his thumb. His hands knew her, the sleek curve of her body from ribcage to hips, the dip at the small of her back, the resilient, round pillows of her behind when he urged her closer as they danced.

If he closed his eyes, he could feel her warm breath against his face.

He opened them, then jerked as he realized it really *was* her warm breath against his face. She was leaning over him to take away the tray. "You're sleepy," she said. "You need to rest."

With the view of her pretty breasts pushing against the clinging fabric of her shirt in his sight lines, he didn't think there was a chance in hell he'd be resting anytime soon. Sleep would be out of the question unless it was to dream about kissing her mouth, cupping those breasts and rubbing his thumbs over her nipples to bring them from soft blossom to tight buds.

In Las Vegas, she'd danced so close to him he'd felt the hard little berries brush against his shirt front and had barely stopped himself from hauling her, he-man style, over his shoulder and into his hotel room. After their marriage, though, she'd run off before they'd had a chance to share in any connubial bliss. No wonder she was still stirring up his libido, now that he was so close to her—and lying in a bed. Lucky he was temporarily incapacitated.

Though, hell, was he? What did a man need to make love? Not his ankle or his foot, anyway. And obviously, he thought, shifting on his mattress, the most relevant portion of him was working just fine.

Shifting again, he watched her walk toward the door with the tray. Did Izzy know about that cute little sway of her behind?

"Why did you offer to do this?" he suddenly asked. He knew why he'd taken her up on it. If he lost sight of her again, who knew how long it might be before he could track her down in order to end their farce of a marriage? And more, he wanted a chance to dissect exactly why they'd followed Will and Emily's crazy idea and gotten married five minutes after their friends. He hoped that by breaking down that decision, the attraction he'd felt for the woman wouldn't have a chance to ever come together again.

She shrugged. "Would you accept it seemed like a good idea at the time?"

Like his notion that bringing her into his everyday life would prove there was nothing left of the attraction he'd felt for her in the land of lust and lost wages, he thought. They said whatever happened in Vegas was supposed to stay in Vegas, after all.

His gaze tracked the sensual roll of her hips as she kept on walking, and the sexiness of it gave another undeniable tug to his libido. Which just went to prove there was no damn truth in advertising.

Chapter Three

Owen ignored his mother's long-suffering sigh and watched Izzy enter the master bedroom carrying yet another tray—this one bearing two glasses of white wine for the women and two bottles of handcrafted beer for Owen and his dad. He hadn't taken any meds since yesterday, so Owen figured he could enjoy a good brew.

His mom shot him a disgruntled look and turned her attention to the younger woman. "Isabella," she said, "your new husband's being very close-mouthed about your wedding. Please tell me a detail or two."

"Well…" Izzy bent to put the tray onto the narrow coffee table in the room's sitting area.

There was a couch, an easy chair that he was sitting on and an ottoman that was being used to prop up his lower legs, as well as a second matching chair, all gathered around a fireplace. Owen's dad had busied himself setting a small fire inside it when he'd first arrived. Now that he'd helped Owen in and out of a shower—thank you, plastic stool and a water-proof covering for his cast—his father kneeled to light the kindling and logs. As the autumn dusk settled outside, the reflection of the flames provided a camouflage for the blush Owen suspected was warming Izzy's cheeks.

"Our wedding?" Izzy repeated. "I, um…"

June Marston took the wineglass the younger woman handed over and returned an easy smile. "At least tell me about your dress."

Izzy shot Owen a look. Oh, yeah. Her dress. While like every other man he knew he wasn't particularly style-conscious, no way could he forget that dress. Strapless. Spangled. Low cut in the cleavage area. High cut in the leg area.

And fire-engine red.

In Vegas you could rent just about anything, and he'd shelled out a couple of twenties for ten minutes with a poof of white stuff that she'd pinned in her hair as a veil and a bouquet of white roses she'd held in her hand while they repeated their vows. He remem-bered thinking she looked as sweet and spicy as pep-permint candy, and his mouth had watered in anticipation of sampling her flavor.

"My dress, uh…" The next look she shot him snapped him out of his happy little reverie. *Get me out of this,* it said.

He supposed she didn't want to tell his mother she'd married him wearing a barely there dress and a pair of scarlet, spike-toed high heels that had made him swallow, hard, so he wouldn't let out his groan of lust—or "approval," as some others liked to term it.

Owen cleared his throat. "Mom, that reminds me. Izzy wants *you* to tell *her* something. She was asking about what I was like as a kid, and I thought you'd be the best source for that."

Izzy latched onto the idea in a way that would have been flattering if he hadn't known she just wanted to avoid the subject of their impromptu wedding. "I'd love to hear everything you can tell me about him."

Owen glanced at his father, now seated beside his mother on the couch. The older man wore a half-smile and sported an amused glint in his eyes. *Nice dodge,* he mouthed to Owen.

You could fool some of the parents some of the time….

And this time he'd succeeded in veering his mother onto a different track. He relaxed with his beer, letting her talk of his Little League years, then seasons of peewee football, followed by details of his high school endeavors.

"Salutatorian," his mother told Izzy. "He graduated second in his high school class. From there he went on to college where he was an economics major, heading for an MBA degree. Which I always considered a very useful field of study."

"Unlike how I'm employed today," Owen couldn't help put in, "because doing things like, I don't know, saving property is just so…irrelevant."

His mother frowned. "You know I didn't mean it like that."

She probably didn't, but he still had a sharp chip on his shoulder left over from the discussions he'd had with his parents and grandfather years ago when he decided against a master's degree and for a place in the fire academy instead. He watched Izzy rise from her chair to perch on the arm of his.

"Not only property," she said, touching his shoulder. "You save lives, too."

But not Jerry Palmer. That knowledge rushed in on Owen in a sudden, cold wave. Nausea churned his stomach and he felt clammy again.

"Owen?" His father was looking at him with concern. "Are you all right, son?"

Glancing around their small circle, he could see identical expressions on the faces of Izzy and his mom. "I'm fine," he said, forcing a half-laugh into his voice. "Well, except for the fact that I'll have to put off beating you at golf again for a few weeks, Dad. Though by the time you get back from your cruise I should be up to it."

When the other three continued to study him with narrowed eyes, he lifted his hands, even the casted one, and pasted on what he hoped was a grin. "What's there to be upset about? I have an unexpected vacation, a fire in the fireplace, the company of a beautiful woman and my loving family."

Maybe his grin worked. His mother gave a little nod and then turned to Izzy again. "Speaking of family...I'd like to hear all about yours, too."

"What can I say?" Izzy's smile looked as effortless as his had been difficult.

What could she say? It occurred to Owen that she'd never said. Not in Vegas—where admittedly they'd been living in a moment that had little room for family histories—and not in the three days she'd been in this house with him, though he'd been sleeping a lot as he tapered off the pain meds.

He slanted a glance at her now, happy to keep the conversation steered away from himself and how he was feeling. Guilty. Queasy. Damn downcast. None of these made for good conversation.

"Izzy?" he prompted when she still didn't speak.

She shrugged, that smile still curving her mouth. "I'm Italian."

"Yes," his mother said. "And your mother and father—"

"I have the pair of them," Izzy confirmed. "Can I get anyone more to drink?" She made to rise.

Owen placed the weight of his cast over her thigh

to hold her down. "You wait on me too much as it is," he said. "People can help themselves."

"That's the point of me being here, Owen," she answered. "To take care of you."

"A wife doesn't consider taking care of her husband a burden," his mother said. "And a husband would feel exactly the same way. Wouldn't you be there for Isabella if she was stuck in bed, Owen?"

He looked up into Izzy's face and the answer to his mother's question struck him with full force. No matter how mad he was that she'd left him, if Izzy was stuck in bed, if she couldn't get away from him like she'd done in Las Vegas, he'd use the opportunity to do more than make her meals or bring her the remote control. If she were on that bed over there, he'd be doing his damnedest to seduce her into letting him have more of those sweet kisses they'd once exchanged. He'd be exerting all his influence to let her let him undo those little buttons marching down the front of her shirt until he could look his fill at her pretty breasts.

Yeah, some things didn't stay in Vegas. Like lust.

Her thigh hardened under his touch and he heard the little catch in her breath. Her tongue reached out to make a nervous flick along the fullness of her bottom lip.

He'd want to do that, too.

"I'd like to give them a call," his mother was saying. Izzy's eyes went wide and her gaze shifted from his face to the older woman on the couch. "What?" she said.

"If you'd give me their number, I'd like to phone them and introduce myself as your new mother-in-law. Maybe they're available to come for a visit soon so we can all get acquainted."

"Oh…well…" Her thigh started jumping as her knee bounced in a jittery movement. "That's not, um…"

Not a good idea? He supposed she'd kept the news of their wedding as secret as he had. And while he could mention that to his mother, and then flat-out inform his parents that this marriage was a tempo-rary situation just waiting for a permanent solution, he…well, he didn't feel like it. Because…

Because his mother might take the truth as a reason to apply the screws and get him out of his place and into the penthouse in San Francisco. He didn't want that.

Because stating the bald-faced truth about their marriage to his family would surely banish Izzy from his life. And he didn't want that, either. Not now. Not yet. Not when he supposed they had forms to fill out and papers to sign.

He stroked his fingertips over Izzy's nervous leg. "Mom, we don't want visitors right now."

"But—"

"Think about it, Mom. This is really my and Izzy's honeymoon."

Izzy's leg stilled. Her gaze jumped to his. The

fire's flames reflected warmly on her apricot skin—damn Bryce, he was never going to get that fairy comment out of his head—but there was another flush warming her skin, as well.

Embarrassment, or that "approval"?

It didn't matter, not when just looking at her could have him remembering past the need to end their marriage, remembering beyond the argument in the Vegas hotel lobby, remembering back to that incredible, undeniable physical attraction he'd experienced the moment they'd met. It overrode every sensible thought, every angry response to what she'd done.

Izzy licked her bottom lip again. His fingers tightened on her thigh.

Owen's dad cleared his throat. "June, I think that's our cue to head on home. We still have some packing to finish up, if I'm not mistaken."

Owen knew it wasn't smart to be feeling this, but he couldn't seem to extinguish the rising heat. Catching Izzy's hand, he brought her fingers to his mouth. "Good idea, Dad," he said, brushing his lips against her knuckles.

That small hitch in her breath reached Owen's ears, and that little sound seemed to reach lower, too, where his body demonstrated so very clearly that not every part of it was broken.

"I'll…I'll just show your parents out," Izzy said, her gaze locked on his.

Owen squeezed her fingers. Attraction, not good sense, ran the show right now. And it didn't want her moving an inch from him. It wanted her close, and hell, Izzy *was* still his wife. "You stay right here, baby. They know the way."

Owen's parents were rising to leave and Izzy really felt as if she should accompany them to the front door, but she found herself pulled down into Owen's lap instead. "What—"

"Play along," he murmured as he nuzzled her hair. "Or else they'll linger and we'll end up confessing one of our wedding guests was a pretend Priscilla Presley."

She squirmed, because she was ticklish right behind her ear and his breath was so hot and his— well, something hard was pressing against her bottom.

"Bye, Mom, Dad. Have a great trip," Owen called out. His voice sounded hoarse and she told herself it was from smoke, not sexual promise. "Be sure not to write. Don't phone."

"Owen," Izzy started to protest, but he put his mouth over hers, cutting off her words. Reminding her of what it was like to kiss him.

Good. Kissing Owen was good. His uninjured hand cupped her cheek and kept her mouth turned to his. His tongue painted the seam between her lips and it was as if she didn't have a will of her own. She opened for him, and even reached out her wet tongue to his.

At the touch, a sizzle shot through her system, a jagged, hot sensation that had her gasping for breath. Her mouth jerked away. She swallowed, her eyes staring into his.

They were so close she could see that the edges of the cut at the bridge of his nose were drawing together. He could have died, she thought again. Owen could have died.

His hand shifted from her face to curl around the back of her head. As he speared his fingers through her hair, he brought her mouth close to his again. Close enough to brush his lightly, setting off more sparklers.

"Owen," she said, though she didn't know why saying his name gave her such satisfaction.

"Shh," he murmured. "Make this look good. They may tiptoe back up the stairs, and we want to look like real honeymooners, don't you think?"

Right. She wasn't sure why she was agreeing, but it didn't really matter when it was just like Las Vegas again, with the incredible feelings she experienced in his arms welling up, buoying her on a combined tide of mental well-being and physical excitement.

Izzy stroked her hands over his thick hair and she heard him groan as she opened her mouth and took his tongue inside again. Heat blossomed over her skin, and she pressed closer to him, even though she knew more closeness wasn't going to cool her down.

The sound of a distant door slamming stilled them

both. "Hey, bro!" Bryce's voice. Steady footsteps said he was coming up the stairs.

Izzy jumped and made to move off Owen's lap, but he held her there. "This is embarrassing," she told him.

"It will be more embarrassing—at least for me— if you get up right now, honey." He stroked a hand over her hip and she felt her face heat up again as she realized her body was covering up what had happened to his.

"But I'm too heavy."

He half groaned, half laughed. "Believe me, that's not what I'm complaining about right now."

Bryce bounded into the bedroom, grinning and appearing not the least put out by finding his brother and Izzy snuggled up on a single chair. "What's up?"

Owen slanted her a glance, one eyebrow winging high. "Want to answer that one?"

Bad. Bad boy. She sent the message with a quelling glance—they taught a course on it in librarian school—then tried to appear casual and not at all a little uncomfortable in her current position. "We just had a visit from your parents."

"And now you," Owen said. "Bryce, it's at least an hour to here from your office. Why the hell have you come?"

"Is that any way to greet your loving little brother?"

"Well, yeah, considering I have a life and that you should get one outside of your assistant, your financial reports and your refereeing between Grand-dad and Dad. If you're taking off early it should be to visit a woman."

"Who says I'm not?" Bryce smiled again, one hundred bright watts of masculine appeal that he shot straight at Izzy. "How's my beautiful fairy today?"

Her heart rocked a little under all the male allure, but probably because his ultrasexy big brother had already set the thing tumbling with that string of surprise kisses. "I'm—"

"Completely immune to your dubious charms," Owen finished for her. Then he frowned as Bryce picked up his beer bottle and drained the half-filled bottle dry. "Hey! That's mine."

"You know I always want whatever you have," he said, sliding his teasing glance toward Izzy's face again. "If I can't play with your wife—"

"Which you can't."

"—then sheesh, don't begrudge me some of your beverage."

Owen was shaking his head, and though Izzy sus-pected he was amused by his brother's antics, he had his casted arm secured against her middle. With his other hand, he adjusted her a little so that her head fit under his chin. She felt him press his lips on the top of her hair.

Bryce was beaming at them both. "I do like to see you so happy, bro."

She would have craned her neck to look at Owen,

but he had her clamped too closely to him. Did he appear happy? She wondered, because over the past few days, more than once she'd caught him looking very much less than that. Moody and brooding described it better, as if there were a dark cloud hanging over his head that was poised to drench him in a downpour.

She was pretty sure he wasn't sleeping well. But when she'd asked him about it, he'd made clear that his nighttime habits were off-limits.

"Happy?" Owen stiffened, then patted her hip in a dismissive gesture. "Yeah, well. Could you move, Iz? My legs are going numb."

Of course Izzy did as directed, and it gave her an opportunity to check out that "happy" herself—and realize it wasn't the way she'd characterize his expression. Not at all. A minute ago he'd been exchanging passionate kisses with her, but now he looked as if he'd much rather be alone. His gaze was remote, his eyes focused on something she couldn't see.

She found herself dropping to the arm of his chair like before, then flicking a glance in Bryce's direction.

He looked worried now, too. "Did I say something wrong?"

"I don't know what you're talking about," Owen replied, his gaze still on that faraway place.

"It just seemed to get a little, I don't know, chilly in here." Bryce frowned, studying his brother.

"Stoke the fire, then."

With a shrug, Bryce ambled over to the brass log carrier set on the hearth. There was some newspaper wedged behind the stacked logs, and he pulled it out. "Wait a second. You don't mean to burn today's copy of the *Paxton Record* here, do you? It doesn't look as if you've read it."

Owen made a dismissive gesture. "I don't want to."

"Mr. News Junkie turning down info? I know it's just the local rag, but you're as addicted to that as your daily dose of those big-city papers you read online."

Bryce was holding it out, but it was Izzy who took the sheets from him. She remembered bringing it in this morning, but she'd just tucked it on Owen's breakfast tray and not given it a second thought.

Now that she saw the odd stiffness in his body, though, she looked down at the paper with suspicion. Above the fold, a photo of a fireman in full gear. *Jerry Palmer,* the caption read. The top story was coverage of his funeral, which had taken place the day before.

Her stomach folded in on itself. Oh, no. "Owen. I wish someone had let us know about the service…"

His face gave nothing away. "I knew about it. The captain called."

"We could have found a way to go—"

"It's okay." He was shaking his head. "Everyone understands."

She didn't understand. Why hadn't he mentioned it? Was it because he didn't want to be seen by his friends and colleagues beat up and battered, or was there something else turning in this man's head?

Bryce didn't seem to be any more enlightened than Izzy. Though he'd finished building up the fire, he still stood by the hearth, gazing on his brother's face, a line between his eyebrows. "Bro…"

Owen curled a hand around Izzy's waist and pulled her into his lap again. Then he bent his head to place a hot kiss against the side of her neck. She shivered, half because it felt so good and half because she knew he was using the move as a way to dodge Bryce's scrutiny.

"Be a bro back and get out of here, will you?" Owen asked.

Bryce didn't appear ready to be dismissed, though. He crossed to the couch and dropped onto the cushions, stretching out his long legs. "Like you said, it took me over an hour to get here from the office. You're not going to kick me out after less than fifteen minutes, are you?"

Owen took Izzy's face in his good hand and turned her lips to his. The kiss he gave her was chaste compared to some they'd shared, but she felt her tight stomach start to unfurl again, even knowing he had something else on his mind besides a renewed acquaintance with her mouth.

Owen's lips lifted. "You don't mind being a third wheel, Bryce?"

"I mind being BS'd," his brother replied. "Is something bothering you, Owen?"

"Yeah, I can't kiss my woman without you looking on."

"Really, Owen," Bryce answered, his eyes narrowing. "Is something biting your butt about what happened that night?"

"What night? Last night?" He laid another soft kiss on Izzy's bottom lip. "Last night when I was alone with my wife?" He caressed her shoulder with his hand.

The same hand that he'd used last night to morosely flip the channels on the TV remote, rarely responding to her in anything other than grunts. She might as well have been a doorknob for all the attention he'd paid to her. The day hadn't been so bad, but as the night descended, as it was doing now, his mood seemed to go down with it.

"I'm talking about the night of your…accident," Bryce clarified. Then his voice quieted, all his earlier humor gone. "Are the memories of it bothering you?"

Owen appeared to swallow his impatience. "Look. I'm good. The fact is, I don't even remember much, okay? I remember studying for a class Will and I are taking on haz mats, I remember the alarm, but after that it's all sorta smoky." He put on a grin that Izzy would swear was forced and shifted his gaze her way. "Hey, librarian, I punned."

"You did." She shot a look at Bryce, then turned back to Owen, not knowing what to think.

"I get a prize, don't I?" And he swooped in to take

it, laying a dramatic kiss on her mouth. Another show, but she went along with it anyway. Fine. It was hard to turn down a kiss that potent.

"Okay, okay," Bryce said as they came up for air. "I get the hint. You two lovebirds want to be alone."

"Thanks for coming." Owen settled back into the cushions of his chair. "Next time, call first."

"Yeah, yeah," the younger man grumbled, waving a hand over his shoulder.

Then he was gone, leaving Owen and Izzy alone. She looked at him, but he was looking at the flames now roaring in the fireplace. A log popped, and Owen jolted, as if a ghost had jumped out and yelled "Boo!"

"You're faking," she heard herself say. God, he *was* faking.

His gaze jumped to hers. "What?" he demanded.

She focused on his face, taking in that bleak expression once more in his eyes. "You're faking. You faked to your family that our marriage is real. You faked to your parents that we're having ourselves a 'honeymoon.' And now you're faking that you're feeling any kind of 'good' about what had happened the night of that fire."

His eyes had narrowed to slits. His uncasted hand was curled into a tense fist. "It's none of your damn business, Izzy."

"Owen—"

"Why don't you just move to a hotel? From there

you can figure out what we need to do about this marriage, then we'll sign the damn papers."

"Your signing hand is in a cast," she pointed out.

And it wasn't just his body that was damaged. She knew now that something deeper was hurt, as well. And Izzy Cavaletti owed this man her help until he healed—all the way. "So I'm sticking," she told him.

Of course, he didn't look very happy about it.

She raised her brows. "Think about it, my friend. Do you want your parents and Bryce here hovering? Or just me?"

She had him there. She knew it.

Except he was looking angry again, instead of grateful, and there was no sign of the man who had kissed her silly just a few minutes before. "Fine," he finally ground out. "Stay. But if you're not in my bed, Isabella Cavaletti, then you stay the hell out of my head!"

Since sharing his bed was about the worst idea she could think of, Izzy welcomed the distinctive ring of her cell phone—"Bohemian Rhapsody"—and hurried away to answer it. Her retreat gave Owen the last word, but that seemed the safest course.

Chapter Four

College football played on Owen's big-screen TV. He was lying on his bed, pretending to be immersed in each play, when all he saw were figures of blue and red scrambling on a green field. He made himself blink every once in a while to keep the colors in focus, but he let the rest of his consciousness drift, thinking about nothing, willing himself into a comfortable catatonic state.

Izzy moved into the periphery of his vision and he drew his eyebrows together, as if the success of the defensive line was tantamount to victory for the free world—or at least as if he had some cash riding on the game. Anything to get Izzy to go away and leave him alone.

"Look who's here," she called out brightly, waving a hand. "And they brought lunch."

Owen slid his gaze in her direction. Damn, there was a "who" all right, two of them, and they were beaming smiles and bearing bags. He felt obliged to smile at them, because at least they'd serve as a temporary buffer between Owen and all the things he didn't want to think about. "Will," he said, greeting his best friend and colleague at the Paxton F.D. "And Emily. It's nice to see you again."

The last time he'd seen the smiling woman had been in Vegas, as matron of honor to Izzy, his bride.

Will gripped his right hand, giving it a strong squeeze. "You said you were doing well on the phone, but Emily said she had to see you in person."

Emily frowned and shoved her husband aside to kiss Owen on the cheek. "It was all his idea," she whispered. "Not that I didn't want to see you myself, but apparently he feels it necessary to hide behind me in order to preserve his macho image."

Owen could certainly understand that. Right now he was all about preserving his macho image, which wasn't easy when a man was laid up, with a lousy memory and a temporary wife he was forced to depend on for his every mouthful. Except this time Will and Emily had brought a meal. "What's in the bags?" he asked, glancing at Will.

His friend was finishing rearranging the furniture in the living area of the master bedroom suite so that Owen could remain propped on the bed yet still be part of the group when they settled onto the sofa and chairs. "Subs from Louie's," he said, and grabbed up the remote on the bedside table to thumb off the TV.

"Hey!" Owen said. "I'm into the game."

Will blinked at him. "You never watch college football."

"It's a new habit." A new habit that was better than watching his wife and *much* better than talking to her. No, it wasn't that he didn't want to talk to Izzy. At the moment, he didn't much want to talk to anyone. He took a big bite of the salami-and-cheese sandwich Emily handed to him on a paper plate. "Put it back on, Will."

With a shrug, his friend complied, but he muted the sound. Owen frowned, but what could he do? He supposed he could take fifteen or so minutes of innocuous conversation.

"So are you all moved into Will's?" Izzy asked Emily.

She nodded and started chattering about painting a bathroom. Owen tuned out, then realized that his best friend was staring at him again. "What now?" He grabbed up a napkin and wiped his chin. "Mustard?"

"I'm just waiting for the 'I told you so.'" Will glanced over at the two women, who were immersed in their own conversation.

"Huh?"

Will chewed a bite of his own sandwich. "The last time we really talked was on the night of the fire."

The night that was only that smoky memory to Owen, and hadn't he established that he liked it that way? "Busy time," he mumbled.

"We were studying for the haz-mat course we're enrolled in. I was bemoaning my married state and wondered aloud how two such smart guys as ourselves could have gotten hitched in Vegas. You know, that big mistake of ours."

"Huh," Owen grunted. He remembered also vowing that he was going to track down Izzy after that very shift ended. Goes to show he should have been more careful about what he wished for. He should have been specific that tracking her down didn't include taking her into his home.

Okay, fine, he'd agreed to letting her stay here. But he hadn't realized how pretty she would look in the morning, and how sexy she'd look at noon and how good she'd smell at night, straight from the shower. And he hadn't considered how talkative she would be, too. She was a librarian, for God's sake! He expected more of her nose in a book and less of her nose in his life.

She'd casually asked him a couple of questions about the fire. The name Jerry Palmer had passed her lips a time or two.

He didn't want to talk about the fire or Jerry.

"You asked me," Will said, breaking into his thoughts, "if I was so sure that what we'd done in Vegas was a mistake."

"Of course it was a mistake," Owen blurted out. Then he realized the women had gone quiet and that both of them were looking at him. Great. He'd just insulted his best friend and his best friend's wife. Not to mention the woman he'd married, too.

"I mean…I mean…" He shoved his plate off his lap. Hell. "No offense meant, okay?"

Will calmly took another bite of his sandwich. "Best damn mistake of my whole life." Reaching over, he ruffled the ends of Emily's hair. She beamed back sexy sunshine that softened her husband's face.

Izzy was the one sending him a dirty look. Her usually warm brown eyes were cooling, and that plump bottom lip of hers was pushed out in disapproval. "I'm sure the newlyweds appreciate your best wishes."

He swallowed his groan. "Look—"

Emily hopped up, interrupting his apology. "I brought chocolate chip cookies, too. C'mon, Iz, help me get them." She dragged her friend up by the elbow.

As the women left the room, taking the remains of the sandwiches and plates, Will grinned at Owen. "That's right. She said chocolate chip cookies. My wife bakes."

Wife. "But…but…" Regardless of what he'd expressed on the night of the fire, could this really be his best friend's happy ending? "Are you absolutely sure you want to be a married man?"

That, after all, had been the opposite of what Will wanted for himself as they'd headed for Vegas going on six weeks ago. Finally freed of the responsibilities of raising five younger siblings, Will had professed to be ready to take up the reins of a wild bachelorhood.

Will propped his feet on the nearby ottoman. "I *want* to be married to Emily."

And she was already living with Will, just as Izzy was living with Owen. Didn't Will find all the female companionship distracting? The soft patter of their footsteps, the heady smell of their perfume, the way they looked in jeans, or a robe or even a towel turban? But then, Will got to work out his distraction between the sheets, while Owen had to ignore his by watching college football on TV or pretending to take another dozenth nap.

"You okay, Owen?"

"Huh," he grunted again, and grabbed up the remote to thumb up the sound on his set. More little insects scrambled across the green screen. Go... whichever team was losing. He was identifying with the underdog these days, big time.

"How're things with you and Izzy?"

"I don't want to talk about it." Remember, he didn't want to talk about anything! Why else did Will think he had the volume up loud enough to hear the announcers drone on about their glory days throwing the pigskin around? Good God, was there no one more self-involved than a sports announcer with a pretty face and a half-dozen seasons in the NFL?

"What about the night of the fire? The night that Jerry died and we were hurt?" Will asked.

We were hurt. Oh, crap. Yeah, there was someone more self-involved than those bull-necked bobble-heads on TV. And that would be him. Will had been injured that night, too—he'd gone through his own harrowing experience. "Are *you* okay?"

"Twisted ankle, already all healed up. Nothing close to what you're dealing with." He looked at his feet, propped on the ottoman, then he looked back over at Owen. "The worst part was when I was trapped under that metal awning. I had a few bad moments wondering if I was going to be crushed under the metal or cooked like stew over a camp stove. Put a few things in perspective for me. My brothers and sisters. Emily."

"Yeah," Owen replied. He had bad moments, too, recalling that hazy night. What had he done wrong? How had he let Jerry down? Surely there was some-thing…

"Tell me, Will," he said gruffly. He couldn't retreat to the land of silence any longer. There was no way he could duck the thoughts in his head. "Tell me about that night."

Will frowned. "You remember."

"I can't…" Owen rubbed a hand over his hair, wishing he could still put off the truth forever. "I don't have the details straight. But I must have made an error in judgment."

"No." Will's adamant voice came clearly through the bedroom doorway, halting Izzy in her trip back to the bedroom with Emily and the cookies. "It wasn't you, Owen. You didn't do anything wrong. That damn fire was responsible for Jerry's death."

Izzy's heart flopped in her chest. Oh, no. Oh, God. This is what she'd been worrying about. She shifted closer to hear better, then felt her friend yank her back by the arm. "Downstairs and to the kitchen for us," she whispered.

"But…" But then she let her words subside. Owen would have clammed up if she and Emily returned, and it was important that he get out whatever he was bottling up inside him. His emotions definitely needed a release.

And she could use the respite from her own. A little chat with her best friend should be the soothing balm she needed.

The two women retreated to the kitchen, and Izzy set down the tray on the counter. "Shall I make some tea?" she asked her friend.

Emily smiled. "Really? You? Tea? Quite the domestic goddess you've turned out to be."

"You should see what I can do with those little

coffeemakers that come in hotel rooms. Three-course meals—though all with the distinctive seasoning of Sanka."

"Ew." Emily leaned against the countertop as Izzy bustled around the kitchen. "So, what's new besides your new stint as 'Isabella Cavaletti, Home Nurse?'"

Izzy gave a little shrug. "Not much. I heard that my *Zia* Sophia passed away."

"Oh, Iz…"

She shrugged again. "She was ninety-seven when she died. I lived with her in third grade—so, twenty years ago? Funny lady. She made a mean ziti and never rose before noon."

Emily frowned. "Never rose before noon? Who got you up for school? Made your breakfast?"

"The saintly three of me, myself and I." She caught the look of sympathy in Emily's gaze. "Girlfriend, it wasn't Dickens. There were clean, folded clothes in the drawers and Pop-Tarts in the kitchen cupboard."

"Still…"

"A mean ziti can overcome many nutritional challenges." The kettle was starting to whistle, so Izzy hurried to the stovetop.

"Do you need some time away from Owen to attend the funeral? I'm sure Owen's brother would help out, since his parents and sister are on that cruise. If not, Will or I—"

"Oh, no." Izzy waved off the offer. "*Zia* was laid to rest about four months ago. I only heard because

I made a call to one of my cousins last week. I was concerned because my mother's number hasn't been working."

"Izzy." Emily took a breath, seeming to get a hold of herself. "All right, the homicidal urge over the way your family forgets about you is passing. Wait— did you say your mother's number wasn't working? Is *she* all right?"

"Yes. She's on a trip, packing for a trip, unpacking for a trip, planning her next trip. One of those." Her parents had led tours throughout Europe for the past thirty years. "She got a new phone and a new number for reasons not quite clear to me in the fifteen seconds we had to talk before her flight was called."

"And your father?"

"He was reading a newspaper, but apparently gave a pinkie-wave when he heard it was me on the phone."

Emily heaved a sigh. "They're not—"

"Anything different than they've ever been. It's when you start expecting more that you get disappointed by people."

"Some people *won't* disappoint you, Iz. Some people will be there always and—"

Izzy shut her up with a brief, hard hug. "Sure. Like Will is there for you, Emily."

Emily's eyes narrowed. "Is there some other family thing you should be telling me about?"

"No! You already know all about my family 'things.'" And the last thing that would relax her was a rehash of her relatives. "So, spill all about marital bliss."

"You're married, too, Izzy."

"And I'm going to have to do something about that, I realize. Did you get very far in finding out what it takes to annul—" She broke off at the odd expression crossing her friend's face. "Let's not talk annulments then. Let's talk happy husbands and winsome wives."

"'Winsome'?" The word made Emily grimace. "What the heck are you talking about, Isabella?"

"I don't know." She laughed. "I know nothing about how this coupledom thing is supposed to work."

"Is that how you see you and Owen? Are you a couple now?"

"No. That wedding thing was impulsive, spontaneous, and we place the blame entirely on you and Will."

"Hey, we didn't force that ring on your finger."

Izzy smiled a little at the memory of Owen beside her, the flash of his smile and that wild—and absurdly right—feeling she'd had as he slid the narrow band down her left ring finger. Common sense hadn't kicked in until the next morning, when he'd caught her in the lobby, trying to sneak out of the hotel. She'd been in the checkout line, tugging on that matrimonial symbol. "Did you know window cleaner is the best method to remove a ring?"

"I'll put that in my reference librarian files," Emily said, rubbing her thumb over her own wedding band. "Though I'm planning to keep this one on forever."

"I believe it."

Emily frowned a little. "Owen didn't seem to."

"It's just that he's in a cantankerous frame of mind," Izzy answered. "He's been pretty much set on moody since the day we walked in here."

"Will thinks he's upset about Jerry."

"Me, too," Izzy admitted. "And maybe beyond the grief that you would expect. But I don't know what to do about it."

"Chicken soup sans Sanka flavoring?"

"That's the best I have to offer so far." Though her mind drifted to those kisses they'd shared since she'd moved in. Granted, they'd been more for show than for seduction, but the sparks had been there all the same. Their Las Vegas experience had been similar. An instant, fiery attraction that at the time had seemed serendipitous and delightful. The sensation of his arms around hers had been just like the books said, a "coming home" sort of feeling that even someone who'd never had a real home could recognize.

On the dance floor, she'd fit her cheek in that hollow where his shoulder met his chest and she'd be as comfortable as if he were her pillow, but also tingly and twitchy at the same time. Her skin had shivered at his slightest touch, and when he kissed that sensitive corner of her jaw, her knees had gone soft.

"Izzy. Izzy!"

She blinked, coming down to earth as Emily sharply called her name. "What? What?"

"Our heroes are calling for dessert," she said. "Where were you?"

"Oh." She put the teapot on the tray, added mugs, made room for a cold jug of water and two glasses. "Here and there. You know me. The proverbial rolling stone."

They climbed the stairs, but reaching the landing, Izzy transferred the tray to her friend. "I forgot napkins. Take this in and I'll be back in a jiff."

It was slightly more than that because she had to find a new package and then practically gnaw her way into the shrink-wrapped plastic to get to the rainbow of folded paper. She clutched a handful as she approached the doorway of the large master suite.

The sight there made her pause. Emily sat in Will's lap, just as she'd sat on Owen's a few nights before. Will's arm was curled about his wife's waist in a gesture that was protective and possessive. They both wore playful expressions and were feeding each other cookies as if they were pieces of wedding cake.

The tenderness of the moment had Izzy's heart flip flopping uncomfortably in her chest again, as if someone were turning a pancake. She'd grown up in a number of households during her childhood, and though most were those of aging female relatives, a time or two she'd been in a home led by a married couple. The husband-and-wife teams had always fascinated her. They were Italian households, so there were often a lot of loud voices and chaos in the kitchen, but the few times she'd witnessed a moment like this between a man and a woman it had skewered her heart.

Because she didn't know how to make that happen for herself. When she'd seen it, she'd tried memorizing the moves and deciphering the dynamics, but she'd been aware that her background was too full of *Zia* Sophias and solo Pop-Tart breakfasts to comprehend the ins and outs of the couple thing.

Still, it was pretty to look at.

Her gaze drifted toward Owen. He was apparently immune to the sweet domestic drama playing out just a few feet away from him. His attention was focused on the football game on the screen, and he didn't look as if his discussion with Will—*I must have made an error in judgment*—had offered him any ease. His expression was stony and when he shifted on the bed, he winced.

Her heart rocked again and she had to force herself to stride into the room, wearing a smile. "Hey," she said. "It's time for your pain relievers, Owen."

He didn't look away from the game. "I don't need anything." His voice was surly.

"Except a mood transplant, maybe," she murmured, dropping the napkins by the lovebirds and heading for the bedside table where the big bottle of ibuprofen sat.

"I heard that," he said, still not looking at her.

"Oops." She made a big play of putting her hand over her mouth. "Did I say something I shouldn't have?"

His mouth twitched, then his eyes shifted her way.

Their startling blue slammed into her, and it was she who rocked this time, her whole body, rolling back on her heels as she saw the spark of amusement catching fire in his gaze. "Okay, I'm being inhospitable, as well as cranky, and you're an angel to put up with me."

She took in a careful breath to give herself time to camouflage the way that reluctant, self-deprecating humor affected her. It was as good as a spin on a Las Vegas dance floor. Her head felt just as dizzy.

For the next half hour, he applied himself to being a more genial host. He turned off the TV, he accepted a couple of pain tablets and three cookies, he complimented Emily and poked at Will. That was like Las Vegas, too, the way the two couples meshed with such ease.

Izzy truly relaxed for the first time since moving into Owen's house.

All four of them were smiling as Will and Emily bid Owen goodbye. Izzy followed them down the flights of stairs, all the way outside to Will's truck.

"Oh, I almost forgot," Emily said, whipping around. "I brought you something."

"A present?" Izzy grinned. "For me?"

Emily's mouth turned down in a grimace. "Well, not exactly a present, but maybe things you'll be just as happy to see."

"Huh?"

Will was already scooping a cardboard box out of the bed of the truck. Emily leaned in to grab another and place it on top. "I'll put them in the living room," Will said, starting off again.

Izzy watched him with resignation. "Are those what I think they are?"

"Hey," Emily said. "You should be happy to get the clothes. I hope they'll be suitable for this climate, but they should be fashionable, since you just shipped them to me to hang on to right before we went to Vegas. The other box is full of books, I think. I've had it for a few years."

"Right," Izzy said. "Thanks."

"What's the matter?"

"Nothing." What could she say? She couldn't complain. There were more than half a dozen friends all over the country who never refused her request to store some stuff for her. And she probably could use the clothes.

"Iz?"

"I'm good. Thanks," she said with false brightness. "You've done me a huge favor!"

Emily was looking at her with suspicious eyes. Izzy made her mouth stretch wider into a big smile. Her relaxing respite was over, but her best friend didn't need to know that. Izzy didn't want anyone to know how much it dismayed her to think of her belongings catching up with her—especially at Owen's.

Chapter Five

Owen was enticed down one flight of stairs by the smell of some kind of simmering sauce that had to include tomato, onion, garlic and basil. Two days had passed since Will and Emily's visit, and he was damn tired of the four walls of the master bedroom suite. He'd started watching medical programs on the Discovery Channel, and the odd conditions high-lighted by some of the shows were starting to seriously disturb him.

He found his wife in a corner of the living room, her back turned to the staircase as she bent over a couple of cardboard boxes. Her position tightened her khaki pants across her backside and Owen smiled to himself. Yeah. Way better view than what was available upstairs.

Settling on the last step, he gave himself a few minutes to indulge in a purely masculine occupation—appreciating the physical charms of a beautiful woman. He wasn't going to feel guilty about it, either. For God's sake, he was a guy after all, a bored one at that, and it wasn't a crime that Isabella Cavaletti's sex appeal could spark a pleasant smolder in the center of his libido.

He might be down, but he wasn't dead.

Two days ago her attractions had been stretching his nerves thin, but since that visit from their respective best friends, Izzy had been more businesslike. Instead of her cheerful chatter, she'd turned quiet and polite—downright preoccupied.

He'd decided against prying into her change of disposition. It was no concern of his.

So he could just sit on the step and ogle the outside of her appealing package and leave her inside alone. His gaze followed the line of her spine as she went from bent over to cross-legged on the floor beside the boxes. She reached inside one and pulled out a hardback book. Her shiny black hair swung forward on each side, the split revealing a patch of smooth skin at the nape of her neck.

The spot looked soft and vulnerable and was perfectly sized for a man's mouth. He let his mind wander to the idea, his hand rubbing the stubble on his jaw. If he were smooth shaven, he might place a kiss there, as his hands slid down her sides to her slim hips. She would be warm and pliant as he drew her back against his body, crossing his arms over her flat belly so that rounded butt of hers was tucked against his hips.

As she sensed his erection just layers of denim and cotton behind her, she'd push back, giving her hips a little wiggle while making a sound that was supposed to be a moan, but was much closer to a sob…

A sound that was supposed to be a moan but was much closer to a sob?

Where the hell had that come from? But then he knew, because he heard it again—Izzy's shoulders trembled and she let out another quiet, choked-off sob.

"Izzy?" he said, without thinking. "Is everything okay?"

She whipped around, and that's when he realized maybe he should have thought first. Maybe he should have thought to take himself back upstairs and leave her to whatever was on her mind. He wasn't supposed to be concerned with the inside of her package even though it was fairly obvious that from the spiky-lashed and tear-drenched chocolate of her eyes, Izzy wasn't too happy.

"How did you get down here?" she asked.

"One stair at a time," he admitted. "On my ass."

"Owen!" she started to scold, then, apparently realizing there were tears on her cheeks, she dashed them away with the backs of both hands. "Owen, you shouldn't be doing that on your own."

"I've been on my own a lot the past couple of days," he heard himself grumble. Oh, hell. Now he sounded like he was complaining about her lack of attention when he'd been wishing for that very thing since he'd let her back into his life.

She made a face. "I'm sorry, I know you must be bored. I've just felt a little less…talkative than usual."

He was such a rat. There she was with tears still drying and she was apologizing to *him*. "What's the matter, honey?"

"Nothing." She shook her head, and scooted around on her bottom to face him. "Not a thing."

He glanced at the book in her lap, then flicked his gaze toward the boxes behind her. "What do you have there?"

"Oh. Emily brought them over. She's been storing the boxes for me. One contains some clothes and the other a bunch of books from my childhood."

"Yeah? What's the one you have there?" Curiosity about a book wasn't curiosity about *her*, he told himself.

She held it up. "*Eight Cousins,* by Louisa May Alcott. One of my favorite books as a kid, along with the sequel, *Rose in Bloom.*"

He knew Louisa May Alcott, of course, but he had never heard of these two titles. "Does some annoyingly good little girl die?"

She put a hand on her chest and made a mock gasp. "Are you referring to Beth in *Little Women?* For shame, to cast aspersions on one of the most beloved fictional characters of all time. I cried for hours when I read that book the first time."

"Yeah? Well, boys, when they are forced to read that book or watch that movie, we use our imaginations to invent ways to hurry that dreary thing to her ultimate destination." But Izzy had mentioned crying, so he figured he could bring it up. "*Eight Cousins* must have a storyline like that one if you're teary-eyed now."

An embarrassed flush crawled up her neck, and she made another quick swipe at her cheeks. "No, no. It's a cheerful story about an orphan girl who is taken in by her large family and becomes a much beloved member—particularly by the seven boy cousins she's never met before."

"So why'd it make you cry?"

Her gaze slid away from his. "Call me sentimental. I haven't seen this copy in a long time and it reminded me of how much pleasure I got out of reading it as a child."

Remembrance of pleasure would make her sob? It didn't jive, but hey, he'd promised himself he wouldn't pry.

So he lifted his head and sniffed the air. "Something smells really good." He remembered in Vegas that she mentioned coming from a large Italian family, no surprise given her last name and the Mediterranean warmth of her olive skin and big brown eyes. "Is that something from your childhood, too? A woman named Cavaletti surely learned her talent in the kitchen at a young age."

"Both my *nonnas* and a *zia* or two could make a grown man weep with what came out of their stock pots."

Weep? Hmm, more crying. "Yeah? What about your mom? Or is she a rebel like you and skipped out on the cooking lessons?"

"She skipped out on a lot of things," Izzy murmured, but then her gaze narrowed. "Did you just call me a rebel?"

"Ms. Just-Say-No-to-Dewey? What do you think?"

"I think you might be right. Though, truly, moving on from Dewey is—" Breaking off, she laughed. "Don't get me started on the Dewey decimal system. We'll be here all night and I won't even notice your eyes glazing over."

"So what will we talk about then? I *am* bored."

"I don't know." She tucked her hair behind her ears and he found himself fascinated with the tiny gold ring threaded through the rim of her left one.

Rebel, all right. No run-of-the-mill piercing for Isabella Cavaletti. She had a different kind of adornment, one that made him think of that sweet delicate shell of ear and how if he let himself follow it with his tongue, he could suck on her tender lobe without getting a mouthful of jewelry.

It would just be a mouthful of Izzy.

Clearing his throat, he shifted on the step, then shifted his gaze off her pretty face. "Um…uh…" The boxes. He shook his head, trying to clear it. "Why do you have Emily storing your stuff?"

"Oh." She looked embarrassed again. "Would you believe I don't have my own place?"

He blinked at her. "What?"

"I shamelessly take advantage of my friends, and every one of them ends up with a box or two or three of Izzy-belongings. My work means that I travel all over and I don't have an actual home base, if you know what I mean."

No. He had no idea what she meant. "You don't… you don't have an address?"

"I have a P.O. box, but I take care of my bills online. It seems odd to a lot of people, but it works out fine for me."

"What about…" He couldn't wrap his mind around it. "Television. Car. Coffeemaker."

"I rent a car when I need one. Most hotel rooms come complete with TV and coffee service."

Still… "You *are* a rebel. Or should I say a rolling stone?"

Izzy shrugged. "Good phrase. I use it myself. I'm definitely footloose, that's for sure. I travel all over the country and enjoy the different sights I see and the friends I make."

Yeah, but for how long did she enjoy them? She

moved from place to place and, unlike a turtle, didn't even bother carrying her house on her back. He remembered Bryce had told him that Izzy had arrived at the condo with only a single small suitcase.

"So you really like living like that?"

"It's good," she said, sounding defensive. "It's a good life."

"I guess." If you didn't like roots or stability or your very own Wii game system. Not to mention a place where your relatives could track you down… Okay, maybe he could see an upside.

But he suspected Izzy couldn't see a thing, because her gaze was back on her copy of *Eight Cousins* and he could detect the distinct glint of tears in her eyes again. He found himself scooting back a step, and cursing his boredom again, because coming down the stairs and seeking her out had been a mistake. What he'd seen and heard—what he'd found inside Izzy—was hitting him right where he didn't want her anywhere near.

His heart.

In the master bedroom suite, Izzy took plates off the tray that Bryce had carried up the stairs and passed them to the two brothers who were sitting at places set on a card table she'd found stashed in a closet. Bryce pretended to swoon as he breathed in the smell of the lasagna that she'd made from the sauce she'd simmered two days before.

"I love your pretty fairy wife," he told Owen. "She's beautiful, she cooks and she even told me I don't have to worry about doing the dishes later."

"Stop flirting," his brother answered. "And damn right you're going to do the dishes."

Bryce groaned. "Me and my big mouth. Would it aid my cause if I complained about the looooong board meeting Granddad presided over today? I doodled through an entire pad of paper."

Izzy pulled out her chair and sank into her seat as Owen gave Bryce a considering look. "The day you waste time doodling is the day I put on ballet slippers and dance in *Swan Lake.*"

Bryce clapped his hands over his ears. "Not another word. Don't burn that image onto my brain!"

Owen glanced at Izzy. "Bryce can take in the details of a meeting, plan another and write up the report on a third all at the same time."

"Not to mention managing my fantasy baseball team," Bryce said, around a bite of lasagna. "Oh, God, this is good, Izzy. Really, I'm *so* marrying you."

She had to smile at him. "But I'm already married."

Bryce's eyes brightened. "About that…"

"Don't go there," his brother warned.

Don't go there. But they had gone there, Izzy thought, for no less than a thousand times, and then had not even gone on to discuss the next step—an annulment—since she'd moved into Owen's condominium. Of course, they'd been pretty much keeping to their corners these days. Though she knew Owen was going stir-crazy, she hadn't felt much like being his entertainment or distraction. That box of books that Emily had delivered seemed to sit on Izzy's shoulders, weighing her down. It was good to have Owen's brother here to give them both another focus.

"Did you hear that, Isabella?"

She started, directing her attention toward Bryce again. "What?"

"I was saying that you two have a reprieve from the Marston machine even when the 'rents get back from their cruise. Right after, Mom's on tap for a benefit she's organizing and she's roped Dad into helping her with the last-minute details."

Izzy thought of the elegant older woman. "Something for the symphony, I suppose?"

"Nah," Bryce answered. "She abhors the symphony."

Owen smiled, and Izzy instantly noticed. He hadn't been doing much of that lately, and it looked good on him. He had strong white teeth and the smile crinkled the corners of his eyes.

"Mom has the pearls and the blue blood, but to give her credit, she's no snob," he said. "She really abhors the symphony just as much as she loves the opera, Springsteen and the Stones." He looked over at Bryce.

"She's a piece of work," they said together, then laughed.

"Dad's favorite phrase," Owen explained.

The brothers shared a smile that forced Izzy to stare down at her plate and swallow a sigh. There was a wealth of family memories and familial closeness in the way Owen and Bryce spoke to each other and spoke about their parents. It made her want to grab a book and escape like she'd done so many times as a child. Inside the pages of a story, she wasn't the outsider, the charity case, the person others felt sorry for.

Even if the book was about an orphan like Rose of *Eight Cousins* and *Rose in Bloom,* the character wasn't left to fend for herself. In books, Izzy had always found her happy ending right along with the protagonist.

"By the way, I thought of another one," Owen said, reaching across the table to touch her arm with his hand.

She looked up. "Another one?" His gaze was trained on her face and she wondered if that was concern she saw in his eyes. It made her skin feel hot and she was suddenly aware of his fingertips on her wrist. Each pad sent an individual streamer of sensation up her arm that then ribboned around her body. Her now-tight lungs struggled to bring in a breath. "Another one what?"

A little smile playing at his mouth, he sang softly, to the tune of "Rudolph the Red-Nosed Reindeer." "You'll go down and hit a tree."

"Hey," Bryce said, frowning. "Are you making fun of me?"

Owen grinned. "Just how you mangled the words to your favorite Christmas carol. And remember this other immortal line of the same song you misheard—not to mention mis-sang? 'Olive, the other reindeer.'"

"Oh, yeah. For years, I never could figure out why Olive didn't make it into the movie."

Owen shook his head. "Olive the reindeer, lost on the cutting room floor. No wonder I've always been considered the brainy brother in the family."

"Hah!" Bryce said, but he looked stymied for a comeback.

Izzy had to laugh, her low mood rising. Was that what Owen had been after? Was he attuned to her that closely? She rallied, trying to fit in with the light-hearted conversation.

It was what she'd done from childhood, after all—making a small place for herself where none was before. "They're called Mondegreens, you know," she told the two men.

"What?" Bryce asked.

"Misheard lyrics. In 1954, a woman named Sylvia Wright wrote a magazine article confessing that she'd misheard the lyric of a folk song about an unlucky earl, 'and laid him on the green,' as 'and Lady Mondegreen.'"

"Ah," Bryce answered. "So there's a name for the

infamous line Owen once sang at summer camp—
'He's got the whole world in his pants.'"

Izzy decided to be loyal and stifled her laugh.
"Hey, I know someone who for years thought the
refrain for that old TV show theme song was 'The
Brady Sponge, the Brady Sponge.'"

"No one could be that dim," Owen scoffed. Then
he did a double take, his gaze narrowing on her face.
"Wait, the 'someone' was you?"

Heat shot up her face. "I was, like, six or something."

"Yeah, but 'The Brady Sponge'? And you said you
sang it that way for years. At least Caro and I clued
in Bryce right away about Rudolph not hitting a tree."

"Yeah, but you let me wonder about Olive for half
my life," his brother grumbled.

Once again, their exchange tickled Izzy's funny
bone. She let herself laugh now, appreciating the
echoes of amusement on the faces of the men sharing
her table. She was good at this "fitting in and making
others feel comfortable" thing—no matter how temporary the circumstances for it were.

"Really, Izzy," Owen said, shaking his head. "I'm
trying to wrap my mind around this, because it would
seem to be a family-wide shame that should have
been corrected immediately. What kind of siblings let
you sing 'The Brady Sponge'?"

Oh. "I thought you knew. I'm an only child." And
for all *Zia* Sophia or *Nonna* Angela knew, it *was*

"The Brady Sponge." The only programs the elderly ladies watched on TV were *The Price Is Right* and their afternoon soaps.

Owen frowned. "I wasn't aware."

"Probably because he heard an Italian last name and assumed—well, we all know how wrong assumptions can be," Bryce said, his expression pious. "I, on the other hand, make it my pleasure to learn a woman—um, a person—on an individual basis."

"Stop, Bryce," Owen said. "Before I backhand you with my cast."

"I'll tell Mom," his younger brother taunted.

"And I'll—"

"Stop, stop," Izzy cut in, amused by their brotherly byplay. As always, what she'd never had fascinated and bemused her. "Bryce, your brother's assumptions, if he actually had any, are not that far off the mark. There's a gazillion Cavalettis. Grandparents, great aunts, uncles, aunts and cousins."

"Eight?" Owen asked softly.

Her gaze dropped and she toyed with her fork, unwilling to let him see how his ability to connect the dots of her life made her just a little...nervous. "Close," she said. "They're all quite a bit older, though." And then there were *Zia* Sophia and *Nonna* Angela, who were so old they thought girls still wore girdles and garter belts.

Owen's fingers tangled with hers on the tabletop.

"So you were the runt of the litter?" His smile was kind. "Though I can't imagine you being down for long."

That was her secret weapon. Never letting anyone see that she was down. Pretending, whether it was from within the pages of a book or within the home of some semireluctant relative, had been Izzy's strength against insecurity. "Nobody can resist me for long," she asserted.

Owen's fingers tightened on hers. "I'm a living example," he said mildly.

Bryce shot up from his seat. "Maybe I should get going on those dishes and then let myself out," he said.

"No." Panic fluttered in Izzy's chest. "No, Bryce. I made apple cobbler for dessert. You have to stay for that." *You have to stay and be the buffer between me and Owen.* Though she knew he was desperate for entertainment, it was dangerous to allow it to be *that* kind of entertainment.

"Stay, Bryce," Owen ordered, his voice soft, his gaze fixed on Izzy's face.

Bryce stacked the plates. "Fine. I'll take these downstairs and bring up—"

"You'll take those downstairs, load the dish-washer, do whatever scrub is necessary on the pots and pans and *then* bring up dessert," Owen said.

Without further comment, Bryce took the dirty dishes down the stairs. Owen looked after his brother's retreating figure. "How much I enjoy play-ing the older brother card."

Izzy smiled. "You didn't have to. I don't mind dishes."

"But I find that at this moment I mind being deprived of your company." He toyed with her fingers, braiding his with hers, unbraiding them, braiding them again. She felt every stroke and tickle, the nerve endings between her fingers seeming to stand on alert to absorb every cell-to-cell contact.

Her breath shortened and she felt her breasts swell and the tips tingle. Did he notice?

"I see what's going on with you," he said.

She twitched. "What?"

"You work too hard, Isabella," he said. "Food, chat, flirtation with my brother." The smile in his blue eyes said he was joking about that last bit. "You're here with me, your husband. You don't have to pretend anything."

But she'd pretended most of her life! Pretended feeling secure, pretended not minding being left behind by her parents, pretended a cheerful, friendly, you-can-be-comfortable-with-me attitude. She was supposed to be all that for Owen while he recuperated from his injuries. The runaway bride owed him that, after all.

"You don't owe me anything," he said.

Did he read minds, too?

His fingers curled around hers, held tight. "Are you okay?"

"I…I don't know," she heard herself whisper. But

that wasn't right, because until she met Owen, Isabella Cavaletti always knew that the way to keep others happy was to appear to be happy herself. The girl someone took in—and this wasn't all that different, was it?—couldn't afford to become demanding or temperamental.

She steeled her spine and drew her hand away from Owen's. "I'm completely fine."

He studied her face. "You've got that down pat."

Her heart seemed to sort of cave in on itself. No one had ever detected how often she acted a part. "I don't—"

Owen put two fingers over her mouth.

Okay, it really shouldn't feel like a kiss.

It felt like a kiss.

"You've been alone too long, Iz," Owen said. His hand dropped from her lips and then he was leaning across the corner of the small table so that his mouth was just a breath from hers.

"Not now. Now I'm not alone, Owen." Her skin rose in bumps as if she were experiencing a cold breeze, while her skin actually felt fevered. "I'm… I'm here with you."

He smiled against her mouth. "Exactly."

But before the promise of a kiss could take her away from reality, Bryce saved the day. He strode back into the room. "Who's ready for sweets?"

Chapter Six

As he drifted off to sleep that night, Owen was aware that Bryce had interrupted a crucial moment by bringing in the apple cobbler. During that meal with his brother he'd realized that despite her runaway status, not only was Izzy sexually attractive to him, but he also plain *liked* the woman. Her good humor, her knowledge of odd facts—Mondagreen!—and her moments of emotional vulnerability appealed to him on more than just the libido level.

As Bryce left that evening, she'd kissed him on the cheek. When she'd wished Owen good-night shortly afterward, she hadn't touched him at all.

Which made him admire her brains, too. When the most permanent thing in a woman's life was her P.O. box, then she had no business getting too tangled up in the man with whom she shared a marriage certificate.

They were really going to have to do something about that, he thought, closing his eyes....

He was standing on the roof of a burning structure. Adrenaline pumped through his veins as it did during any firefight. But there was an added kick to the natural drug flooding his system, because this time, he knew. This time, he was keenly aware that at any moment he'd take an elevator fall and drop into the maw of a many-tongued beast roaring in the depths below his fireproof boots.

Jerry was going to fall with him.

He peered across the roof and through the smoke toward his friend. Maybe he could warn him. "Jerry! Jerry!"

His gaze found the other man. Oh, God. His heart shuddered. Jerry was out of uniform! Instead of being protected by full turnout gear as Owen was, the other man was in jeans and a T-shirt. Were those flip-flops on his feet?

Owen started yelling again through his mask. "Jerry! Get the hell off the roof! Jerry! Jerry!"

His buddy looked up, finally heeding Owen's frantic calls. A grin broke over his grimy, ash-darkened face. He gave Owen a jaunty salute, and then—

The roof opened like the gates of hell and Jerry was gone.

"Jerry!" Owen scrambled toward where he'd last seen his friend, but felt the surface beneath his feet give. He was going down, too. His stomach rose toward his throat as he fell. Bad, he thought. This was going to be—

He jerked awake.

Disoriented, breathing hard, he jackknifed to a sitting position. It was darkness surrounding him. Not smoke. Not fire.

His bed. His bedroom. He'd survived.

Only Jerry was dead.

He fell back to his pillows and flopped his forearm over his eyes. God. His mouth was dry and he felt as if he'd just finished a five-mile run with Will and Jerry dogging his every step as they always did during physical training.

But Jerry would never run another step.

Owen groaned, squeezing his eyes tighter shut, though aware that couldn't stop the replay of his dream and of Jerry, that second before he'd fallen through the roof. His grin. His happy-go-lucky wave.

His death.

Owen shoved the covers aside, needing to get out from under their suffocating weight. He swung his legs over the side of the bed. He needed more air, water, something.

Before Bryce had left that night, he'd moved the

furniture to give Owen objects set at strategic distances apart so he could use them for support as he hobbled to the bathroom. He reached for the first, but instead of his fingers finding the edge of the bedside table, his cast swiped the lamp. It hit the floor with a deafening crash.

"Damn!" he cursed, then dropped back to the mattress. There wasn't much hope that Izzy hadn't heard the noise. He had no doubt that she'd come running.

The light in the hallway between the bedrooms snapped on. There was a pattering of footsteps, then his door popped open. "Owen!"

"I'm fine," he said, maneuvering himself beneath the blankets again. "I'm sorry I woke you."

She took a few steps inside the room. "What happened?"

"I'm clumsy," he said, glancing over at her. Then his heart stopped. He didn't know what he would have thought Izzy would wear to bed. A T-shirt big enough for a linebacker? A granny nightgown?

Even his libido couldn't have come up with something like this. Below her tumbled hair, her body was mostly uncovered in a pair of babydoll pajamas—he knew the term from a long-ago former girlfriend who'd worked at a lingerie store—that was a filmy, spaghetti-strapped top worn over a matching pair of boy shorts.

She must have noticed his sudden, tongue-hanging-out interest. Her bare feet shuffled a step back as one arm flew up to cover her chest. "I pack light and I pack, um, little," she said. "I get, uh, hot at night."

"I'm not touching that remark. And don't look so nervous, because I'm not planning on touching you, either," he said, scowling. Just before he'd nodded off, he'd been glad he'd managed to keep his mitts off her, right? Though that was certainly the last of the sleep he'd get tonight, thanks to the disturbing night-mare followed by this chaser of an electrical jolt to his libido.

"Can I get you something?" she asked.

"Water, if you wouldn't mind," he said, trying to sound more human. "There's a glass in the bath-room—and my robe on the back of the door."

In a few minutes she was back, and she handed him the full glass and then leaned down to pick up the lamp and replace it on the table. His flannel robe was belted around her waist and its hem hit her shins. He breathed a sigh of relief, and then another when she straight-ened. The plaid lapels criss-crossed at her throat, ef-fectively covering her from neck to nearly toes.

He downed half the water in one chug and then set the glass on the bedside table. "Thanks. And again, sorry to have disturbed you."

She stared down at him. "You're not going to be able to get back to sleep, are you?"

"It doesn't matter."

"But it does matter." She sat on the edge of his

mattress. "You need a lot of rest because your body's been traumatized, not to mention your psyche—"

"Psyche?" he scoffed. "I'm a man, sweetheart. I don't have a psyche."

She didn't even pretend to find him funny. "Your mind, then. When a friend dies like that—"

Something hot rose from his belly like a red tide. "I told you to stay out of my head, Izzy." Yeah, he was physically weakened, not to mention impotent against the damn dreams and the dark moods that were blanketing him, but he didn't want her pecking at his broken pieces. "Just go away."

He knew he sounded like an abrupt, ungrateful SOB again. Just what he was.

With only the light from the hall filtering into the room, he couldn't read her expression. Her body language said "stubbornly staying," as she didn't move her cute little butt an inch. "How about a bedtime story?"

"For God's sake," he ground out.

"No, really. Let me tell you about Melvil Dewey. Did you know he was instrumental in siting the 1932 Winter Olympics in Lake Placid, New York?"

"Never knew, never cared," Owen answered.

His dismissal didn't dismiss her. For a second he'd thought he'd won his solitude, because she stood up. But then she made her way around the king-size mattress to the other side of the bed. Under his astounded gaze, she propped the pillow against the headboard and stretched out beside him. There was a healthy thirty inches or so between them, but hell, they were sharing the same bed!

"Well, then this should have you snoring in no time," she continued calmly, as she crossed her legs at the ankles. "While Melvil was working in the library at Amherst, he started designing a hierarchical system for the books that would classify all human knowledge. He came up with the decimal-based scheme. There are ten top-tier or 'main' classes that are divided into ten subordinate sections. Each one of those one hundred subordinate topics are broken into ten more divisions. That's a thousand sections that can be referred to by an integer. And each of these numbers can be infinitely divided again using fractional numbers. Now…"

He tuned her out then, though the fact was his attention had begun to wander when she'd said "decimal-based scheme." Not that he had anything against numbers. But with her so close, her slender figure flat against the same mattress that supported him, he could only think of her body. He could only think of that slip of nightwear she wore beneath his utilitarian robe. It was apricot colored, he thought, which reminded him of Bryce's chocolate-and-apricot fairy, which only made him think of all the flavors of Isabella Cavaletti. The ones he knew, and the ones he'd yet to sample.

The disturbing nightmare, his frustration over his

physical condition and her irritating stubbornness over not leaving him alone with his sleeplessness, all of those were receding as Izzy took over the forefront of his focus. He could smell a faint note of her perfume, he could sense the warmth of her skin just a few inches away, he could hear her words wash over him, which made his mind jump to her mouth and the way it felt against his. Pillowy soft, with that wet heat inside.

Oh, God. That made him think of Izzy's other hot, wet places. His erection hardened to full arousal.

One wrist was in a cast, and he couldn't put his full weight on his feet, but there was another part of him that was obviously in fine working order. And he couldn't help heeding its sudden, insistent call to action.

Setting his teeth against the erotic ache, he reached over with his good arm and found her hand with his. She jumped a little at his touch, but he soothed her by brushing his thumb across the top of her knuckles.

"Um, Owen?"

He caressed her hand again. "Keep going. I'm listening." *I'm lying, but what the hell?* Because he could tell her temperature was climbing and he could hear the way her breath was coming quicker in response to his hand on hers. This was the instant magic they'd made in Las Vegas. Toying with the cuff of the robe she wore, he pushed it farther up her arm and let his fingertips drift after it, tracking a line from her wrist to the tender inside of her elbow.

Her breath caught. He let his hand drift back, trailing it to her fingers and then back up again.

Her legs made a restless movement, the edges of the robe opening to reveal her bare legs to a point just above her knees. His blood surged in his veins, as if she'd suddenly gone naked.

His gaze traced the olive skin as if he were licking a line down her shin. Her legs moved again, and the robe revealed another few inches of Izzy's thighs. Without thinking, he slid his hand around one of them, cupping the taut muscle on top and letting his fingers press against the sleek inner surface.

He heard her swallow, then she valiantly continued with her sleep-inducing—hah!—lecture. "I think you'll like this part the most," she said. "He was an advocate for a simpler spelling system for the English language. At one point he considered writing his own name as *M-E-L-V-I-L D-U-I*."

He moved his hand, stroking her leg now, and saw the way her thighs parted ever more. Under the pads of his fingers, he felt her telltale goose bumps.

"Um, Owen?" she said again, her voice fainter this time. "Do you… Are you… What are you thinking?"

Of only one thing, for good or for bad. Only one damn thing. "I'm thinking ol' Melvil would completely approve," he said, "when I tell you that I would like to *H-A-V S-E-X*."

* * *

Izzy's heart was beating harder than it had in those few seconds after she'd heard the crash of Owen's lamp and made it to his bedroom to discover he was all right. Her skin was tingling from the slow washes of goose bumps rolling from the point where he touched her thigh. *H-A-V S-E-X,* her brain repeated.

Desire had been pooling low in her belly from the instant he touched her hand, and at that thought— having sex with Owen—the heaviness there throbbed.

"We shouldn't… We don't… But…"

"Yeah," he whispered, his hand still tracing mysterious patterns on her skin. "All that."

"Then why?"

"Because it's a long, dark night. Because I remember what it felt like to dance with you in Vegas, and I think we'll do this dance well, too. Because I could do with a little human contact." He rolled on his side, and he lifted his casted wrist so those fingers could brush the hair off her forehead. "Take your pick, Isabella."

His palm flattened on her thigh, and he leaned close to press his mouth briefly to hers. "Take your pick or say no. Whichever you want."

But it was never the way she wanted! She'd spent the last few years trying to make things her way after a childhood of being passed off and shuffled over, in a manner that made her feel she had to be quiet or accommodating or easy to get along with, whatever the new living situation required of her. Only since she'd started her career in library consultation had she really been able to order her world the way that pleased *her.*

And she'd never wanted to want a man like she wanted Owen Marston.

But she did want him, and here he was, just inches away, his gentle touch sparking blazes along her nerve endings, like those signal fires that ancient peoples used to spread news.

Of good tidings?

Of danger ahead?

"Just a little human contact," he whispered again, and her heart squeezed, ridding itself of the last of her objections.

It was the thing she needed, too—and often. Human contact, human comfort—the loving touch of a parent, even the playful shove of a sibling—would have been welcome during those lonely childhood years. Books were magic, and they had taken her away and given her hundreds of new worlds and new characters to be—but they couldn't provide the warmth of a body. They were not a substitute for the strength and heat of a man to whom she wanted to offer her matching softness and need.

So here was a temptation she wasn't willing to pass up. An opportunity to share the long night with someone who made her insides tremble with just the briefest of kisses. But *brief* was the operative word. They'd been briefly in the same orbit, they were going to be briefly married and this interlude of contact and comfort would be brief, too.

Brief, lightweight, not meaningless, but not full of heavy implications, either. It would be a pleasurable way for two people to fill a long, dark night.

He traced her upper lip with two fingers and she tilted her chin to catch the pads between her teeth. She felt him tense, and when she licked across his skin, he groaned an answer to her caressing tongue. His other hand left the inside of her thigh and traveled to her far hip so that he could roll her toward him. In a smooth jerk, their bodies were flush.

She sucked on his fingers and he groaned again, pulling them free of her mouth so he could use the damp tips to paint her lips. "This was the first thing I noticed when I met you. Soft and full and the color of summer plums."

"I was wearing a bikini, and you were looking at my *face?*" she teased. Teasing, smiling, flirtatious. That was just the way she wanted this interlude to go.

"The second time you were wearing a bikini," he reminded her, "and I promise I was suitably impressed." The back of his hand skimmed her throat and then followed the center of her body to subtly loosen the belt around her waist. "But the first occasion we met was over drinks, and I think we were both a little put out that our two friends had dragged us to meet a total stranger."

"Oh, not me. Emily always connects me with the

cutest hunks. I can't tell you how many pickups she's found for me at these librarian conventions."

He punished her sass by leaning in and biting her lower lip. She squealed a fake protest as a hot arrow shot from her mouth to her womb. "Hey, don't damage the kisser."

His hands paused in the middle of stripping the robe off her shoulders. "'Don't damage the kisser'? Is that librarian-speak?"

"It's…it's…" She had no idea what it was, because the pathway from the thinking part of her brain to its speech center was suddenly experiencing gridlock. Owen had slid the flannel free of her skin and now the only thing covering her was the filmy fabric of her shortie nightgown and matching panties—and the heat of Owen's gaze.

He cupped one breast and rolled his thumb across the already hard tip. The flesh tightened and she felt herself swelling, become even more sensitive with each light pass of his thumb. "Owen…" she breathed.

"The second thing I noticed about you," he said, "was that you have a strong reaction to cold."

"What?" She wanted to laugh, or maybe she wanted to hit him. "That was the second thing you noticed? Do men really pay attention to…to…stuff like that?"

One corner of his mouth kicked up. "My brothers-in-slavedom-to-our-sex-drives might not appreciate me admitting this, but, yes, we really pay attention to 'stuff' like that. Right next to *dog* in your library's fat fancy dictionary, you're likely to find a photo of a guy who looks just like me."

He'd not stopped stroking her nipple during the confession, so she had a difficult time being as appalled or offended as she supposed she should be. Instead, she found herself leaning toward him, silently begging for more than that subtle touch.

"What can you tell me about women?" he whispered, his mouth tracing her eyebrow, the rise of her cheekbone, the line of her jaw. "Is there some confession you'd like to share?"

She tried to come up with something funny or teasing or fun, but all she could think about was the tingling tip of her breast and the maddening way he was really not even touching it. Yes, not really touching it at all, she realized, as her focus centered on the movements of his maddening thumb. His flesh wasn't making contact with hers. His palm barely cradled her breast, and his thumb was merely moving the gauzy fabric of her nightwear across her hard nipple.

"Isabella? A confession?"

Enough of fun, funny, teasing. "If you don't really touch me, Owen, I'm going to scream."

Instead of obeying, he let out a low, sexy laugh, then rolled again, landing flat on his back, with her on top of him. "So at least I know a little more about Isabella. She's demanding, impatient, single-minded..."

He was the one teasing now. But she was miffed

at him anyway for being so in control when she was so obviously losing her grasp on her dignity. She rose up, a knee on either side of his hips, determined to put a little distance between them.

Owen stole that determination away as he instantly scooted down on the mattress and took her nipple in his mouth. Surprise short-circuited her brain. Her body arched, her shoulders jerking back and her bottom shooting up. He groaned against her flesh, sucking harder as his casted arm lay across the small of her back and his other palm cupped the raised curve of her behind.

He took his mouth from her and she moaned. "We're not done, sweetheart," he said. "I promise. But you're going to have to help me out again, Isabella. As much as I'd like to strip you myself, my cast will just get in the way."

She hesitated, a little shy, a little nervous. He palmed her bottom again. "Isabella, get naked and then I'll take you in my mouth again."

Desire burned through her veins. Her hands shook as she undressed under his watchful gaze. Her stomach fluttered, because naked suddenly didn't seem lightweight or fun or funny. It seemed personal and intimate and maybe more than she could handle if the other human on the end of "contact" was Owen Marston, who had thrilled her from the first moment their eyes had met across the crowded casino.

His hand slid along her ribcage, encouraging her

back into position. "Oh, sweetheart. Everything about you is so pretty," he said. She was trembling, but shyness and nerves evaporated the moment he took her breast into his mouth.

Her body bowed again, heat flashed across her skin and Owen groaned as his other hand lifted to toy with her other nipple. Her belly sank lower, brushing against the hard erection she could feel beneath his cotton boxers. She put one hand to the waistband and wiggled her fingers under to find the silky tip.

His hips shifted upward at her touch and his mouth tightened on her nipple. They both groaned.

His mouth moved between her breasts as she continued to caress him. "Sweetheart," he said suddenly, his voice low and tight. "No more. No more or this will all be over."

But she liked the fact that he was begging her this time, and she rolled off him against his protests, just so she could strip him as naked as she. Then she crawled up the mattress, finding her inner tease again, licking his hair-dusted shin, taking a nip at his knee cap, pressing kisses against his muscled thighs.

His hand found her hair as she pressed baby kisses all around his groin. His fingers bit into her scalp when she wrote a message with her tongue on his hard length. When she reached the tip, he yanked upward on her hair, bringing their bodies flush, their mouths within kissing distance.

Owen Marston had not lost his talent for kissing.

He laid them on her, one after one, feeding the sweet drug of intimacy to her, until she was hot and wiggly and so wet and swollen between her legs that when he touched her there with one long finger it slid inside so easily he immediately added another.

They were groaning against each other's mouths, needing no words to share confessions, telling secrets with their bodies and it was all so good, so right, so simple. It was like a "Dui" version of how sex should be, and when he whispered instructions to her, telling her where to find a condom and then telling her to lift up and slide down on him, she didn't feel embarrassed or exposed, or any of the dozens of emotions that moments like this between a man and a woman could sometimes bring.

She only felt pleasure.

Chapter Seven

Owen sat on the edge of the made-up bed to pull on his clothes after his shower. He'd woken alone, but there was the smell of coffee rising up the stairs and a note left on the pillow where Izzy had lain.

It was composed of a single word—a Dui-esque *THNX*.

It made him smile to look at it, and to think of what had passed between them, when together they'd transformed the cold darkness of his nightmare into the velvet cocoon of shared sexual pleasure. First thing this morning, he needed to convey a "THNX" of his own. She'd been what he'd needed the night before, and this morning he could revel in a sense of well-being he hadn't experienced since before the night of the fire.

He felt like himself again, the laid-back, calm-in-a-crisis, impervious-to-pressure Owen Marston who'd headed out with his head on straight the night of that last call. He wanted to keep a firm grasp on that—and on that man.

From the bedside table, his cell phone rang. He didn't bother checking the screen; he just put the phone to his ear and then swallowed his groan when he heard the raspy voice coming through the speaker. "Have you cooled down yet?" his grandfather demanded.

Owen recalled that the last time he'd spoken with the old man, he'd hung up on him. It was a minor miracle that Philip Marston had let this long pass without another call. Owen probably owed Bryce a beer or two or twelve for running interference for him.

"I'm good, Granddad," Owen said, swiping Izzy's note from the bedside table and stuffing it into his pocket. She'd apparently made the bed while he was showering, and he was glad she hadn't tossed the scrap of paper. It was tangible proof that he was a man on the mend. "How are you?"

"Annoyed, impatient, concerned."

Owen grinned. "And so self-aware, too. What's got your dander up?"

"Well, you, of course! I promised your mother I wouldn't pester you...."

So it was his mother Owen had to thank for his grandfather's uncharacteristic—though obviously now over—period of radio silence. Unfortunately, she didn't go for the easy beer payoff, which made him more than a little uneasy.

"...but hell," his grandfather continued. "You're my eldest grandson, and it's not like I don't read the newspapers!"

The non sequitur clearly stated the old man was agitated. Usually he was extremely, and sometimes obnoxiously, direct. "Granddad," Owen said, "I'm having a little trouble following you."

"Did you hit your head when you fell?"

"No." He frowned. "I just don't see how me being your eldest grandson and you reading the business pages have anything in common."

"They have everything in common. And it's not the *Wall Street Journal* that I'm talking about. It's the *Paxton Record.*"

Tiny carpenters had invaded Owen's brain and were tapping on his skull with their tiny hammers. He pinched the bridge of his nose between his thumb and forefinger, trying to force the pain away and remember that last night he'd had the best sex of his life. Izzy on top, her warm flank in the palm of his hand, her incredible molten center sliding down on him. The carpenters faded away and he took in a slow breath.

"Did you hear me, son? The *Paxton Record.*"

"You're irritated by the score of the high school football team? I don't think they've been the same since Bryce graduated—"

"This isn't about your brother, who did the right thing and joined the family business. This is about you!"

It's what Owen had been afraid of, ever since the last phone call he'd had from his grandfather, the one during which he brought up the old argument about Owen's career choice. The carpenters set to work again. "Granddad—"

"Did you or did you not go to college intending to join the business?"

"I did. You know I did." Maybe if he let the old man get it out of his system, they could drop this familiar quarrel for good—or at least for now. "And I interned every summer and listened to you talk about the company at every family dinner. But it just wasn't for me."

"How do you know?"

"I know because when I worked there it drained my enthusiasm and my energy. And I know because after the first hour at the fire academy I had found it again." Not only energy and enthusiasm, but purpose and pride. There was nothing wrong with what his father and Bryce and Caro had chosen to do—involve themselves in and expand the business Philip Marston had started. It just wasn't Owen's choice.

"You were good at it," the old man grumbled.

"And Bryce was a damn good quarterback, but you're not all over his case for not trying out for the NFL."

"I told you, this is not about your brother. And damn it, I would have been all over his case if he had set his sights on the NFL. Do you know how many of those players limp off the field with debilitating injuries that affect them for the rest of their lives?"

Owen slid his fingers in his pocket to touch Izzy's note. *Remember last night. Remember that smile on your face this morning.* "Granddad, what does this all have to do with me?"

"I'm coming by to see you today."

"No."

"Nonsense. Would you prevent an old man from assuring himself his favorite grandson is recovering?"

"Bryce is your favorite grandson."

"Today it's you."

Owen rolled his eyes. "I need my rest."

"You're getting plenty of rest. And your mother told me you have a nice health worker living there with you, making sure you don't overtax yourself."

Well, he might have overtaxed himself a little last night… "Wait. What? Health worker?"

"Some young woman. Misty? Betsy?"

"Izzy," Owen corrected, wondering what he was going to owe his mother now. He should have known she'd kept quiet about his marriage or else his grand-father would have been on his doorstep immediately, eager to meet the mother of his great-grandsons. "Her name is Isabella."

"Well, I assume she's taking good care of you."

He touched the note again, sniffed the coffee in the air and swore that he smelled French toast and maple syrup. "The best."

"So I'll see you in a few minutes."

"What? You're more than an hour away."

"I'm talking to you from the limo. I'm in Paxton right now."

Between the little carpenters and the old man, Owen's good mood was taking a serious beating. "Tell me you're joking."

"Not at all. I want us to have a serious, face-to-face discussion."

Oh, God. "About…?"

"Now that you know the potential consequences of this career of yours, I'm going to persuade you to see reason and quit."

Here they went again. "No."

"A man died, Owen."

"Don't you think I know that?" he burst out. His own loud voice obliterated the last of his well-being. "Don't you realize I can't stop thinking of that?"

Fine. That was the damn truth of it. That Jerry was gone had been hovering over him like a black cloud since he'd come to in the hospital.

That Jerry was gone *and* that Owen hadn't been able to prevent Jerry's death. All his training, all their equipment and experience, none of it had been able to stop the outcome. It was just like that damn nightmare, when even aware of what was about to happen, Owen hadn't been able to stop Jerry from going down.

"And son, I read in the paper…" Philip Marston cleared his throat. "I read in the Paxton newspaper that your colleague, he was younger than you."

"A couple of years."

"And that he was married."

"I went to their wedding," he heard himself say. "The bride's name is Ellie." He thought of her apple cheeks and her sparkling blue eyes. Even in a wedding dress and veil, she'd looked hardly older than a teenager. She and Jerry had been high school sweethearts and he'd worn that same jaunty grin at the altar that Owen had seen on his face in the nightmare.

His grandfather's voice lowered to a gruffer note. "The young widow is eight months pregnant."

The carpenters synchronized their hammers, assaulting Owen's skull with a single joint blow. He squeezed his eyes against the pain. "Yes." Eight months pregnant. Oh, damn it all, yes.

It was that fact he'd been avoiding facing since he'd learned of Jerry's death. It's why he hadn't moved hell and high water to make it to the funeral. It was why he'd not called Ellie, or sent a separate floral arrangement besides the one the station had added his name to and the other that his mother had sent from the entire Marston clan.

He hadn't wanted to think about it.

Jerry had been so psyched to be a dad. He swore he was going to be the kind who read to his toddler every night. He'd coach if the child was into sports, he'd applaud if the kid was into dance recitals, he'd listen to squeaky violin lessons and make a hundred kites catch wind.

Jerry said he'd had that kind of father himself and wanted to give his son or daughter every wonderful childhood moment that he'd experienced. Jerry's dad had passed away five years before. Jerry two weeks ago.

Leaving no one to do all those things for Jerry and Ellie's child because Jerry had died.

And Owen survived.

Why?

He hadn't wanted to ask himself that question because he knew there was no good answer.

Why?

Why?

He forced the question from his mind. "Look, Granddad—"

"I'm walking up your front steps, Owen," the old man said. "You better tell your young woman to let me in."

And remind her not to give away that she was Owen's wife, he thought, hobbling toward the bedroom door. Great. His positive mood was gone for good. He touched the note in his pocket. And now he'd found the perfect way to extinguish hers, too.

Izzy hauled in a deep breath before opening Owen's front door. She knew who was on the other side. Philip Marston. His grandson, the man she'd slept with the night before, had just called her up the stairs in an urgent voice and explained that his grandfather was moments away and that she'd been identified as the "health worker" by his mother. For reasons of their privacy, Owen supposed, or their sanity, he'd added.

He'd looked tense and tired, the exact opposite of how she'd felt upon waking up. She hoped it was the unexpected arrival of his grandfather that was affecting his mood, but…well, she just wasn't going to worry about it. Her state of mind was buoyant, and she planned on keeping it that way.

Why not? She'd been wondering for weeks about what she'd missed out on with Owen, and now she knew. Yes, as he'd suspected, they danced on the mattress as well as they did in the clubs in Las Vegas. Satisfying one's curiosity could be a positive experience.

On her next breath, she pulled open the door. The impression of a tall, gray-haired man flashed through her brain before she found herself flat on her back on the floor, a yellow monster hanging over her.

"Nugget," the man scolded. "Is that any way for a Marston to act?"

The big dog swiped her chin with a wet tongue, then pranced backward to stare at her with big brown eyes. Izzy cautiously sat up.

"Granddad? You brought the dog?"

Izzy glanced back to see Owen on the upper landing. Then she returned her gaze to the canine standing at attention, close enough that she could feel his breath wash over her face.

"It's okay, Izzy," Owen said.

Mr. Marston frowned down at her. "Not afraid of dogs, are you?"

"Um…I don't know any dogs. Not, um, this close and personal, anyway." The elderly ladies she'd most often stayed with had been cat people. She slowly climbed to her feet, and, one eye on the dog, held her hand out to the older man. "I'm Isabella Cavaletti, Mr. Marston."

His shake was brief and businesslike. "Good to meet you. And this champion yellow Labrador is none other than Marston's Golden Nugget."

"Or, as we find more appropriate, the Nug," Owen added.

"Okay," Izzy said. The dog looked more like a "Nug" than a champion. He was still watching her with his doggy eyes and his tongue hanging out. "Would everybody, um, like some breakfast?"

"You're not here to wait on us," Owen started.

His grandfather spoke over him. "Just coffee for me, please. Black. Owen, your mother said you're headquartered upstairs during your recovery. Can I help you back to bed?"

"I don't need to lie down," his grandson grumbled. "But come on up, Granddad."

To her dismay, the dog hung around in the kitchen while she put together a tray. Did he somehow think she was suspect? Could he tell she was a counterfeit "health worker"?

Then she happened to knock a piece of bacon off a plate, sending it toward the floor. Nugget, aka "the Nug," caught it in midair. She stared at him. "You're not suspicious, you're a mooch."

He didn't appear to take offense. In fact, he kept even closer to her as she put Owen's plate on the tray, the coffees, and then carried the food and beverages up the stairs. She found the two men around the small meal table she'd set up. Trying to remain unobtrusive, she put Owen's breakfast in front of him and then placed the mug of black coffee at Mr. Marston's elbow.

She and the Nug were ready to slink off when Owen caught her wrist. "Stay," he said, his tone soft.

His grandfather glanced up at her. "By all means. Maybe an objective viewpoint is exactly what we need."

Izzy avoided both men's gaze. Objective? Could she possibly be nonpartisan when she'd spent the night before in Owen's arms? "I, um…" But her protest, such as it was, died, as she lowered herself to the free chair. Even without looking directly into his eyes, she was aware that Owen's tense, tired expression had turned grim. She couldn't ignore that, could she?

He was her husband, after all.

"I'm just explaining to my grandson, here, that it's time to reconsider his choice of career."

Izzy glanced at Owen. "Well—"

"It was fine for a time, but…"

She glanced at Owen again. His face was expressionless. She remembered the conversation he'd had with his mother, when he'd defended his job as a firefighter, but now he didn't look interested in sticking up for himself. "I think he likes his work."

"Because he hasn't truly considered the consequences," Philip Marston said with a wave of his hand. "Young men believe themselves immortal. It's biology. The brain isn't sufficiently formed to foresee the risks of a particular action."

"Well, that's true of many adolescents," Izzy agreed. "But you can't lump into that group every single person who pursues a job that involves some personal risk."

Owen's grandfather's eyes narrowed. "Tell me again how you came to be a home health worker?"

She ignored the question. "We need our first responders. Surely you would admit that."

The elder Mr. Marston frowned. "All first responders aren't my grandson."

Izzy looked over at Owen. It was obvious he

wasn't listening to their exchange. His gaze was un-focused and trained on some inner movie screen, and uneasiness trickled down her back. It made her voice sharp. "You don't give your grandson much respect," she said, more direct than her usual Izzy's-here-to-please style. "His work is important."

"Hah." The older man sent her another piercing look. "Well. You're awfully loyal for a temporary, hourly employee."

That caught Owen's attention, and he looked over. "Leave Izzy alone, Granddad."

"What?"

"Leave Izzy alone," Owen ground out.

"I'm not bothering her," his grandfather replied in a mild voice. "Now, Nugget on the other hand…"

She glanced down and had to laugh. She'd been so caught up in the conversation that she hadn't realized the beast was resting his head on her lap. When it came to canines, bacon must hold a special power.

"I don't know anything about dogs." Her hand caressed the buttery fur on the top of his head.

"I thought I explained all about them last night," Owen murmured.

It startled another laugh out of her, but then it died, as "last night" came back to her: Owen's grin, his touch, the intimacy of the darkness and his caresses.

In the silence surrounding them, his grandfather humphed. "Nothing anyone has said negates my concerns, Owen. Your coworker was killed."

His grandson stilled. "You keep saying that."

"Because it's true."

And Izzy could see the knowledge of it wash over Owen. His posture didn't change—it remained straight and strong—but she could see anguish ripple across his face, deadening the color of his eyes and setting his mouth into a grim line. His gaze unfocused again and she knew he was once again tuning them out.

She leaned forward. "Owen…"

Her voice jerked him out of his reverie. He blinked, his gaze focusing on her. "Jerry's wife, Ellie, is expecting a baby in a few weeks. Maybe any day now, I'm not sure."

"Oh, Owen."

"She's a widow. That baby won't have a father."

"Exactly my point," Philip Marston boomed. "You'll get married soon. You'll have a child. Will you still take the same risks with your life? I say leave now, and get back into the family business where you belong."

You'll get married soon. You'll have a child.

Of course he would. She and Owen would undo their whim of a wedding and he'd find himself a real wife.

That couldn't be her, because she couldn't see herself settling down. She didn't know how to do it. How did anyone trust someone else with their heart?

"Maybe you're right, Granddad," Owen said. "I'll be thinking about that."

Izzy barely heard him. She pushed out of her chair, murmuring something about cleaning up the breakfast dishes. With the Nug dogging her footsteps—so that's where the phrase came from, she thought—she returned to the kitchen. There, she stood, unmoving, as Philip Marston's words repeated in her head.

You'll get married soon. You'll have a child.

Yes, she wasn't part of that picture, was she? She caught sight of her reflection in the silver surface of the refrigerator and her hands went to her belly. Really, she couldn't see herself that way. Pregnant and barefoot? No.

Pregnant and wearing those cute slides she'd spied at Nordstrom the other day? Well…

No!

And…yes.

The dog pressed up against her thigh and she rubbed the top of his head. "I'm crazy, right?" she whispered.

Because there was a picture forming in her mind. Izzy, the perpetual outsider, having her very own family. Being someone's wife.

Owen's wife.

The Nug whined, the sound popping that aberrant mental bubble. With a sigh, she glanced down at the dog. "Yeah, I know. You're hoping for more bacon to fly through the air, and when pigs do that very same thing is when I'll allow myself to rely on someone for that forever-after thing."

On another sigh, she moved to the sink and started dealing with the dishes, not allowing herself to get caught up in the domestic intimacy of it all. "It may be like playing house," she told the Nug, who continued his crumb surveillance, "but it's not my house, and this is definitely not the way I would play it anyway."

Nobody was supposed to have to cook *and* clean up, after all. "Which just goes to show I'm merely the hired help. The health worker, right, Nug?" Even Owen's mother had figured out Izzy wasn't wife material.

The doorbell rang and she was glad for an excuse to hurry away from her own thoughts. She swung open the door, only to see a mail service truck lumber off. On the doorstep were four large cardboard boxes.

Frowning, she checked the address.

It was Owen's, all right.

But the name on the *To:* line was all wrong.

Isabella Cavaletti Marston.

Chapter Eight

Owen groaned from the easy chair by his bedroom window as he watched his brother stride over the threshold, his arms full of bound reports. "Tell me those aren't what I think they are."

"You told Granddad you were thinking about joining the company," Bryce said, dropping the stack at Owen's feet. "What, you thought he'd forget about that?"

"I didn't think he would have you bring me homework, like you used to do when we were kids and I missed a day of school."

Bryce settled in the matching chair. "You never

missed a day of school, remember? Perfect attendance, six years running. God, I hated you for that."

"Wasn't my fault you didn't remember that girls
have cooties. That's where all those coughs and colds
come from, you know."

"Well, the one who I think is sick now is you. Sick
in the head."

Owen narrowed his eyes at his brother. "What do
you mean by that?"

With a nod, Bryce indicated the window. "Why are
you up here moping and not down there with her?"

"Down there" was the courtyard they could see
below. Izzy had discovered the neighbor's cat sun-
ning itself on the bricks and she was crouched beside
the fluffy creature, alternately petting it and letting
it bat at a long piece of yarn she held.

"Yeah? What excuse could I give?"

"That you, too, want to pet a—" He broke off at
Owen's sharp glance. "You have a dirty mind! I was
going to say 'pet a cat.' Yeesh."

"I'll just bet."

Bryce grinned. "Speaking of gambles…I never
really got a chance to hear the full story about your
whirlwind Vegas, uh, vacation. You went for the adventure and came home with—"

"Nothing," Owen ground out. "You know that."

"But then five weeks later this pretty woman trips
into your life and claims she's your wife. Don't you

think I've been patient long enough? Don't I get all the details now?"

"Since when are you like a teenage girl at a slumber party?"

"Since you turned so close-mouthed and crotchety."

Bryce said it with his usual smile on his face, but Owen still felt the sting. *Crotchety* sounded old and cranky, and damn if that wasn't the way he felt. "I hate being cooped up."

"But you're cooped up with a babe. C'mon, surely I don't have to spell out ways to lift your mood."

The thought didn't lift Owen's mood. He'd woken up two days ago, feeling about as good as a man could, and then his grandfather had called and he'd remembered what the sex had pushed aside.

Jerry Palmer, imminent father-to-be, was dead.

And Owen still couldn't figure out why he was alive.

"If you're not in any hurry to seduce the lovely Isabella, I think you're going to have to tell me how she ended up as your wife."

Owen stared through the glass at her profile, the smooth curve of her cheek, that plum-colored purse of her mouth. Her fingers swept through the cat's fur and he remembered them buried in his hair as they sank into yet another kiss. "The usual way," he answered. "Elvis asked. We said 'I do.'"

"No. Way." Bryce hooted. "I love it. Golden Boy Marston, Granddad's favorite, the one Mom loves best, the guy Dad envies because he doesn't have to deal with the old man on a daily basis, was married by an *Elvis impersonator?*"

"Who says he was an impersonator? And so you know, Priscilla can play a mean Wurlitzer organ."

Bryce started laughing, hard enough that Owen couldn't stop his own smile. "You're not kidding."

"Would I kid you about the complimentary, post-ceremony, grilled peanut-butter-and-banana sand-wiches?"

"It's so bad, it's good." Bryce leaned close. "Tell me there are pictures."

"There are pictures." He put up his hand to stop his brother's next question. "But no, you can't see them. Izzy took them with her, and knowing her habits, I'd guess they've been shipped to some friend of hers in Timbuktu." Yet, he discovered he was still smiling. As rash as their decision to marry had been that night, he'd enjoyed the hell out of himself the entire time.

From the moment he'd met her, he'd enjoyed the hell out of himself. But who could believe some-thing like that could last?

He had.

"So what happened?"

"Hm?" Owen looked over at his brother.

"What happened? A second ago you were wearing one of those Perfect Attendance Award smiles and then next thing you look like someone told you the principal was taking away your traffic patrol captain's badge."

He stared at his brother. "You really did hate me during our school years, didn't you?"

"Nah. You've just always been a hell of a brother to follow after. And if you were going to buck the family and go for a job outside the company, why couldn't you have chosen to be a shoe salesman or something? Not that all work isn't honorable, but hell, bro— A firefighter. I'll be in your shadow for the rest of my life."

"You're so full of BS." As if Bryce was in anyone's shadow. "And I don't know how long I'm going to be with the department anyway."

Bryce wagged one foot. "Pull the other one. I don't care what you told Granddad, but you're not leaving the Paxton F.D. *And,* you're not putting me off my slumber party sensibilities. I'm still waiting for the details. What happened between you and your bride that she went running?"

"She went running." Owen spread his hands. "I caught her in the hotel lobby as she was hotfooting it out of the place. She looked scared. I acted certain. She got mad. I got madder. Next thing I know—"

"She doesn't look scared when she looks at you now."

"Yeah, instead she looks sympathetic. I'm her pity project."

Bryce shrugged. "Maybe you need to show her that you still have some moves."

He'd shown her his moves. Moves weren't the

problem. Things between them had been good in bed. Better than good. He knew that. But what came after?

He hadn't gone looking for a repeat. And not just because they hadn't resolved or even discussed their marriage. That was just one of the pile of issues that was taking up the front and center of his head.

"Well." Bryce slapped his palms on his thighs. "Gotta go. I delivered your spelling and math as ordered. Except, oh, yeah, there's this little question I believe you should be addressing. In regards to entering the family business: What the hell are you thinking? Write up five cogent paragraphs and get back to me."

He passed Izzy in the doorway, pausing only long enough to grab her by the shoulders and buss her on the cheek. "Yum. You smell good. When you want the better brother, let me know. In the meantime, I think you should take the big guy over there to the fire station. Someone needs a little face time with his team."

Izzy blinked as Bryce strode away, then came farther into the room. Her eyebrows rose as she took in the mountain of materials that the other man had left behind. "Most people recuperate with lighter reading. I have several recommendations for you. Do you like mysteries? Thrillers? Or, if you're serious about heavier fare, I know a great biography of one of our founding fathers."

"These are some of the company's financial reports," Owen said. "Granddad sent them over."

"You're not really thinking—" She broke off. "But it's none of my business."

"Yeah."

And it was none of his business to absorb how beautiful she was, even in a pair of sweatpants and a T-shirt. Even those brief few minutes in the sunshine had spread a layer of rosy warmth across her cheekbones…or maybe she was thinking, like he was, of how they'd been together that night. Of how the kisses had gone on forever and how seamlessly they'd joined and how he'd felt her orgasm pulsing around him as she came.

Sex had been as easy and as right as that first moment in Las Vegas. As well matched as their dancing. As hot as every glance they'd shared before they'd said "I do" while the rhinestones on Elvis's suit glittered in the disco ball light of the chapel.

She looked out the window. "Is Bryce right? Do you want to go to the fire station?"

The heat kindling inside him went cold. "I don't know if I should go back there." He didn't know if he *could* go back there.

"Owen…"

"What?"

Her gaze stayed trained on the window. "We didn't talk about the other night."

"That's right." He touched the outside of his pocket. He'd made a habit of carrying around her

THNX, sap that he was. "I appreciate what you shared with me. That night…it was a tough time."

"I know."

"And you…?"

She shot him a quick glance. "You know darn well I have no complaints."

"Good."

"Good." Her gaze cut his way again. "But…"

"But?"

"Does this need to be said?"

That it could never happen again? That it had been a huge mistake? That he was an idiot for not being able to keep her taste, her scent, the feel of her silky skin out of his head?

He steeled himself. "Does what need to be said?"

"That it's okay to delight in being alive."

"I…I don't know what you mean."

"It's all right to have enjoyed what we did, Owen. It's all right to have enjoyed our…pleasure. You have nothing to feel guilty about."

Owen stared out the window. Would she still say that if she knew? Would she say it was all right if she knew that every cell of him wanted to "delight in being alive" again? Right now. Tonight. Tomorrow.

But that *was* wrong, wasn't it? She was temporarily here. He was temporarily needing her near. And he was afraid that all that "delighting" that he wanted was just an excuse to get away from what really needed to be done: Facing all the questions about his future.

* * *

The next day, Owen felt so suffocated by the four walls around him that he gave in and agreed to go to dinner at Will and Emily's house with Izzy. Though he didn't want to talk shop with Will, he was fairly certain he could avoid what was happening down at the station by using the two women as a buffer.

His plan was to settle himself on the couple's couch and keep quiet.

His worries were needless, he realized, when he limped into the house, using the cane that he'd been given by the orthopedist. No one was going to be expecting him to maintain his end of a conversation because there were too many of them going on. He and Izzy were not the only dinner guests. Will's siblings were in attendance, too, along with a variety of spouses, girlfriends and roommates, which made it easy for Owen to hide behind the noise and chaos.

As she'd been doing lately, Izzy wandered off, leaving him alone. When they were at his place, she didn't hang around him, either. He supposed she read a lot of the time. He knew she talked on the phone often. It rang a heck of a lot—so much that the distinctive ring tone was starting to rub his nerves raw. Probably some of her calls were business related, and he'd brought up the fact that he was causing her trouble on that end—giving her the chance to say she needed to leave him—but she'd waved the concern away.

Too bad he couldn't bring up her other phone calls and have her wave away the concern he had about those, too. But that would mean admitting he'd been listening. That would mean admitting he was a little, um, well, irritated shouldn't be the word, but it was, by the many times she'd been thrilled to hear from "Greg" and "David" and "Brad." Of course, there'd been calls from "Jane" and "Sally" and "Taylor," too, but—but wait, "Taylor" was a name that could go either way, meaning yet another possible hash mark under the column entitled "Male Callers," right?

The sofa cushion beside his bounced as a younger man dropped into the other corner. As tall and dark as his brother, but as skinny as only a twenty-and-change guy could be, Will's sibling Tom gave him a quick smile. "Yo. Owen."

"Hey, Tom." Owen smiled back, because Tom wasn't the type to take conversation into any uncomfortable territory. He wasn't likely to ask about the fire or about Jerry or about when Owen expected to be back on the job at the station. "How about those Raiders?" he added anyway, just to direct the conversation into a nonloaded area.

The other man groaned. "Did you have to bring that up?" he asked, his expression pained.

Owen did a quick mental review. It was early in the season, but the team was doing about as expected. "What's the matter? Did you make a bad bet with someone on last week's game?"

"This week's game," Tom mumbled. "I have tickets."

"And you have to work?"

"And I have a girlfriend," the other man said with a sigh.

"Oh," Owen answered, amused. "She doesn't like football?"

Tom slid lower onto the cushions, as if misery was yanking at his ankles. "At the moment, she doesn't like me."

"Sorry to hear that."

"Yeah," Tom said morosely, his gaze going distant. Then he jerked upright. "Wait, wait. Who's that?"

"Huh?" Owen looked in the same direction. "Who's what?"

"Oh, baby. The world is looking up. Chic-lookin' dark-haired chick just flitted into the kitchen. She has a very, *very* cute butt, and maybe Mr. Tom can find a new seatmate for Sunday's game."

Owen reminded himself that Tom was just acting his age and gender. It didn't help. "Was she wearing jeans and a red sweater?"

Tom's grin was appreciative. "*Tight* jeans, and—"

"She's with me," Owen growled.

"Oh." The younger man's smile died. "Sorry. No disrespect and all that."

"Fine."

Tom cast another speculative look toward the kitchen. "Except—"

"Taken." Guilt at the claim bounced right off him. "Irrevocably taken."

"I got that," Tom said, "the minute your expression turned all ugly."

Ugly? Owen tried smoothing out his face.

"I just wondered if maybe she could introduce me to someone. I've still got those tickets."

"So you and your girlfriend...?"

"Gretchen." Tom turned morose again. "Who am I fooling? I don't want to meet anyone else. I don't want to go with anyone but her to the game."

"Then you better make up with her or give away those tickets."

"Yeah." He glanced over at Owen. "I fell for her the minute I saw her. I was at this friend's birthday party and Gretchen walked toward me. I didn't have some perfect-girl image in my head. You know, this tall, or this colored hair, nothing like that. But here comes this girl and she tucks her hair behind her ears and her eye catches mine and I step closer and...well, she just smelled right, you know?"

"Sort of," Owen answered. He was such a liar. That's how it had been with Izzy. She'd walked up to him, put out her hand, and it had been just like Tom and Gretchen. It had just been right.

Or at least he'd thought so.

"Who could believe in love at first sight?" Tom continued, shaking his head. "But it happened to me."

That's not what had happened to Owen! It had been right, but right for the moment, right for the weekend, but not right for…right for… Damn! This was exactly the kind of conversation he didn't want to be having with Tom *or* with himself.

"Why don't you phone Gretchen?" he suggested. "See if you can get back in her good graces?"

Tom brightened. "You think I should do that?"

"Yeah. Find a nice private corner and give her a call." And let me return to my peace and quiet.

To his relief, Tom thanked him for the advice and wandered off. Owen was alone again, alone with thoughts that wanted to wander again toward Izzy and rightness, but he refused to let them. A little kid toddled by with a small car in hand, and he allowed his casted wrist to be used as a roadway.

"There you are!" a voice called out.

He and the kid both jumped, then looked at Emily. She was smiling at the little guy. "Your mom's looking for you," she said. "She has a cup of pretzels for you."

A plaster roadway was no match for pretzels, apparently. The toddler hurried off and Emily sat in the place previously occupied by Tom. "I'm sorry we've been ignoring you."

"No problem." He couldn't be impolite and say it was what he'd been hoping for, could he? With a gesture, he indicated the hustle and bustle as people moved in and about the room. "I'm enjoying the chaos."

Emily smiled. "It terrified me at first. I was an

only child, and the first couple of times I found myself at a Dailey clan event I was overwhelmed."

Maybe that was why Izzy had integrated so well into this party atmosphere, leaving him as the solo man on the sofa. Coming from a large family like this, she was likely accustomed to the commotion. Emily looked in fine form herself.

"You're good with it now, though," he said, tilting his head. "You look very good with it." Both Emily and Will shone with the same light he'd noticed beaming from them in Vegas. "You and Will."

"Yes." Just then, the man in question passed through the room and her gaze followed him. As if he felt it, he suddenly pivoted, walking backward while he shared a look with his wife. He gave her an intimate smile, then exited the room, causing Emily to turn back to Owen. "And you and Izzy?"

"Can we talk about something else?"

Her brows rose. "Uh, sure. How about those Raiders?"

"Tom has tickets to Sunday's game, I know that."

"But he's on temporary outs with Gretchen," Emily answered.

"Yeah. But I think he's on the phone over there…" Owen turned to indicate the corner where—

Where Izzy stood, her shoulder leaning against the wall, her cell phone at her ear. He swore he could read her lips, and on that smiling mouth was the name of yet another hash mark for the "Male Callers" category. "Who is John?" Owen demanded.

"What?" Emily asked.

He couldn't stop himself. "Who is John—and Greg and David and Brad? There's likely more, because that damn phone of hers is ringing all the time."

"Am I the only one who thinks she needs to get a little more varied with the ring tone? Aren't you sick of 'Bohemian Rhapsody'?"

Okay, he knew he shouldn't press it. He was, after all, the one who wanted to not talk about Izzy. "Emily," he heard himself say anyway. "The woman takes more phone calls in a day than the department takes training runs in a year."

Emily laughed. "Yeah. You must be *really* sick of 'Bohemian Rhapsody.'"

"I thought they were calling regarding work, and then I thought they must be that large family of hers checking up on her, but she says they're all friends."

"They're not her family, that's for sure."

"Huh?"

Emily glanced over at Izzy, still chatting in the corner. "They forget she exists most of the time, I think."

"What are you talking about? She said she comes from this big Italian family. She implied they were the close-knit group you immediately think of when—" He broke off, frowning at Emily's compressed lips and shaking head. "They're not close-knit?"

"Not with Izzy. Maybe I shouldn't tell you…"

"Maybe you should," he insisted. "What's the deal?"

"Izzy won't thank you for feeling sorry for her…"

"I know how unpleasant it is to be felt sorry for. Don't worry about that. Just spill it, Emily."

"She's adopted." Emily darted a glance at Izzy and lowered her voice.

Owen had to lean closer to hear her over the hubbub in the house. "And?"

"And her parents quickly lost interest in having an infant. I think it was a passing phase, they fancied the idea of a child, but they run a tour agency—"

"She said that. Global excursions, particularly to Europe."

"Right, and they discovered that a baby put a crimp in their business plan. So they shuffled her around to various relatives, moving her from one Cavaletti to another to another. I don't think she stayed anyplace for more than a year or two."

Izzy. He tried imagining her circumstances. "Didn't anyone think that was cruel?"

"I don't know what they thought. I only know they let Izzy live with a succession of mostly maiden aunts and elderly widows. I think twice in her life she spent summers with families with kids. In essence, she raised herself."

Oh, Izzy.

"So instead of counting on the Cavalettis, she's made a family of friends for herself all over the country."

"The ones who hold on to her stuff," Owen said.

"Yeah. You know about that?"

"Boxes have been showing up at my place."

"Oops." Emily looked like she was biting back a smile. "I might be guilty of, um, letting it slip out that she's had a change in circumstance."

"It's making her crazy, having all her things showing up."

Emily's head tilted and her eyes narrowed. "Is it making *you* crazy?"

"No." *Izzy* was making him crazy—her scent, her mouth, the memories of the two of them in bed—but not those cartons that kept arriving on the doorstep.

"Izzy's good at getting people to like her," Emily said.

"Probably because of all that moving around she had to do," Owen surmised.

"Probably," Emily agreed. "But I'm not sure she allows herself to depend on anyone, in case they disappoint her like her parents and relatives."

From the corner of his eye, he saw Izzy move past the couch and out of the room, her phone no longer in evidence. "She has so much," he murmured. "Beauty, brains, charm out the wazoo—"

"But no trust," Emily interjected, pushing to a

stand. "I don't know that she can believe that anyone will make a lasting place for her in their life."

Owen wasn't, that was sure.

Though he shouldn't feel guilty over it, because that was the way both of them wanted it. She'd made that clear the day she'd run from him in Las Vegas. His runaway bride was back, but it was only to end their marriage.

Chapter Nine

Izzy was using her foot to shove the latest delivery away from the front door when Owen hobbled down the stairs. His eyebrows rose. "Another box?"

Heat crawled up her neck. "Somehow this address got out. Blasted e-mail loops."

"How many is that now?" he asked, sitting on one of the steps.

"Nine." She kicked at it, moving it just an inch or two. What was in this one? She couldn't remember. "I should just take them all straight to the Salvation Army."

"And lose your Louisa May Alcott books? Why would you do that?"

Izzy waved her hand. "All that happy family/happy romance was the stuff of childhood fantasy. I'm grown-up now." She knew the score and knew the difference between what a child longed for and what an adult could depend on. She glanced over at Owen, still aware of the embarrassed heat of her face. "I'm sorry for the inconvenience."

"Not inconvenient for me. You can store them in the garage, if you want. Indefinitely."

Indefinitely. But there was a definite between them, a definite end date to this interlude. To their marriage. She snuck another look at him and noticed how tired he looked. Not sleeping again, she figured. His gaze was fixed, unseeing, on the shelving in the living room that held the vintage firefighter memorabilia.

And that reminded her…

"Say," she said, giving the box one last push with her foot so it was out of the way of the door. "How about we go for a drive? You can show me all the Paxton, California, scenic locations."

They could both use a diversion. She certainly wanted to think about something other than the belongings that were catching up with her. She had to be ready to leave at a moment's notice; it had always been that way for her, and too many things would only make it harder when she had to pick up and go.

Shoving the thought away, she noted the remote expression on Owen's face and the shadows under his eyes. He needed a change of place, too. "Let's get out of here, Owen."

"You'll have to play chauffeur," he reminded her.

She slapped on a grin, trying to lighten both their moods. "There's nothing I like better than to drive a man…crazy."

A smile ghosted over his mouth as he got to his feet. "You've got it down pat, sweetheart."

Heat washed over her again, across her face and down her body so that her skin felt too tight beneath her jeans and sweater. That night in his bed had been an aberration, but that didn't stop her from remembering every moment of it, from the first sure thrust of his tongue to the gentle withdrawal of his erection from the still-pulsing liquid center of her body.

She cleared her throat. "I could use some fresh air," she murmured.

"Won't help," he offered. "Last night I opened my window and stuck my whole head out and it didn't erase any thoughts from my brain or take my temperature down a single degree."

Oh, and as if that little comment cooled *her* off. She ignored him as she brushed past on her way to retrieve her purse. His low laugh was as good as a touch, though. It ruffled through her hair and traced like a fingertip down her spine.

Bad man.

Being closed up in his SUV didn't help matters much. Yes, they each had their own bucket seat, but this close she could smell his shampoo and see the strength of his long legs from the corner of her eye. Forcing her attention to the road, she said, "Where to?"

He directed her to his elementary school first. It was a typical, somewhat sprawling, suburban public school, with handpainted notices about the upcoming Fun Run and Halloween Festival taped to the surrounding fence. It was Saturday, so the fields were full of knee-socked little kids playing soccer. They moved about the grass in huddles and she and Owen idly watched their antics for a few minutes from the parking lot.

"So you spent kindergarten through fifth grade here?" she asked.

"Yep. Then I went to the junior high that's down the road and the high school beyond there. Go Paxton Panthers."

"I'll bet you were a jock."

"My mom already told you. In high school I played football and ran track. But I was a smart jock, remember? Salutatorian."

"And modest, too," she teased.

He reached over and yanked on the ends of her hair. "Hey, when a guy doesn't have his full mobility he's got to keep his ego pumped."

"Ah." She trained her gaze out the window, not daring to look at him. "So that's what you call it."

He groaned. "You're heading into dangerous territory, pretty girl."

She shook her head. "I wasn't one, you know. I

wasn't a jock and I wasn't pretty, either. I was brainy and I wore glasses and I was the kind of girl the guys never looked at twice."

"Now that's a lie."

"Really."

"You just never caught the guys looking at you. I noticed that about the bookworms. They should have glanced up from the page a time or two."

Izzy glanced over at him now. Big mistake. That…that *thing* that had been between them from the first moment in Las Vegas flared to life again. Her breath caught and her thigh muscles clenched, and she felt herself tremble as he reached over to play with her hair. His fingertips brushed the rim of her ear as he tucked some strands behind it, then toyed with the small gold ring there.

"You're so damn pretty now, Isabella," he said.

They both moved at once, each leaning toward the other. Her mouth tingled, in anticipation of his kiss. "Damn pretty," he said again, his breath washing over her lips.

Thunk!

They started, and straightening, Izzy saw a soccer ball roll off the hood of the car. "Whoa," she said.

"Wake-up call," he muttered.

Checking her watch, she turned the key in the ignition. "Where should we go next?" Someplace that wouldn't allow for that inconvenient intimacy to arise between them again. Those waters were dangerous.

"Let's check out the old homestead."

He directed her through suburban streets with green lawns and mature trees that had leaves just turning to autumn's colors. There were kids on the sidewalks on bicycles and people walking dogs, and if she could have put it all in a bubble with little white flakes, it would have made a perfect snow globe.

She sighed as he indicated a house on a corner with wraparound grass and large trees anchoring each end. "You actually grew up there?"

"I actually grew up there."

"But your family lives in San Francisco now."

"After Bryce graduated from high school, Mom and Dad moved into the city. But before that, we were right here, doing the whole small-town thing."

Izzy sighed again. Add seven boy cousins and she would have been in heaven in such an environment. "Is that a treehouse?"

"Yep. We even rigged a bucket on the end of a rope so that we could haul up snacks that my mom would bring out to us. On Halloween, once we were past the age of trick-or-treating, we put up ghosts and ghouls inside and made our buddies pay us a quarter to go through it."

"Oh, Owen." She smiled over at him. "It must have been great."

"Yeah." He shrugged. "But the city has its pluses, too. If I go to work for the family company, I'll probably move there to avoid a long commute."

"You're still considering that?"

He hedged. "I'm reading all those boring reports."

"But—"

"I remember you commenting a couple of days ago it wasn't your business," he said, scowling.

"Yes, but—"

"And it *isn't* your business, Izzy."

She scowled back. Fine, then. They might not have a discussion about what he should do, but she still had a little demonstration up her sleeve. With a twist of her wrist, she restarted the car.

"Where now?" he asked.

"I'll head downtown. See what's up."

The Paxton "downtown" was three blocks of small shops and restaurants with the city administration building and the central fire station at the northern end. As they neared the main thoroughfare, they found that the road was barricaded and people were lining the sidewalks.

"What's going on?" Owen asked aloud.

He'd still been ignoring the local newspaper, but she hadn't. "Parade," she answered. She swung into the parking lot of a bank, digging into her purse to give the attending Boy Scout the five bucks the troop was charging for a prime location. Just as the first marching band passed them, she was turning off the engine and setting the emergency brake.

She snuck a look to her right. Owen had gone expressionless again, his face betraying nothing as the groups marched past. There was the junior high jazz band playing something—pretty badly—from their places in the back of a pickup. Tiny gymnasts came next, in spangled leotards and carrying a banner that read "Paxton Pixies." Next up was the obligatory horse riders in flashy chaps and silver-studded finery, their animals' hides gleaming.

Then a mixed group of Boy Scouts and Girl Scouts, carrying a sign:

Paxton Fire Department: 100 Years of Service 100 Times That Many Thanks from Paxton Citizens!

The crowds on the sidewalk cheered, then cheered louder as a fire-engine-red fire engine slowly rolled down the street. Firefighters, including Will, Izzy noted, leaned out of the vehicle, throwing candy at the parade watchers.

"Let's go," Owen ground out.

"Don't you want to enjoy—"

"For God's sake, Izzy, give me some credit," he said. "I know what you're trying to do. But surely you realize I didn't do the job for the parades."

"Why did you do the job?" She cleared her throat. "Why do you do the job?"

He opened his mouth. Closed it. Opened it again. Then he ran his hand through his hair. "I don't know, damn it. I don't know the why of anything anymore."

The words tore at her heart. Dangerous territory, indeed. She twisted the key in the ignition and blinked away the sting of tears in her eyes before backing up and leaving the parking lot. Though she was pretty sure no matter how many miles they put between themselves and this place, there was no getting away from the uncertainty he'd just shared.

Owen didn't protest when Izzy made another stop before returning to his place. Privacy wasn't what the two of them should risk right now. He was equal parts angry and horny, and she'd been rubbing against him in both the right and wrong ways all morning.

They were either going to get into a full-fledged fight or they were going to get into bed. Neither was a good idea, and before meeting Izzy he would have thought he had enough control over himself to make sure what he didn't want didn't happen.

But she added points to his blood pressure just by the way she looked in a pair of old jeans and black boots.

And he was the one who prided himself on his calm demeanor and his cool under pressure.

"I thought we could have some lunch," she said, pulling into a parking space of the lot beside a small Italian restaurant. "Every time I drive past this place the smell makes my taste buds start crying."

It did smell delicious, he had to admit as he limped into the restaurant, using the cane that it still annoyed him to be relying upon. He knew the food tasted just as good as it smelled; he'd been there a time or two with a date, though he decided against admitting to that. Frankly, when he slid into the booth opposite the woman he'd married, he couldn't picture any other woman's face across the table.

They both ordered. When the waiter was gone, she toyed with the stem of her water goblet. "Owen…"

His attention was focused on her fingertip, the one that was ringing the base of the glass. He remembered her small fingers caressing his chest, the way they stroked the back of her hand against his jaw, how she'd gripped the ends of his hair as she rode him in sweet, cowgirl style.

God, he'd loved to see her do that again, while still wearing those shiny black boots…

"Owen?"

He blinked, bringing himself back to the moment. Oh. Right. Lunch.

"What?" The word came out rough.

She blinked, blushed. "About earlier…about at the parade…"

His temper shot up again. "Damn it, Izzy—"

"I wanted to say I'm sorry." She reached across the table and touched his hand with those seductive fingertips of hers. "You were right, I was wrong. I had no business putting that in your face or asking you any kind of questions at all."

Her apology deflated him. He slumped against

the back of the banquette. "Izzy…" Without a clue where to go next, he let the word die.

She curled her fingers around his and tightened them. "Don't be mad."

He swallowed his silent groan. Mad might be better. But this, her touch, her big, brown eyes, they only made him have other kinds of feelings, ones that were just as hot, but even more dangerous than anger. "I'm not mad," he said, slipping his hand away from hers and curling his fingers into a fist that he placed on his thigh.

Away from temptation.

Their food arrived, and he applied himself to his meal, aware of the awkward silence between them. He wasn't going to break it. If anger wasn't in the air, awkward would do just as well. He would nurture anything that would keep the distance between them.

As they finished the food on their plates, the wait-staff arranged tables nearby, creating a long stretch that was soon filled by what appeared to be multiple generations of one family. One large, Italian family. Dark hair, dark eyes, a plethora of people whose looks reminded him of Izzy's.

The group attracted her attention, as well. As she pushed her nearly empty plate to the side, she watched them pass around menus and swap chairs. A small child began to wail and was instantly picked up by an older lady who could have been its grandmother or great-grandmother. She unearthed a package of crackers from somewhere, and the child leaned against the lady's big bosom and contentedly munched, tears drying. Two older youngsters started a loud squabble until a man—their father?—reached over and cuffed them lightly on the tops of their heads.

Izzy looked back at Owen and their eyes met. They both smiled. "Look familiar?" he asked.

Her smiled died as a strange expression passed over her face. She hesitated, then stole another glance at the family next door. "Oh, uh, sure. The Cavalettis are like that. Big, happy, everybody with a place at the table."

Owen stilled, his fork halfway to his mouth. He'd meant that the family resembled Izzy in appearance, not that her family had been a loving, happy group like this one. From what Emily had implied, that hadn't been the case at all. In fact, Izzy had spent most of her childhood on her own.

"There's nothing better than feeling part of a close-knit clan," she continued.

Which, Owen realized with a jolt, explained why *Eight Cousins* had been her favorite childhood book. That had been her fantasy as a kid. A big, happy clan that made room for every member at the table. He laid his fork on his plate, his appetite gone, as he thought of how lonely she must have been and how she was still telling herself stories to fill up that old void in her life.

"Izzy," he said. "Isabella." He reached across the table to find her hand.

It curled in his, small and delicate, and something filled his chest, making it hard to breathe. He looked down at her ring finger, remembered sliding that narrow gold band down the short slender length, and he replayed the moment in his head, recapturing just how he'd felt under the disco lights at the Elvis Luvs U Wedding Chapel.

A trio of emotions had bubbled inside him. Anticipation, exhilaration and a sense of inevitability that he'd not even attempted to escape. He'd not wanted to hesitate; he'd only wanted to hold her.

He rubbed his thumb over her knuckles. Her eyes met his and he could see her pupils widen. He slid the pad of his thumb between her fingers, stroking over the silky inner skin. Her breath was moving faster, and he could see her breasts rising and falling beneath her sweater. His pulse started to throb in time with the movement.

Anger hadn't helped. The awkwardness between them was gone. That strong sexual pull was back, and he didn't think he had a chance of keeping distant from her now.

"Remember what I said about fresh air not helping?" he asked softly.

Her nostrils flared and she nodded.

Maybe if she wasn't so beautiful, he thought. Maybe if he didn't remember that the silken texture of the inner surface of her fingers exactly matched that of the inner surface of her thighs. But he really thought it was that independent exterior of hers that he now knew protected such a vulnerable core that got to him.

She was bravado and beauty and loneliness and… lust.

Yeah, like him, she felt that, too.

He could see it in the flush of her face and the way her tongue slipped out to wet her lips. Any second thought he might have had evaporated as he stared at her plush, tempting mouth. Her throat moved as she swallowed.

"Owen…?" she whispered.

"Yeah?"

"The fresh air didn't help me, either."

His hand tightened on hers. Then he smiled and released her fingers so he could reach for his wallet. He threw some bills on the table. "Let's go home."

As he slowly limped toward the door, leaning on his cane, he decided they both deserved what pleasure they could find together. Yeah, it might be temporary, but they were grown-ups. Each of them had their reasons for agreeing to more human contact. Izzy, because she lived her footloose lifestyle that likely made connections few and far between. And him, because of that parade. Because—

"Owen."

He halted, looking toward the sound of the voice. In the booth he was passing, a man rose. "Mick," Owen answered. He shifted the cane to his casted hand so he could meet the grip of his captain, Mick Hanson.

"It's good to see you," Mick said.

"You, too." Even though Owen felt guilty as hell for the way he'd been ducking the other man's calls in the past couple of weeks, he managed a smile that he directed to everyone in the booth. He recognized Mick's two school-age kids, Jane and Lee, as well as the young woman who'd been their babysitter since Mick's wife died five years before.

He remembered Kayla as a pretty college coed, but now he could see that she'd turned into a very attractive woman. For a second, Owen wondered if Mick had noticed that, too, though something told him it was unlikely.

"Nice to see you kids," he said, then he smiled at the woman. "And I like the new haircut, Kayla."

Mick's head whipped toward the babysitter. "You have a new haircut? Since when?"

Jane rolled her eyes in the way of daughters everywhere. "Since two weeks ago, Daddy."

"Oh." Frowning, Mick returned his attention to Owen. "I'm glad I ran into you. You need to come by the station this afternoon."

"No." He tried softening his instant refusal, even as his gaze strayed toward the restaurant's front door where Izzy was hovering. "I have a friend. We have plans…."

"Bring the friend. Postpone the plans," Mick insisted. "There are people who need to see you."

"But…"

"Bring the friend," Mick said again, his tone of voice brooking no argument. "Postpone the plans."

Sighing, Owen nodded, even though he realized that what he needed distance from, more than Izzy, more than anything, was what his boss had just ordered him to do.

Chapter Ten

Izzy told herself she was glad that Owen wanted to stop by the fire station after lunch. Bryce had said he needed to visit his coworkers, and apparently his captain thought the same thing. Even better, it gave her head a chance to take control over her hormones. They'd been a short car ride away from ending up in bed again, and that would have been a big mistake.

They were nothing more than casual friends, when it came right down to it. And you didn't need to read a lot of books or listen to therapists on afternoon TV to know that turning casual into sexual opened up a can of worms. Sort of like marrying someone after a three-day acquaintance.

"Pull in over there," Owen said, indicating a space in a parking area between the main fire station and the city's municipal building.

"It looks new," Izzy observed, studying the attractive stucco building with its simple landscaping and three wide bays for emergency vehicles. Bunches of balloons waved here and there in the breeze, and the double front doors were flung wide open.

"It is new," Owen said. "A recent bond issue provided the money. That's why there's an open house today. Not only because it's the hundredth anniversary of the department, but also to give the public a chance to tour the facilities."

He didn't appear eager to visit himself, however. As they watched people wander in and out of the building, he stayed glued to his seat. Then, with a sigh, he reached for the door handle. "You ready?"

Um, no. Because watching him wage this little war with himself wasn't helping her head take control of the situation. Now her heart was getting involved, too, aching a little to see how hard it was for him to face the place and the people he'd worked with.

Each step across the asphalt only served to tighten her nerves. She'd asked him, while they were watching the parade, why he was a firefighter. He'd answered, *"I don't know, damn it. I don't know the why of anything anymore."*

The man was second-guessing how he'd spent the past years of his life and what he was going to do with the next ones. She couldn't imagine, just from the way Bryce had reacted, that getting into the family business was something that would suit Owen. And she could easily see him bumping heads with the elder Mr. Marston on a daily basis.

Would that be as satisfying as the important work of a first responder?

She glanced around, realizing he wasn't beside her any longer. Instead of walking up the path that led to the front door of the facility, Owen was halted at the bottom of it, his jaw set, his expression grim. Her heart squeezed again and she retraced her steps.

"Owen?" She touched the back of his hand.

He shook himself and gripped his cane tighter. "Let's go in," he said, starting forward.

"All right." Without thinking twice about it, she wove her fingers with those of his sticking out of the cast. "Let's go in."

Of course that gesture wasn't casual. Maybe it appeared friendly, though, because as they breached the threshold to the fire station, the first person they ran into by the front desk—Will—didn't even blink to see them so connected.

"Owen." He grinned, but didn't reach out for the customary handshake.

She wondered about that for a second, until she realized that Owen wasn't stretching his palm toward his friend, either. No, he was still holding on to his cane and Izzy like lifelines.

He didn't even notice, she thought, glancing over. She didn't think he noticed Will, either, because his attention was focused exclusively on an enlarged photograph set up on an easel at the far corner of the building's foyer.

A photograph of Jerry Palmer.

There was a massive pile of flowers and stuffed animals and hand-lettered notes at the foot of the easel. As they watched, a boy, accompanied by his mother, placed a bear dressed in a firefighter's uniform beside a mass of autumn-colored chrysan-themums.

The child turned, and his gaze snagged on Owen. "Mom!" he said in a loud voice, tugging at her sleeve so he could tow her in their direction. "Look, it's Mr. Marston."

The boy's mother was blond and shapely, in cropped jeans, sneakers and a V-necked T-shirt that revealed a little too much cleavage, if Izzy were asked to offer an opinion. Her glossy mouth turned up in a delighted smile as she and the boy surged forward.

"Owen!" she said, reaching out both hands.

Oh, so *now* he let go of his wife and allowed the blond cutie to squeeze his fingers. "I'm so glad to see that you're on the mend," she said, beaming.

He smiled back, though it did look a tad auto-matic. "Better every day," he said, and then he reached out to ruffle the boy's hair. "And thanks for the get-well card you sent, Ryan. The licorice, too."

The kid glanced up at his mom and then back at his apparent hero. "It was Mom's idea. *I* wanted to lend you my game system, but she said with your broken arm and all…"

Owen held up his cast. "Just the wrist, but it does seriously affect my *Halo* score."

"Can I sign it?" Ryan asked, looking at the bright blue plaster with the envy only a kid could have for such a device. "You don't have any signatures. You're supposed to have people write their names and stuff."

"I suppose you're right." Owen put on another of those forced-looking smiles. "Why don't you be the first?"

The boy's grin split his face. "Mom, do you have a pen?"

She shook her head, and then Will stepped in. "Ryan, come with me and we'll rustle up a marker."

The two took off, leaving Izzy and Owen and Ryan's mom, who for the first time seemed to notice someone other than Izzy's husband. Her gaze ran over Izzy, from the top of her hair to the heels of her boots.

Straightening her spine a little, Izzy was pleased that while her jeans were on the battered side, her black boots were new and oh-so-much chicer than the other woman's soccer-mom footwear. Okay, Izzy wasn't all that proud of herself for the thought, but the blonde was, well, blond. And busty.

The busty blonde held out her hand to Izzy. "I'm sorry, I didn't catch your name. I'm Alicia Ayers."

Alliterative Alicia wasn't wearing a wedding band. "Izzy Cavaletti," she said, shaking hands.

"I know Owen because, well, he saved our lives."

"Did he?" Izzy turned to look at the man in question, who had been hailed by another firefighter and was slightly turned away.

"Ryan and I were in a rollover car accident a few months back. We landed upside down in a ditch and the first to arrive on scene were Owen and Jerry Palmer." Her pretty mouth turned down. "They stayed with us and kept us calm until the right kind of equipment was brought to pry us out."

"I'm glad you were both okay."

"Me, too." The blonde's gaze darted to Owen again. "We've been friends ever since. I'm divorced, and Ryan has taken a real shine to Owen."

"I'll bet." And Izzy bet that Ryan wasn't the only one who had taken a shine to the man who was now extending his cast for the boy to sign. She looked back at the divorcée, whose gaze was resting fondly on the—boy?—man? "Owen is surely easy to, um, like."

"So…" The other woman looked back at Izzy, paused, then shrugged, as if she'd lost a debate with herself. "How are you two acquainted?"

Izzy glanced at Owen again. Someone had pulled up a chair for him so he could get off his feet. He had his cast propped on his knees and was watching while the youngster drew a picture along the plaster. His expression was open, easier than it had been since she'd come to Paxton and found him lying in the hospital bed.

It reminded her of how he'd struck her in Las Vegas. A big man with a big smile, friendly and confident enough not to hesitate to greet his best friend's girl's best friend. He hadn't hesitated to dance with her, kiss her, make her crush on him just a little, and just enough to get her to go ahead and say "I do" when Elvis stood before them with his guitar strapped across his chest and a Bible in his hand.

So Izzy didn't hesitate now. Fully aware she could claim a casual friendship with him, or even "home health worker" status like she had with Mr. Marston, she instead looked the pretty divorced woman right in the eye and said, "I'm his wife."

Hey, it was only the truth, wasn't it?

The woman's baby blues flared wide and then Izzy felt the heat of a stare on her backside. Uh-oh. She didn't think Owen was admiring her bottom, not at the moment anyway. He was more likely aghast at how she'd just complicated his romantic life with Alicia.

But had Cutie Pie been making him grilled-cheese-and-tomato sandwiches? Had she been pouring his milk over ice? Had she spent a night in his bed and—

Oh. She didn't want to go there. She didn't want to know if the woman's gratitude had been expressed in ways other than greeting cards and candy.

"Isabella?" The low note in Owen's voice did not spook her. It did not.

She just had a sudden hankering for some of those refreshments she saw stacked on a table across the foyer. "Excuse me," she said, with a polite smile for the divorcée. Owen she didn't dare look at. "I'll be back in a few minutes."

Just as soon as she got her emotions under control. First it was lust and now it was jealousy. Goodness. She needed to work on her perspective. She scurried away, heading for the bin of bottled water. As she reached for one, her hand collided with that of someone else.

"Oops," she said, and looked into the face of another woman. Younger than Alicia. Younger than Izzy. She had red-rimmed eyes, and the tip of her nose was pink. Her belly stuck out like a beach ball.

And Izzy was assaulted by yet more emotions as she surmised the identification of the very pregnant person with whom she was playing tug of war with a bottle of water. Her eyes pricked in sympathy and her stomach rolled as she thought back to the tragic fire.

This had to be Ellie Palmer. Jerry's widow.

Izzy's head had no control over the knowledge that speared straight into her heart. This young woman had lost her husband that night, just as Izzy could have lost hers.

* * *

Owen looked after the woman running away from him, for a moment distracted by the upside-down heart shape of her cute, denim-covered butt. And Izzy thought boys hadn't noticed her in high school. That might only be because she wasn't looking behind her as she walked off.

"So, you're married?"

Alicia's voice jerked his attention her way. "Uh…"

"You never mentioned it." Two lines appeared between her brows, and the sharpness in her voice had her son glancing up from the dragon/tiger/eagle—it could have been any or all—he was penning on Owen's cast.

"It's sort of a recent thing."

She was still frowning. "You didn't strike me as a man interested in marriage."

Funny, because he'd never thought about the marriage deal one way or another. His parents had a great one, and he'd probably taken it for granted, because he hadn't considered how he would achieve such a partnership like that for himself. It wasn't that he was against it, exactly, but…

Alicia was right, before he hit Las Vegas and looked in the velvet-brown eyes of one Isabella Cavaletti, he hadn't thought about himself and marriage at all. But then he'd met her, touched her, smiled into her eyes, and there had been that connection. They'd instantly clicked in a physical way, and then there

was their mutual misheard lyrics idiosyncrasy—
"Hold me closer, Tony Danza." Which of course
sounded like a damn stupid reason to wed a woman,
but there he'd been, at the altar, a big ol' contented
grin on his face.

"There!" Ryan crowed, straightening from the
work he was doing on Owen's cast.

Owen looked down at the creature crawling across
the plaster. "Looks great. Thank you."

The boy grinned. "It's your warrior. With your
arm broken and your legs not one hundred percent,
this guy'll step up and do your battles for you."

"Hey, I appreciate it." Owen smiled, because the
kid made him think of Bryce. And looking at the
kid's towhead, it made him think of…himself.

Good God. It made him think of himself as a father.
Damn. There was a completely new, completely baf-
fling idea. A boy like Ryan. A mother, like…

Like…

His gaze lifted. A mother not like Alicia. And not
that there was anything wrong with her. She was
beautiful and a devoted mom. But when he thought
about the next generation, his next generation, he
could only think of one woman…

Hell. He was thinking of Izzy, of course.

And he needed to find her. Be near her. Now.

With a gentle hand, he ruffled Ryan's hair.
"Thanks so much for what you drew." His gaze lifted
to Alicia. "Thanks so much for…"

He broke off. Because he couldn't articulate what she'd demonstrated. It wasn't fully formed in his mind, not yet. It still was a vague, amorphous…something.

Alicia was looking at him, her mouth quirked in a bemused smile. "Well, congratulations on your marriage," she said. She looked over his shoulder and he glanced back, seeing that her gaze had drifted to the enlarged photo of Jerry. "And remember that we shouldn't waste time with anything but happy."

The happy that the dead man couldn't experience anymore.

On that, Owen's upbeat mood surge disappeared. But not the need to find Izzy. She was his means to getting home, he told himself. That's why he needed her more than ever.

Pushing up from the chair he was in, he accepted the cane that Ryan immediately handed him. "Thanks, pal," he said, his right hand closing over the handle. He gave the kid a smile that felt as forced as he was sure it appeared.

Looking around the small crowd in the foyer, he saw Izzy's dark head. Focusing his gaze there, he threaded through the people, touching the back of her shoulder once he reached her.

She turned. There were tears in her eyes.

"Sweetheart." He frowned, his hand trailing down her arm. Concern for her added to his own low mood. "What's the matter?"

Izzy shifted so that he could see she'd been conversing with another young woman. Oh. Oh, God.

Ellie Palmer.

Images slammed into him again. Fractured pictures from that night and from his recurrent nightmare. He smelled smoke and he heard shouts and the gnawing, crunching sound that flames made as they ate at a structure. His vision dimmed and it was only Jerry's grin he could see, flashing on and off like the strobe on top of the fire engine.

"Owen. *Owen.* Are you okay?"

He blinked, startled to find himself outside the station and limping across the parking lot toward his car. Izzy had her hand in the crook of his elbow, above his cast, and was leading him like a blind man.

Embarrassment shot through him. He stumbled, and Izzy clutched tighter, keeping him upright.

"Are you okay?" she asked again.

He felt like such an idiot, he couldn't look at her. "I'm fine," he managed to get out. "Just fine."

"You're not," she answered, unlocking the passenger door for him. "And I know it. So don't even try the macho baloney with me."

He climbed into the car instead of answering. Once she was in her seat, she shut her door then started the car and pulled out of the parking spot. "I thought I was going to lose it, too, when I first realized it was her," Izzy said softly.

He kept staring out the window.

"Then I decided that my little breakdown wasn't going to help. So we talked about the baby. It's a boy. She's going to name him Alexander Gerald Palmer. Alexander is the name of Jerry's dad."

Owen's hand tightened on the crook of his cane until his knuckles were white. He couldn't think of one damn thing to say.

"She and Jerry painted the nursery with pale-blue and yellow stripes. It's all ready for the baby."

Jerry's baby. The baby he would never see.

"And—"

"Damn it, Izzy!" he burst out. Emotion broke over him again, like a cold, clammy sweat. "Do you think this is what I want to hear?"

"No," she answered, her voice quiet. "But I want to help, and your wall of silence isn't making things better, either. I know you're hurting, and I'd like to find some way to make it better."

Her words, her tone, took the fight out of him. It wasn't her fault. It was his, wasn't it? That night of the fire, he should have foreseen, he should have felt that things would go south. As Izzy drove, he ran everything he could remember through his head. It continued to be hazy in some places, but he forced every memory back that he could, from the first moment of the call until he'd felt the world cracking beneath his feet. How had it all gone so wrong?

He was barely aware that they'd made it home and that he and Izzy were slowly climbing the stairs to the bedroom. Still preoccupied with the past, he dropped down onto the edge of the bed. "I should be the one who's gone," he murmured, finally articulating the thought that had been hounding him since he woke up in the hospital.

Izzy sat on the mattress beside him. He looked into her eyes, their velvet darkness trained on his face, and for the first time spoke the words that had been sitting like acid in his belly for the last four weeks. "I would give anything to go back and have the one who is alive be Jerry."

She brushed her fingers through his hair, pushing it off his forehead. "I know," she whispered. "I know."

It was the exact right response, he realized. She didn't try talking him out of the feeling, she didn't try telling him that he should be happy he was alive, which he'd either told himself a hundred times or had heard from his family and friends. Izzy accepted his words, even seemed to understand them, and he couldn't begin to tell her how grateful he was for that.

Her fingers combed through his hair again and she leaned up to press a gentle kiss on his mouth. It was sweet, as understanding as her words, as soothing as her touch, but it ignited him all the same.

His good hand came around to the back of her head to keep her mouth centered on his. He deepened the kiss, surging into the wet heat of her mouth. He needed this, too, her understanding and this powerful sexual connection of theirs.

"Izzy?" he murmured against her mouth.

"Yes." She was already pulling the tails of his shirt out of his jeans. The fabric slid against his belly, making him shudder. Her small fingers went to work on the buttons even as he tried yanking off her sweater with his one good hand.

Their frantic fumbling might have been funny, and under other circumstances they might have laughed, but seriousness lay over them like a blanket. It slowed their movements, too, so that when they finally were naked from the waist up, it seemed like it took a week for her to respond to the press of his hand on the smooth, hot skin of her back. When the hard tips of her nipples finally met his chest wall, they both gasped.

They collapsed onto the mattress, their mouths meeting, melding, the heat between them making it imperative that he get them out of their pants. His hand popped open the snap of her jeans and yanked down her zipper. A small triangle of cherry-red fabric distracted his purpose and he slid is hand beneath it—to find her already hot and wet and so soft that his fingers curled into her as he groaned his approval against her mouth.

She bucked against his hand, her torso twisting against his so that her nipples dragged through the hair on his chest. He slid another finger into her, filling her, and her hips jerked hard. His thumb easily found the center of her pleasure at the top of her flowered sex. He rolled over it, once, twice, while Izzy moaned into his mouth.

She grabbed his wrist. "Owen, stop. I'm…almost, I…don't…"

Yeah, she was almost there. He could feel it in the tension of her muscles and see it in the flush on her face. "But I do, Izzy," he said, continuing to stroke the sleek heat between her legs. "I do need this."

After the disastrous outcome of that fire, he needed to have control of something, and taking charge of her pleasure was calming the roil of emotions that had been churning in his gut all day. Drawing his mouth away from hers, he trailed it across her cheek, her ear, and then down her neck. She bowed into him, her body squeezing his invading fingers, her breath coming fast. He glanced up, their eyes met, and he watched the orgasm crash over her.

Still half-broken, in that moment Owen felt whole.

But there was more ahead. She wiggled out of her jeans, helped him with his and then they were together on the bed, their bodies moving in that dance that came to them so naturally.

He kissed her mouth, he buried his nose in the perfumed smoothness of her neck, he let her rock him into his own burst of pleasure and then into…peace.

That's what she offered, too, he realized.

He'd been able to tell her the darkest secret of his soul and she'd responded with the intimacy of her body. This is what marriage was about, he decided, as he watched her drift into sleep on the pillow beside him.

You shared it all, and the other person took you in. Your partner was your shelter when you needed that, was your peace when that was paramount, was in your corner no matter how unwinnable the fight.

This was what love was about.

And love was exactly what Owen Marston realized he felt for his wife.

Chapter Eleven

Izzy heard the uneven limp of Owen behind her. "What are you doing?" he asked.

She smiled to herself and continued through the door that led down the steps to the garage, a box in her arms. "I'm learning a new language while teaching myself tiddly winks."

"Okay, fine. Laugh at me." He sounded out of sorts, but nowhere near the dark mood he'd been in after their visit to the fire station a few days before. This one was more of a boyish, it's-a-rainy-day-and-there's-nothing-to-do variety. He was walking better and his wrist was starting to itch beneath the plaster.

"He's bored," Izzy whispered to herself as she

hitched the box higher in her hands and set it on one of the two towers she'd created. This latest carton had been delivered that morning, but she'd moved the others down here before. There were twelve altogether now, and at some point she was going to have to find a new storage spot for them. There were other tasks on her list first, however.

She climbed the steps only to find Owen waiting for her at the top. Leaning on his cane, he wrapped his casted arm around her back and pulled her close for a kiss. With a little sigh, she melted against him. For better or worse—just like their marriage vows—they'd been sleeping together since the fire station visit.

"You got up too early this morning," he complained, nuzzling a sensitive spot below her jaw. His mouth skittered down her neck. "Let's go back to bed."

Goose bumps broke over her skin. Yes. They could go back to bed and she could pull him over her body just like warm covers and make the world go away. But no, today she had made plans that required looking the world in the eye.

Owen couldn't hide anymore, and she was going to have to find a way to break that truth to him.

She broke out of his hold instead and tromped up the stairs toward the third level that housed the bedrooms. "Later," she said, looking down at him with a smile.

He groaned in mock frustration. "Isabelllllla."

She laughed. He drew her name out like that when she did things to make him crazy, like order him to stay completely still while she inspected the heated skin of his chest…with her tongue.

Up in the room where she kept her things but no longer slept, she started folding the small pile of clean laundry on her bed. She didn't hear Owen until he spoke from the threshold of the door. "What are you doing?"

His brows were lowered and there was a frown on his face. "Izzy?"

She had no idea what he was talking about. She looked around the room. It was neat and clean, and her small suitcase, sitting open on top of the long dresser, was, as always, well organized. With a short pile of T-shirts in one hand, she crossed to it and tucked the clothes into the appropriate corner. "Is there something wrong?"

"Why are you packing?" he asked.

"Packing?" She frowned, then realized that he must never have peeked into the bedroom she'd slept in when she'd first arrived. "Oh. This is just…just how I live. Out of suitcases. I never put things in drawers."

He crossed the carpeting to sit on the end of her bed. His hand idly played with the small heap of not-yet-folded underthings a few inches away. She watched him toy with the delicate lace on a pair of just-washed thong panties that she vividly remembered him stripping off her one steamy night.

He'd parted her legs, then kneeled low so he could taste her there. "Sweet," he'd said, looking up. "Hot." She'd already been on fire, her nerve endings crackling and sparking like live wires after a storm.

But the storm had been yet to come. He'd bent down again, holding her knees wide so that he could keep her open as he tongued and tasted her there, coiling the desire inside her belly until it moved lower and lower and then spun out in a great frenzied whiplash of a release.

Now, she turned away from him so he wouldn't see how affected she was just by him touching the clothes that weren't even on her body. That would tighten his hold on her, if he knew. And everything she'd been planning was about loosening the ties between them.

"Izzy, sweetheart."

"Hmm?"

"Look at me," he commanded.

If she refused, he'd make something out of that, too, so she whirled around and gave him a brilliant smile. "What?"

He was twirling a tiny pair of leopard-print panties on his forefinger. An unholy grin lit up his face. "These make me want to growl."

Heat shot up her face again and she stomped over to grab all the underwear, including the pair now dangling from his finger. She shoved the handful into an interior pocket of her suitcase. "There. All done. Now can we please leave behind the topic of my clothes?"

He shook his head, his grin dying. "I still think it's odd that you haven't unpacked the entire time you've been here."

"I told you. I always live out of my suitcase." It made it so much easier to move out and move on, a lesson she'd learned early. "If you don't keep your belongings close, you might inadvertently leave something of value behind."

There was a long pause. "Oh, Isabella," he finally said. "Sometimes you sucker punch me without even meaning to."

"I don't have a clue as to what you're talking about." The way he was looking at her made her stomach jump up and down in a very unpleasant manner, she thought, frowning at him. "I've been traveling this way since childhood—"

"Exactly." He caught her hand and drew her close to him. "Let's talk about your traveling childhood."

"I don't have time for that."

He yanked on her hand, pulling her onto his lap. "Sure you do. I was talking to Emily a while back, and—"

"I need to go make lunch." Izzy struggled to get up, but his cast was pressed against her waist.

"We can have a late lunch. Or I can make lunch. Or we can go out to lunch. Let's forget about lunch altogether and talk."

"I've invited someone over." She bit her lip. She'd meant it to be a surprise, but that probably wasn't fair anyhow.

Owen groaned. "If you say it's my grandfather…"

"It's not."

"Are you sure? Because I know Granddad has been calling you, my lovely home health worker, for daily updates."

She smiled, because something about the older gentleman tickled her. He was loud and brash and absolutely devoted to his grandson. "And don't I cover for you every single time? I tell him you're napping or showering or—"

"Bryce said you once told Granddad I was behind a closed door with a *Playboy* magazine and couldn't be disturbed."

Her mouth fell open and she scrambled off his lap. "I did no such thing!"

Owen laughed. "Okay, then Bryce made that one up." He brightened. "Tell me it's my brother coming for lunch and I can think up some fitting way to pay him back. Like, you made brownies for dessert and now he doesn't get any."

"No, it's not Bryce, either," she said.

Something on her face must have warned him. He sobered, his gaze narrowing. "Who is it, Isabella?"

She retreated for the door, her fluttering heart joining the up-and-down movement of her stomach. "It's Jerry's wife. It's Ellie Palmer."

He stared at her.

"You didn't speak to her at all at the fire station that day. You took one look at her and walked out. So she called yesterday to see…to see how you were." Izzy wiped her palms on her thighs. Her other attempts at interference hadn't worked, but this time it had to. "What could I say?"

"'Come over for lunch' doesn't seem the most natural first response." His expression was closed off and he'd crossed his arms over his chest. "But hey, whatever. I'll get out of the house and out of your hair so you two women can chat."

"No, no! You…you haven't been driving."

"Then it's about time that I do." He made to rise.

She leaped over to push him down by the shoulders. It was imperative he meet with Jerry's widow. It was the necessary final step in his healing process. Once he was emotionally whole again, Izzy could finally walk away from him.

The longer she put that off, the harder walking away would be for her. "Owen, you know you need to speak with Ellie."

"No, I don't."

"Even if just to tell her what you know about Jerry's last evening."

"I'm sure other people have told her all about that. We had enchiladas. Somebody at the station just loves to make enchiladas."

"You had another nightmare last night," she told him. "I think that means you've got to face—"

"Stay out of my head, Izzy." His voice was low and controlled. "Remember? We made that deal?"

"*If* I stayed out of your bed," she reminded him. "But I didn't, did I? So when I say you've got to stop disassociating—"

"'Disassociating'?" It was Owen who stood now, and he headed for the doorway. "What's that supposed to mean?"

"You don't want to talk about the fire, you don't want to face Jerry's widow or visit the station, let alone think about going back there to work."

"Are you calling me a coward?"

"No, of course not, but—"

"Because the lily-livered one is you, darling. Making up stories about your perfect family life. Telling tales that aren't true so you can keep *me* out of *your* head."

Her heart stuttered. "This is not about—"

"You married me but you couldn't even commit to twelve hours as my wife before you had to run away." Owen's blue eyes burned. "I know why now, though, don't I? You just told me. You just told me that you have to keep all your belongings close so you don't leave anything behind by mistake."

"Owen…"

"I was a damned fool that day for believing I'd found the woman I wanted to marry and whom I'd love for the rest of my life. It had only been three days, a Las Vegas weekend, but I was willing to gamble my future on you Izzy. Yeah. I certainly was a chump."

She swallowed. "Owen…"

"Because you're too afraid to take that same kind of chance. You'll never risk your heart, will you, Izzy? You'll never let anyone close enough to touch it."

She left. She took that suitcase of hers—all packed up as if she'd planned this all along—and walked out on him. Owen couldn't blame her—

Hell, yes, he blamed her!

But he wasn't surprised. After all, after Vegas he'd figured her to be his once and future runaway bride. Going after her was an option, but what was the use? He might think himself in love with her, but she didn't want to be married to him. And hell, after how he'd failed Jerry, Owen wasn't sure what he wanted for himself.

But he wasn't a coward. Shoving his hand through his hair, he nursed his bad temper and thought of all the ways that Izzy had been wrong about him.

He hadn't been distancing himself from the fire. It was all too real, every day, every minute in his head. Where did she think his survivor's guilt came from?

Oh, yeah, he knew what it was. And he was aware he was experiencing it. So he tried telling himself it was the fire that was at fault for Jerry's death. Some-times he believed it. Other times, he couldn't understand how all their training, their physical fitness, their equipment couldn't have made a difference and kept that young man, that young man about to be a father, alive.

It was then that he couldn't imagine going back to the job that he'd loved because he couldn't believe in the point of it any longer. He didn't have faith that his actions could make a difference.

And he was afraid there wasn't a person or a way to talk himself out of that feeling. Even Izzy, even thinking that he was in love with Izzy, hadn't budged that bleak shadow on his soul.

The doorbell rang.

Izzy? God, he couldn't stop himself from hoping it was her, because even though she'd run over his heart twice on her rush to get out of his life, the stupid thing was still beating.

He wasn't fleet on his feet, but he hurried as quick as he could, flinging open the door to see Jerry's widow. Ellie Palmer.

Hell. He hadn't thought she'd be arriving. After the argument, he'd assumed Izzy would call Ellie and renege on the invitation. But here she was, looking pale. A small smile curved her lips. "Hi, Owen."

"Hi. I—" What could he say—"Come in"—but that?

The very, very pregnant woman's movements were slow as she crossed the threshold and gingerly sat down on the chair he indicated. She tugged the hem of her maternity dress toward her knees as her gaze roamed the room. "Um, Izzy invited me over."

"Right, right." Shoving his hand through his hair, he took a seat on the sofa opposite her. "She had to step out."

"Oh. Will she be gone long?"

"I'm not sure." *Probably for the rest of my life.* "What I can do is have her call you when she, uh, gets back."

She shook her head. "It was you I wanted to talk to anyway." Her hand smoothed over the huge bump of her belly. "Do you think I could have a glass of water?"

"Oh, sure. I'm sorry…can I also get you something to eat?"

"No." She grimaced. "I couldn't eat. The water sounds great, though."

He limped away. "Coming right up."

She watched him as he returned from the kitchen and crossed the living room with her glass. "You're moving around pretty well."

"Yeah." Jerry wasn't moving at all. She didn't say the words, but Owen heard them in his head anyway. "And you, you're feeling all right?"

Her free hand, the one without the water glass, rubbed her stomach again. "Okay. Sort of like an overstuffed olive, though."

He managed a laugh at her little joke. "You have family coming to help when the baby's born?"

She nodded. "My mom and dad. Maybe I'll move closer to them afterward. I'm not certain." When she brought her water to her mouth, he noticed her hand was shaking.

Nerves because she was talking to him? "Are you sure you're feeling okay, Ellie?"

"I just want to tell you about Jerry. About how much he liked working with you."

"Oh." *Oh, God.*

"He always said you were the calmest in a crisis. The guy he liked by his side when things were heating up."

"I couldn't save him." The words came from the deepest pit of Owen's belly. "I'm so damn sorry, Ellie. I didn't see, I didn't know, I wish…I so wish…" He closed his eyes, replaying it all again. The darkness, the fire, Jerry's grin. The memory stung his eyes and he squeezed them tighter.

Owen could remember the details clearly now, every one. He saw that truth, that there had been nothing he could do to forestall Jerry's death, but the fact of it still clawed at him. "Ellie…"

Glass shattered.

He jolted, his eyes flying open. Across from him, the pregnant woman was standing, broken glass at her feet. Wetness stained her maternity dress.

"Don't move," he cautioned, rising. "I'll clean up the water and the glass, but I don't want you to risk getting cut."

She was looking at him, her eyes round. "That's not all that happened. I got to my feet and…"

"And…? Ah." Understanding dawned. "Your water broke."

Her head bobbed up and down in agreement. "I…oh, boy." Her hands clutched at her belly.

Owen hurried to her. Contraction pains already? "Deep breaths, Ellie. Deep breaths."

Her eyes widened. "It's really hurting."

"I know," he said, keeping his voice soothing. "Let's get you down the hall. There's a bedroom in there where you can lie down while I find some dry things for you to wear and call your doctor."

She held his arm as they made the few steps down the hall and then squeezed tighter, causing them both to halt as another contraction hit. "Um…"

He kept his gaze on hers and breathed in and out, trying to silently encourage her to do the same. "You're okay," he said softly. "You're okay."

When the pain passed, he moved as quick as he could, hurriedly laying down some towels when she protested about getting onto the bed. Then he went upstairs to retrieve a T-shirt and sweat pants, and helped her back up and toward the bathroom where she could change.

She had another contraction on the way in, interrupting her recitation of her doctor's name and phone number. Before he'd even had a chance to dial it, the bathroom door was back open. Ellie stood there, in only his big T-shirt, which fell all the way to her knees.

"Um…Owen…" There was a clammy sweat on her face, and when he reached for her, she grabbed on to his fingers in a viselike grip.

As he helped her stretch back out on the bed, he decided that dialing 911 was a sounder idea.

When he hung up the phone, she was having yet another contraction. "Owen," her voice was faint. "I think…I think…"

He squeezed her hands. "Don't worry. I know how to deliver a baby, though I'm sure the para-medics will—"

"Owen!" her voice rose to a breathless squeak. "I think the baby's coming."

"All right. Keep breathing, honey." He met her gaze. "Do you want me to check?"

She nodded vigorously, and then her back bowed as another pain overtook her.

In the bathroom he found another big towel to give her modesty. When it was draped over her legs, he tucked into the kitchen where he thoroughly washed his good hand and wrapped plastic wrap around his cast and other fingers. Then he returned to the bedroom and gently positioned Ellie in order to assess the situation.

Good Lord. He glanced up to see her anxious gaze on his face and flashed her a reassuring smile. "Well, you might want to prepare yourself for a boy who doesn't have much patience for authority figures. I don't think he's going to wait for the EMTs to arrive."

The corners of her mouth quirked in an answering smile. "Like father, like son."

Alexander Gerald Palmer slid into Owen's waiting hands like he was a football delivered by an extremely proficient center. He didn't share that little tidbit with the baby's mother, but as he placed the infant on Ellie's chest, he thought he felt Jerry's presence somewhere, grinning with approval.

That damn grin of Jerry's. Unforgettable.

But he and Ellie were grinning, too, he realized. She shared hers with him and then went back to crooning to the baby. Owen enjoyed the sight for a moment, then heard the commotion at his front door.

Grateful to give the reins over to the personnel who did this kind of thing on a more regular basis, Owen let them in, then retreated to his kitchen while they checked out mother and child. He wasn't alone long. Word must have gotten out, because soon Will and others from the station were milling about his living area, anxious to hear the news.

"I'm telling you," Owen said to his friends. "It's Jerry's boy. He came into the world whistling."

"You look like you're ready to warble something yourself," Will answered. "I haven't seen you smiling like that since…since before."

The comment didn't dissipate Owen's exuberance. "I don't just feel good. I feel great." His training had been worth something again. When the moment came he'd found faith in his ability to handle the situation and help Jerry's widow while she did the important work of birthing her baby. It did make a man want to whistle. Maybe sing a few bars of misheard lyrics.

Yeah. *Hold me closer, Tony Danza.*

He swallowed a laugh and reveled in how damn good it was to delight in being alive.

Chapter Twelve

"There's a lesson to be learned in all this, right?" Izzy said into her cell phone. She moved about the anonymous hotel room, opening her suitcase by rote, as she pondered why burnt orange seemed to be the favorite color of all business-hotel interior designers throughout the country.

"That you can't run away from your problems?" Emily questioned. "Though I think the nuns in *The Sound of Music* trademarked that one."

"No." Izzy frowned. The bedside alarm clock was a model she wasn't familiar with. Tack on five minutes to make sure she figured out its mechanics.

Oh, but that's right, she didn't have anywhere to be at any particular time. Not for another week.

"I think the lesson here is that a woman shouldn't get married in Las Vegas."

"Worked out pretty well for me," Emily reminded her.

Izzy sighed. "Okay, maybe that *I* shouldn't get married."

"Period? Or just in Nevada?"

She didn't dare answer the question. She just kept moving about the hotel room, performing her usual tasks: turning back the bedspread and blankets; pulling the light filter curtain so the room wasn't too bright yet wasn't too dark, either; unfurling the towels in the bathroom from their decorative, yet inconvenient, snail-like design.

"Izzy?"

"I'm here." She gazed around the room, trying to figure out something to do with herself next. All her usual make-herself-comfortable actions were complete. Unless she suddenly changed course and developed an itch to unpack—as if that was going to happen—then she was out of busy work. Except…

Sitting herself at the desk, she reached into its drawer for the complimentary stationery and pen she knew she'd find there. "Tell me everything you know about a Nevada annulment."

"Izzy…" There was a wealth of doubt in her friend's voice.

"Please spare me the warning or the lecture or whatever it is you're about to say. I need something to occupy my mind, and the annulment has now found its way to the top of my agenda."

"I didn't look into it with much diligence," Emily confessed.

"That's okay. I just need a starting point."

"Until it's actually granted, you shouldn't enter any beauty pageants."

"What?" The answer startled a laugh out of her, though she wasn't finding much amusing about the past hours of her life.

"You've got to be single to enter most contests like that, and even a quickie wedding in Vegas can mess up your reign if you win."

Izzy held the phone away from her ear for a moment and frowned at it. "What are you talking about?"

"Just one of the pitfalls of research librarianship. I start pulling on a thread and it leads me to the darnedest places."

"Let me get this straight." Izzy rubbed at her forehead. "You were looking into how to end your marriage to Will and you found out about beauty contest rules?"

"I told you, I didn't look into it with much diligence."

"I'll say."

"Hey," Emily defended herself. "You have the same skills that I do, and you've managed to not even find out that much. At least I had the excuse of being in love with my husband and in my heart of hearts not wanting the marriage to be over at all. What's yours?"

"I'm not in love with Owen!" She heard the strident tone in her voice and tried too late to calm it. "I can't be in love with Owen."

"Okay, okay," Emily soothed. "Relax. I remember a little bit more about the annulment rules. If one or both of you is under eighteen without a parent's consent, the marriage can be annulled. Bigamy gets you out of it. Consanguination."

Since they both were thirty, never married before and not related by blood, those were all out. "What else?"

"Drug or alcohol addiction."

"I don't wish for either one of those. Is there another circumstance?"

"Hmm…I think if the marriage was the result of threat or duress."

Izzy pursed her lips and tried imagining the scene. *Your honor, this man's kisses put me under such duress that I didn't hesitate to say "I do."* She sighed. "Do you have anything else?"

"Well…" Emily was quiet a moment. "Fraud might do it."

"Fraud?"

"Yes. You tell the judge Owen misrepresented himself somehow. There was a famous celebrity marriage that ended in just over fifty hours when a pop singer convinced the judge that she and her non-groom hadn't had an honest discussion of where they would live or if they wanted kids, that sort of thing."

Izzy penned the word on her piece of paper. *F-R-A-U-D*. Then she wrote it how Melvil Dewey might have. *F-R-O-D*. Then she crossed them both out.

It was true that they'd never discussed where they might live or anything about children. But… "There's no one less a fraud in the western half of the United States than Owen Marston," she said. "He's a firefighter, for goodness sake. The kind of man who devotes his career to helping others. Every day he's out there saving lives and property."

Okay, she knew she was preaching to the choir, because Emily's husband, Will, was just such a person, too, but she couldn't let the words go unsaid. She rose from the desk chair to pace about the room. "I could never stand before anyone and tell them Owen was a fraud."

"Okay," Emily said again. "I get you on that. But Izzy…"

There was a note in her friend's voice that told her a lightbulb had gone off. Emily, bless her fact-finding little heart, had thought of something.

"What?" she demanded. "But what?"

"Are you sitting down?"

Izzy huffed in impatience, but she threw herself onto the end of the bed. "Yes. Now out with it."

"Well, Iz," Emily said slowly. "What about Owen going before the judge and testifying that the one in this marriage who perpetrated a fraud was you?"

Izzy's stomach whooshed to her toes. She tightened her fingers on the phone and pressed the flat of her other hand to the mattress. "Me? Why would you think he would say that about me?"

"You weren't really serious about the marriage at all, were you?" Emily asked.

"I don't know why—"

"You were scuttling from the hotel when dawn broke."

Izzy's breath didn't seem to reach her lungs. "You left Las Vegas, too," she pointed out.

"I tried to contact Will. And I knew that I was going to be living just a few miles from him. He knew he was going to be able to find me. You didn't even give Owen your cell phone number."

Because she was scared! Because she was scared that if she heard his voice she'd be seduced again by the fantasy of all that she'd learned never to believe in. A man, a marriage, a family that didn't just see her as an inconvenience or an obligation.

How could she trust that? How many times when she was five or eight or ten had she let herself think that her current caretaker loved her and wanted her and would love her and want her forever? Each time she'd been disappointed when a different car would drive up and she'd be shuffled to yet another person who didn't really care.

There at the new place she'd turn on the charm, she'd make herself small or quiet or helpful, whatever was required, and yet it still was never enough.

She had never been enough.

"Izzy? Izzy, you know I love you."

"Yes," she said dully. "Yes, I know that." She had found good, close friends, and she cherished them, though truth to tell, even they weren't the same as what she'd pretended for three days in Las Vegas that she could have with Owen.

"So you know I don't like saying this," Emily continued. "But I'm right, aren't I? It was you who went to the altar under false pretenses."

"Yes," she said again.

"You didn't believe in a lifetime with the man."

"Yes," she agreed again.

"And you weren't the least bit in love with him."

Izzy took a breath. The agreement to that sentence just sat on her tongue.

"Iz?"

She stayed silent.

"You weren't in love with him, right?" Emily insisted. "You *aren't* in love with him, right?"

Wrong.

Izzy put her head in her hand. She'd been wrong about so many things, but it was too late…for her and Owen.

And for her crumbling heart.

* * *

At the sound of the doorbell, Owen continued his phone conversation with Will. He pulled open the front door to find his brother, whom he gestured inside. "I'll work shifts for you. I'll cut your damn lawn for a month. Just get me her cell phone number."

Will started to hem and haw, but Owen interrupted him. "She walked out on me. And took my car. For God's sake, I at least need to demand my ride back."

Bryce waved his hand in Owen's face. "You need Izzy's cell phone number?"

Cupping his hand over the phone, he addressed his brother. "Yeah. And don't say anything about me being stupid not to have it. I get that."

Bryce grinned. "But *I* have *it*."

"Never mind, Will," Owen said into the phone, hanging up and looking at his brother expectantly, his fingers hovering over the keypad. "Go ahead."

Grinning, Bryce dropped onto the couch and stretched out his legs. "Wait a minute. Aren't we going to negotiate? You were offering to cut Will's lawn."

"I'll cut important parts of your body off if you don't give it to me right now."

"Ouch." Still grinning, Bryce crossed his legs. "But c'mon, bro, I do you a favor, you do me a favor…"

Owen took a breath. "Fine. Here's the favor— I'm not going to join the family company, where I would have swiftly risen in the ranks to become your boss and then taken great pleasure in canning your irritating ass."

Bryce sat up straight. "Really?"

"Really. So thank me for saving your career by giving me Isabella's phone number."

His brother dug in his front pocket for his phone. "I see a man retaking control of his life."

"Yeah." He paused, then felt his mouth curve in a smile like it had been doing about every fifteen minutes since the day before, when Alexander Gerald Palmer made his way into the world. "I helped deliver a baby yesterday."

"No kidding. Anybody's I know?"

"Jerry's wife. Jerry's son." It still felt damn good to know that he'd been able to help Jerry's widow. The experience had given Owen back his juice, the motivation and the energy to return to the work that was his life's calling.

And the motivation, energy and determination to try to get a certain wife to return to his life, too.

The way he figured it, now that his head was finally back in working order, was that Izzy had gone AWOL in Las Vegas because she was afraid to believe they could have a real marriage. But she hadn't disbelieved enough to start proceedings to end it, either. That said something. "Give me the number, Bryce."

His brother rattled it off and Owen punched it into his phone. Then he hesitated, and added the number to his address book instead of directly dialing Izzy. Still considering, he glanced at his brother again.

"I figure you owe me more," he told Bryce.

"What? Why?"

"It's a big thing to save a man's job, not to mention his standing in the family. Look, I'll keep quiet about the emergency birth thing, if you give me a couple hours of your time."

Amusement sparked in Bryce's eyes, but he made a show of grumbling. "Want to make a bet that we'll all be sitting around the turkey at Thanksgiving and you'll somehow let it slip?"

"Right now there's only one thing I'm willing to gamble on," Owen replied.

He wanted his car back. Of course he wanted his car back, Izzy acknowledged. It was mortifying to recall that she'd driven off in it and then never given the vehicle another thought. Her mind had been occupied elsewhere.

She was in love with Owen, and she'd blown it.

The worst thing about the situation, she thought, as she pulled into his driveway, was that even if she could replay the last four weeks, she didn't see herself doing anything differently.

You could know that you were in love.

You could see that you'd had a chance at something you'd never expected to touch.

But you could still be unable to make yourself reach out and grasp it.

Her foot caught on a pile of flattened empty boxes stacked against the garage and she gave them a little kick before marching toward the front door. It felt like an execution was in the offing, but she wasn't going to let him know that this meeting would be the lethal injection to her heart.

It wasn't his fault that she couldn't be the kind of woman he deserved. She could work at being friendly, fun and pleasing, but for the life and marriage he wanted she had to be trusting and open. For too long she'd only had herself to rely on, and she couldn't see herself learning to rely on someone else.

As she reached the front door, it suddenly opened. She took a hasty step back, then saw that it was Bryce, who looked a little sweaty and dusty. He smiled, then swooped in to grab her up for a kiss on the forehead. "Later, little fairy," he said, then breezed past her at a jog.

She gazed after him with a sad smile. "I didn't get a chance to say goodbye," she murmured to his retreating back. It was likely she'd never see him again.

"Tears?" a voice said at her back. "Don't tell me you're crying over my little brother."

She blinked rapidly and then spun around. "Of course not." There was going to be no sentiment during this meeting. She'd hand over the keys and they'd exchange thoughts on how best to end their marriage.

Owen backed away from the threshold. "Come inside."

On the small table in the shallow foyer was a huge arrangement of pale-blue roses. Maybe two dozen. She stared at the flowers, wondering who had sent them, and then immediately thought of single mom Alicia. Had she stepped up her courtship of Owen despite Izzy's laying claim to him?

Or had he called the other woman and explained their not-really-a-marriage himself?

"They're from Ellie Palmer's parents," he said, his gaze on her face. "Yesterday, during the visit you arranged, we had a surprise special delivery on these very premises."

Izzy's eyes widened as she deduced his meaning. "What? The baby? Born here?"

"Yep." He smiled. "The baby. Born here."

"Wow. They're okay?"

"They're okay. I'm okay."

She studied the relaxed expression on his face. He looked different. Happy. Purposeful. The tightness in her chest eased a little. It appeared as if the old Owen—the man she'd married—was back.

"Let's sit down for a minute," he said.

Following him in, she tried breathing slow and easy. He sat on the couch, and she took the chair opposite. Something seemed different, besides his newly relaxed demeanor, but she couldn't quite put her finger on it. Frowning, she reached out to place his keys on the table between them. "Sorry about taking off with your car."

"No problem." He scooped up the metal ring and immediately pocketed it.

She frowned again, annoyed with herself for not thinking to call a cab to pick her up here at a certain time. Now she'd have to have Owen drive her back to the hotel or stand around on his sidewalk while she waited for a taxi once they were through.

Oh, well. She wiped her palms on her thighs and took a quick breath. "We should talk."

He nodded. "We should."

She looked down at her hands as a silence stretched between them. "I've started looking into the annulment laws."

"Yeah? Me, too."

Why did that hurt so much? She twisted her fingers together. "There's a couple of possibilities."

"No. No, there's not."

Her gaze jumped up to meet his. His expression was unreadable, but his face was so handsome and so…so *dear* to her. How had this happened? How had she been so stupid as to fall in love when she was the kind of person who couldn't let herself count on forever?

"The annulment idea won't work," Owen said.

"Oh, but I think we can find something in our circumstance that fits—"

"We've been living together, Izzy. I admit I'm no legal expert, but from what I've read, the fact that we've been living together—and sleeping together—puts the kibosh on that plan."

She slumped against the back of the chair. Yesterday, after her conversation with Emily during which she'd confronted the truth that she was in love with Owen, she'd stopped thinking about a way out of their marriage and just wallowed in self-pity.

And really bad room-service pizza.

She held her palm to her stomach as if it were still burning a hole there. "Really? There's a clause about living together?"

Owen nodded. "Think so."

Her eyes closed. That meant they needed a divorce then. The idea of it only served to wound her ready-to-be-executed heart. An annulment could be something to forget about, since it legally ruled that the marriage had indeed never occurred. But a divorce made it real.

A divorce made it real that she'd wedded the man she was in love with and that she didn't have what it took to stay married to him. Bryce had once called her a woman who made do with less. Had he been right?

"Izzy," Owen said softly. "Isabella."

She willed away the tears stinging her eyes. Swallowing hard, she looked at him. "What is it?"

"Izzy…"

Her gaze snagged on a quilt folded over the arm of the sofa he was sitting on. It looked familiar. She frowned at it, then scooted forward on her cushion so she had a better view. It certainly was a quilt. In the colors of her alma mater. The alma mater she shared with Emily.

As a matter of fact, it appeared to be the very quilt that Emily had made for Izzy the year after they'd graduated.

Eyebrows raised, she looked at Owen. He was watching her, and something in his expression made her run her gaze around the room. Some of the firefighter memorabilia on the bookcase had been rearranged. There were more books on the shelves now, including *Eight Cousins* and *A Rose in Bloom*.

Her books.

She rose to her feet, her insides unsteady as she toured the house. In the kitchen were some hand-embroidered tea towels that one of her *zias* had given her when she turned eighteen. Down the hall, in the room Owen used as a home office, her framed college diplomas hung on the wall next to his. Photographs that she'd taken over the years were set about, too. With a tentative fingertip, she touched one. It wasn't a figment of her imagination.

Then she whirled, sensing Owen behind her. He

stood in the doorway, his gaze trained on her face. She looked away, because what she was feeling was too big, too scary, too hard to speak of. He moved aside as she approached the door and then trailed her up the stairs to the next level.

In his bedroom, she found the clothes that had been in boxes in the garage hanging in the closet. A pair of scruffy slippers shaped like jalapeño peppers that she'd had since high school and never gotten around to throwing out peeked from under the bed.

Owen cleared his throat. "There were some god-awful flannel granny nightgowns. I took the liberty of tossing those."

She still couldn't look at him. Her gaze hit on another familiar item. It was propped on the pillows in the center of the bed. One of her friends had em-broidered the heart-shaped thing for her eons ago. "My night has become a sunny dawn because of you."

Blinking rapidly, she turned her head, only to find something that sent the tears cascading down her cheeks. On the bedside table—on the side that *he* slept on—was a beautiful frame. And inside it—their marriage certificate.

Her gaze jumped to her side of the bed, and there, in a matching frame, was a photograph from their wedding. Magnetlike, it drew her, and she took it in her hand, her vision blurring so that she couldn't see the image of the two people who had found each other through some unexplainable intersection of luck and fate.

It didn't matter. She remembered exactly how the couple had felt.

Happy. In love. Ready to face the future together.

She wiped her face with the back of her hand and then looked over at her husband. He was smiling at her, and she guessed that he knew his gesture had been the exact right thing to get through to her. The exact right thing to make her believe.

"You made a place for me here," she said.

"Because I want you in my life," Owen answered. "Forever. Do you think the rolling stone can settle down awhile?"

She sniffed, and had to wipe at her wet face again. She'd lived nowhere because there'd been no one she'd felt like this about. "I like Paxton. You know I'm in love with you."

Grinning now, he came closer. "I counted on it." He placed the photograph back on the table and then took her into his arms.

"I can count on you." The knowledge was the sunny dawn that warmed every lonely and empty corner of her soul. After a childhood filled with un-reliability, it was this that she needed. To know that she could count on him. He'd proved it to her, hadn't he, by putting her things side by side with his. "I can really, really count on you."

"Yes. On my support, on my partnership. On my love."

Izzy hugged Owen to her, hearing his heart beating steady in her ear. "I am going to make you so happy," she said fiercely. "Wait until you see how stubborn I can be about that."

He tipped her face up for his kiss. "No more running?"

"Only to you," she answered. "Always."

* * * * *

RODEO BRIDE

BY
MYRNA MACKENZIE

Myrna Mackenzie grew up not having a clue what she wanted to be (she hadn't been born a princess, the one job she thought she might like because of the steady flow of pretty dresses and crowns), but she knew that she loved stories and happy endings, so falling into life as a romance writer was pretty much inevitable. An award-winning author, with over thirty-five novels written, Myrna was born in a small town in Dunklin County, Missouri, grew up just outside Chicago, and now divides her time between two lakes in Chicago and Wisconsin—both very different and both very beautiful. She adores the internet (which still seems magical after all these years), loves coffee, hiking, attempting gardening (without much success), cooking and knitting. Readers (and other potential gardeners, cooks, knitters, writers, etc.) can visit Myrna online at www.myrnamackenzie. com, or write to her at PO Box 225, La Grange, IL 60525, USA.

CHAPTER ONE

DILLON FARRADAY was coming. "This morning," Colleen Applegate whispered, staring out the window at the long drive leading from her ranch to the rest of the world. And the reason he was coming was going to tear her heart apart, she thought, glancing down at the baby monitor, her lifeline to the child she'd grown to love as her own.

She'd never actually met the man, but what she knew worried her. He was drop-dead handsome, rich and, therefore, probably used to getting his way. He was from Chicago and might frown on Montana ranch life. Moreover, he was a soldier, used to harsh ways, and Colleen knew all about harsh men. This one had been injured in battle six months ago, so he might not be in the best of humor. All of that information was public, readily available on the Internet.

Beyond that, however, things got murkier. Dillon was recently divorced from Lisa, a former local who had gone to school with Colleen, and three months ago Lisa had shown up at Colleen's door with her new baby. "I can't do this," she'd told Colleen, "but you're perfect with babies, and you've always wanted one. Take care of him, please, for now."

Colleen had wanted to say no, but a baby had been involved. She'd reluctantly agreed to keep Toby safe.

"By the way," Lisa had said, before she left, "I sent a note to Dillon at the hospital where he's laid up, so he knows about the baby's existence. He might or might not want to see Toby someday, but…the baby might not be his. Biologically, that is."

Then Lisa had run, so that small cryptic bit of information was almost all that Colleen knew. Except for one more thing. That question about whether or not Dillon might want to see the baby? It was no longer a question.

In a brief, terse telephone conversation yesterday he had introduced himself, said that he'd been released from the hospital and indicated one thing more: he was coming to Montana and he expected Colleen to docilely hand sweet little Toby over.

There was only one problem there. Dillon Farraday might have a legal claim, but Colleen had never been a docile woman.

Moreover, she had questions, and she intended to get good solid answers before she simply handed over an innocent baby, one she loved, to anyone, especially to a man she didn't know or trust.

Dillon parked his black Ferrari in front of the long, low log house. The beauty of the mountains was behind him, but other than this lopsided house and the outbuildings, there were no signs of civilization for miles around. Why on earth had Lisa left the baby here? And why had she waited so long to let him know of the child's existence?

The same questions—and possible answers—had been swirling through his head for weeks, but he had spent a lifetime learning to bide his time, to think things through to their logical conclusion and then to act when the time was right. His marriage to Lisa had seemed to follow the same pattern, but in reality it had been the one glaring exception and an obvious mistake. But now that he was capable of walking a reasonable distance, driving a reasonable distance, the time was definitely right for lots of things he hadn't been able to take care of before.

He would have his answers…and his son. Colleen Applegate couldn't legally deny him, and she probably knew that. She hadn't sounded happy to hear from him when he'd called yesterday.

Too bad. She could have touched base with him anytime during the past three months and she hadn't bothered to do that, so her opinions didn't matter. All that mattered about Colleen Applegate was that she had his child.

Dillon pulled himself from the car, took the darned cane he was still forced to use and approached the house that appeared to have been put together haphazardly, like a child using two different sets of blocks that didn't fit together. There were two front steps. Sloping steps. Those would be a problem. He didn't like anyone seeing him struggle, so when the door opened and a woman stepped out onto the slanted porch, he stayed where he was.

"Ms. Applegate?" he asked.

"You're half an hour early," she said with a nod.

Somehow Dillon managed to conceal his surprise at her appearance. Lisa had always been friends with women who were a lot like herself: model-thin and petite with skillfully made-up faces and expensive clothing that accentuated their willowy figures. Colleen Applegate was tall and curvy with messy, riotous blond curls and little if any makeup. She was dressed in a red T-shirt, jeans and boots. There were no signs of vanity about her. No smile, either, and her comment clearly indicated irritation.

For some reason that made him want to smile. Maybe because of the interest factor. He'd been raised to command, and people had been tiptoeing around him all his adult life.

His employees, his soldiers, apparently even his ex-wife. But this woman wasn't tiptoeing. Not even slightly.

"Traffic was light," he said with a smile and a shrug.

She looked instantly wary. He supposed he could understand why. This situation had to be uncomfortable for her at best. If she'd grown attached to the baby, it would be worse than that. He noted that she had brown eyes…expressive eyes that signaled a woman who had trouble hiding her thoughts. "You know why I'm here," he said.

"You made that clear yesterday."

Dillon studied those pretty brown eyes. He had seen a lot of pain in the past year, his own physical pain the least of it. This woman was in pain.

He closed his eyes and tried to pretend she was the enemy. No use. *Damn Lisa for bringing another person into this. If she'd wanted to punish him for neglecting her when he traveled for work and went to war, that was fine, but a child? This woman who was clearly emotionally affected by all this?*

He looked at Colleen. "I want my child." His voice was low, quiet, a bit raspy. "Can you blame me?"

She bit her lip and shook her head. Those eyes looked even sadder. "No." The word was barely a whisper. "Come in. He's sleeping."

"Just like that? Don't you want proof that I am who I am? Identification?"

Something close to a smile lifted her lips. "You're a millionaire and a war hero, Mr. Farraday. That makes you easy to find on the Internet. I don't actually need proof that you're who you say you are."

He nodded.

"But I'll look at your identification. To verify your address and any other particulars I might not have thought of. I want all of this done right. Every *i* dotted and every *t* crossed. I have questions. Lots of them, but none of them have to do with a photo ID."

"What kinds of questions are they, then?"

"Whether you'll be a good father, whether Toby will get everything he needs."

The obvious, automatic answer would have been to say that Toby would be given all that money could buy, but Dillon knew all too well that money was never enough. His upbringing and his failed marriage were proof of that. Colleen Applegate was right on the money with her qualms. He couldn't even argue with her.

And despite her invitation to come inside, she was still standing in front of the door as if to guard his son from him.

"I intend to be a good father," he said, and prayed that he could live up to his intentions. Children were fragile in so many ways.

Colleen still didn't budge.

"I meant that," he said.

"I'm not doubting your word, but—"

"But you don't know me," he suggested. "You know my public history, but you don't know what kind of man I really am. Is that it?"

She hesitated. "Something like that. I don't mean to be rude, but I've gotten used to worrying about Toby. I have to live with myself after I turn him over to you, and he's still so little."

"Understood," Dillon said, even as a small streak of admiration for Colleen Applegate's determination to guard his child crept in.

She needed reassurance. He needed his child. The fact that so much time had already passed, that he'd missed so much…

Anger at these circumstances shot straight through Dillon. Disregarding his appearance and his own embarrassment at his weakness, he struggled up onto the porch and moved to within a foot of Colleen, towering over her despite her height.

"I understand your reticence," he assured her. "I see your point. Here's mine. Toby *is* my son. And while I have no experience whatsoever at being a father, I intend to do everything in my power to make sure Toby is happy."

Dillon held her gaze. He noted the small flutter of her pulse at her throat. He knew that his height and stoic demeanor often intimidated people, but while Colleen was noticeably nervous, she was still standing tall and proud. However reluctant he was to give ground to this woman, he had to admire her for not wilting before his anger. Still, the worried look in her eyes eased. Just a bit.

"He's sleeping," she reminded him, as if she had to get the last word in.

He fought not to smile. "I won't wake him."

Colleen sighed. "He's a light sleeper, but his naptime is almost over, anyway. Come inside." She finally turned and opened the door, leading him into the house.

There was something about the way she moved that immediately attracted his attention. It wasn't a sway, the kind of thing that other men reacted to. It was both less and more. Tall and long-legged, she moved with confidence, sleekly and quietly making her way through the house.

Instantly, his male antennae went on alert. The attraction was surprisingly intense. Also wrong, given the situation. Obviously his months in a military hospital out of the mainstream were having an effect.

That was unacceptable. He was here for one reason only, to find his child. And even if he weren't, he'd been betrayed by women too many times to jump in blindly again. A man who had been betrayed by his mother, his first love and his wife should have learned his lesson by now.

I have, he thought. Women were out, at least in any meaningful way.

So he concentrated on being as silent as Colleen, trying not to knock his cane against anything. The baby was asleep in the depths of this rambling house. This very old, and in need of repairs and paint, rambling house, Dillon noted, as Colleen came to a stop outside a door.

"Here," she whispered, touching her finger to her lips.

Dillon came up close behind her. The light soap scent of her filled his nostrils. He ignored his own body's reaction and stared into a room unlike the others he'd passed through. The walls were a robin's egg blue. Clouds and stars and moons were stenciled on a border that circled the room just below the ceiling. A sturdy white crib with a mobile of dancing horses hanging above it sat in the corner, and in the crib lay a chubby little child in a pale yellow shirt and diaper, his skin rosy and pink, his fingers and toes unbelievably tiny.

Toby Farraday, Dillon thought. His child. His heir. He had had many people in his life, but none, not even his parents, certainly not his wife, who had truly been his.

He glanced down at Colleen, who, despite the fact that she had been living with Toby for months, seemed totally entranced by the sight, too. She glanced up at Dillon. "He's beautiful, isn't he?" she whispered.

Her voice was soft and feminine and the way she had looked at the baby, the fact that they all seemed to be closed up in this cozy, warm, safe cocoon…

Was an illusion, Dillon knew. Safety and security of that type weren't real. He couldn't afford to fall into that kind of thinking, not now when he had someone other than himself he was responsible for. Reality was key to avoiding disillusionment for his son…and for himself.

"Is that one of your questions?" he asked.

She blinked. "Pardon me?"

"You told me you had many questions. Is asking me if my son is beautiful a test? If I should say no…"

Anger flashed in her eyes. "Then you'd be a liar."

"Ah, so it was a test," he said, his tone teasing. "Yes, he's beautiful, Ms. Applegate."

She grimaced. "No one calls me that."

He had the distinct impression that the last time someone had called her that, it hadn't been a pleasant experience.

"Then yes, he's beautiful, Colleen. And I'm not lying."

"Good. I'm glad you feel that way because…" Those deep brown eyes filled with concern again.

"What?"

"I hate to even bring this up…but before I completely turn him over to you, there's something that has to be asked. There's a potential problem."

Still she hesitated. He was pretty sure he knew why. Given the fact that there was nothing in the public history she had read that could have caused her to worry, there could be only one thing remaining that was making her this uncomfortable.

"Ask," he demanded, the single word clipped and cold.

Colleen took a deep, visible breath and looked right into his eyes.

"What if Lisa…there might be a chance…I wouldn't ordinarily even bring up something so painful and so…not my business, but as I mentioned, I have to make sure Toby's okay, and…what if he isn't your biological son?"

Anger pulsed through Dillon even as he told himself that her question was a valid one for a woman who saw herself as the sole protector of an innocent baby.

"If you think I haven't heard that my wife had…intimate friends even before we divorced, then you're wrong. If you're suggesting that I would take out my displeasure on a baby, then you haven't really done your research on me after all and you haven't been listening to me. And if you think for one second that this changes things, then let me tell you that it doesn't. Whether Toby is my biological son or not, he's legally mine. I was married to Lisa when he was conceived, and the law is clear on my claim to him."

His words and tone would have cowed most people. But Colleen didn't drop her gaze even one bit. She was, he conceded, acting like the proverbial mother bear, even if Toby wasn't hers.

"I'm not the type of guy who would let that make a difference. I no longer have a wife, so what Lisa did or didn't do doesn't matter to me. What I have is a son. He's not responsible for his parentage. No one ever is." Thank goodness.

Colleen visibly relaxed. "Thank you. Some men wouldn't feel that way."

"I'm not those men." His last words may have been uttered a bit too loudly. Toby made a small, unhappy whimpering sound.

Faster than light, quieter than the dawn, Colleen was across the room. She reached down and gently stroked the baby's arm. "Shh, you're safe, sweetheart," she whispered. "I'm here. No one will hurt you."

Almost instantly, the baby calmed. He pulled one fist up to his mouth and began to suck his thumb. He slept, his long lashes fluttering back down over those pale, pretty cheeks. Colleen gazed down at the baby with what looked like true affection. Had any of his nannies ever looked like that when he was growing up? Dillon wondered. No, some of them had been decent, but not even close to being that involved. He hadn't expected them to, hadn't even known it was possible. Still, this was…nice, even though her attachment to the baby was clearly going to be a problem.

Colleen looked up into Dillon's eyes, that naked pain evident again. Dillon wanted to look away. He forced himself not to.

She stood straight and tall, proudly defying him while she still could. For an Amazon she didn't look even slightly out of place in this room full of small things. He noted the stuffed animals in a sun-yellow crate, the changing table with diapers and lotions, the piles of baby clothes on top of a child-sized dresser, the toys and books. A night-light shaped like a lamb. Now, he remembered that he'd passed a stroller on the way in, a bright blue playpen in the living room. Where had all these things come from?

As if she'd read his mind, she moved toward him. "We need to talk," she said.

"My thoughts exactly."

"We have about thirty minutes before Toby wakes up in earnest. He's like clockwork and then he'll want to be fed." She ushered Dillon toward the living room, where she perched on a chair that had a lot more years on it than anything in the nursery. Dillon sat down on a tired old sofa.

With the playpen taking up a lot of the space, the room seemed small, tight, not quite big enough for two adults. Dillon looked at Colleen, and now, without the foil of Toby to concentrate on, she looked nervous, rubbing her palms over her jeans.

Dillon's gaze followed her hands down her legs. He ordered himself to think of the business at hand, not what Colleen Applegate's long legs looked like when they weren't encased in denim. There were important issues to deal with here. "Did Lisa give you money to take care of Toby?"

"Why would you think that?"

"Babies cost money. They take time."

"I haven't even had any contact with her since the day she dropped him here. He was only a week old. She didn't want him. I didn't even think of asking for payment. He was a baby with no one to love him."

"But you've obviously spent a fair amount of money. You'll be compensated."

She glared at him. "I don't want it. That would be like selling him." Those strong, sturdy hands were opening and closing now.

"All right. I won't insult you by offering again. Just tell me this. Why you? I'd never even heard of you before. Lisa never spoke of you. Were you good friends?"

Colleen shook her head, those messy curls brushing her cheeks. "We grew up in the same town and we went to school together, but no, we weren't friends at all. As for why, she seemed frantic, trapped and, well, this is a small town and everyone here knows me. It's no secret that I've always wanted children, but…"

"But you don't have any."

"No. I don't." It was clear that there was more to this part of the story than she was saying, but Dillon had no right to ask more. She had given him a valid answer.

"Lisa said that she couldn't be a mother to Toby," Colleen continued, "and she didn't say much more. She didn't stay long, and she seemed worried at what your reaction was going to be, as if she wanted to be gone before you got here."

"Which is why you have a number of questions of your own," he said.

"Partly, yes."

"Those questions you were asking earlier…you think I abused my wife or that I would once I knew that she had cheated on me?"

"I don't know you. I know there are men who can be abusive, with or without a reason. And even when abuse doesn't involve hitting it can be brutal and harmful." Something about the tone of her voice, the way she looked away when all along she'd been facing him head-on, led Dillon to believe that Colleen had had personal experience of such men. Something shifted inside him. Anger at his own kind filled him.

"I'm not a perfect man, Colleen, but I've never intentionally harmed a woman or a child, and I wouldn't."

She studied him as if trying to read his mind to see if he spoke the truth. Her eyes were dark and unhappy but she sucked in her lip, blinked and gave a hard nod. "Okay," she whispered. "I mean, I don't have a choice do I, but…"

Suddenly she leaned forward and opened a drawer on the end table next to the chair. She pulled out a sheaf of papers. Pages and pages of papers.

"These are things you need to know. Routines. Details on what went on during his first few months. His preferences, his quirks, his fears. Medical things. He was jaundiced when Lisa brought him here, and until recently, he was colicky, but if I wrapped him up tight in a blanket and rocked with him, eventually he would go to sleep. He takes a nap in the morning and one in the afternoon and…who will do all these things?" she asked suddenly. Then just as quickly she shook her head. "Forget I asked that. You're a wealthy man. You'll hire some…some nurse or something."

Someone who doesn't love him yet, she meant to say. Dillon was sure of that.

Gently, he took the stack of papers from Colleen. There were all kinds of notes. A description of Toby's first smile, his first laugh, which was just last week. His feeding schedule. More.

"You're right. I'm a wealthy man. I can hire a nurse." Just the way his parents had. A whole series of nurses and nannies who had come and gone. He didn't want that for his child.

"You could teach me what to do." The words just popped right out of nowhere. Dillon had no clue why he'd even said the words, but…

"I could take care of him," he added.

As if she wasn't even thinking, Colleen suddenly reached across and touched his hand. "That's incredibly sweet."

Dillon wanted to laugh. Sort of. "Have you looked at me, Colleen? No one on earth, least of all the people in my business or the men under my command, have ever called me sweet."

"I know." She looked down at where her hand lay on his, as if she regretted the move but didn't know how to take it back. "I didn't mean it quite the way it sounded. What I meant was, you don't have a clue what you're saying. Despite all your accomplishments, taking care of a baby is different from anything on earth you've ever done."

"I suspect that it is. So show me, Colleen."

"Now?"

"I've been away from my business for a long time. There are people I trust in charge, and they won't mind waiting for me a little longer. I have time for you to teach me."

Colleen worked hard at controlling her breathing. Dillon Farraday's hand was warm and strong and very masculine beneath her own. Not that she had any business noticing. Quickly, she pulled away. "I don't feel comfortable having a man in my house."

Strange man. She should have said strange man. But she had meant what she said. She didn't want *any* man here. This whole house was her haven, her shelter, her barrier.

"You have other buildings. I could rent one."

For the first time she allowed herself to smile. "Some of them have animals in them, some have tools. You aren't exactly the type to bunk with the hired hands I employ."

"Don't judge a man by his looks, Colleen."

No, she never did. Looks could deceive. "I won't."

"Good. Then you'll let me stay here a few days? You'll train me in the basics so I can be a good father to Toby?"

"What will you do when you go back to Chicago? You'll still need someone."

"What do you do when you have to work around the ranch?"

"I bundle him up and take him with me or I find people I trust implicitly to help."

"Then I'll do that. Colleen?"

She looked straight into those ice-blue eyes and her heart began to pound fast. He was the most gorgeous, intimidating man she'd ever met. Not in the usual sense of the word. It wasn't that she thought he'd physically harm her, but something far different. He was the kind of man who could hurt her emotionally, and she was pretty sure that it wasn't just because he would take Toby. The smartest thing to do would be to run, to say no, and yet…

"You'll give me warning before you take him away?" she asked, trying to adjust to the sudden shift in plans.

She should be jumping at this, latching on to it. Dillon wanted to learn how to be a good father. That was a good thing, the best thing for Toby, and she would at least have a bit more time with the baby.

And with the man.

Colleen shoved that thought away. She hoped her face wasn't flaming. In the past, *her* past, well, a woman like her could easily look pathetic when she was attracted to a man, especially a man who was totally out of bounds.

"Will you let me stay?" he repeated. "Will you tutor me until I've got everything down pat and until Toby and I feel comfortable together?"

"You know I can't say no to that."

He smiled at her, and heat rushed through her. "Then say yes, Colleen."

She didn't even remember saying the word. She felt faint and sick and nervous, as if her body was not her own. But she must have said yes, because Dillon had gone outside and he was pulling a suitcase from his car.

A man was going to be staying with her here at the Applegate Ranch. She wondered what he would say when he discovered that all her employees were women.

CHAPTER TWO

MAYBE he should have stayed inside and read all that paperwork that Colleen had for him to pore over, but the enormity of what he was doing had finally hit, and Dillon needed a few minutes to regroup, so he stood on the porch leaning on the crooked railing as he looked out across the land. He'd spent a lifetime learning to control his emotions. Those lessons had served him well in business, and this past year with all that had happened, the merits of guarding his reactions had hit even harder.

But Colleen Applegate's passionate loyalty to his son had been unexpected. It had caught him off guard, which was most likely why he had made that uncharacteristically impetuous declaration that he wanted her to give him parenting lessons. He was already regretting that decision and yet, she was right. He didn't know a damn thing about caring for a baby and he wasn't about to let just anyone take over that task.

He swore beneath his breath. "What a mess."

The door opened behind him and when he turned to look at Colleen the expression on her face told him that she had, most likely, heard his last comment. Her chin was raised in defiance, and a trace of guilt slipped through Dillon. None of this, after all, was her fault.

"I apologize for the way that sounded."

All the defiance slipped away from her. "I doubt this was what you had anticipated when you thought about having children."

"I hadn't actually thought about it too much."

She studied him. "You didn't want a child?"

It hadn't been that so much. "I felt...unqualified. Still do. But he's here, and just because I hadn't anticipated him doesn't mean I don't want him. He's never going to feel as if his birth was a mistake, so don't even think that I'm heading down that path. I'm taking this job seriously."

"Job?"

"Dad."

Colleen gave a curt nod. "Okay, Dad. Let's get you settled. Then we'll get right to the father lessons."

Dillon saw now that she had a bundle of quilts in her arms. He reached out and started to take them from her but she shook her head.

"I can carry a few blankets," she said.

"I'm sure you can. You run a ranch. You tend to my son. You have employees. But just because you can doesn't mean you should. I'm not a guest and I'm sure having me living here is an imposition that wasn't remotely in your plans for this week. If you won't let me compensate you for Toby's care, at least let me pull my weight." *Take back some of the control you've lost these past months,* he told himself. He'd grown up having no input into his parents' decision to farm him out to disinterested keepers. As a child, his quest for affection had only resulted in a roller-coaster ride of brief bouts of interest followed by long periods of apathy from both his parents and the people they hired to keep him fed, occupied and out of their way.

So, when he'd grown up, he'd turned to something ever dependable: logic and control. The precise environment of engineering never failed him. The reliability of being able to predict and control outcomes, and the measured skills involved in running a company and commanding troops, had been a perfect fit…until the events of the last year had blindsided him.

That time was over. He was not a man given to highs and lows and he'd made a mistake choosing someone as volatile as Lisa. Somehow, he'd missed who and what she was, just as the soldier walking ahead of him hadn't seen that land mine that had taken his life and injured Dillon. But, from now on, Dillon was putting the lid back on his emotions and regaining control of his life in even the most basic ways. He tugged on the quilts.

To his surprise, Colleen didn't let go. "This visit wasn't in your plans, either, I'm sure. And just so you know, so that there won't be too many surprises, ranch life's difficult," she countered. To her credit, she didn't glance at his leg, though he knew that was at least part of what she was referring to.

Dillon had a feeling that Colleen was one of those surprises. Was the woman really worrying about the welfare of the man who'd come to take the baby she clearly coveted?

"I'll let you know if it gets to be too much."

A small smile lifted her lips. "Somehow I doubt you would admit any such thing. You're an infuriatingly determined man, Mr. Farraday, but all right." She turned over the quilts.

He smiled slightly at her tone, but he didn't apologize. "Just Dillon will do. If you'll show me where I'm staying while I'm here, I'll get settled so that we can get right down to that crash course in fatherhood."

She hesitated. And hesitated some more. "The bunkhouse is occupied."

"And you don't feel comfortable having a man in your house," he remembered.

She looked uneasy. "I know that seems silly when I'm

an independent woman who's been running a ranch for years, but—"

Dillon raised one hand to silence her. "You don't have to apologize or explain anything to me, Colleen. It doesn't sound silly. You're careful. That's good." Although he could tell from her expression that her concerns went deeper than simply being careful. Not his business. Nothing he needed to know about.

"Still, you're here to learn about taking care of Toby. You'll want to be near when he wakes up in the middle of the night. I have an enclosed back porch, and at this time of year you won't need heat. You won't have to worry about anyone intruding on you there. There's a door separating it from the house and a sleeper sofa that's...I'm sorry, I can't lie. It's *almost* comfortable."

Dillon wanted to smile, but she was clearly a bit embarrassed at her refusal to let him all the way inside her house. "I've been a soldier, Colleen. I've slept in the mud from time to time, and I'm used to less than comfortable circumstances, so I'm sure I'll be fine sleeping on the porch."

"Is he really staying?" a voice rang out. Dillon turned to see a big iron-haired woman making her way across the grass toward the house. "Gretchen said you called and told her that he was, but I didn't believe her. It's been a long time since we had a fine-looking man visiting the Applegate," the woman told Dillon.

Dillon glanced from a suddenly pink-faced Colleen to the older woman. Colleen raised her chin and drew herself up.

"Millie, this is Dillon Farraday. He's—"

"Toby's father," the woman said. "Yes, I know."

"Millie is my right-hand woman," Colleen explained.

"She means that I cook, I clean, I mend and I take care of Toby when she has other duties to tend to," the woman said. She shoved out one large hand. "I can handle all the jobs that a man can handle, too, but…I miss having a man about the place. It's been a long time since I heard a deep voice around here."

Dillon shook her strong, weathered hand. "I thought Colleen said that she had other workers. Ranch hands. I assumed—"

Colleen sighed. "Millie, go get them. They must be in from their chores by now, anyway."

Without another word, Millie whipped out a cell phone, punched a few keys and just said, "Yes, now."

Immediately, Dillon heard female voices in the distance. He looked up to see two twentysomething women exit a building that had to be the bunkhouse. They headed toward the house.

"Wow, Mil, he's gorgeous. In a kind of rugged way," Dillon heard coming through the phone before Colleen reached over, plucked the phone from Millie and clicked it shut.

"I could have done that much," Colleen told her right-hand woman.

Millie shrugged. "Made more sense than running all the way back to the bunkhouse."

"Dillon might have needed some time to prepare himself," Colleen said. She stepped in front of him as if to protect him when the duo drew closer. He countered and moved to her side.

"Gretchen and Julie, this is Mr. Farraday," Colleen said. "He'll be with us for at least a few days. I'm pretty sure he doesn't bite, so show him what he needs to know if he asks. All right?"

"Of course. Will he be eating with us?" one of them asked.

"I normally eat in the bunkhouse," Colleen explained to Dillon. "It's just easier for Millie if we're all in one place, and the bunkhouse kitchen is newer and roomier. But for now," she said, turning toward the women, "I think Dillon might prefer it at the house with Toby. They're just getting to know each other."

Disappointment registered on at least one of the faces.

Then the girls smiled and waved goodbye as they went back to the bunkhouse.

"I'll bring the food over soon," Millie said as she followed the girls.

Silence set in.

"I suppose you're wondering why I have only women working here."

He was. "I suppose you have your reasons and that they're none of my business. If you think I'm going to offer criticism, you're dead wrong. Some of the best soldiers I ever met were women and there are a number of fine female engineers working for my engineering firm. Besides, even though I don't know anything about ranching, your ranch looks as if it's in pretty good shape." In fact, the ranch looked significantly better than the house. Clearly, she was pumping her profits back into the business.

"Gretchen and Julie are young, they're strong, they're knowledgeable and they need this ranch to succeed as much as I do, so they put their all into it," Colleen said. "This is their home. They belong here."

And he didn't, Dillon knew. He and his shiny expensive car didn't belong here, but this was where he was going to begin again.

"Thank you for letting me stay and I'll tell the women thank-you when I see them again. I've already disrupted their routines by having you switch the meal. We don't have to do that."

She studied him carefully with those dark, serious eyes. "No, I think we do. Toby needs to get used to you being the one he focuses on. It will be easier for him if there aren't too many other distracting faces around at mealtimes. Not that he really eats meals exactly, but I make sure he's with us at the table. Being together at mealtime is important to a family."

He wouldn't know about that. His family had not been

anything like a real family. "Is this my first lesson?" he asked with a smile.

He had clearly caught her by surprise with that question, and Colleen's cheeks pinked up again. Some women looked less attractive when they were flustered, but not this woman. When she took a long, deep breath, drew herself up to her full, impressive height and opened her mouth slightly as if choosing her words carefully, there was something utterly fascinating about her. As if she was concentrating all of her being into choosing those words. A sliver of heat slipped through Dillon…which wouldn't do at all.

Colleen shook her head, her curls brushing her shoulders. "I'm afraid I get carried away sometimes. The girls—the women, I mean—have been working here a couple of years, and since Julie is only twenty and Gretchen is twenty-three, a full five years younger than me, I guess I've gotten too used to doing that prim schoolteacher thing. Bad habit. I didn't mean to lecture, so no, that wasn't your first lesson."

Prim schoolteacher? Dillon couldn't help thinking that with Colleen's generous curves, *prim* was the last word that came to mind.

A strange, small sound suddenly filled the air. Automatically Colleen and Dillon both glanced down at her baby monitor.

It was the first time Dillon had heard his child's voice. "He's crying," Dillon said with wonder.

"Yes. And *that's* going to be your first lesson." Colleen held the door open. "You're going to hold your son," she said as Dillon brushed past her. The combination of her low, husky voice and the prospect of finally meeting his child face-to-face nearly made Dillon's knees buckle.

He'd faced disasters in his life, business barons and scenes in battle he'd prefer to forget. He had been suited to what he'd face in business and in battle. He had been trained and at least partially prepared for them. Nothing, he thought, had prepared him for the responsibility of molding a life that was so young and fragile.

He really was going to be dependent on Colleen, this woman he found far too intriguing. Bad move. He didn't do intriguing anymore, so somehow he had to learn all she could teach him as quickly as possible. Once he and Toby were on their own, they could sort everything else out and forget that this woman had ever been a part of their lives.

Everything about Dillon was too big, Colleen thought as she led him back to Toby's room. He was tall, his shoulders were broad, his hands were big with long fingers, his legs were long and well-muscled. Even with the limp, he seemed powerful and strong and she felt small. She never, ever felt small. That had been her mother, her charming, petite, pretty and utterly helpless mother, who had not passed along her genes to gawky, awkward, big-boned Colleen.

All of her life she'd wanted to be small. And now? Now, with Dillon behind her, dwarfing her, she just felt vulnerable. More awkward and self-conscious than ever. As if she'd just now realized that she was a woman. And all because Dillon, with that warrior's body of his, was most definitely a man.

"This way," she said, feeling instantly stupid.

Dillon chuckled, and Colleen felt her neck growing warm. "You're right. I guess I didn't need to direct you. You've been in here before," she conceded.

"And then there's the crying," he said dryly.

She couldn't help herself then. She laughed, too. "Your son does have a good set of lungs."

"Does he...does he cry often?"

She stopped, turned, and nearly ended up right against

Dillon. Close, too close to that muscled chest. Colleen tipped her head up. She *never* tipped her head up to a man. She never got that close. "Babies cry." Her voice came out in a whisper, slightly harsh. She cleared her throat. "Toby probably cries less than most. He's a happy baby."

"I wasn't criticizing." Intense blue eyes stared into her own. She struggled for breath. "I just didn't know. I wouldn't even know what was normal for a baby. No experience."

Somehow she managed to nod, her head feeling oddly wobbly on her body. She needed to back away, to quit staring into those mesmerizing eyes. She was making a fool of herself. That was so not acceptable.

Colleen took a step backward away from Dillon. It wasn't far enough. She still felt locked in that blue gaze.

One more step.

He lowered his gaze slightly, turned down the intensity. "So, he's happy?"

Ah, back in safe territory. She managed a small smile as she turned back and began moving toward the room again. "Come see. He's especially cheerful and cuddly when he first wakes up. As long as he wakes up on his own timetable, that is."

She stepped through the doorway and Dillon came up beside her. Toby was on his stomach, and as soon as he saw Colleen his crying turned to a soulful whimpering. His gaze slipped over to Dillon, and a look of distress came over his face.

Dillon sucked in a visible breath. Colleen felt for him. A man's first meeting with his child should be a wondrous thing, not a sad one.

"He's scared of me."

"He hasn't seen many men, and you're a rather large one. You have a deeper voice. You might need to soften it and speak more quietly at first to keep from startling him."

Toby was visibly upset now.

"I've made him cry more. You should pick him up."

"Ordinarily I would," she agreed, "but right now we need to soothe him without upsetting him, and if I pick him up and then turn him over to you, he'll howl for sure."

"What should I do then? I don't want to hurt him or scare him more than he is."

Colleen didn't really know. She loved babies. She particularly loved *this* baby. Still, she ran on pure instinct most of the time the same way she did with her horses or other animals. She had always had terrible instincts where men were concerned; awful luck. She'd made very bad decisions or had others' bad choices thrust on her, but this was one decision she couldn't afford to muck up. Despite the fact that Dillon was going to take Toby away from her soon, she couldn't sacrifice the child in a lame attempt to make the man retreat.

"Stay close to me," she told Dillon. "Toby's used to me, and he's…well, he's very young. Maybe if he associates you with me, an extension of sorts, he'll accept you more quickly."

"Will that work?"

"Maybe."

She heard what sounded like a low curse and looked to her side.

"Sorry," he said. "I'll have to train myself not to do that. I've been living the life of a soldier too long."

Colleen nodded. She couldn't begin to imagine what his life had been like, what kind of hell he had been living in when his leg had been damaged so badly. And she didn't want to. She was doing all this for Toby, she told herself. Not for Dillon.

But as she moved toward the crib, she slowed enough so that Dillon could stay with her without lurching too much. Reaching the crib, she turned to Dillon. "I'm going to soothe him a bit. Just stay close, speak quietly and don't make any sudden movements."

Dillon didn't answer. His gaze was locked on his child.

She reached down and stroked her thumb across Toby's cheeks, smoothing away the tears that were rolling down his tiny face. "It's all right, sweetheart," she said. "This is your daddy. He just wants to meet you."

Quietly, quietly, she spoke, she caressed, she slowly felt Toby begin to relax. He stopped crying.

"All right, you touch him now," she told Dillon. "Gently."

And suddenly she was very aware of how close she and Dillon were standing. His warmth was up against her. She breathed in, and the scent of his aftershave filled her senses, pungent and male and…her hand trembled slightly.

Dillon reached out and placed his big hand next to hers. Toby was small, and Dillon's thumb brushed against her fingers.

Colleen felt suddenly dizzy. Every nerve ending in her body snapped to attention. She swallowed.

"I'm going to let go now," she whispered, turning to her left. She looked up and found her lips only a breath away from Dillon's.

Don't feel. Don't even dare to think of him as anyone who could ever be important to you, she ordered herself. Men had brought her nothing but pain. Her father who had taken risks and had died suddenly, breaking her heart. Her stepfather and stepbrother who had verbally abused and taunted her, making her life a misery. The man who had pretended to love her, but had really loved her land and had left her for a wealthier woman.

She'd been caught by surprise when each of those relationships had bitten her, but with Dillon, she already knew he was too great a risk. Allowing herself to feel anything, even simple lust, was just setting herself up for disaster. She couldn't face that kind of crippling disappointment again.

Slowly, Colleen forced herself to breathe, to enforce control over her reactions.

She tried a simple, shaky smile.

"I'm ready," Dillon said.

Colleen blinked, then realized that he was referring to flying solo with Toby.

She lifted her hand off the baby's warm back. When she glanced down, he was staring at her and Dillon with those big blue solemn eyes. Quietly considering the situation.

The baby shifted his attention to Dillon.

His lower lip quivered. He let out a cry.

"Oh, Toby," she said, then automatically turned to Dillon to explain that things would get better soon.

But Dillon wasn't paying attention. He automatically reached down and lifted the little bundle into his arms, curving Toby into his big body.

"I've got you, slugger," he said. "And I won't ever hurt you. I won't let you down or leave you. I won't let anyone harm you. Ever." His words were a low, quiet whisper. He stared into those blue eyes, cupping the baby close. "You're mine, Toby," he said. "We're father and son. We're going to be buddies and make our own little world, just you and me."

On and on he went, that deep, soothing baritone whispering promises, bits of nothing. It didn't matter, because the baby was reacting to the secure hold Dillon had on him and the hypnotic tone of his voice. Slowly, Toby stilled, quieted.

"Are we good, buddy?" Dillon asked.

As if he understood the question, Toby let out a watery coo.

Dillon looked over the baby's head straight into Colleen's eyes. His smile was brilliant, gorgeous and oh so sexy. "You're one heck of a teacher, Colleen," he said.

The smile went right through her, and her body reacted as if she were on a thrill ride. Out of control, her heart flipped right up into her throat, sending pleasure through her even though she knew there would eventually be a sudden drop that

would bang her about. A man who could so easily produce a
reaction like that must have been one heck of a commander,
one heck of a CEO, one very talented…

The word *lover* came to mind, but she blanked it out of her
mind. That smile of his, that darn smile…

I am in so much trouble, she thought. On so many levels.

CHAPTER THREE

DILLON stepped out on the porch and found Colleen trying to open up a sleeper sofa that looked as if it hadn't been used during the past century. The mechanical parts were putting up a good fight as Colleen tugged.

"I don't mean to insult you," Dillon said. "Given the fact that you run a ranch, you're clearly capable and probably strong, too, but…"

He reached down and touched Colleen's hand. Her skin was softer than he would have expected from a woman who did physical labor. Caught off guard, his body immediately reacted to that softness, that warmth, this woman. The fact that they were standing next to what was going to be his bed didn't help the situation any. Irritated with himself, Dillon put the brakes on his reaction to the best of his ability.

Colleen must have had her mind elsewhere, because as his words faded away and as he moved up beside her, she let out a tiny gasp and let go of the metal handle, backing up a step. Good. He didn't want to continue to be that aware of her. He definitely didn't need to be thinking erotic thoughts about her.

"I didn't mean to startle you," he said, as he gave a tug on the handle and the bed pulled partway out.

"You're not supposed to be doing that," she said.

He looked over his shoulder at her as he lowered the legs of the bed to the ground. "Why?" he asked, turning to face her.

She hesitated. He knew that she was thinking of his cane and his injury. He hated that.

"You're…you're a guest," she said.

"I'm an intruder."

"That would only be true if I hadn't agreed for you to stay, but I did. I'm totally in control of the situation."

He smiled at that.

"What?"

"I don't think either of us is in control of the situation. You had a baby dumped on you out of the blue. I had a wife who divorced me, then kept my child from me. Now you've, unexpectedly, been asked to house a man when it's obvious that that's not something you and your employees are used to."

A small smile lifted her lips.

"What?" he asked.

"That was so polite the way you put that, the fact that we're not used to having men around. As you could see from some of the women's reactions, it's not that we dislike men. At least not all men. We've just…all of us have had bad experiences, so we're taking a break. Some for the short term and some for forever. Julie's on the road to being engaged, so her break's over and she'll most likely be leaving soon. But for the most part, yes, this place has become a bit of a haven for women who need to drop out of the bride game."

"I've never heard it called that."

"Me either. I just made it up. But it's true that even in this century, most women grow up thinking they'll probably eventually get married."

"You?"

Her smile seemed to freeze. "I had a little more unconventional upbringing. I lost my father early, my stepfather and stepbrother were, to put it nicely, bullies without souls and my failed engagement…well, let's just say that I have major trust issues and I won't ever be a bride. I don't want to be. So, I guess you were right, after all. I do steer clear of men."

"Except for Toby."

"He's a baby."

"He won't always be a baby."

"I know." She sounded sad.

"You don't want him to grow up?"

"Of course I do. I just—I won't…he's yours, Dillon. Not mine."

She wouldn't see him grow up.

"I'm sorry about that." And he was. Genuinely. She cared about Toby, and already Dillon was inclined to think favorably of anyone who liked his child.

"It's not your fault," she told him. "You'll take him away when you go, and if I were in your shoes…if he were mine, nothing would stop me from taking him home and claiming him. You shouldn't even think about apologizing for that, just as I'm not going to apologize about the fact that I'll miss him when he's gone."

"Good. I prefer honesty." He'd had too little of that with Lisa. Or maybe he'd been the one lying, thinking they were a match when they were no more suited than he and Colleen Applegate were.

She nodded. "Well then, the honest truth is that this bed is probably *not* almost comfortable as I implied earlier. Looking at it now, I'd say you're going to have a very restless night."

He shrugged. His comfort was the least of his worries these days. "I assume you'll want to lock the door, but will you call me if you need me in the night?"

For a second those dark eyes looked startled and sensually aware. That wouldn't do. Not when he was already too aware of her as a woman. His concentration from here on out had to be on Toby. Unlike his parents, he would put his child first. He would actually care. His choices would be made carefully, logically. No whisking women in and out of his life. No risking Toby getting attached to someone who was temporary. In fact, no more risking making the kind of mistakes he'd made with Lisa. Besides, Colleen definitely wasn't the kind of woman who would welcome a drive-by fling. Apparently she wouldn't welcome any kind of fling. A good thing.

"I won't need to call you. I've been handling things for three months," she argued.

"Yes. But I'm here now."

For several seconds they stood there, toe-to-toe. It was obvious that she didn't want to give up her control. Maybe it was because of those soulless men she'd known. No matter. He sympathized but he couldn't compromise with his son.

"I'll call you if there's an emergency," she said.

Which wasn't exactly the same thing, but it would do. He and Colleen were going to be tangling with each other for the entire time he was here, Dillon thought.

It should have made him angry. Instead he was intrigued. *Watch it,* he told himself. *This woman is fire.*

Unfortunately, he seemed to be attracted to fire, because when she turned to leave he had an insane urge to call her back.

Dillon lay on the sleeper sofa the next morning and scrubbed one hand through his hair. He was tense and uneasy in more ways than one and none of them had much to do with the bumpy metal frame of the sleeper sofa biting into his back.

No, sleeping on Colleen's porch last night, he had discovered that the walls of the house were thin. There might be a door separating him from the building, but with the porch only covered by a screen, he'd been privy to a view of the windows.

Even with the extremely faint and undefined shadow showing through on her light-dimming window shade, he'd been able to tell that Colleen's bedroom was just off to his left. He'd heard her humming and had been unable to think of anything except for the fact that she was getting ready for bed.

Heat had seared him as he'd tried to force himself to think about the business matters he needed to tend to when he had time tomorrow.

And when he'd awakened moments ago, his first instinct had been to look toward Colleen's window. His first thought had been to wonder if she realized how her silhouette had fueled his fantasies.

Don't be an idiot, he told himself. The woman had a ranch to run, a baby to take care of, employees to supervise and a clueless man to train as a father. She had too many things on her plate to add seduction to the list. Besides, there wasn't a coy bone in her body that he could tell, and with her ranch located off the beaten path, no one would, under ordinary circumstances, ever see anything at all. If she even thought about the possibility that he'd caught a glimpse of her body's outline on the shade, he knew she'd be appalled. She was already uneasy about him being in the house. Those pretty caramel eyes of hers might spark amber when she looked at him, but if not for Toby, she would never have let him into her house at all. This ranch was clearly a hideout for wounded women and Colleen's reasons for mistrusting men seemed to go deep.

He understood her need to steer clear of unwise entanglements. Caring for Toby, making sure he had free and clear custody of Toby and preserving his business for Toby was all Dillon could concern himself with from now on.

With that admission, he shoved himself up off the couch, slipped on his jeans, got up and knocked on the door.

When Colleen opened it, she was wearing a white fluffy

bathrobe that had seen better days but still reminded him that she had only recently been lying in bed. Her hair was slightly tousled as if some man had plunged his fingers into all those untamed curls. With that image, Dillon's good intentions took a nosedive. Somehow he forced a good-morning smile to his lips.

She smiled back, even though he noticed that her hands were fidgeting with her belt.

"Where's Toby?" he asked, trying to get his mind back on track.

"He's a very early riser, so he's already been up for a while and had his breakfast."

Dillon frowned. "I should be doing that. Feeding him, I mean. I'll have to get up earlier. I apologize."

She wrinkled her nose. "Don't apologize. It's your first full day of daddyhood. Besides, I love being the one to give him his first meal of the day. He's so alert and fun to watch. Not that I won't willingly turn the task over to you. You have the right, and yes, you need to get used to his hours, but for today, it's fine. Millie's reading to him."

Dillon lifted a brow. "Isn't he a little young for books?"

She laughed, the sound deep and husky and delicious. "You say that as if he's already graduated to sneaking the underwear sections of the Sunday ads. Babies like to be cuddled, and while they're being cuddled, they especially like listening to you and feeling your voice as it rumbles up through your body. Add in the bright colors of a picture book and you've got a winning activity. Plus, Millie loves reading to him as much as I do. She has children but they're all grown and none of them want to have kids."

An odd, sad sensation slipped through Dillon. "I'm lucky that you and Millie were the ones to take him in. Not every woman would have cared for him the way the two of you have." Including, apparently, Toby's mother.

"I think most people, when faced with a child in need, grow to love that child at least a little."

"That hasn't been my experience."

She blinked, and he realized that he had let something slip that he had never shared, because he wasn't referring only to Lisa's treatment of Toby but his own childhood experiences. Bad move. It was the kind of remark that seemed to require an explanation, but he wasn't prepared to share more than he had already offered, so he merely shook his head, dismissing his hasty words.

Colleen looked troubled but she merely nodded. "You'll probably want to spend as much time as possible with Toby today. I think just being with him and letting him get used to you will be enough for one day. You're the first male in his life, so after you've had breakfast and taken a shower or whatever else you need to do, I'll let Millie know that you're on dad duty until nap time. She'll step in if he needs his diaper changed. Later today will be soon enough to tackle the big stuff."

"You think I can't handle it yet?"

Her lips curved up in an entrancing smile. "You told me you'd slept in the mud, so I'm sure you can handle a little mess. I'm just not sure if Toby's ready to be traumatized by a crooked diaper yet."

Dillon couldn't help smiling back at her. "Already criticizing my skills, Colleen?"

"Everyone needs practice. Have fun." With that, she turned toward the back of the house. When she came back a few minutes later, Dillon was finishing his breakfast. He looked up.

Colleen was wearing blue jeans that weren't exceptionally tight, but that emphasized the length of her legs and the curve of her hips. The cherry-red shirt tucked into the jeans fit where a shirt should fit a woman. She was wearing some sort of green polished glass on a black satin cord around her neck, and he remembered seeing it yesterday, too. In fact, there seemed to be a lot of brightly colored polished glass in the house. Sun catchers and wind chimes hung here and there, the golds and reds and blues and greens turned warm by the light.

"I have to go into town for supplies," she said, "but I'll stop in before I head out onto the range again. Toby will go down in an hour or so. Then he'll take another nap this afternoon, so if you have other things to do, that would be a good time to see to them."

"Don't worry about me. I'll figure it out or I'll ask Millie. Toby and I will be great. Everything's fine." Except for the fact that he had—again—noticed too many things about Colleen that he found attractive. What was wrong with him? He had no intention of getting into a long-term relationship with a woman again, so he needed to get this "problem" under control.

His phone rang, and Colleen gave him a wave as she headed for the door. Dillon looked down and wanted to swear. The call was from Lisa. She hadn't called him since she'd asked for a divorce and even then she hadn't called. He'd gotten the message in an e-mail. So why was she calling now?

Anger filled him. Lisa was one of those people who changed their minds about what to wear ten times and then spent all night worrying that they had made the wrong choice. Had she heard that he was coming to Montana to get Toby? How would she react to that? Would she change her mind and decide that *she* wanted the baby now?

By the time he'd decided that there was no point in speculating about anything at all about his ex-wife and never had been, the phone stopped ringing.

Ten seconds later, the phone in Colleen's house began to ring. She had already stepped onto the porch and was just closing the door, but she turned around, came back inside and looked at Dillon. Then she walked toward the phone and glanced at the number registered there.

Slowly, she raised her chin and looked into Dillon's eyes. "It's her," she said. She didn't have to say more.

"I realize that this is your house, but I just think you should know right now," he said, "that I'm not letting her near Toby."

Colleen frowned, those pretty brows drawing together. "You shouldn't drag your child into a battle between you and your ex-wife." Somehow, the way she said that made him think she had some experience of such things.

Slowly, Dillon shook his head. He walked over to her and stared down into her troubled eyes, taking her hands in his own. "This isn't about Lisa ending our marriage. We were people whose goals and interests were too different for us to stay married, and I should have realized that before I proposed. We weren't a logical fit, but I asked her to marry me, anyway, so I'll take my share of the blame for the failure of the marriage.

"But there's something else I can't forgive. She walked away from Toby when he had barely entered the world. She left him and didn't seem to care what became of him. It couldn't have been money. I gave her money in the settlement. She just didn't want him. She didn't even mention that he was on the way, so I'm not letting her change her mind and try to take him from me now. Especially not when she could change her mind again and do a one-eighty a few days later. What's more, I'm not apologizing even though I know she's someone from your past, so don't ask me to."

"You're forgetting that since I've known her longer, I may know even more of how she operates," Colleen said. "Lisa used to go through men like sticks of gum that lost their flavor quickly. The only time she came back to a guy the second time was when she thought he had something to offer her that she had overlooked the first time around." She kept her chin high as she stared directly into his eyes and dropped this nugget into the conversation.

"Yes, that was her on my cell phone," he told her, answering the question she hadn't asked. "So, I'm one of those men she's contacted a second time. What do you think she's overlooked that she's come back for? Do you think she's developed an urge to raise a baby?"

Colleen's smile grew taut. "I'll help you," she said.

"Why?"

She hesitated, then let out a deep, audible breath. "I suppose I have lots of reasons and some of them aren't exactly admirable, but the main one is that Toby is a sweet, adorable little boy and…Dillon, he's just a baby. A total innocent. No one should get to dump him and then turn around and pretend it never happened. When she left here, she didn't even leave any way for me to get in touch with her in case something happened to him. It was…I don't know…as if she didn't even care."

He digested that bit of information, and indignation for the child in the other room seared his soul. Toby wasn't old enough to know his mother had abandoned him at birth but someday he *would* be old enough to realize the truth, and that would hurt him. Dillon wanted to swear, but he was a guest here and he needed to behave.

"Are you going to call her back?" Colleen asked.

"No. Sooner or later I'll have to talk to her, but not today. I have other calls to make while Toby's sleeping. Things to do with my firm."

Colleen looked slightly uncomfortable. She fidgeted with her belt buckle. "I'm sure you have lots of things to do, business you need to get back to, and during the night, it occurred to me…"

He waited.

"Babies sleep a lot. There's a lot of downtime," she said. "And you're a man who's used to being busy."

Dillon raised a brow. "How did you reach that conclusion?"

"You were a soldier who led other soldiers. You built structures and started running a company when you were barely out of college and still going to grad school. That's all in your bio on the Farraday Engineering Web site. In fact, I think one of the articles said something about how you specialized in multitasking, but ranch life moves at a slower pace. That could be a problem. You might get bored here really fast."

"Meaning I might want to leave here after only a few days."

"Yes."

"And take my son with me."

Her eyes looked stricken. "Yes."

"Maybe we should set a specific date. I do need to make sure that I know what I'm doing as a father, and I'm more than grateful that you've agreed to help me with that, but I can't stay here too long. Being an absentee owner of a business has drawbacks, and while I did my best to take charge when I was bedridden, now that I'm mobile, it's past time for me to take back the helm of the firm. If I name a time frame, at least you'll know when the end is coming. Will that be best?"

Slowly she nodded.

"Three weeks?" he asked.

"That sounds good." But her voice was a bit tight. Obviously, letting go of Toby would be difficult for her. "Now," she continued, "is there anything you need while I'm in town? Something that will make the hours when Toby's napping pass more quickly? Books? Newspapers?"

He laughed. "Pamper the rich, bored male, you mean? Eventually there will be things I'll need, but I'm not sure what will be on the list and when I know, I'll have everything delivered."

She looked startled. "That won't be necessary. I have a pickup truck."

"Yes, but I don't think a load of lumber and roofing shingles will fit in your truck."

"Lumber and shingles? I don't understand."

Dillon smiled. "I'm more than just a rich man, Colleen. I'm an engineer. I know how to build things and build them right. I can fix your porch."

She blushed prettily. "I'm afraid I can't afford it right now."

"I can."

"But you're a—"

He put his finger over her lips to stop her from saying *guest*.

"You're helping me. Let me help *you*. I'm going to do this," he said. "And a few other things, starting with replacing that sleeper sofa."

Now, he had her attention. She crossed her arms over chest, which was supposed to make her look stern, he was sure, but only served to draw his attention to her pretty breasts. "I can't let you do that much," she said.

"You can't stop me, Colleen. I'm a man on a mission. Now go do whatever you need to do."

And stop looking so adorable, he thought as she walked away.

CHAPTER FOUR

How am I going to survive this man? Colleen thought as she drove toward town. He had only been here less than a day and already he seemed to fill up her house.

What's more, when she got to town she found that word of Dillon's arrival had already spread. "Buying a lot of food, are you? Stocking up?" Alma Anderson asked at the grocery store. "Yeah, a man will eat you out of house and home, especially if he's a big man. *Is* he a big man? Is he staying long?"

Colleen pasted on a smile that didn't say anything but seemed to satisfy Alma.

"Wow, I can't remember the last time I associated the word *man* with you, Colleen," Barb Seltzer added. She was getting ready to expound on that and probably ask more questions when Colleen cut in.

"Sorry, gotta run, ladies. Business to tend to."

But it was the same everywhere she went. The town had never had anyone rich in their midst, at least not anyone who was planning to stay more than a day or two. "I saw that car when he drove through town yesterday," Bill Winters said with a long, low whistle. "A man would do a lot for a sleek, fast car like that. A brand-new Ferrari? Pricey. I never thought to see one in Bright Creek. So…that guy at the house, this Dillon Farraday, Lisa's man, I guess he's pretty used to having the best, eh?"

"Um," Colleen muttered, loading the rest of her supplies into the truck.

"Of course he's used to the best," Harve Enson said. "He married Lisa, didn't he? And Lisa was the best we had to offer. Certainly the prettiest I always thought. Lisa was the Lupine Festival queen, wasn't she? And the homecoming queen? She was the lead in all those plays and had the most boyfriends before she ran off to Chicago to go to college. You went out with her, didn't you, Rob?" he asked his son, who had just come out of the hardware store next door.

"Who?" Rob asked.

"Lisa Breckinridge."

"I went out with her once, before she started dating that college guy three years older. Why do you want to know?"

"Her ex-husband is staying with Colleen."

Rob raised his eyebrows and looked at Colleen as if Harve had just announced that she was really from an alien planet. "I don't get it. Why is he doing that?"

"He's come for his baby, Rob, not for me," she said between gritted teeth. It was patently obvious that Rob couldn't think of any reason a good-looking man would be visiting her.

"I didn't mean that in a bad way," Rob mumbled, and to his credit, he blushed and looked uncomfortable. "I just…I mean…"

"Forget it, Rob," she said, letting him off the hook.

"The point is," Harve continued, "the man is used to champagne." Harve suddenly looked at what Colleen was doing.

"Colleen, I don't know why you're buying so much stuff. He's come for his kid and how long will that take? A man like that won't want to stay in a little do-nothing town like Bright

Creek. For sure he won't want to stick around long on a little horse ranch. No disrespect, Colleen," he said. "You're the best horsewoman around and you rent out the best fishing pond of anyone, but unless this guy's a fisherman, there's not much of what he's used to at your place."

Which seemed to be the general consensus and was, in fact, the truth, so Colleen shouldn't let it sting so much.

"We'll see," Colleen said. "He's staying for three weeks, so I'd appreciate it if you'd all stop gossiping about him. If we don't act like do-nothings and gossips, he won't think that's what we are." Hastily, she threw the rest of her things in the truck and headed for the driver's side door.

"Three weeks? What's he going to do?"

She kept moving. She was *so* not going to bring Toby further into this than she already had. Dillon probably didn't want to broadcast the news that he had asked her to give him lessons in something most people considered basic knowledge. Announcing that might embarrass him, which might result in him leaving and taking Toby away from her immediately.

Besides, while everyone already knew that Toby was Lisa's son and that she had been married to Dillon, they also knew Dillon had been away at war last year. And so far no one had openly questioned the paternity of Lisa's child. *At least not in my presence,* Colleen thought. Maybe because Lisa apparently still held legend status here despite leaving her baby with Colleen. Maybe they assumed—or hoped—Lisa had a good reason for deserting him. So, if it protected Dillon and Toby, Colleen could live with the lie that Lisa was the best of Bright Creek. That meant not even venturing near the topic of Toby, Dillon and Lisa any more than she had to.

"He says he's going to fix things on the ranch."

Harve and Bill exchanged looks. "By himself? Colleen,

hon, did you explain to him how long that place has been falling down around your ears?"

No, she had not. She still had some pride, and the beginning of the demise of the ranch house went back to the worst time of her life, when her mother had remarried and brought darkness to their lives. It was not something she wanted to drop into a conversation with Dillon.

"Dillon says he can do it," she said. But as she started to open the door, she heard words that she wished she hadn't.

"A one-man reclamation team raising those old buildings from the dead? This I have to see. Besides, if he's going to be here for a while, I sure would like to take a ride in that car."

Harve told Rob what Dillon had been driving, and Rob let out a low whistle. "Man, that's sweet."

"Yeah, I wonder if he'll let us inside it."

"I don't think—" she began. But Harve and Bill were already walking away, lost in their plans. And even Rob, who was still standing on the sidewalk, had a speculative gleam in his eyes.

Uh-oh, Colleen thought as she got in the truck and drove away. If one person came, more would follow. Colleen had a feeling that Dillon hadn't counted on having an audience gawking while she instructed him. And as the woman who had uttered the words that were surely the start to the Bright Creek equivalent of the Gold Rush, it was up to her to head off the townspeople and divert their attention from Dillon. The man needed to learn to change diapers, not give test drives of his car.

He's not going to thank me for this, she thought.

The sight that met Colleen's eyes when she drove up to the house made her heart flip around and her breath catch in her throat. Dillon stood next to her porch, which was already looking sturdier. He was shirtless, a hammer was snagged in the back belt loop of his jeans and he was holding Toby up against his naked chest. He was, in short, gorgeous. A man feast for a woman's eyes, the best the male species had to offer visually. A lot of bests in Dillon's world, Colleen thought. His car. His ex-wife.

Darn it! For half a second, Harve's words about Lisa being the best slipped in before Colleen hastily tromped that sucker of a thought down. As a woman who had been hurt too much and who wasn't most men's idea of perfect femininity, she might not want to enter into the bride game, but she still liked to look, and no way was she going to let thoughts of Lisa spoil this brief, perfect moment.

Dillon looked up and smiled, those ice-blue eyes focused on her. "Welcome back," he said.

She couldn't help smiling at him even though she knew it wasn't smart to make these exchanges a habit. They left her too warm and yearning for things she could never have.

"This isn't finished," he said, indicating the porch that certainly already looked much straighter than it had. "Might take a few days. Until then, you'll need to use the side door."

Colleen nodded slowly. She wasn't sure where to look. His direct blue gaze was compelling. His bare chest made her feel even warmer than she should on such a warm day. The fact that she wanted to step closer made her feel as if she really should take a step back. In the end, her dilemma was solved when Toby began to babble and buck and hold out his arms to her.

"Little traitor," Dillon said affectionately, winking at his son, and just like that he lifted Toby, dropped a kiss on the top of his silky baby hair and turned him so that the baby could see Colleen better. "Don't worry, big guy. She'll have some time for you, I'm sure. See there, I told you she'd be back."

Toby's response was to blow a bubble and wave his arms around.

But entranced as she was with the child she loved, it was

the man's easy manner with him that held her attention. Dillon had never had a child. Most men would be at least a little tentative at first. The new fathers she'd met always were. But not Dillon. Toby looked totally right and comfortable held against his daddy's big body.

Big, half-naked body, Colleen thought, then immediately wished she could keep a lid on her thoughts.

"I need to put a shirt on now that I'm done for the day," he said as if he'd read her mind. He looked down at Toby, then at Colleen, a question in his eyes. "Not that I'm abdicating my paternal responsibilities or anything, mind you, or that I'm foisting him off on you, but…"

"Here," she said with a smile and reached out to take Toby from him. "As if I'd complain. He's a treasure. Right?" she asked the baby, who promptly crowed and smiled and stuffed his fist in his mouth.

"Nothing like a compliment from a lady, is there, Toby?" Dillon asked as he snagged his shirt from the railing and slipped it over his shoulders. "Did you get everything you needed?"

"Yes, but I need to talk to you about something."

"Not a problem. Why don't you show me a bit of the ranch? I'll get a hat for the big guy here."

"I'm impressed. Most men wouldn't have thought of the fact that a baby is more sensitive to the sun."

"Yes, well, don't give me too much credit. Millie's the one who reminded me. I could only bring him outside to sit with me if I promised to stay in the shade."

"But you learned quickly."

He laughed. "You should teach school. You're good at giving pats on the back for small accomplishments."

"School? You must have been talking to someone. It's no secret around here that I've wanted to start a ranch camp for girls for several years. I'd especially like to be able to give at-risk girls from the city who've never been near a ranch the chance to see how empowering this life can be."

"Why don't you do it?"

She shrugged. "Money. A proper building for them to sleep in. Maybe a fear that I might not be good at it."

"Never know until you try, will you? Of course, that's easy for me to say, but it looks as if you've already made a start with Gretchen and Julie. Millie told me that their father was an abuser and you were aware of that when they came to work for you."

"Yes, but they *do* work here. And they'd grown up on a ranch. I didn't have to teach them anything or expose them to a lifestyle they'd never lived. All I did was give them a job."

"Is that all?" he asked, a teasing tone in his voice. "Just a job where they don't have to live in fear. Millie told me that you also gave *her* a place to stay when her husband died and left her with tons of debt."

"Millie makes more of things than actually exist. Besides, the women are my friends. They give as much as they get, so even if their situation helped spawn the idea for the ranch camp, it's nothing like bringing girls here who've never even seen a horse and trying to teach them some basic skills. It's not the same as being in a situation where I might actually harm someone if I do or say the wrong thing. With Julie and Gretchen, there was nothing I needed to teach them about raising, riding or caring for horses."

"Just horses? I thought you were a cattle ranch."

"No. When my mother, stepfather and stepbrother died in a small plane crash while I was at a rodeo, and the ranch passed to me, I sold the cattle and some of the land to pay bills. We're a small horse ranch with a number of sidelines. We have an orchard, we open our section of the creek to fly fisherman, Gretchen and Julie make and sell flies and Millie has a small bread-making business. Basically, if we have the time and know-how and we can make money off of it, we try it."

While they were talking, they made their way to a pasture where horses were grazing. One of them, a white one, whinnied and slowly ambled over to the fence.

"Hey, Mr. Peepers." Colleen shifted the baby to her side to keep him away from the horse and stroked the aging animal. "He's a sweetheart. Mr. Peepers and I did some fine barrel racing together."

"So, you're a cowgirl. A rodeo queen."

"I *am* a cowgirl, a horsewoman. These are my babies." Instantly, she wished she could call back the last comment. Already Dillon suspected the truth: that she couldn't have children and that it broke her heart. She'd seen it in his eyes when they'd discussed her desire for babies yesterday. And she didn't want him feeling sorry for her. There were enough people in town who already did that and always had. It set her apart and made her too different. It created barriers she'd never understood how to breach. She needed to turn the conversation in a different direction, so she might as well discuss what she'd brought him out here to say. "I love my life, Dillon, and my world here. I've made it all myself, and I'm responsible for whatever happens here. So, I have to tell you, I might have done something wrong and made a mistake when I went into town. One that will affect you."

She explained about Bill and Harve and Rob and the car. "I should have made them understand. Argued more. Made it clear that you weren't here to give tours of your Ferrari."

"Don't worry about it."

"No. I was the one who made the mistake. I want you to know that I won't let them come on my land to pester you."

"They're your neighbors."

"Doesn't matter. They're just being nosy. That's not right."

He turned her around and placed his hands on her shoulders, the baby between them. Her entire body felt as if it might melt at his touch. "When I leave here, you have to live with your friends and neighbors. It's only a car. I don't mind giving a test drive to a couple of your neighbors. Seriously not an issue with me."

She was still unconvinced. "They might ask a lot of gossipy questions about Toby and Lisa."

"Then I just won't answer. Do you always feel this responsible about everything that happens here?" he asked.

"No. Yes. I guess I feel I have to. This ranch is my whole world. It's what makes me who I am, and these people…the women…if *I* fail, they lose their livelihoods when they've all already had to face too many bad things in their lives."

"But it's me you're trying to protect this time."

She shrugged. "Maybe you could use a sanctuary for a few weeks, too. Just because you're rich doesn't mean you've been exempted from the tough stuff. It couldn't have been easy marrying Lisa and losing her. Or going to war. Or being wounded."

Toby had fallen asleep and was listing to one side in her arms. Without a word and with seemingly little effort, Dillon took him and tucked him against his shoulder. Then he reached out and slid one palm along Colleen's jaw.

He had a magic touch. She wanted to lean right into his palm, step up against his body. Instead, she forced herself to simply look into his eyes.

"I doubt that divorce is ever easy for anyone, but I've had a long time to think about it, and I think my marriage was doomed from the start. I can't even really blame Lisa. She has that princess aura, and I chose her thinking she would be a good wife for a businessman the way other men choose a suit off the rack. But she wanted someone more exciting than I was, someone more willing to make the rounds of the social circuit and less of a workaholic and I should have realized that from the start. When I got called back into service and went overseas, she was livid about the fact that I didn't fight my tour of duty. As for the rest…no, none of that was easy, but still easier than a lot of other people who went to war have had. From that perspective, I can't complain."

"Are you just being nice, trying to make me feel better and forget that I messed up? Because I *did* mention the car and your work on the ranch. Now Harve Enson thinks you're some foolish guy who's easy prey and he's going to stalk you just because he's bored and has nothing to do with his time."

He stared down into her eyes, his own that unsettling blue. "If I really wanted you to forget something, I'd try a more drastic approach."

"What?"

He shifted the baby and leaned into her, sweeping his arm around her waist. "I'm not easy prey," he whispered when his lips were just a breath away from hers. "What I am is curious. Maybe even a bit fascinated."

He touched his mouth to hers and his touch was so…hot, so…she didn't know what. It was like nothing she had ever felt before. Like jumping your horse over a barrier so high that you weren't sure you could land safely. Fear and elation and excitement all mixed together. And when it was over, there was definitely an insane desire to do that dangerous thing all over again, she thought as he pulled away, leaving her lips aching.

"That was…what was that about?" she asked.

"It was probably about following through on a bad idea even though you have an incredibly delicious mouth, Colleen."

Her lips were still burning. Her body was still aching. Now she knew what kissing him was like and what she'd been missing and would never have. Darn it, she'd have been better off not knowing that.

"We shouldn't do that again," she whispered.

"You're probably right. I seem to have bad luck with the women of Bright Creek. Probably best to keep my distance."

And just like that, she remembered one more reason why she had to stay smart about Dillon. He was temporary. He would leave her in the dust. He had never been for her and never would be. And thinking of him was only going to take her mind off her own concerns and very real goals of keeping the ranch running and saving money for the ranch camp.

"Let's go get the baby out of the sun and then later today, after I'm done with my work, I'll give you some more lessons," she said. "Some basic stuff."

"Basic. All right. I can handle that."

Hours later, Colleen was struggling to keep a straight face as Dillon stared down at his son and then looked at the diaper he held in his hand.

"An interesting contraption," he told his son.

Toby stared at him with those huge blue eyes and jabbered something unintelligible.

"The tabs go in the back and fasten in the front," Colleen said helpfully.

"Of course they do. Toby just told me so. Didn't you, buddy?"

Toby just stared.

"Oh sure, go quiet on me *now*," Dillon said. "Just when I'm looking for a little support here." He smiled, and Toby responded to his daddy's smile, giving a delighted little squeal.

"All right, then. Let's get this on you." Dillon lifted Toby's tiny bottom and slid the diaper under him. He brought the front of the diaper up and looked at the left of the diaper and then the right. He brought the sides of his hand up and sighted along it.

"The tabs…" Colleen began.

"I know. In the back, fasten in the front," Dillon repeated.

"Then what are you doing?" she asked gently.

"I'm measuring."

Colleen couldn't keep from chuckling. "Dillon, it's a diaper, not an engineering project."

Dillon gave her a patient, measured look. "Toby, she doesn't understand that we are men, and we have our own way of doing things."

"What she understands is that if you don't fasten that diaper on soon, Toby is going to respond to all this fresh air, and we'll have a lot of cleaning up to do," she said, raising a brow.

Dillon gave her a wry grin. "Have I mentioned what a wise woman Colleen is, scout?" he asked his son. "Of course, you already knew that. Let's get you diapered up."

When he was done, the diaper was almost perfectly straight, but not quite. He eyed it with a frown.

"Don't be so hard on yourself," she said. "You did great, and it's going to get easier…until he learns to crawl and wriggle away," she teased.

Dillon laughed. He scooped his son up into his arms. "I can hardly wait." Then, his expression grew serious. "Thank you for helping me, Colleen. You're a good teacher."

"I didn't do anything."

"Yes. You did. He's happy. That's all you."

She wanted to tell him no, that Toby had been born a happy child, but her throat was closing up. She *needed* to ask him not to praise her, for fear she might do something foolish and take it too much to heart. She could not start yearning for praise from Dillon.

Finally, she found her voice. "Thank you," she said quietly. "I guess…it's time for Toby's story and bed. Then…I have some written material you might find helpful." Which was such a stupid, inane thing to say, but he nodded, took Toby and headed for the rocking chair.

Soon the sound of his deep, hypnotic voice could be heard in the kitchen where she had retreated so that Dillon could have some private time with his son.

She was alone in a way she hadn't been for the past three months. Maybe she'd never been this alone, Colleen thought. Because now she had experienced joy, a special kind of joy. And she craved it.

Get over it, she told herself. *Be happy with what you've been lucky enough to have been given. And stop moping. There's still a lot to do today. And maybe this would be a good day for you to go back to eating at the bunkhouse.* She was spending too much time alone with Dillon.

But by the time the day was done and the lessons were over, Millie had gone to bed with a headache, the women in the bunkhouse had made their own dinner and she and Dillon were all that was left.

"I'm not much of a cook, but I can manage something," she told him when he came back from putting Toby in his crib.

"I'd offer to do the honors, but I've never learned how."

"You've always had servants, haven't you?"

"It goes with the territory. My parents were too self-involved to cook. I was too busy. Fortunately, there are people who will cook for you if you pay them well."

She was pretty sure that he paid better than well. Before he'd come here she'd done her homework on him. She'd seen his name on one of those Web sites where people gossiped about which celebrities were lousy tippers at restaurants, and Dillon was a legendary highly generous tipper.

"I can help," he offered, but the thought of him being next to her while she cooked…after that kiss…well, she'd probably have a brain meltdown and slice off a finger or two.

"Go. Ramble. Read. Do something," she ordered.

He smiled and wandered out of the room. In a minute, she heard the noise of glass doors opening and closing and went to see what the commotion was. He had opened the china cabinet and was setting the table.

"You really are a rodeo queen." He motioned to the trophies and ribbons he'd had to move to get at the dishes.

"Well, everyone has to be good at one thing," she said.

He frowned at that. "I'm sure you're good at many things."

Automatically the sound of her stepfather telling her that she was good for absolutely nothing, that she was ugly and useless and that he couldn't believe someone as pretty as her mother had given birth to her, dropped in. She hadn't allowed that thought for ages.

"I was a great barrel racer back when I had the time to practice," she said as if she was trying to force that opinion down someone's throat.

"I would have liked to have seen that."

"I—" Colleen's words were cut off by the sound of Dillon's cell phone ringing.

He looked at the display. "Unfamiliar. Probably a wrong number, but…"

He clicked it on. Colleen went back into the kitchen to give him privacy.

"What's this about, Lisa? Yes, I know you called earlier. You're in Europe. Fine. Where am I? I'm with my son."

Lisa, Colleen thought. Maybe Lisa wanted the baby even though she hadn't asked one question about him these past few months. Or maybe she wanted Dillon again. A woman like Lisa tended to get the things she wanted.

With an extra dollop of force, Colleen slammed the pan onto the stove.

"Lisa, we haven't talked in a year. What exactly do you

want now?" Dillon continued. "I see. Well, you do what you have to do."

Colleen took out another pan and banged it on the stove, too. She wanted to scream, "Tell her not to call you here." But she didn't.

"I'd say this conversation is over," Dillon said.

Another pan. And another. And…

Colleen sensed rather than saw Dillon come into the room. She whirled and looked at him. He was leaning casually against the far wall, as if he'd been there all day and could stand there for another entire day. He looked as if nothing at all had happened.

"How can you be so calm?" she asked.

"I'm not, but tonight I'm too tired to think and react logically, and at the moment I have no recourse other than to keep tabs on her whereabouts. I already knew she was in Europe before she told me."

"What did she want?"

"She seemed to want to tell me that she'd been planning to come back to the States, but that she didn't have enough cash to make the trip and I—"

He paused.

"What?"

"How are we going to eat all this?"

Colleen looked down and saw that she had taken at least six pans out of the cabinet. They were squeezed together on the big commercial stove.

"I was angry," she said. "Really angry." She suddenly couldn't help smiling. "If Lisa had been here, I would have…"

"You would have what? Fed her to death?"

Colleen's smile grew. "Hey, I said that I wasn't a good cook, but nobody ever died from my cooking."

"I'm oddly reassured."

But Colleen wasn't. Standing here alone in the kitchen with Dillon, she felt vulnerable. He'd asked her earlier today what she was good at, but at this moment, staring at him across the room this way, all she could concentrate on were his lips. She wanted to be good at kissing Dillon Farraday. She wanted to forget that any adults other than the two of them even existed and she wanted him to kiss her again.

And since that wasn't going to happen, Colleen simply opened the refrigerator, pulled out a little of this and a little of that and hastily made two sandwiches. She handed one to Dillon.

"I do happen to make a darn good sandwich," she told him, trying to turn her thoughts back to the mundane.

"Looks delicious. I'll be sure to savor it." Which certainly didn't sound as mundane as it should have. In fact, when she woke in the middle of the night from a sound sleep, she realized that she had been dreaming that she and Dillon had been locked in a fierce embrace.

Surely it was just the newness of having a man in the house. "Tomorrow I will be so over this phase," she promised herself. No more thinking about Dillon beyond teaching him his duties.

CHAPTER FIVE

DILLON awoke to the sound of hushed whispers in the other part of the house. That was Colleen's low husky voice. Already he knew it. Already he was regretting having touched her…and yet not regretting it at all. For all her tough cowgirl ways, there was something very soft and vulnerable about her. And her skin was equally soft, her lips warm and womanly.

And my mind is where it has no business being, he thought. There were too many things to do today, too many important things to tend to. And some things he needed to talk to Colleen about. Despite his seemingly calm demeanor last night, Lisa's sudden reappearance worried him. Lisa, he'd discovered early in their marriage, had a reason for everything she did. She was good at masking her ambition behind a smiling facade but she was very ambitious. All his instincts told him she wanted money, and the tool she might use as leverage was a baby.

All that had passed through his mind last night, but he'd put off telling Colleen because…maybe because he hadn't wanted to upset her.

That wasn't like him. He had never shied from getting right to the tough stuff. When he'd been growing up, the only way to get his parents' attention had been to aim right for the jugular and cut directly to the heart of whatever topic he'd needed to take care of. He'd been that way ever since and it had stood him well in business and in war. Even in his personal life, he had jumped right in, met and married Lisa within a matter of weeks. But with Colleen, who had erected barriers the minute she'd met him and didn't have any qualms about making him abide by rules, he thought, looking at the offending door that separated him from her, he found himself wanting to ease into topics. With her shields up, she was hard to read at times, so going slowly was important. She tried to be tough. He knew she was strong in many ways, but he also sensed that she could be easily wounded. He could fail her, and he didn't want to either hurt her or fail her, not when he was pretty darn sure that she'd had more than her share of men doing that kind of thing.

But we still have to talk about things, he thought. Money and attention were Lisa's weaknesses, he'd learned. And now that he was back on his feet and able to be approached about giving her more funding, Lisa was probably going to be trouble. He would need to protect Toby. Things could get ugly, and he didn't want any of this spilling over onto Colleen. Unfortunately, given her affection for Toby, he wasn't sure how to protect her. Anger that the woman he had once trusted enough to marry might betray him again and roll over Colleen in the process made him want to swear.

Blowing out a breath, he rolled over, grabbed his clothes and got dressed. Then he padded to the door and gave a rap.

The door opened and he found himself facing Millie holding Toby, who had milk on his face, partially running down his bare baby chest and trickling into his diaper. The baby perked up and made happy smacking noises when he saw Dillon.

Dillon's heart flipped right over, and he held out his arms. Millie handed over Toby.

"Looks like breakfast was a winner," Dillon said, giving his child a kiss. "It also looks like I'll be taking my first lesson on giving you a bath."

Millie chuckled, but he wondered why she was the one feeding Toby. Colleen had told him only yesterday how much she liked feeding Toby his breakfast.

"Where's Colleen?" he asked.

Millie hesitated.

"Is this one of those 'none of my business, because it has nothing to do with me' occasions?" he asked.

No. The answer was clearly no, even though Millie didn't speak. Her hesitation told him that Colleen's absence *did* have something to do with him. Did this have something to do with that thing about the car Colleen had mentioned yesterday? And if he asked, would he get an answer?

Fire fast and catch her off guard, he thought. *She'll either tell you something or think you're totally crazy.*

He smiled down at his son, then quickly turned toward Millie. "Is there any chance there are visitors coming today?" he asked with as much of a frown as he could muster with a baby pulling on the button of his shirt and slobbering on his arm as Toby bent over and tried to chew without teeth. "Colleen seemed to think my car might bring some…um… crazed fans out of the woodwork."

Millie's eyes opened wide. "Now, you're not to worry. As soon as the first man showed up a few minutes ago, Colleen headed down to the entrance to make sure no one tried to sneak up here."

"She's guarding the Ferrari?"

"I wouldn't exactly say guarding. Just telling everyone to back off. People are curious, but Colleen says that you and Toby are our guests, you're our responsibility and she doesn't want those men bothering you when you and Toby need some

quality bonding time. Jokes might be made. Or they might try
to coerce you to let them drive your car. In other words, she feels
that our neighbors aren't minding their manners. But don't
worry. She has her shotgun, and Colleen hardly ever misses."

Dillon blinked.

"Dillon, I'm just kidding, hon," Millie drawled. "Not about
Colleen hardly ever missing, but about her having her gun.
Colleen doesn't *need* a gun, but she *is* down there reading the
riot act to the locals who came out to poke around and ask
you nosy questions."

Which was totally wrong. She had done him a favor loving
and caring for his child for the past three months, and now
she was teaching him how to be a good father despite the fact
that he was taking Toby away from her. Last night she had
patiently sat down with him and given him a crash course on
car seats and other safety issues. She had shepherded him
through his first diaper change and assured him that Toby
would let him know if he got the thing on too tight.

Dillon looked down at his son's milky face and gave him
a kiss. "I'll be back," he said and he held Toby out to Millie.
"Can you man the baby while I go give Colleen a hand?"

"You can't do that. You're supposed to be a—"

"Don't say *guest*. Everyone keeps saying that. That's an
order."

Millie shrugged. "Sorry. We're just trying to be hospitable."

"And I appreciate it. But things will run more smoothly if you
simply accept the fact that I'm used to taking charge and being
responsible for my own actions and welfare. I'm not good at
being a taker. At least I hope not. Now, where will I find her?"

"Probably down where the entrance to the Applegate is.
Colleen won't stop the fishermen from going through, but
she'll want to make sure that no one decides to wander up to
the house to snoop around."

He nodded. "Toby?"

"Of course," Millie said. "And…thank you. It's nice that there's some man who doesn't automatically assume that Colleen should be capable of doing everything. People have always taken advantage of the fact that she's a doer. She takes on too much. Not that I should complain. If she hadn't been the kind of person she is and taken us in, who knows what would have happened to us, but…yeah, I'm glad you're not simply taking her for granted the way everyone in town seems to."

Interesting. Dillon was certainly going to find out more about that topic when he got a few minutes, but for now, it seemed that Colleen was off fighting dragons for him. He was grateful, but he just wasn't a dependent sort of guy. Couldn't ever be.

As he started out the door, Millie called to him. "The fastest way to the entrance is straight across the south pasture and through the orchard. If you take the road, it's a lot farther."

"Thank you," he said as he took off toward the entrance. Despite the uneven ground and his uncooperative leg, he moved as swiftly as he could, given that he had left his cane behind. He wasn't sure what this was all about, but he knew this much. If he weren't here, Colleen wouldn't have to take care of the extra work of making sure he wasn't "bothered." Which was crazy, given the fact that he *was* bothered and hot and all kinds of attracted to her every time she got close to him. A man wanting to ask him about his car? Or even watching him struggle with a diaper? That was easy stuff. Not wanting to touch Colleen? Far too difficult.

When he entered the orchard, the first thing he noticed was a striking sculpture of metal and what looked like broken bits of glass. It glittered in the sun, the glass tinkling in the breeze. Other bits of colored glass hung from the trees amidst the glossy leaves, the budding fruit and the gnarled branches. It was a bit like a living art gallery, but Dillon didn't stop, because midway through the orchard he heard Colleen's voice.

"Harve, now I know you didn't come here to fish. You only fish on Saturdays and the occasional Sunday. If you're here during the week, it's to spy on Mr. Farraday."

"He's rich. He's probably used to people staring at him."

"I don't think that anyone ever gets used to people staring at them and asking nosy questions. Besides, where he's from people probably don't make him feel like some sort of bug under a microscope. There are lots of rich people in Chicago. Lots of interesting cars, too."

"Oh, come on, Colleen. We're not going to bite him."

"No, you're going to bug him. The man just got home after being in the hospital, he's still recuperating and he wants some alone time with his son while they get used to each other. He doesn't need to become an oddity on display. And I don't want you asking him any questions about Lisa, either. I especially don't want you doing *that*, and after what I heard in town yesterday, I know that you will, so don't tell me otherwise. Rob, is that you? Don't you have a job?"

"It's my break time."

"Well, break time's over. Now, all of you go on back to town. Sooner or later Dillon will show up, and then and only then, if he wants, he'll answer your questions. The Applegate should be a sanctuary, though. Off-limits."

"You're a harsh woman, Colleen. And getting snootier every day. Why is that guy staying here, anyway? We all know how you feel about men on your place, and he's sure not a ranch hand."

"No, Harve, and neither am I. I'm the owner and I call the shots, including who I invite here." Her point was clear. Dillon had been invited. They hadn't.

"Maybe you're trying to keep us away because you

wouldn't mind getting engaged again, this time to a rich man who could spend his money on the Applegate and turn it into a moneymaker. If you keep him to yourself, no other woman can snatch him up the way it happened with Dave."

Intense silence met that comment, followed by some throat clearing and someone swearing beneath their breath. At that point, Dillon decided it was time to make an appearance. He slipped between the last of the trees, coming out just to the east of the entrance to the Applegate. His eyebrows rose. There were at least half a dozen cars jammed up at the entrance, all blocked by Colleen's pickup truck. She was standing in the bed, her blond curls fluttering in the breeze, and looking glorious in her obvious anger. Good. Because if someone had hurt her and brought her to tears, he'd just have to hit them and he wasn't in nearly good enough physical condition yet to dodge quickly if it came to that.

"I'm going to try to forget that you said that, Rob," Colleen said, but her voice seemed strained.

Dillon moved forward. He stared directly at Colleen, who looked startled, then started to the edge of the wagon bed. He shook his head.

"Hello, Colleen. I don't mean to interrupt this meeting, but I was out taking a walk and it's sure a nice day, isn't it? You've got some great scenery here, too. I'm really glad I got out of Chicago to see it."

He turned to the men. "Hi, everyone. I'm Dillon Farraday."

There was some throat clearing, some shuffling. Some calling out of names. Harve Enson, Bill Winters, Rob Enson. More.

Dillon nodded. "I'm glad to make your acquaintance, but I couldn't help overhearing part of the conversation as I was walking through the orchard, and I think some things may need clearing up. For the record, Colleen has been the perfect hostess to me, and I've been a total pain of a guest," he said, using the hated word. "I dropped in on her out of the blue, and she's been caring for my baby for three months, which has to have cost her some work hours. In spite of that, she's made me feel welcome. So, while I really want to be a model visitor to your fine state and not make any unnecessary waves, I have to tell you that I would really take exception to anyone who criticized Colleen or embarrassed her or gave her any grief for taking Toby and me in. I'd definitely have to do something about that," Dillon said.

By now, everyone was looking at him. A small buzz of voices began in the crowd, and Colleen uttered something Dillon couldn't make out, but sounded like a muffled curse. She crossed her arms.

Dillon would have liked to have climbed up to stand in the back of the truck with her, but he didn't trust his leg to enable him to do that without him falling and looking like a fool. Right now, a commanding presence was called for.

"Well, now, Dillon, we all know better than to insult Colleen. She can ride a horse or shoot a gun better than any of us can," one older man said. "And when she was younger, she could beat up the boys if they messed with her. Rob here didn't mean anything by his comment. He was just irritated and not thinking straight. Nobody set out to insult Colleen, and they wouldn't. She's one of us."

"And I'm not," Dillon said with a smile.

The man looked startled. "I didn't mean it that way. I just meant…I meant that we all like Colleen. She's almost like one of the men."

Dillon frowned. Colleen was definitely nothing like a man, but since she didn't look happy to see him, and he had a distinct feeling that he'd already undermined some of her power simply by showing up here, he wasn't going to point

out the fact that she was very obviously and achingly female.
Or at least he wasn't going to point that out yet. That time
might still come along.

"But I'm glad you showed up, Dillon, because we wanted
to meet you. Colleen, it looks like we win, after all," one of
the men said.

Now Dillon was sure that he'd made a tactical error by
showing up. He didn't care about the darn car or even about
becoming a tourist attraction, but he did care about
Colleen's pride.

"I *didn't* bring the car you wanted to see," he pointed out.

"But you'll let us see it, won't you? Most of us don't have
the money to be allowed near enough to even test drive a car
that costs well over a hundred grand. And based on your
reaction to Rob's comment, I can see that you're a good guy,"
the man who appeared to be Harve said.

"I'm glad you think so. And I *will* bring the car into
town…eventually. Right now Colleen and I have too much to
do. No offense, but I need her right now worse than you need
to see my car."

Some grumbling ensued. Dillon heard some man muttering that he had been talked into driving all the way out
here for nothing and now had to drive all the way back
home with no gossip to tell his wife. She wasn't going to
be happy with him.

"What do you need Colleen for?" someone suddenly asked.

Dillon looked the man right in the eye. He could have
simply laid the facts out in black and white. He wasn't the least
bit ashamed that he had asked Colleen to tutor him in how to
be a good dad, but the fact that all these men seemed to feel
that it was their right to treat her as if she had no privacy…

"That's between me and Colleen," he said. "But I'll tell you
this much. She's teaching me to be a better man. She deserves

to be treated with respect. You need to back off from bothering her about me."

Colleen opened her mouth. She didn't look happy, but then she shook her head and shut her mouth.

"*We* need to go," she told him. She jumped down from the bed of the truck and climbed in.

Giving the men a nod, Dillon opened the passenger door and, using mostly his arms, leveraged himself smoothly into the vehicle.

Behind him, he could hear quiet conversation as the men returned to their trucks and cars. "Do you think they're dating?"

"No."

"Yes."

"No. Bill, the man was married to Lisa. Colleen's great, but she's a…I don't know what the term is nowadays, but she's a tomboy."

"He wasn't looking at her like she was a tomboy."

"Uh…"

Dillon couldn't catch the rest. Doors slammed, cars took off. He glanced to his left and saw that Colleen's color was high.

Interesting.

She headed off toward the house. "You shouldn't have done that."

"What?"

"Defended me. Come down to help me. Threatened to take action if someone insulted me."

"I didn't like their tone."

"I didn't, either, but they're mostly harmless. Most of this bunch is retired and they're bored. You're different and new and exciting. Something to see. Something to talk about."

"That doesn't excuse them trampling on your pride."

"I would have handled it. I'm used to handling it. I can hold my own."

"I didn't say you couldn't, but you came down here to protect me. I'm not letting you take risks for my sake, not when I'm perfectly capable of and used to taking my own risks."

Colleen stopped the truck.

"I know that, but…Dillon, I *have* to be in charge on the ranch. You're only here for a short while but I'm here forever. I'm responsible for lives—of people, of animals, of this whole operation. I'm responsible for everything that happens here. I can't be seen as weak and dependent on a man to step in and help me when things get tough."

Her tone, the memory of a few snippets of conversation, her comments about her stepfather, Rob's comments about her wanting to get engaged *again*, Millie's concerns about how people treated Colleen…

"Tell me…this hasn't always been a choice, has it? You've had to become strong, to establish yourself as unbending?"

Colleen stared at him through eyes that reflected old wounds, but her jaw was tight. "I've agreed to help you, I'm *glad* to be able to help you, but I'm not one of your employees or your soldiers. You can't simply command me to give up my secrets."

Because she was right, because his request might have been out of line and too personal and also because she looked petrified at the thought of telling him anything personal, guilt slipped through Dillon.

"You're totally right about that," he said.

"I have to stay in control. This ranch, everything that happens on it, it's personal to me. I just…my father…he loved this ranch. He died when I was young, and my mother was fragile and weak and ended up marrying a man who seemed strong but was merely mean and lazy. He and his son belittled me constantly, and she said nothing. He didn't let me do much other than work, except for the rodeo. That he allowed only because he felt it made him look good when I won.

"But I had one retreat. This ranch. My stepfather wasn't that interested in it other than letting it support him, and he was slowly leaching it of all its operating cash. Some of the older ranch hands who were still around taught me everything they knew, and this ranch became my sanctuary. Years later, when my mother and stepfather and stepbrother died in a plane crash and the ranch became wholly mine, a man asked me to marry him, but when I found out that it was the ranch he wanted, not me, I broke things off. Almost immediately, he married another woman who gave him what he wanted. So, this is my world. I control it and everything that happens here. It's where I fit, and it's the other women's home, too. If I fail with it, they lose their home.

"So, I can't fail and I can't quit. Succeeding, however, means I have to be in charge of things. The buck stops here. Always."

"Meaning that having a man step in to protect you takes something away from you."

"Well, it *was* nice," she admitted. "I'm certainly not used to a man stepping up to defend me or threatening to protect my honor and reputation."

"Ouch. I sound like a domineering jerk."

"Maybe, more like a warrior."

"Colleen, I really am grateful to you for all you're doing for me and Toby, and…"

She looked over at him when he paused.

"There's something else I have to tell you. I don't really want to because I hate to worry you," he said. "I know how you feel about Toby."

Instantly, she sat up higher. "Is he sick? What's wrong?"

He shook his head. "He's fine. At least he was when I left. But Lisa…I think that Lisa is going to be a problem, one I'm going to have to address, like it or not. Considering the fact that she left him here, and she's already called you, you might get sucked in. I'll try to keep that from happening."

"Didn't I just tell you that you couldn't protect me? You know I'll help. Whatever I can do, I'll help you."

He reached out and traced his fingertips down the soft skin of her jaw. "And you said that *I* was a warrior. You just jump right in without any thought to your own welfare, don't you?"

She shrugged. "It's a bad habit, one that's gotten me in trouble from time to time."

"Maybe, but it's also incredibly appealing." He shouldn't be touching her. Ever. She was married to her ranch for better or worse. He had a life and a business in Chicago, and this…this flood of sensation she called up in him owed nothing to logic. Because logic told him that neither of them wanted a forever kind of relationship. It also told him that she would be hurt by anything less.

That left no outlet, no way forward, no way for him to touch her without guilt. Besides, he was *not* going to be another one of those men she'd known who hadn't cared about her feelings.

But suddenly she reached out and grasped the collar of his shirt in both hands. "You shouldn't say things like that," she whispered. Then she pulled him close for a quick, hard, mind-numbing kiss. A fantastic kiss that left his lips burning, his head spinning and his body craving more. Much more.

"We both wanted to do that, didn't we?" she asked when she pulled back just as fast as she'd started. There was uncertainty and a trace of vulnerability in her voice.

"Oh, yes, we did. Still do," he said with a grin.

She let her breath out. "Well, that's about all I can stand for today. I need to concentrate on work."

"You're the boss," he said as she put the truck in gear and headed back to the house. "You're in charge."

Which was good, because Dillon was beginning to think that he wasn't in charge of himself at all where Colleen was concerned.

CHAPTER SIX

COLLEEN felt as if she was having an out-of-body experience. Dillon made her too aware of herself in ways that she wasn't used to. That kiss…had she really kissed him? Just like that?

She had. The darn man just made her crazy with his insistence on treating her as if she was some kind of precious porcelain when everyone knew she was a tough woman. But that kiss. She'd been tempted beyond all belief to touch him, and when she had, the heat and emotions and desire that had slammed through her had been overwhelming. Too much. She hadn't known what to do about them. And she still didn't.

Well, no, that wasn't true. What she needed to do was ignore them. Sooner or later Dillon would leave.

In the meantime, she'd try to get back to doing what she did best. Taking care of business and people. As she'd told him, she'd already spent large portions of her life taking charge of others. Her stepfather had been a total jerk, but he'd been right about one or two things. Colleen had been awkward. She'd never been a girly girl.

But she *was* a fighter, one with a purpose. This ranch was her kingdom. And right now, something other than the too potent energy swirling between her and Dillon was disturbing her kingdom. And she was going to do something about it.

It was late. The bunkhouse had already gone dark, but she could still hear Dillon moving around. Going to the door leading out to the porch, she knocked.

He answered the door wearing a black T-shirt and jeans. She couldn't help noting the strength in his biceps, but she didn't want to notice that. It wasn't why she'd sought him out. "We should talk about Lisa," she said.

"Name the place."

Not here. He'd already pulled out his bed. They could sit in the kitchen, but the night was warm. The kitchen felt hot and sticky. He'd almost finished with the front porch today, but the swing still hadn't been hung.

"The picnic table in the yard will do. It's close enough that the monitor will pick up Toby if he wakes, but far enough from everyone else that no one will hear us. And it's out in the open."

He smiled at that.

She felt her face growing warm. "You're safe," she said, tipping her chin up. "I don't intend to jump you again."

"Did you think I was worried that you might?" he asked, raising one eyebrow.

She thought…no, she wasn't thinking straight at all right now.

"Let's go outside," she said.

He led the way. The stars had come out and stretched across the sky in a navy-and-white-spangled blanket that twinkled and glowed. Dillon held out his hand to help Colleen up onto the table and, without thought, she took it. His big fingers closed around hers, his warmth flowed into her. She breathed in deeply, trying to control her reaction, to slow the sparks that were zipping through her.

Concentrate, she told herself.

"Tell me about Lisa," she said. "I know her, but we weren't close. Mostly I remember Lisa as the star of Bright Creek, the girl every other girl seemed to want to be when we were growing up."

"Even you?"

"Not the way other girls did. I wouldn't have liked having that much attention turned on me. I was always awkward, as if my body was a bad fit. I still feel that way lots of times, except when I'm on a horse. But what I wanted doesn't matter. What does Lisa want? And how is that going to affect you and Toby?"

"I hope it won't affect us much at all. I'm hoping that we can just go on with our lives, but those aren't the vibes I'm getting from Lisa. And what I'm hearing about her doesn't bode well for Toby and me." He shook his head.

"Tell me," she said.

"I gave her a very generous settlement, more than what was required legally, but my sources tell me that she's running through it quickly and living beyond her means. Not an easy feat, but she appears to be doing it. The baby…she *never* expressed a desire for a baby. She left him with you with no way of reaching her but suddenly, as soon as I showed up here and met him, as soon as I fell for that cute little guy, she called me when she had never called before."

"You think Toby is a bargaining chip for more money?"

"I hope I'm wrong about that. And it's not that I'm worried about the money so much. It's how far she'll take this."

Colleen knew just what he meant. "When we were in school once, Esme Hawkins got a dress that was the prettiest I had ever seen. Esme had never had so much attention before in her life, I don't think. But when we were out playing at recess, Esme tripped over Lisa's foot and got her dress all dirty. It looked like an accident, Lisa didn't try to hide the fact that it had been her foot that had gotten in the way, and she apologized profusely. I wouldn't have thought anything of it at all, except the very next week Lisa came in wearing an equally pretty new dress. As if she had to prove a point and reclaim her title. Maybe it was a coincidence, but there were lots of those coincidences over the years. Nothing serious, just Lisa having to always be the one and only. Lisa flirting with the male teachers, complimenting the female teachers who were the toughest graders on their hair and nails and clothes. There was something about her that made even adults want to win her favor. But she is, as you've heard, the best in Bright Creek, so maybe I simply have a vivid imagination. I shouldn't be speculating when I have no proof."

She glanced up. Dillon was looking down at her, the moonlight shining in his eyes. "Did you have an experience similar to Esme's with Lisa?"

Colleen laughed. "No. Lisa liked me or at least she didn't bother me. I posed no threat to her crown whatsoever. I was interested only in books and broncs and the Applegate. Well, back then I was still interested in boys."

"And, of course, now you're not." He took her hand and rubbed his thumb across her palm.

She shivered and gave him a look. "Being interested and following through on being interested are two different things. I try to be smart."

"You *are* smart. You read people very well." He released her hand.

"Do you mean that your experience of Lisa was similar to mine?"

"No." He shook his head. "I wasn't entranced by Lisa at first. I was too focused on my work and my company. In some ways I was like Lisa."

"You wanted to be the center of attention?"

"I needed my company to succeed. When I was growing up, I had no anchor. My parents barely knew I existed half the time, and the nannies they hired came and went. I was untethered, adrift, combative and unhappy. I wanted structure, but there wasn't any. There was nothing and no one in my life to hold my attention until I discovered that the family business held the answers.

"Engineers can make the seemingly impossible possible. They can harness science and math and change life for the better. The company and what it stands for, a logical, well-ordered set of rules that, when applied, can create something that works to make the world a better place, gave me a sense of purpose and control when I was seriously adrift. It still does. I live by logic. My company represents a world that performs according to prescribed rules. Outcomes can be anticipated. Applying those kinds of rules with predictable outcomes is how I live my life, too. Letting my emotions control me when I was young had been disastrous for me when I finally faced the fact that my parents didn't care about me and never had. I didn't have a single soul who cared that I was even alive, and the dark feelings that followed that admission nearly destroyed me. I did risky, crazy things. I started down a path that would have ended in tragedy or prison if I hadn't had the good luck to have a run-in with a police officer who convinced me that my life *could* get much worse if I let it. Deciding to concentrate on my work and my duties was the solution that saved me. Unfortunately, with Lisa, who seemed like a sensible choice for a man like me, I read her wrong."

Colleen nodded. "Well, Lisa is a pretty good actress. People see what she wants them to see. And they're blinded by her beauty."

"I don't remember being blinded by beauty or an overwhelming passion. I had simply reached a time in my life when I wanted someone who would fit the part of my wife well and I didn't consider how we would fit *together*, I suppose."

She smiled. "Well, at least your initial decision sounds as if it was based on logic."

"What's happening now with her and Toby isn't. She left him and now she's calling, but without any obvious purpose. I don't know what she's planning, but I know that I won't let her use him. He's not a bargaining chip and if she intends to try to make him into one, I need to have a way of blocking her. Her desertion of him should carry some weight with a court if it comes to that, but…"

"But as I said, Lisa's a convincing actress," Colleen interjected. "In a custody battle, she might throw herself on the mercy of the court and claim a change of heart after she'd been apart from her child for a while. And she might win. So, you need a plan."

"A logical plan. One that makes sense and ups my odds of winning, because I don't intend to lose my son."

"Then you need to make a fantastic home for him. A haven. You need to show the world that he comes first with you, that you're focusing all your attention on providing a safe and secure environment."

Dillon smiled.

"Why are you looking at me that way?"

"That's what you've made here. A haven."

She shrugged. The moon was rising. Dillon looked like a beautiful man-god in the moonlight, his sharp male jawline shadowed, inviting the curve of her hand to rest there.

Look away, she told herself. Think of something else.

"You have a home in Chicago, don't you, where you could make a life with him?"

"I haven't been back there yet, and I gave the house to Lisa in the settlement. I'll need more than just bricks and mortar, though. I was raised in a huge house, but it wasn't a home."

"Still, it's a good place to start."

"Which is true. I'll begin looking for one tomorrow."

Good. And yet, that meant he would begin to think of leaving. Maybe even before the three weeks were up. He might have no choice. Colleen's heart clenched at the thought.

"That's very sensible," she said.

He took her hand. "This isn't." He kissed her palm, and butterflies did aerial dives in her stomach. "Thank you for giving me some direction, a calm, reasonable approach. You should come to bed," he said, standing up. "It's late."

She hesitated.

"I meant come inside and go to your own bed, Colleen," he stressed. "I wasn't trying to seduce you, much as I'd like to."

"I'll come inside. Soon," she promised. And she watched him walk away from her. What were the words he'd used? Calm and reasonable? She only wished she felt that way, because Dillon made her feel a million things, but none of them were either calm or reasonable.

CHAPTER SEVEN

DILLON knew the minute Colleen came in the door an hour later. He couldn't fall asleep until she came inside. In spite of the fact that she'd lived here all her life, in spite of the fact that they were miles from anywhere with no threats in sight, he needed to know she was safe before he would allow himself to rest. And even once she came inside, he didn't rest easily. The memory of her sitting in the dark beside him with the stars overhead haunted him. Had he turned just a bit he could have drawn her into his arms.

What if he had kissed her and taken it further than mere kisses?

"Then you'd have to shoot yourself, because you would hurt her," he muttered. The last thing she needed was a transient man trooping into her life, messing with her emotions and then heading out of town. Wasn't he already mad at the men who had used and abused her in the past? Did he really want to join their ranks?

Keep it simple, Farraday, he told himself. Just do what needs doing.

She had made a helpful suggestion about the house. And it was a good way to keep his mind on something other than touching Colleen.

So, the next day when he had finished putting the last touches on her porch, he called a Realtor in Chicago.

Three days later, he had an entire folder of information, but he still didn't know what he wanted and needed, because he'd never been a father before. So, when lunchtime rolled around, he tracked down all the women and asked if they would give him their expert advice.

"You want our help?" Colleen asked.

"I trust your judgment."

"Sounds good to me. I love looking at houses," Millie said.

"Oh, yeah. And in this case, with money no object, it's like pretending you really can have all the cool things you would, in reality, never be able to afford in real life," Gretchen said.

"Do you have any specific considerations, features you'd like?" Colleen asked.

"I was hoping all of you could help me draw up a master list of what would be the perfect house for a grown man and a baby, if such a house even exists. Then we'll go from there."

He and Colleen exchanged a look. He knew that this ranch house, even with all the work it needed, was the perfect house for *her*.

"Okay, I'll bite," Julie said. "It's obvious that, since money is no object—I take it that it isn't—that you should have lots of space. There will be sleepovers, eventually, you know. Gretchen and I once got to have a sleepover when Mom was still alive. I'll never forget that we stayed up all night watching princess-themed movies. It was fantastic."

"It was," Gretchen said. "We had everyone bring stuffed animals and we put on a play. That was before daddy burned all our things to punish us."

"Oh, sweetie," Colleen said and gave Gretchen a hug. Gretchen hugged her back and then Julie joined in.

Dillon looked as if he wanted to punch someone. "I don't

mean to denigrate your family," he told the women, "but some men don't deserve to have children. I'm sorry you had to go through that."

"I'm just glad Toby has a father like you," Julie said. "Toby's never going to have to feel scared. He won't have to give up his childhood because his father's a jerk."

But, of course, Colleen thought, Toby's mother wasn't as nice as Dillon. Dillon had to win. And Lisa had a habit of hitting below the belt. They had to make Dillon's case as tight as possible and he had to present as the perfect father providing the perfect home.

"Gretchen, what do you think would help?" she asked.

"I'd vote for a big yard with room for a playground," Gretchen said. "A garden with flowers. Even guys love flowers, even if they won't always admit it. And there should be at least one tree with some branches that are low enough for a kid to get a leg up when he climbs. If it's got a nice crook where a tree house could be located, so much the better."

"And a big kitchen," Millie added. "Boys eat a lot. Or my sons did when they were growing up. Besides, you'll probably have birthday parties. You'll need space."

Dillon smiled. He looked over the women's heads to Colleen, who hadn't joined in yet. It was obvious that her ranch-hand friends were getting in the spirit of things.

More suggestions flew. A playroom. A theater. A library. A basketball court. The list was growing so long Dillon knew it wouldn't be possible to include everything. But the women had moved beyond their sad memories. They were having fun and so was he.

But when someone suggested a good staircase to slide down, Colleen looked into Dillon's eyes. She stood up and walked over to him. "Make it safe," she said. "That will be important. And…make sure it's the house that *you* want. The kind of place you'll want to come home to every night, one that feels like a comfortable fit. You'll be living there, too, you know. What's most important in a house to you?"

Dillon stared down into Colleen's face. He was close enough to touch her, but of course he wouldn't, not with everyone here. What was most important in a house to him?

A big bed. He nearly groaned. Had he really thought that? He hadn't said it out loud, had he?

Looking around, he could see he hadn't. The women were still waiting for him to answer.

"A house with a sturdy front porch," he said, "and an enclosed back porch with a top-of-the-line sleeper sofa."

Laughter greeted his comment, but Colleen wrinkled her nose. "All right, you can buy a new one. The one you want. As long as you take it with you when you go. It will be yours."

Despite his good intentions, he reached out and touched her face. "I was kidding, not complaining."

"I know. But it *is* an awful mattress."

"Why? Have you tried it lately, Colleen?" Gretchen asked, and he turned to see that she was teasing, but also wide-eyed with curiosity.

"Gretchen," Colleen warned.

"I'm afraid I'm the sole occupant of the killer sofa bed," he said, winking.

"I think you just like to complain about it to make me feel guilty," Colleen said in a teasing tone.

Everyone laughed again, and Dillon realized that he felt at home in this group of women. Too much at home. That wasn't good. He couldn't start doing stupid things now. Getting emotionally wrapped into this group, or especially into Colleen, would only end in disaster for both of them. She had her base and her sanctuary. He had his. She had obligations. His were different. There was no middle ground, and she didn't want a man.

The Applegate was and might always be "no males" territory. He and Toby had simply been granted temporary sanctuary.

As if he knew that his father was thinking about him, the baby, who was cuddled up against Millie, began to babble.

"What's that, Toby? You think your dad is right about that sofa bed?" Dillon asked.

Colleen wrinkled her nose. "Don't you go putting words in my baby's mouth."

And just like that, the atmosphere changed.

"I meant *your* baby, of course," Colleen said.

"Don't be sad, Colleen," Millie said. "I'm sure that when he takes Toby back to Chicago he'll call. He'll make sure that Toby stays in touch over the years, won't you, Dillon?"

Before he had a time to open his mouth, to breathe, to think, Colleen held up her hand. "Do not answer that," she said. Which was good because he didn't know how to answer. He knew that maintaining contact with a woman who drove him insane with desire but to who he could never make love or marry would be a kind of hell.

"And don't any of you make Dillon feel guilty about Toby," she said to her friends.

"Of course we wouldn't, Colleen," Julie said. "It isn't Dillon's fault that you can't have a baby of your own."

And that was when the chandelier fell on their heads. Metaphorically, anyway, Dillon thought later.

For a long moment time seemed to stop. No one breathed. No one spoke. Even the clock on the wall seemed to stop ticking.

"You didn't know," Millie said to Dillon.

"Why should he? It isn't exactly the kind of thing I was just going to drop into a conversation over lunch. And besides, there was no reason for Dillon to know. It was an accident I had *years* ago. It's not his fault I can't have a child, and there's nothing he can do about it."

She turned to Dillon and pasted on a smile. It was totally phony. He knew it. She knew he knew it. But what she was telling him was that she didn't want to talk about it. How could he not honor that when the topic was one that was so painful for her?

And Toby was starting to fret, to twist in Millie's arms and whimper, as if he was absorbing the charged atmosphere and was frightened.

Automatically, as if she'd done it a thousand times and probably had, Colleen turned to the baby, a look of love and concern on her face. Quickly she moved toward him, but then she stopped suddenly just two feet from Toby, who was waving his little hands in distress.

Colleen looked suddenly smaller, her shoulders more rounded, her head dropped slightly.

She turned away from Toby and looked at Dillon.

"You need to hold your son," she said. "Now, I'd better get some work done." She smiled sadly. Then she quietly left the room.

As Dillon cuddled his child he realized that something elemental had happened here. Colleen had decided that it was time to start letting go. She would begin to transfer the care of Toby to him in earnest.

And she would begin to back out of the picture.

This should have been a moment of pride for Dillon, the fact that she trusted him enough to turn control of Toby over to him.

Instead, when he heard the front door open and close a few seconds later, he simply wanted to go after her, stop her, wherever she was going.

In fact, he must have made a move toward the door, because he felt a hand on his sleeve. Millie was shaking her head.

"She'll probably be working all night in her shop."

When he frowned in confusion, Millie smiled. "I guess she

didn't tell you. Colleen's an artist." She gestured toward the beautiful decorated glass vases that were in every room in the house. "The wind chimes, the sculpture…that, more than anything, has kept this ranch going when times got rough. Colleen can't create a child, but she creates beautiful things nonetheless."

"I didn't know," he said. It occurred to him that there were lots of things he didn't know about Colleen.

Things he wanted to know but never would. As he left the room and headed toward the nursery with Toby, he reached up and touched one of the chimes that hung in the doorway. Its soft sounds were like music. Sad but very sweet and very beautiful.

Just like the woman responsible for them.

Colleen didn't spend all night in her workshop. In fact, she had done very little work when she put her tools down and faced the facts. She had behaved badly, stealing the happiness from what had been a fun afternoon.

Dillon was buying a house for him and Toby, she and her friends had been given the honor of helping him decide how to make things special for them and she had walked out just when things had come to fruition. It wasn't as if she hadn't spent years living with the knowledge that she couldn't produce a child.

No, her sudden sadness had been because the house represented the beginning of the end. Dillon would be leaving soon. Not that that was a surprise exactly, but she hadn't expected that sharp pain that had hit her when she'd realized how fast time was flying. She'd just had to get away.

And now you have to go back, she told herself. *The man probably thinks you're acting crazy or that you're rolling in self-pity.* Which she was…a little bit. And that just wasn't going to continue. She was not that kind of woman.

"So, suck it up, Applegate," she told herself. "And go help the man do what he needs to do."

She opened the door to the house quietly. The curtains were open in the bunkhouse, and she could see Millie reading by the window, so Colleen knew that only Toby and Dillon were in the house.

She went directly to Toby's room, but no one was there. Then she heard a low baby gurgle.

And then a deep male voice mimicking the gurgle. "Oh, you are so talented, buddy," Dillon said. "That's a tough sound to make. How about this one?" He made a buzzing sound like a bee.

Colleen poked her head around the door. Dillon was sitting on a blanket holding Toby in front of him. Toby was studying his daddy very solemnly with those big blue eyes.

"No? Not that sound? Okay, about this one?" He leaned forward and very gently made a raspberry noise against Toby's tiny tummy. The baby's eyes got big and round and then he squealed and grabbed a handful of Dillon's hair.

"You little squirt," Dillon said, disentangling himself and smiling at his son. "You are going to be trouble when you grow up, you know that? And I'm going to love you no matter what."

Toby blew a bubble. He smiled.

It was a beautiful thing to see, this big man and this tiny baby enjoying each other's company. Then she realized that she was snooping. She hadn't even announced her presence.

"You're going to get a stiff neck sticking your head around corners that way," Dillon said, making her jump and squeal almost as loud as Toby had.

She came all the way into the room. "I didn't mean to keep my presence a secret and I wasn't spying," she protested. "Well, maybe just a little."

"Uh-oh, Toby. I wonder how much of our conversation she

heard. She probably knows our secrets now. We may have to tie her up and hold her prisoner."

Toby's eyes followed every movement of his father's head and mouth. He made a very small grunt.

"Toby says we must show lenience to the princess who has sheltered us and given us asylum." Dillon put his hand in front of his face to block his mouth and spoke to Colleen in an aside. "My son has a heart of gold, it seems, but I was kind of looking forward to having you as my prisoner," he teased.

"Toby, pay no attention to your daddy's antics. He's crazy." She leaned closer and smiled at the baby, who gifted her with one of his most beatific smiles.

"You're an angel, sweetie," she told him, "but it looks as if you're wearing part of your dinner." Milk had dribbled down his neck.

"A slight incident with the bottle," Dillon told her. "I was just going to give him a bath. We were just waiting."

"For what?"

"A how-to session," he said. "It occurred to me that reading your instructions on how to give a baby a bath while in the midst of actually carrying out those instructions might be tricky, given all the water and soap and slippery baby and instruction sheets. What if I smudge the paper and can't figure out what to do next?" His smile was huge, his teasing tone was seductive.

She reached out and placed her hand on his jaw. "You don't have to do this, you know."

This time he didn't smile and he turned into her hand slightly, his beard scratching a bit. She loved the sensation. Her heart did a flip. "Don't have to what?" he asked. "Give the baby a bath?" His voice echoed through her body right down to her toes.

She shook her head slowly. "You don't have to be careful

with me. You don't have to make me laugh, although I like laughing with you. You don't have to shy away from the difficult topics. I can't have a baby. You know it. I know it. We've said it out loud, and that's not a problem. I'm not made of glass. Okay?"

"Not glass. Flesh and bone and…I'm sorry. I just can't ignore the fact that you've been hurt, Colleen."

"You can't change it, either. I know that all too well. It was a freak riding accident where I ended up cut up. When the doctors told me that I'd never have children, it stunned me at first, that riding—something I love so much—could take the thing I most wanted. I got angry, and I hated the fact that I was broken when I'd never let anything break me before. So, I got back on my horse and spent a lot of time riding the range and screaming at the sky that first year. I channeled my anger into my racing, but finally I realized that I could fight and yell all my life and it wouldn't change a thing. So, I put it behind me—mostly—and I need you to put it out of your mind, too. I would hate it if you pitied me or were careful with me because of this. So, Dillon…don't be careful."

For several seconds, tension filled the air as he stared at her, studied her.

"Dillon, I mean it."

He muttered a curse and looked to one side.

"Dillon?"

He swung his head around, his eyes dark and fierce. "All right."

She frowned. "That could mean a lot of things."

"In this case," he said quietly, "it means I won't be…careful."

Which sounded so much more dangerous than he probably meant it to, Colleen was sure. She nodded and managed a shaky smile. "So, okay, yes," she said, determined to change the subject and the mood. "I'll show you how to give a baby a bath. It's not difficult. You just have to make sure to put everything out that you need ahead of time, because you can never leave him alone in the tub. I'll show you how to make sure the temperature of the water is right. And I just know you're going to be a whiz at this. Because you like to talk and tease. And Toby likes to listen to people talk and tease while he takes a bath."

"Ah, another one of those teacher-type pats on the back," he said, allowing her to move beyond the "Colleen can't have babies" topic. "I'm starting to like those."

And because she was starting to like a lot of things about Dillon, far too much, Colleen made herself get right to the task. Dillon talked to his son the whole time he was cleaning him up, but the excitement of having his two favorite people to himself at the same time was clearly too much. His arms flailed more than usual, and by the time they were through, both Colleen and Dillon had generous splashes of water dotting their clothes. Toby, of course, was adorable and dry in his little towel with the hood.

"Thank you for the lesson. I think I've got the hang of it now, but you'd better go put on something dry."

"Oh, I'm okay," she said. "I can handle a little water."

"Maybe so, but I'm not sure that I can, or that I can be trusted," Dillon said, looking pointedly at her shirt where, she realized as she looked down, the outline of her bra was visible through the damp cloth.

Her eyes opened wide. She crossed her arms over her chest. "You," she said to Toby, "need to learn to bathe with more decorum and less splashing. You've embarrassed your daddy." And she leaned forward and kissed the baby's forehead. "Excuse me. I'll just take your advice and go put on something dry, change the scenery," she told Dillon.

He smiled and leaned forward and kissed her right beneath the ear. "The scenery is beautiful. It's the observer who isn't sure he won't reach out and grab, given the chance. Not that I'm saying I would have gotten the chance or anything, mind you."

"You'll never know now, will you?" she teased as she left the room.

"That thing she told you about not splashing?" she heard Dillon say to Toby. "Don't listen. Splashing is fun, although that may be totally a guy thing. That's us, buddy. You and me. We're guys. Colleen, now, she's a woman. A beautiful woman," he clarified. "Especially beautiful after bathtime."

Colleen blushed all the way to her room. And in the middle of the night, she woke up, remembered Dillon's comment and blushed some more. She definitely needed to start pulling away or at least to work harder about not getting too close.

Think of staying away from Dillon as just another ranch chore, a goal, she told herself. *Something you just need to do.* But when she closed her eyes, she felt his mouth on hers, and her goals…she couldn't even remember what they were.

CHAPTER EIGHT

FIVE days later, the tension climbed a little higher, but this was nothing like the tension caused by her reactions to Dillon, Colleen thought as she hung up the phone and reviewed the conversation that had just transpired.

She had been meaning to call Lisa back ever since that first day when her phone had rung. Despite her anger at Lisa leaving Toby, a part of her had hoped that the woman had had some sort of valid reason. But what kind of valid reason could there be for abandoning your child and leaving no forwarding address…or not telling your husband or even your ex-husband that you were expecting his child until you had already delivered the baby?

So, despite the fact that the number had been on her phone's call log, she had put off contacting Lisa. Given the order of things, Lisa had probably simply been trying to reach Dillon, anyway. And she had already done so. At least that was what Colleen had told herself…until the phone call from Lisa this morning.

"I hear that Dillon is staying at your ranch," Lisa had said.

Colleen took a deep breath and considered her words carefully. She knew that Dillon hadn't mentioned that fact in his phone call with Lisa. "I assume you've spoken to someone in town."

"I still have a few contacts there, yes. They don't know everything, though. So, why is he there?"

For some reason Colleen didn't want to tell Lisa that Dillon was taking lessons in parenting. If he wanted her to know that, he'd tell her. Besides, Colleen was afraid to tell her. Lisa was Toby's mother. She had rights, and one of those rights was to come ask for her baby back. There was no law stopping her. If someone else had something she no longer had, if Toby's value increased because Dillon wanted him, she might decide she wanted Toby, too.

"Dillon's a guest," Colleen said noncommittally.

"The Applegate never was a guest ranch."

Colleen could have told Lisa that it still wasn't, but that would only call up more questions. "I'm always adding new sidelines to the Applegate. Horses are expensive to keep."

"But Dillon is your only guest. If there had been others, Bill would have told me."

Colleen frowned. So Bill Winters was the one spilling his guts to Lisa. Not a surprise, since he'd always wanted to date her.

"How long do you think he's going to stay there?"

Probably not long, but…

"I have no idea," Colleen said, but she was wondering why Lisa hadn't asked one question about Toby.

"How's the baby?" Lisa asked, as if she'd read Colleen's mind.

Perfect. Adorable. A total love. How could you leave him that way? Colleen thought. "He's doing well," she said.

"I can't come get him just yet," Lisa said. "Maybe when my situation changes." Which made Colleen's blood turn cold. If Dillon's contacts were right, Lisa was partying hard in Europe, not worrying about her baby. But, when she wanted something—if she should ever decide she wanted Toby— Colleen had no question that Lisa could "change her situation"

at will, play the part of remorseful mother and play it convinc-
ingly enough to fool a judge who was in charge of determin-
ing the terms of custody.

"Let me offer a friendly word of warning," Lisa suddenly
said. "Dillon's an attractive man and a wealthy one, but he's
also used to calling the shots. He isn't easy to handle, even
for someone who's experienced and knows how to handle
men. I know you don't have that kind of experience,
Colleen. I know a lot. I would be careful around Dillon if
I were you."

Colleen felt as if bands of fear and indignation were squeezing her heart. "It's nice of you to worry about me, Lisa."

At that moment, Dillon walked in the door. Those bands
closed tighter. And on the other end of the line, Lisa was
laughing. It sounded like light laughter, but Colleen thought she
heard a hard edge to it. Or maybe that was just her imagination
because she was afraid Lisa would someday try to reclaim Toby
on one of those whims she and Dillon had discussed.

Lisa, Colleen mouthed to Dillon.

"Of course I worry about you, Colleen," Lisa said. "No one
knows better than I do that I took advantage of your kindness,
but I'd hate to see you hurt by Dillon. And you will get hurt
if you start thinking of him romantically. But then, you've
never really been the romantic sort, have you?"

"No, I'm not romantic. You don't have to worry about me
falling in love with Dillon," Colleen said, and she knew that
her words were as much to reassure herself and Dillon as they
were to stop Lisa from any more warnings.

"Good. I was really concerned for you when Bill told me
that. Since you're taking care of Toby, I feel kind of protective toward you, and if I thought you were in danger of getting
your heart broken by Dillon, I'd feel responsible. After all, he
would never even be there if not for me. Maybe I should have

left Toby with someone older, but you seemed like the right person at the time."

Colleen felt anger rising in her. She felt threatened, and she wanted nothing more than to tell Lisa off, but there was Toby and there was Dillon. Both of them would suffer if Lisa decided to…act like Lisa. Colleen couldn't do anything that would incite her to get angry and take action.

"Well, I really appreciate that, Lisa. I do," Colleen lied. "And, thank you again. But I really have to go now. A ranch takes a lot of time and effort and I have a foal that desperately needs tending to. I'm sure we can talk more later."

She hung up without letting Lisa even say goodbye.

If Dillon hadn't been standing there, Colleen would have pressed her hands against her heart. She would have leaned over, put her hands on her knees and taken deep breaths to keep from getting dizzy. She had hung up on Lisa Farraday, who had the power to harm Dillon and Toby.

"What did she want?" Dillon asked.

What could she say? He had been there when she made that declaration about not falling in love with him.

Colleen turned to him. "I think she wanted to make sure I wasn't poaching what she still thinks of as hers. I think I just became Esme Hawkins and you're the pretty dress."

Dillon looked unconvinced. "You're forgetting that Lisa was the one who divorced *me*."

No, she wasn't forgetting that. If Lisa hadn't divorced Dillon, the two of them would still be married. Colleen hadn't forgotten that. And wouldn't. But that wasn't what he was trying to say.

"Lisa may not be married to you anymore, but this is her town and her territory, and she is, as I mentioned, still the queen here. That means no one takes her place. Even if she divorced you, that may have just been the impetuous, scorned woman reacting. She probably didn't like it that you put your work before her pleasure, so she was punishing you. Knowing Lisa, she probably assumed she could come back and remarry you whenever she wanted, and you'd go along with that the way other men have. She'd have more power over you, because you would have learned your lesson. That's pure speculation based on her past performance, of course, but no matter what, she wouldn't want someone from here to waltz in and take what was once hers. And I…I think she may have threatened me. I definitely hung up on her. That's not good."

"Are you afraid of her?"

Colleen examined that statement. "Not for me." Lisa couldn't take anything from her, Colleen realized, because she didn't *really* have anything Lisa wanted. "But for you and Toby—I don't want to antagonize her. She could make things difficult for you."

"Regarding custody."

"Yes."

"I've thought of that. I'm hoping we can reach an amicable arrangement."

They stared at each other for a long time. "What kind of arrangement do you want?" she asked.

"One where I get him all the time."

"You don't want to have to go to court over this."

"If what you say is true, and I believe it may be, then no. I like situations where I control all the variables. But, in the event that I might have to go to court—and it could come to that—I want to hold as many of the cards as I can."

"You need to demonstrate that you're the perfect dad." In Colleen's eyes, he was already that. But she wasn't a judge.

"I don't want to leave even one stone unturned."

She nodded. "Then we'd better consider all the possibilities, we'd better make sure you're as knowledgeable about raising a child as we can make you and we'd better make sure we cover all the bases and get you into the perfect setup back in Chicago as soon as possible."

Dillon suddenly smiled at her, and her heart did a triple somersault. "You are an amazing woman," he said. "You deserve an award, national recognition, a plaque and a spot on television about women who have made a difference. You're certainly being a tremendous help to me and Toby."

How could a woman not fall in love with a man who said things like that? Colleen wondered, then immediately regretted the thought. *She* couldn't fall in love with him. For so many reasons, ranging from the fact that Lisa would punish him if she thought that Colleen was showing an interest to the fact that Dillon really would break her heart to the fact that they lived in different worlds and different lifestyles a thousand miles apart. And both of them were committed to those worlds and those lifestyles. Her place was here. She mattered *here*. What was a woman supposed to do?

"Thank you," she said, doing the simple thing. "Now, I really should get some work done. I'd call Bill Winters and give him a piece of my mind for reporting on me and you to Lisa but he'd probably just tell her that I threatened him."

"I wouldn't worry about the man," Dillon said.

"Dillon, you can't do anything that would make you look…I don't know…violent at a time like this."

He shook his head. "I wouldn't do anything that would cause a problem." Which meant he probably still had some sort of plan.

Colleen looked at him and saw the warrior, the man who dealt in solutions. She could have told him to leave things alone completely, but…

"Who's worried?" she lied with a smile. "Everything here is just perfect."

Except for the fact that she kept wanting to kiss Dillon Farraday, everything was just fine.

"I mean it, Colleen," Dillon said. And just like that, he moved forward, looped his arm around her waist and pulled her so close that their mouths were almost touching. "Leave Bill to me. You're not to get hurt on my account."

"I won't," she lied.

"And I heard what you said about falling in love with me. We may not be in danger of that, but there's this," he said, kissing her so that it was all she could do not to wrap her arms around his neck and hang on. "It's a problem."

"I know."

"I like kissing you too much."

"I like kissing you, too. Too much. And I don't like it one bit. It's not smart and it's only going to cause trouble."

"Agreed. I'm going to have to work on self-control."

"You let me know how that works out," she said.

He smiled at her as he let her go. "So far it's not working at all."

"We'll keep trying." And somehow she managed to walk away on legs that shook. Somehow she kept going and didn't look back.

Until she did.

He was still looking at her. Her body turned to flame. It was going to be a very hot afternoon, she thought as she attempted to get back to whatever it was she really needed to do on the ranch.

What *did* she need to do, anyway?

Kiss Dillon, her misbehaving brain told her.

Two days had passed. Toby was fretting because he'd been awakened unexpectedly from his nap when a branch had fallen on the roof. Dillon felt like fretting, too, but it had nothing to do with the branch. He was still brooding over that kissing conversation he'd had with Colleen. The self-control plan was not working real well.

But that wasn't his son's problem. "It's tough waking up from a nap, isn't it, buddy?" he asked, cuddling his son. "It's tough when you want something you can't have, too, isn't it?" He moved away from the table they were sitting next to so that Toby couldn't reach the sugar bowl he'd been trying to touch. "Like Colleen. We both like her, don't we?"

Toby gurgled.

"I'll take that as a yes."

His son let out a crowing sound.

"Okay, a really big yes. But neither of us can have her. She's got this ranch and…heck, she *needs* this ranch and everything that goes with it. She's got plans. Big plans, ones that don't involve men. Plans that involve staying here and running a ranch with her friends and setting up that camp to teach needy city girls how to ride and ranch. Can't do that in Chicago. Besides, she likes us well enough now, but she likes us partly because we're temporary, you know. She doesn't want to get tied to a man and, well, heck, you and I have plans, too. We've got things we need to do and all of those require being in Chicago. So, we're just going to have to get used to doing without her even if she's helping us a lot, you know?"

He cuddled Toby to him and dropped a kiss on the top of his head. And one of his son's little hands latched on to his shirt. Something about that just choked Dillon up. That trust. Those tiny fingers. He wanted…he wanted to call Colleen inside and show her, to tell her how it made him feel. But it was probably best to keep his distance from Colleen for a while. Kissing her was getting to be a habit, and the truth was that he wanted to do a lot more than kiss her.

That could only complicate things for both of them, and when he left here he didn't want him and his son to be something she would regret.

"It's just you and me, Toby," he said. But just then Toby bucked a bit and kicked his toe into the table. He let out a howl and then a sob that turned into more heartbreaking sobs. His little body shook. He was inconsolable and so was Dillon.

Looking at the little red dent on his baby's leg, he wanted to swear. He had let his son get hurt. Surely Colleen wouldn't have done that. Of course she wouldn't have.

Toby was snuffling and crying, and Dillon got to his feet. He walked out the door with Toby's little body cuddled up against him.

The movement seemed to do the trick, and Toby's cries died down to whimpers.

"Dillon, is everything all right?"

Dillon looked up and found himself standing just outside the corral where Colleen was mounted on a frisky palomino. She looked beautiful up there. She looked right.

"Darn it, I let him get hurt. He kicked into the table and now he has a red mark."

Dillon slid his palm under Toby's leg and showed Colleen. Immediately the worried look in those big brown eyes disappeared and she smiled. "I can almost see it," she said.

From her attitude, Dillon knew that he had overreacted. "Toby, she's making light of our situation. Two clueless guys in obvious need of direction. We're new at this. Doesn't she know that?" he asked, whispering the words against the top of Toby's head, loud enough for Colleen to hear.

Of course, she *did* know. "Looks like you need Dr. Colleen to look at that wound," she teased. "Just let me take Suzie's saddle off and go wash up."

By now Toby wasn't crying at all and Dillon wasn't

worried anymore, but he had come to a decision within the past hour. He needed to talk to Colleen about it.

So, when she came back out, he smiled at her. "Let's walk."

She gave him a questioning look. "You look serious. I'm sure Toby is fine. Babies get little bumps and bruises all the time. You can't blame yourself."

"I don't take my responsibilities lightly, so yes, I can, but Toby's leg isn't what I want to talk about. It's a gorgeous day. Show me what I haven't seen."

To her credit, Colleen didn't mention his leg. Good. He hadn't been using his cane around the house much lately and he had decided to stop using it altogether, because holding a cane and a baby was just not practical. Still, it was probably going to give him trouble or at least ache for a good long time. Too bad. He had no intention of letting that stop him. Especially not now. Just when he was trying to prove that he was the perfect person to keep Toby full-time was no time to appear weak.

Colleen merely gave a curt nod and fell into step beside him, not saying anything. They passed another one of those wild and beautiful glass-and-metal sculptures similar to the one Dillon had seen in the orchard that day. "You're talented," he said. "I know people in Chicago who would pay a lot of money for something like that. How long have you been an artist?"

She looked a bit self-conscious when he glanced at her. "I'm not exactly an artist. I'm a reactionary. I started working with glass back when my stepfather and stepbrother were here. They liked to shoot guns when they were drunk, and they preferred shooting things that were made of glass. It didn't matter if it was expensive or pretty or meaningful. Just as long as it shattered in a satisfying way. I hated that. Not the shooting so much, but the indiscriminate drunkenness of it all. They tended to be that way about everything, and of course, they never cleaned up the glass, so if someone didn't do it, I had to. We had more animals then, and I didn't want them to get hurt. So, to funnel my anger and frustration, I started making things out of the glass. After a while it became a hobby and even after they were gone, I kept it up. Nowadays, I get the satisfaction of breaking the glass myself, so when I'm angry or frustrated, I tend to disappear into my workshop," she said, waving toward a small building.

It wasn't exactly the most perfect building Dillon had ever seen, and Colleen seemed to know what he was thinking.

"I know what it looks like," she said, "but this is one building I don't want you to touch. If it were dangerous, I would have got it fixed, but as it is, I like the slightly mis-shapen structure. It's unpolished and a bit rough."

"I know you well enough by now to realize that that's how you think of yourself. You identify with it."

She hesitated. "I've bonded with it, yes. It has significance to me. It reminds me that I fit here, that I'm a part of all this, rooted here, and that I can never stop trying to make things better. I owe it to the women who live and work here and the ones who will visit one day and hopefully take something meaningful and empowering away if I ever get the camp going. And if any of those girls end up needing an escape hatch, this place needs to be there for them. A rock, a safe place."

More than ever, Dillon understood the significance of this ranch she thought of as her sanctuary. She had to be here to take in lost lambs, those who had been mistreated.

"Toby and I are going to have to leave soon," he said suddenly. "We can't stay much longer."

Colleen stumbled and Dillon reached out one hand to catch her, but she shook her head and quickly righted herself. "Of course. Lisa has called too many times. There's something going on. You'll want to have all your chessmen in position should she decide to challenge your rights as a father."

And he also wanted to make sure that he got out before Colleen started meaning too much to him.

"That's about the gist of it," he said. "I've got the Realtor looking for the house. As soon as she finds one that fits, I want to furnish it, find someone to help me take care of Toby while I'm working and then I want to firmly establish the two of us in that stronghold. There can't be any question that I'm putting his welfare first or that I know what I'm doing."

She stopped. They had made it to the creek, upstream from where the fisherman were, but Dillon could hear them in the distance. "I can't imagine that anyone who knew you would question your dedication to him. Just…Dillon, look at the two of you," she said, biting her lip. When she looked up into his eyes, her own were misting up.

"You've done this for us," he said.

"No." She shook her head. "No one knows better than me that fathers have to actually *want* to be fathers in order for things to work out. This is all you."

Anger that she should have been denied what should have been rightfully hers, that any man should fail to see her value, surged through Dillon, but he could see that she was vulnerable right now. And she was a woman who wanted to be and needed to be strong. She *was* strong, and she wouldn't want him to point out her moment of vulnerability any more than he liked having his weak leg pointed out.

Moreover, he was beginning to think that it would hurt her as much as it would hurt him if he didn't get to have Toby full-time. She'd dedicated herself to helping him. He couldn't let her or Toby or himself down.

"Before I leave, I want you to drill me, to teach me, to quiz me, so that I know at least some of what I should do in any given situation. Most people learn as they go, but with Lisa possibly plotting something, I don't feel I have that luxury."

"We'll burn the midnight oil," she promised. "We'll search the Internet and read all the books. We'll role-play. I promise we'll do all we can. We…all of us care. About Toby."

He stared into her eyes, and he burned to touch her.

Then he *was* touching her, but gently this time, pulling her close enough so that Toby was snuggled high up on his shoulder, his little hands touching both of them, connecting them. "I know you care," he said. "We're never going to forget what you've done for us, you know."

For long seconds they just stayed that way, together. Almost like a family, but…not. Then Dillon felt her take a deep breath. She straightened. "We'd better get started. I'm going to tell you everything I've noticed about Toby that you may not have absorbed yet. Lisa will have the mantle of motherhood to bruit about, but you'll have the details of who your son actually is."

The fact that she'd thought of that, the fact that *she* knew those details and that she was willing to help him in this way…Dillon's chest hurt.

That couldn't matter. "Let's do it," he said. "If what my Realtor tells me is true, we might not have much more than a week, because as soon as the right place comes up, we're there. It won't be quite the three weeks I told you, but—"

"I know," she said. "You have to do it. You have to go."

CHAPTER NINE

IN FACT, Dillon had less than a week remaining. The next morning began with a gloomy sky and even gloomier news that one of his company's projects was in trouble, but his project manager had to leave town next week to tend to important family business. Dillon's presence was needed as soon as possible. He had spent the evening studying all the notes Colleen had given him and as many of the books and articles as they could lay their hands on. He could probably recite information that many pediatricians didn't know, he had the number of the Illinois Poison Center memorized in case of an emergency and he knew all the best medical Web sites and parenting resources.

But this morning, because of Farraday Engineering's problems, he'd been holed up with a telephone and computer and he hadn't had nearly enough sleep. So, Colleen was totally shocked when he came out of the room with a big grin on his face.

"I have something to show you."

She opened her mouth. "Tell me."

He shook his head. "No. It's a surprise, so you have to see."

"I've never been very big on surprises," she told him. Most of her experience with them had been bad. Her father's reckless decision to ride a bull when he had no experience of such things. His death. Her mother bringing home a new husband and son.

"It's not something bad," he promised. "Not a bug or a snake."

"I'm not afraid of bugs and snakes," she told him.

"Liar. At least about the snakes. I saw you when we were watching that nature show on television the other day. You were practically curling up in your chair when that diamondback came on the screen. You don't always have to be tough about everything, Colleen."

"Easy for you to say. They don't have snakes in Chicago. At least not the dangerous kind."

He lifted a brow. "Sure they do. Worse than diamondbacks, too, since they're the human kind. They're more devious."

She gave him a crooked smile. "All right, *show* me," she told him.

Dillon took her hand and led her to his computer. Then he sat down and keyed in a URL. Within seconds a photo of a breathtaking house came on the screen. "It has everything all of you suggested would be necessary and then some," he said, giving her a virtual tour of the house.

"It's…a bit like a dream house," she said, staring at the big white stone building. "Like one of those places on cable television where the rich and famous live." It occurred to Colleen that Dillon actually might well be one of the rich and famous. At least in some circles.

"You could fit another small house inside each of the closets," Colleen said. "And all the windows and skylights make it seem so bright and inviting, but the yard and that huge porch are the best parts, I think."

"I'm glad you think so. I was thinking it would be a great place for a birthday party for Toby when that day comes."

"He'll be a star with all of your friends." Which only

reminded Colleen of just how far apart their worlds were. Of course, Dillon would have lots of friends in Chicago. Women friends. Ones who were going to adore Toby and desire Dillon.

"So, you're buying it," she said, cutting off the sadness that was stealing over her. "That's so wonderful. You're on your way." Even though pain was rushing through her at the thought that he would, inevitably, be leaving soon.

He stared at her, long and hard. "Thank you," he said. "My thanks to you and the other women, too. All of you knew what I needed when I didn't, and I'm grateful."

Over the course of the next few hours, everyone got a taste of just how grateful Dillon was. While he went on an errand and took Toby with him, a delivery truck arrived. Inside were flowers and seeds and bedding plants for Gretchen, a selection of the latest princess-style romance movies for Julie and a whole assortment of gourmet cookbooks for Millie's kitchen.

"That man remembered all the things we said when we were planning his house," Millie said. "Can you believe that?"

Gretchen turned her delighted eyes from the flowers to Colleen. "But what about Colleen?" she asked.

Colleen shrugged. She was so touched that Dillon had gone out of his way for her friends who had so little. And she was sure that Dillon was trying just as hard as she was to put some distance between them.

"I only told him to make the house safe. And he's already making *my* house safe," she reminded them.

It was true. Dillon had put in long hours. After the porch was finished, he had moved on to repair cracks in the walls, checked the electrical and heating systems and fixed what he felt were a few inadequacies. He'd made some changes at the bunkhouse and done some roof repairs on both buildings, driving himself relentlessly whenever he had the time.

"What more could a girl ask for?" she asked her friends.

"Good point," Julie said. "It's not every guy who'll climb up on a second-story roof for a woman. He must really like you."

"I…that wasn't what I meant at all," Colleen said, feeling her face grow warm.

"What did you mean?" A low, masculine voice sounded outside the open window and all the women jumped. Julie squealed.

"Were you eavesdropping on us?" Colleen demanded as Dillon came through the door.

"Absolutely," he said with a grin, catching her off guard.

Her eyes widened. "Aren't you the honest one?" she asked.

"Actually, I wasn't really eavesdropping," Dillon confessed. "Toby and I just got here. We were out on an important mission, weren't we, slugger?"

Toby stared up at his dad, his eyes wide. It was obvious that he was fascinated with Dillon. *And why not?* Colleen thought. *All the rest of us are fascinated.* She did her best not to ask what his mission had been. If he had wanted her to know, he would have said so.

"What mission?" Gretchen asked.

Colleen gave her employee and friend a "shush" look.

"I'm glad you asked," Dillon said. He pulled a bag from behind his back. "Because I really could use some feminine advice. There's this woman I want to take to dinner to show her my appreciation for all she's done for me, but I have it on good authority from Nate, the man who apparently runs the only department store within thirty miles, that there aren't any hot restaurants in town."

Millie snorted. "There are only two restaurants in town and only one of them has edible food."

"You must know Nate, too," Dillon teased.

"I have taste buds," Millie said with a laugh. "They work. If you want to go to dinner, go to Yvonne's."

"Thank you. I fully intend to, but since even Yvonne's doesn't appear to have the panache I was shooting for, I was afraid my gift would fall short."

Colleen wanted to tell him that she didn't need a gift, but since he hadn't said anything about the gift being for her, she couldn't very well do that.

"Fortunately, Nate and Yvonne and I made some special arrangements. Millie, do you think you can watch my little guy here for a few hours?"

Julie and Gretchen were already starting to whisper, loud enough to hear. *Special arrangements. What could those be?* But Millie just smiled. "Yvonne is a good friend of mine," she said. "And of course I'll watch the baby. He and I are book buddies. We love reading stories. Besides, I want to make sure this special event takes place, too."

Now Colleen was getting flustered. "I don't like surprises," she reminded Dillon.

"I know. But this is a good surprise. I hope." Millie took Toby, and Dillon reached into the bag. Inside was an envelope, an ivory silk scarf and a bracelet. The bracelet consisted of gorgeous bits of garnet glass set in gold. A solitary golden heart was centered between the glass and golden chain.

"I asked Nate for the best piece of jewelry he had and he showed me this. I…at first it seemed wrong to give you something you had made yourself, but the longer I looked at it the more right it felt. You have so many of your works here, but only one piece of jewelry." He indicated the solitary bit of green glass on the black satin cord around her neck.

"I keep it to remember who I am and what I need to do and to forget," she said, fingering the delicate bracelet. "But this…it was my favorite, too. Too fragile to wear on a ranch. Nate paid me well for it."

"I hope you'll allow me to return it to you and accept the scarf. You'll have a place to wear the bracelet, since we won't be on the ranch tonight if you agree to accept my invitation."

He nodded toward the envelope and she opened it with clumsy fingers. "'Mr. Dillon Farraday requests the company of Ms. Colleen Applegate at table six at Yvonne's dining emporium at seven o'clock tonight. Dress is semiformal.'"

Colleen's skin felt suddenly tight. Her limbs felt heavy. This sounded too much like a date. But it wasn't a date. She knew that. "Just two friends having dinner, right?" she asked.

He smiled and tilted his head. "I hope you consider me a friend. You've done me a major favor. *Many* favors."

Gretchen's eyebrows rose and Colleen glared at her. "He's talking about Toby," she said.

"I'm talking about Toby," he agreed. "Colleen has mothered him and taught me. But she's also a pretty good kisser," he told Gretchen, who hooted.

"Hmm, telling my secrets?" Colleen asked, trying to keep from blushing. "I haven't said yes yet."

"Say yes," he said. "I want you to have a night on the town. Yvonne is making something amazing, I've been told."

"At her dining emporium, too," Millie added. "I'll have to ask her about that name. Usually she's just plain old Yvonne's or at best Yvonne's diner."

"Tonight's different," Dillon said. He waited.

"I can't disappoint Yvonne," Colleen said softly. "Besides, you've piqued my curiosity. I want to see the difference between a dining emporium and a diner."

"Oh, and there'll be entertainment, too," he promised. "I'll pick you up here in an hour, all right?" Then he winked at her and left the room.

"Entertainment? I wonder what that could be," Julie said. "Yvonne's never had entertainment before."

"I don't know, but I hope he kisses you again," Gretchen said. "He made you blush. I don't think I've ever seen anyone fluster you enough to make you blush. It looks as if it agrees with you."

CHAPTER TEN

DILLON felt like a kid going on his first date…which was ridiculous. He'd dated many women over the years. He might not be good at making a success of emotional relationships, but he had never had a problem getting things off the ground. The only problem here was that with Colleen there was no chance of even the beginnings of a relationship. He had to be careful and keep his desire in check because he could hurt her if this thing between them began to take flight. So, that couldn't happen. He couldn't let himself lose control.

And it wasn't just Colleen who was at risk, either. Already he knew that he wasn't leaving Bright Creek intact. He was going to miss Colleen like crazy when this was over, from that bossy brave way she had of crossing her arms and confronting things that scared her to the way she threw herself into kissing and then in the next minute told him that they couldn't do it anymore.

Colleen was an original, but he had it on good authority that she had never been taken seriously as a woman in Bright Creek. She had always just been one of the guys.

Not tonight. It would be different tonight, and Dillon hoped she wouldn't be embarrassed or self-conscious.

He moved into the living room. And stopped. And just…looked.

She was wearing a red dress. He'd never seen her in a dress. And her hair waved around her shoulders. She looked…beautiful. Stunningly so in a way a more petite, less curvaceous woman couldn't. But really, Dillon thought, it had always been what came from inside that made Colleen truly beautiful. Who and what she was, was written in her eyes, in her smile, in the way she stood and moved. But tonight…

"I like that," he said, when what he wanted to say was "I like *you*." On another day he would have, but tonight this felt too personal. She had wanted things merely to be friendly. So did he. "I see you're still wearing your red cowgirl boots."

"I didn't have any dress shoes that fit and no one else wears the same size I do."

He smiled. "Looks good, though."

She laughed. "Nice save," she told him. "Julie complained that if I ever got married, I'd probably wear these under my wedding dress. They're not her favorites. To me, they look okay…sort of, but I wouldn't go further than that."

"That's because you're not a man looking at an attractive woman."

"That's because I'm honest. I just hope no one laughs when I walk into the restaurant. Maybe no one will recognize me with makeup and a dress on."

Oh, they would recognize her all right, and if there were any men there who had thought of her as one of the guys, they were going to be in for a shock, Dillon thought. He held out his hand. She placed her slender fingers in his. He allowed himself to enjoy her touch for just a minute while they moved outside to the car before he held the door open for her. "Better put the scarf on," he told her.

"Is that what that was for?" she asked. "I thought I was

supposed to wear it around my neck or my shoulders or something."

"You could do that, too, but you'll need it for your hair right now."

She did as he asked, and by the time they pulled up in front of Yvonne's and got out of the car Colleen was nodding. "That was so amazing," she said, gesturing toward his car. "I thought you were kidding about the scarf. The way that thing moves so fast, the wind in my hair…it was incredible."

"Don't tell Harve you already rode in the Ferrari," Dillon teased her. "He'll turn green."

She laughed as she and Dillon walked the few steps to Yvonne's and Dillon opened the door. "Oh, my," Colleen said as they walked inside.

Oh, my was right. He'd stopped in this afternoon, and he had to admit that the woman had taken the money he'd given her and worked a small miracle in a few hours. There wasn't much that could be done about the booths, but Yvonne had covered every table in cloths the color of fine merlot. She'd put wine-colored shades on the wall light fixtures and left the overheads off altogether. White candles burned on every table, and soft music was playing in the background. A few people sat in the booths looking shell-shocked and confused.

Yvonne came out of the back as if on cue, holding menus that could only have been run off today. They didn't look anything like the ones Dillon had seen earlier. Yvonne herself had undergone a change from her customary pale blue uniform with white apron to a tasteful black dress and heels. "Mr. Farraday. Colleen," she said. "Please follow me. Your table is ready."

She led them to a table in a corner, the only table in the room, one that had obviously come from somewhere else. Dillon couldn't remember what had sat in this space this afternoon—a dessert display case, he thought—but this square table set with china and crystal and roses had definitely not been here.

"It's so beautiful, Yvonne," Colleen said, touching the woman's hand.

"You exceeded my expectations," Dillon agreed. "This is just what I had in mind."

"I may be small town, but I'm not small-minded," Yvonne said with a smile. "I know what a romantic dinner should be like."

For a second Colleen looked frantic and distressed, but Dillon touched her arm. "It's okay. I understand that you don't want there to be anything romantic between us," he said. "I'm not your type. But for tonight let me pretend," he said.

As he said it, he turned slightly, drawing Colleen with him. In a booth to their right, a group of men sat, staring. He recognized at least one of them from that day at the ranch when Colleen had blocked the exit. "Evening, men," he said. "I assume by the way you're looking at her that you all know Colleen."

At his words, they gave Colleen a once-over. And then they looked again.

"Whoa, Colleen, I…man, I just saw you at the ranch a week ago, but I wouldn't have recognized you tonight. You look…heck, you look hot. Hotter than Lisa Breckinridge. I mean Farraday," he said, nodding toward Dillon. "No disrespect to your ex-wife," he told Dillon.

Dillon shrugged. "I don't care about Lisa. Just so you know that Colleen is here with *me* tonight."

Colleen turned to the man. "But I'll still remember that you pushed me down in the mud once, Rob," she told him. "And you laughed at me and never said you were sorry."

The man's face turned red. "Well, I am sorry. I was young and stupid back then. And you…you were…"

"Felix Bamrow's ugly stepdaughter? That was what you called me."

"I know I did. I was sorry right afterward. You looked like you were going to cry."

"And then I kicked you in the shins, didn't I?"

"Yeah, you did. I deserved it, too. You want to kick me again? Or call me Harve Enson's ugly son? I'll stand still and let you."

Suddenly Colleen shook her head and gave the man a small smile. Dillon felt as if *he* had been kicked in the *stomach* the way she was looking at that guy. "I was never good at name calling and I don't kick men too much anymore."

"Do you let them apologize years after the fact?"

"Is it just because I'm wearing this dress? Would you have apologized if I'd been wearing my jeans?"

The man hesitated. "I don't know how to answer that. I don't exactly know, Colleen. You look pretty tonight but you still scare me when you're dressed for ranching. You always look as if you hate men, as if you'd welcome the chance to kick a guy or two."

"Maybe I haven't met too many guys who didn't deserve it."

The man nodded. "That's fair. I knew that your stepfather and stepbrother were jerks, and obviously, so were the rest of us." He motioned to the other men at the table, who hadn't said anything but were looking uncomfortable. Then he went back to his meal, but he didn't look too happy.

Dillon silently led Colleen to their table and pulled out her chair. After they were seated at right angles to each other, she leaned to the side and whispered in his ear, "Why did you do that?"

He shook his head, not knowing how to answer. "Do what?"

"Phrase things so that it sounded as if I was some woman you were pursuing. You did it so that those men would pay attention, didn't you?"

"Well, it makes me mad that, up until now, they haven't been able to see what's clear to me. Still, I probably should have consulted with you before I did that. You might not have approved."

"It could have ended pretty ugly," she said. "Rob or one of the others could have said something nasty."

"I didn't think any man could be so big an idiot that he would insult a gorgeous woman."

She frowned. "Rob Enson never thought I was gorgeous."

"That's because he's blind. The truth is that you're gorgeous no matter what you're wearing. The fact that he doesn't see it when you're dressed for ranching just proves he's shortsighted, but believe me, Colleen, no one's so shortsighted and ignorant that they could miss your appeal dressed as you are tonight."

"But you didn't know that when you arranged this, did you?" she asked.

"I imagined what you would look like," he admitted, his voice deepening. Their voices were low so no one could hear, but his tone was such that a few heads turned when he made this comment. He knew he probably looked smitten. Frankly, he didn't care right now, because Colleen was looking at him with those clear, trusting eyes and she was smiling.

"Lisa was so stupid," she said. "While you were away, she must have forgotten how you say such pretty things. She always did need to hear those kinds of compliments."

And Colleen hadn't. She wasn't used to them.

"Colleen, I'm warning you, if you keep looking at me like that, I'm going to kiss you right here in front of the whole town."

"Well, that would be something else they haven't seen," she mused. "Me kissing someone."

Dillon growled.

Colleen reached out and touched his hand soothingly.

"Colleen, this is supposed to be *your* night. I wanted *you* to have the chance to be the queen for once. You get to shine tonight. You're not supposed to be worrying about my reaction."

"The queen? You darn silly man," she said, and when he looked at her, there were tears on her lashes. "You wanted me to have what Lisa had all these years."

"No, I wanted you to have more than Lisa had. Lisa is an illusion, an actress. You're the real deal. People need to see that. You deserve your due."

And then she laughed. Yvonne brought out the special meal she had prepared and Colleen turned to her. "Yvonne, this man is amazing. He did all of this to thank me just for babysitting that cute little baby of his. Isn't he something?"

Yvonne looked at Dillon. "I'm not arguing, Colleen. When he came in here today, I had to fan myself, he looks so good in jeans. Then I found out that he had this all planned for you. If I didn't like you so much we'd have to have a hair-pulling contest over him. As it is, I'm just glad it's you he's doing this for. You're the best. Enjoy the meal and the entertainment."

Colleen wondered what entertainment Yvonne was talking about. Wasn't having Rob Enson all but beg her to forgive him for his crimes entertainment enough?

Yeah, she was going to have to accept his apology before he left here tonight. It just wasn't in her to turn down a request from someone who seemed genuinely repentant. But she knew that none of that would ever have happened if not for Dillon.

She was more than entertained. She was enthralled. Too enthralled. Every time Dillon leaned over and whispered something to her, she wanted to turn so that their lips met. She wanted to wrap her arms around his neck. And it wasn't that he looked so amazingly handsome in his white shirt and black pants that did nothing to hide his tanned throat or the muscles in his thighs. It was Dillon himself, his very essence. The man was just dangerous. She was going to have to pull away or she would go up in a fireball now and be nothing but cinders when he left.

"There we go," Dillon was saying. "Those guys are good."

Colleen looked behind her to see that a trio of musicians had set up in the back of the restaurant. They were playing soft, slow tunes. Dreamy stuff.

"Dance with me," Dillon said and he drew her up with him.

"I don't know how." Suddenly, she was nervous. "I'll look like an idiot."

"I won't let that happen. I'll do all the work. You just shuffle along until you can follow my movements. I promise to keep it simple. And if all else fails, we can always resort to the standby slow dance. Just swaying together."

Oh no. Not that. That would be where she was held up against Dillon's chest, her arms draped around his neck and every cell in her body tight with desire. There was no way she could hide her reactions to Dillon from this crowd in that kind of a situation.

In the end, she didn't have to. Despite the wound that she knew still pained him, Dillon was a superb dancer and he led her through the steps with such ease that she didn't even feel as if she was learning.

In what seemed like mere seconds the dance had ended. She was staring up at Dillon and she knew that her eyes had to be glowing with naked desire.

"Mind if I cut in?" It was Rob, and Colleen blinked. For half a second Dillon looked irritated. No doubt because he remembered what had transpired between her and Rob earlier. He wouldn't let anyone crowd her if she didn't want it. She knew that. But Dillon couldn't afford to mix it up with anyone. The restaurant had filled by now as news of Yvonne's coup spread, and there were probably eyes and ears in this room looking and listening. There would be reports made to Lisa.

"All right, I forgive you, Rob," she said. "Since you seem sincere in your apology, and since you're Harve's son and I like him. You just keep in mind that I'm not a very good dancer. No snickering or name calling."

"I don't do that stuff anymore," Rob said. "And I'm not such a good dancer myself."

Colleen tried to concentrate on the man she was dancing with. She didn't want anyone to notice that her gaze followed Dillon as he walked away, but it was almost impossible for her not to glance his way now and then as the dance progressed. To her dismay, she saw that Bill Winters, Lisa's spy, the man Dillon had told her not to worry about, had come into the restaurant. He was standing in front of Dillon, gesticulating wildly, his hands in tight fists.

"Rob, I…thank you for the dance," she said and stopped dancing.

"It ain't over yet, Colleen." Then he saw where she was looking. He uttered a curse and she knew that there would be no chance to keep this private. Already people were starting to gather round.

"It's just a little too suspicious that all this stuff started now after you came to town," Bill was saying, practically spitting out the words.

"Bill, pal, I don't know what you're talking about. Maybe you need to sit down. You really don't look so hot," Dillon answered.

"I don't want to sit down and I don't *feel* so hot. Why should I when there are pictures of me on the Internet on my knees in front of Lisa begging her to notice me. I don't know where you got those pictures, but I never said those things. I never was in that pose. Those photos were altered, those dialogue balloons were added by somebody and I don't know anybody around here who would have any incentive to do that. Except Colleen."

Colleen did her best to look blasé. "Bill, you know I'm not that skilled with computers. How would I know how to do something like that?"

"And what incentive would she have, Bill? Colleen has no reason to cause you grief."

"You do."

Dillon shook his head. "We've barely exchanged two sentences until now. What would I have against you?"

Bill was looking around wildly now. He obviously couldn't admit that he'd spread tales to Lisa and that he'd spied on Dillon and Colleen when no one was supposed to know that. "I don't know, but nothing like this ever happened until you got here. I want it stopped and taken down."

"You'll have to talk to whoever put it up there," Dillon said. "You'll have to figure out who in town has something against you. That's rough, buddy. When something goes viral, it's next to impossible to stop it. Could take some time. Sorry, but I have to go now. My son gets up early in the morning and I have to be there for him."

"Hey, Dillon, how about showing us that car before you go?"

"Later, Harve. It's dark. You need light to do it justice."

Harve grumbled, but he didn't say more. Dillon smiled. He held out his arm and Colleen took it, falling into step with him. They didn't talk on the way home, but when they were finally in the house, had checked on Toby and were standing at the door that led to the back porch, Colleen looked up at Dillon.

"That stuff with Bill, was that part of the entertainment?"

"That was an extra I hadn't expected."

"Then you didn't put that stuff up on the Internet?"

He lifted a shoulder in dismissal. "I have friends and employees who live for all the quirky sites on the Internet. They know how to use a computer and how to send a message out so that it multiplies and hits its target. I might have indicated that a rumor might be helpful as long as it wasn't anything that would negatively impact Toby and me. Beyond that, no."

"It *was* pretty funny. Bill deserved that."

"I don't want him to think that he can threaten you. Now, he knows there are ways to get at him if he misbehaves."

"Thank you," she whispered.

"It's a little thing."

"Tonight wasn't a little thing. The restaurant and Yvonne and Rob and the music. I felt just like any other woman tonight."

Dillon groaned. "Colleen, you are never going to be just like any other woman. You are so much better."

"You make me better," she said, and then he was pulling her into his arms, his mouth covering hers and it was…so good, so right, so not nearly enough.

Suddenly, Dillon pulled away. "I better go before I do something that can't be called back."

Colleen looked at the door that she locked every night. "I put you out here because I didn't trust you at first, but…"

He stopped her with a fierce kiss. "Lock the door tonight, Colleen. Don't trust me, tonight or ever. This door is all that keeps me honest and away from you. You have to continue to be who you are after I'm gone and if I touch you…too much, I'm afraid it will show. People will know. It will change you somehow and make things more difficult for you. Lock the door."

She took a deep breath. She ignored the yearning in her heart and the pain of what could never be.

"I'll lock the door," she said. But as she put words to deeds, she knew that it was already too late. She'd let him into her heart and she already *had* been changed. The question was, who would she be when he and Toby were gone? What was she going to do?

CHAPTER ELEVEN

THE next morning, everything went south. Dillon was doing one last job, repairing a window that had been leaking during heavy rains when his telephone rang.

He answered it and listened. "Lisa's back in Chicago, Jace?" he said. "All right, I need you to find out what that's all about and what her plans are. Is she staying there? Just passing through? On her way here?"

But he didn't have to wait long for Jace's call. Within hours Lisa herself had checked in. "I'm home," she told him, "and I'm settling in. I'm nesting."

Dillon's blood temperature dropped ten degrees. "What does that mean?"

"Probably what it sounds like. I'm feeling very domestic. Very maternal."

"That's nice, Lisa. That's…fantastic. I'm wondering why you're telling me this."

"Why wouldn't I tell you? You're my ex-husband. We share a child. A child who's grown to be very cute and adorable, I understand." Then she hung up. Dillon swore.

Almost immediately, Colleen was there. She'd been inside with Toby, but now she came outside with him on her hip, which looked…right. He didn't want to even begin to tell her about the phone call. And yet he had to.

Quickly, he relayed Lisa's message. "She didn't ask for money," he said.

"She wouldn't. If she said it, then there would be a record of that, and if money is what she really wants, then she needs ammunition against you. She won't give you any to use against her."

"And if I just flat out offered her money on the chance that that's what she's after, she could use that against *me* in court by telling the judge I tried to bribe her."

They stood there looking at each other. Colleen's lips were nearly white, she was so obviously stressed. Dillon felt panic beginning to rip through him, and yet…he remembered his own childhood, wanting the attention of his mother and father. "If I thought there was a chance that she *really* wanted to be a mother to him…" Dillon began.

Colleen bit her lip, then nodded. "A child should get a chance to know both his parents."

"Yes. If I thought she cared about him even a little, I'd make sure that she had the right to see him. But I'm not letting her take him from me, and if it's only money she's after, if she's trying to somehow use him…" Dillon's voice was hard.

Colleen reached out and touched his arm. "You can't let that happen."

"I'm not going to let it happen." There was no question that it was time to return to Chicago now, not next week. In addition to the problem with his business and his out-of-town project manager, he had territory on the home front and on the baby front to guard. He had to dig in and get ready in case Lisa made a move that would affect Toby.

"Let's go figure out how this is going to play out. What steps you have to take to stay ahead of her when you go back and how you can make this turn out right for Toby. I assume you've already spoken to your attorney."

"Of course. His advice is practical and sound. Don't make any wrong moves. Be a good father and a good person. Make friends. Make connections, especially in Chicago, since I've been away a while. It doesn't hurt to have good, strong character witnesses in the community."

"All right, then, you…you and Toby will go home tomorrow instead of next week. You'll furnish your house and you'll do all the things you've been doing and more." Her eyes were dark. Haunted, but she was standing straight and tall. Not flinching, even though Dillon knew her heart was breaking over the loss of Toby.

Julie was walking past just then. "Dillon and Toby are really leaving, then? For good?"

Those last two words seemed to say it all. They spelled out the finality of this move. He was leaving *for good*. The stark truth of that thought caught Dillon off guard, and Colleen must have felt it, too. She put her chin up the way she did when she was trying to act as if she was unaffected by things that hurt.

Dillon understood completely, because inside he was howling. With rage. With pain. He hadn't been ready to break this off just yet. And not this way.

"But who'll help you set up that big house?" Julie asked. "More importantly, who'll watch Toby when you're at work or just not home? Won't your ex-wife…won't Lisa jump right on that if the person you hire scares Toby or isn't totally perfect? You need someone who's special, someone who Toby is going to love and who is going to love him right back, so you can't just go rushing in to hire any old person."

Dillon had been thinking the same thing. When he looked at Colleen, he knew she had already started to worry about those things, too.

"You really need more time to set the scene and set things up and find someone to help you with Toby," she said, "but…"

But he didn't have more time. What he needed was Colleen by his side for just a little while longer. What he needed was the impossible. He rubbed his hand along his jaw. He couldn't ask her. She had this ranch to run. She'd already given him too much, and besides, he knew that part of the reason he wanted her with him had nothing to do with his child. That wasn't fair to Colleen, not when both of them knew this thing between them wasn't going anywhere.

Colleen exchanged a look with Julie. Then she nodded, some feminine exchange that Dillon didn't understand.

"The others can manage alone here for a short while. If you need me, if you'll let me, I'll help you interview people and find the right person to be a nanny for Toby. I'll help you get your house set up and I'll help you show everyone just how dedicated to your child you really are. I can do this...if you...that is, if you want my help."

Dillon gave her an incredulous look. "I don't know which of the ignorant men in this town killed your confidence, but I'd like to kick every one of them over a cliff. If I want your help...Colleen, do I look like a crazy man? If you're offering, I'm accepting." Even if it was insane. Even if having her near and knowing she would only be in his home for a week was going to be a rough bit of knowledge to live with. A week was one week more than he had had just a minute ago.

"You two are going to have a lot of work to do," Julie continued. "Good thing that house is empty. You're going to have to close on it and furnish it in only days. There aren't even any beds in the place."

"There will be by the time we get there," Dillon said. "You all figure out everything you need to tend to before Colleen leaves. I'll tend to the Chicago end of things and then... Colleen?"

She looked at him.

"Before we leave I have something I have to take care of. In town. If you'd like to go with me and hustle up all the people I've made promises to, I would appreciate it."

Colleen looked confused at first, then she shook her head. "The car. Harve and the others. You don't have to do that, you know."

"Putting someone off until later is one thing, but a promise is a promise. I'm not going to say one thing and do another. Let Harve know that we'll be stopping by this afternoon on our way out of town."

"I will," she said, shaking her head, but Julie was already tugging her by the hand.

"Come on," Julie said. "We have to choose the right clothes for you to take to Chicago."

A look of distress came over Colleen. "Clothes? You know I'm awful at picking out clothes."

"I know. That's why it's lucky you have the rest of us. We'll make sure you don't dress like a scarecrow...or a cowboy. Dillon needs to impress people."

For half a second, a look of terror came into Colleen's eyes before she managed to shutter it. His fearless Colleen, who had faced him down and stood off half a dozen men she thought were going to bother him and Toby, was afraid of embarrassing him by wearing the wrong clothes.

Just let one person in Chicago insult her, he thought, *and they'll have me to deal with.*

And wouldn't that be just great? If he stepped out of line at all...if he ended up in the newspapers or on a police blotter or even in the society gossip pages where he'd appeared before...when he got married...

Dillon felt like swearing, but that wasn't going to happen. He had to be on his best behavior. But he was going to protect Colleen, too. That was just nonnegotiable.

* * *

Tension filled Colleen's soul. She was flying blind here, heading into completely unknown territory and risking her heart in ways she couldn't even begin to imagine. She'd never even been outside Montana before, certainly never to a major city like Chicago. And to go there with a man like Dillon who, from the looks of his car, really was used to the best…

A vision of Lisa came to mind. The best, everyone had always said. A woman who knew how to dress and wear makeup and get her way when she wanted to. And she always wanted to. She wanted something from Dillon, something that might hurt him and Toby.

Not going to happen if I can help it, Colleen thought. So there was no turning coward now. She put the last item in her suitcase and took a deep breath.

"I'm ready," she called to Dillon.

And the next thing she knew all her friends were hugging her.

"Don't get too fond of Chicago," Millie said, looking a little teary-eyed.

"But have fun," Julie said.

"And call," Gretchen added. "Take pictures so we can live vicariously."

Suddenly Colleen felt grounded. Especially since Dillon was watching them with such affection in his eyes. He had been so good to her friends, these women who needed the goodness that had been denied them in the past.

"I'll do my best," she told everyone. "But you know I'm not going to sightsee. I'll be there to help Dillon."

"Yes, but surely you'll see at least some of the city."

Dillon was laughing at Julie's impatient tone. "Don't worry," he told her. "If you think I'm going to keep her chained up in the nursery, well, I hope you know me better than that by now. I have a couple of social events where having an attractive woman on my arm will be a real asset, and of course we'll have to tour the city so Toby can see his new hometown."

Colleen rolled her eyes. "At his age, I doubt Toby's anxious to join the sightseeing set. And you can't take me to a social event. I won't fit in."

"Sure you will, and just in case you're worried about not having the right clothes, I already had my secretary buy you a couple of dresses and put them in the closet at the house."

"Dillon! You can't do that!"

"It's done. And don't deny me the pleasure. I can certainly afford it."

She shook her head. "We'd better get going before you tell me that you've bought me a castle."

"Colleen, why didn't you tell me that you wanted a castle?" he teased.

"I'm telling you now," she said in a teasing tone. "A gold one. With pink turrets and…and a unicorn." Her smile grew. "Hah! Just try to get your secretary to come up with one of those."

And with that, she took Toby from Millie and headed out to the car.

"You are going to be a handful," he said to her back. But he sounded pleased. For some reason that made her heart ache.

When Dillon pulled the Ferrari into a spot in front of Yvonne's, got out and took Toby out of his car seat, Colleen noted that the crowd of retired men in the chairs in front of Yvonne's was bigger than usual. In fact, this was a standing room only crowd. She walked around to the sidewalk and held out her hands for Toby. "I think you'll need both hands free. These men are going to want a show."

"And a ride," Harve said. "If that's possible."

Dillon smiled. "We can fit three at a time. Harve, why don't you drive us around the town, show everyone what this car can do, and I'll explain about the finer points of this vehicle."

"I hear it's made of aluminum," one man said. "That's one sweet little car. I wish my son was in town. He'd love to ride in this."

"Maybe if I'm ever out this way again," Dillon promised. But, of course, Dillon wouldn't be out this way again, Colleen thought. She'd known that all along, so why did her heart hurt?

Deal with it, she told herself and went into Yvonne's with Toby in tow.

For the next forty-five minutes, Dillon gave tours, let the men drive alone and at one point, drove out into the country so that one elderly man could give his grandson a chance to ride in the sleek car. "I couldn't deny a guy a chance to be a hero in his grandson's eyes," Dillon explained with a shrug.

"You're a softie," she said.

He shrugged. "Kids deserve to have a little unexpected excitement now and then."

And so do you, Colleen thought. But for the longest time all he had had was worry. The man had left the business of his heart, gone off to war, been injured and now faced the possibility that the woman who had betrayed him might try to harm him yet again.

If I can help him stop that, I will, Colleen thought. *But how do I stop myself from getting in deeper than I already am?*

CHAPTER TWELVE

IN THE end, Dillon had hired someone to drive the Ferrari home and a private plane to fly him, Colleen and Toby to Chicago. He just couldn't ask her to spend more time away from the ranch than she had to. They were both weary and wary enough already, and Toby was still young for a long, cross-country trip.

Even flying, by the time they stumbled into his house, it was late. Toby was asleep, and Dillon knew Colleen had to be tired, but…

"This is totally amazing, Dillon," she said, wide-eyed. "I don't know who you hired or how they worked so fast, but whoever he or she was, they knew what they were doing. This place is furnished so beautifully." She ran her hand over the honeyed wood of a table.

"And the forest-green and gold against all the hardwood floors makes everything look cozy and warm and inviting. And all those windows…the lights of the city are like a million fireflies. Toby will love it here when he gets old enough to notice the details. Or when he wakes up," she said, kissing Toby's soft baby curls. "I guess we'd better get him right to bed."

But no sooner had they located the nursery and gotten Toby off to sleep than Dillon's telephone started ringing.

He excused himself, took the call and immediately got another one. By the time the tenth phone call had come through, Dillon had had enough. He recorded a new message, begging off until the morning, telling all callers that he and his son were going to sleep and then he turned the ringer down on the phone.

"Looks as though your admiring public has found you," Colleen said softly. "You're home. Or maybe it was business and…I'm sorry, none of this is my affair."

"Jace thought it would be a good idea to broadcast the fact that I was returning to town with Toby, that I had a new house and was putting down deep roots. Most of the calls were old friends and acquaintances wishing me well."

"But not all?"

"One was work. And one was Lisa telling me that she would be over to see Toby first thing tomorrow."

The two of them stared at each other. "We'd better make sure we're on the same page, then," Colleen whispered. "I don't want to say the wrong thing and make a mistake that might cost you everything." She looked genuinely worried.

"You couldn't. Just be yourself and tell the truth. You're here to help me hire a nanny and get settled in with Toby, because Toby is used to you and you know what he likes."

Colleen bit her lip, but she nodded. She took on that serious, determined look that made him want to hold her and promise her that the world couldn't harm her anymore, that he wouldn't let that happen, even though he knew he wouldn't be around to fulfill that promise. "I *do* know what he likes. I *am* here to help you," she said. "Not trying to lie makes it easier. I'm not a good liar, although…"

He tilted his head as she hesitated.

"I would lie through my teeth if I thought it would help the two of you."

And just like that, every good intention he had about keeping his distance flew away on firefly wings. He framed his hands around her face and kissed her. Gently. Once. Twice. More times than he cared to count, because once he started kissing Colleen, his mind turned fuzzy and warm. He was dazed, confused, uncaring of anything except staying with her softness, keeping his mouth against her skin, holding her heat against his body. Giving in. Giving up. He wrapped himself around her, curled her body into his.

And all the time he was doing that, she was stretching forward, tugging him closer, kissing him back. Turning him into a mindless madman, a collection of desires and not an intelligent thought in his head.

"Kiss me again," she told him. "I love it when you kiss me."

He kissed her, and she moaned. She settled against him.

He slid his hand down her side, over her curves. Learning her. Memorizing her. Knowing that he had to memorize her, because soon memory would be all he had. This was…this was insane and he didn't engage in insane gestures. He didn't like things to slip out of his control. He didn't want to want what he could never have. He'd done that already. He'd regretted that too many times, and yet…

"Colleen," he whispered. "You're fire, you're magic. Touching you is like a dream and…"

He felt her shudder and then still beneath his hands. "You're right," she said. "This isn't real. It isn't right or logical or practical or…we both know that this…you and I have a purpose. That's what we both wanted, what we came together for. We're both nervous, fearful of what's going to happen in the next few days or weeks and that's why we're doing this. We have to stop."

Dillon stopped. She was wrong. He hoped she was wrong. He wasn't just using her to avoid facing the uncertainty of tomorrow. She wasn't just a crutch like the cane he had used when he first came to her house. And yet…what was she? She wasn't his, and she…

"You're probably feeling out of place. I know this is the first time you've even been out of Montana," he said. "I shouldn't have taken advantage of that out-of-kilter feeling. Come here. Come with me."

She was shaking a little and he wanted to soothe her, to warm her, but he was afraid of what would happen if he touched her again, so he simply wrapped a throw from the arm of the sofa around her shoulders. He led her to the computer that had been set up in a nearby room, sat her down and clicked on some keys. "Montana's an hour later than we are here," he said. "Everyone will still be awake."

Within seconds, Millie came on the screen and then the other women of the Applegate appeared. Colleen blinked. She turned to Dillon.

"Gretchen and I set it up before you left. They need you to be within reach, and I didn't want you to be homesick. Being able to see them makes it easier, I hope."

She blinked hard a couple of times. "You're making it very hard for me."

"In what way?" Dillon said.

"Before you came to the Applegate, I was happy believing that men were necessary to the world but not people I wanted to let into *my* world. Now, because of you, I've had to change my mind about men. Some of them are worth getting to know."

But as Dillon left the room and left Colleen to her conversation, he wondered why her words didn't make him happy. Of course, he knew the answer to that. Now that Colleen had opened her doors to men, she might meet one she would allow into her heart forever. Some good-looking cowboy might win her someday. He'd help her with her horses, he'd sleep with her in the bed Dillon had never even seen.

And you should be happy for her, he told himself as he tromped up the stairs to his own lonely room.

Instead, he wanted to go downstairs, talk Colleen into sharing his bed tonight and being the first man to tame her and win her. It was a selfish thought, he told himself.

But when the morning came, he hadn't slept it off. Her name was the first thing he thought of when he woke up.

Colleen woke up disoriented. The first thing she remembered was kissing Dillon and wanting him to never stop kissing her. She wanted him to make love with her, and that wasn't something she'd really wanted with any man before.

Which made it a very bad idea, because that meant that he was starting to mean far too much to her. And her time with him was limited.

Besides, today Lisa was coming. Perfect Lisa. Maybe perfect Lisa would want Dillon back. And had Colleen ever met a man who could say no to the woman?

She squinted her eyes closed, trying to block the thought, then got up, got dressed and went looking for Toby. He wasn't in his room.

Barefooted, she padded downstairs. Still no Toby and no Dillon.

"Look who I see." Dillon's deep voice rippled through her body. Toby's coo fanned across her heart. She let herself out onto the deck where the two of them were sitting in the early morning pale light. And stopped.

"Dillon…" she drawled.

"What?"

"Why did you do this? *When* did you do this?"

He didn't pretend not to know what she was talking about. "Hey, I love your sculptures," he said, turning toward the huge yard where several specimens of her work were prominently displayed. There was one in the shadow and dappled light beneath the large branches of a tree and two in full sun flanking a walkway that led to a gazebo. And at the entrance of the gazebo, multiple wind chimes waved and softly chimed in the slight breeze.

"Dillon, I can go months without a single order."

"That's because you don't promote yourself. Your work is never seen. I guarantee people will see these. And they'll love them."

"Are you trying to help me without seeming as if you're helping me?" Of course he was.

"Are you accusing me of not knowing great art when I see it? This," he told his son, "is beautiful and unique, just like the woman who made it. And you and I are lucky we got in on the ground floor before everyone finds out about her and wants a piece of the action."

Toby gurgled.

"Yes, that's what I thought," Dillon said. "He thinks I made a great decision," Dillon told her.

She laughed and shook her head. "Well, far be it from me to demand that someone send back something of mine."

"As if they would. So…are you ready to see the town this afternoon?"

"We're sightseeing?"

"We're being seen. I have it on excellent authority that if we show up in the right places—the zoo, Lincoln Park, the butterfly haven at the nature museum—we'll run in to friends and acquaintances who will, of course, remember later that Toby was getting the best of attention. They might even mention to the local gossip columnist that a well-known businessman has returned to town after a long absence with his very happy, very well cared for child in tow."

She smiled. "Isn't that a bit manipulative?"

"Totally. Ask me if I care. This is my son we're talking about."

"Good point."

"I'll do whatever it takes."

"And so will I," she said decisively.

But when the doorbell rang several hours later, just as they had finally decided that Lisa wasn't coming, Colleen felt less certain of herself.

"Dillon!" Lisa said, rising on her toes and kissing Dillon on the cheek. "You're looking as delicious as ever." She swept past him into the room, all long dark hair, violet eyes and petite beauty.

"Hi, Colleen. Where's my baby?" As if Colleen had been hiding him in a cave somewhere for the past few months.

"Hello, Lisa," Colleen said, but she didn't answer the question. That was for Dillon to do.

"He's still napping," Dillon said.

"Well, wake him up. I can't wait to see him. You won't mind, will you? I'm sure he'll fall right back asleep."

Which wasn't true at all, and Dillon knew it. He'd grown to know a lot about babies during the past couple of weeks and about this baby in particular. Toby was fretful and cranky when he was pulled out of sleep early and it took him a while to adjust. In fact, Colleen could see that Dillon was ready to say no, and she wondered what Lisa would do with that denial. Tell people he hadn't allowed her to see their child?

"Dillon, you're angry with me and who could blame you? I was a failure at being a military wife, wasn't I? I was so lonely when you were gone and…what can I say? I panicked, I filed for divorce. But now I have this pretty baby, and I'm his mother."

No word at all about the fact that she had clearly cheated on Dillon and had abandoned her child in order to enjoy herself in Europe with a parade of men.

Still, Dillon didn't answer. "You're not going to let me see him, are you?" Lisa finally asked. She blinked those big violet eyes as if she were going to cry.

Colleen wanted to tell her to stop it, that Dillon wasn't like other men. He didn't fall for those tricks, but he *had* married her and—

"Lisa," Dillon said, "I don't know what you're doing, but let's at least not play games with each other."

Lisa froze. "What—I don't know what you're talking about."

He scowled. "You threw him away as if he meant nothing to you."

"That's not true! Colleen, tell him how it was."

Colleen wanted nothing more than to tell Lisa how it was, that Dillon was exactly right, that Lisa hadn't seemed to care at all, even though she knew she had to be careful here. Push Lisa into a corner and she would bring out the rusty knives and fight dirty. Still, Colleen had to ask one thing. "Why didn't you even give me any way to locate you? What if something had happened to Toby and I needed your help or at least your signature on medical forms? I can't even begin to understand that."

"Didn't you care anything at all about him?" Dillon demanded.

Lisa's pretty face crumpled. "Stop it! Please…my baby. I came here because…I just want to see my baby."

Dillon's expression was thunderous, but Colleen knew Lisa's methods well enough to know that this was when she was most dangerous, when she was being deprived of something. The truth was that if Dillon didn't do as Lisa said, she could claim that he had kept her from Toby.

So, even though it felt completely wrong on many levels, Colleen stepped forward. "We know you want to see Toby. Dillon's just waiting for him to wake up."

Dillon's frown deepened.

"But, of course, we know how difficult it is to wait in a case like this. You and Toby have been apart so long," Colleen continued, rushing on. "So, we won't wait any longer. I'll be right back." She closed her eyes, crossed her fingers, prayed a little as she moved into the nursery and gently picked up the sleeping baby. He was adorable, he was so sweet, and as usual, he had wet his diaper while he was sleeping. "I'm so sorry, sweetie," she whispered to Toby, "but I really need your help. You'll need to wait just a few minutes until I change you."

Toby woke up and began to blink his eyes and cry in that choking little way that babies do. Ordinarily, Colleen would have sang to him, rocked him. She fully intended to do that, she hated herself for not doing those comforting things for him, and yet—

She walked out of the room to face a fuming Dillon, and Lisa wearing a determined if pale expression. "Here he is," Colleen said, handing Toby to Lisa. She held her breath. Lisa was small, she was pretty and she smelled of expensive perfume. Maybe Toby would like all that. Maybe he'd be just like every other member of the male population. And…

Colleen could barely bear to move on to the next thought, but…if Lisa truly didn't mind this wet and crying baby and opened her heart to him, maybe Dillon would eventually have to let Lisa into Toby's circle. He'd said that he would allow it if Lisa truly wanted it. *Did* she really want Toby? *Had* she missed her baby at all? A part of Colleen knew that she should want Lisa to love Toby. For the baby's sake, she tried to be open-minded, even though in her heart of hearts, it hurt to even try. And she prayed that Dillon would not hate her for having handed his son over to Lisa.

Toby howled. Lisa held him at arm's length. "You're very pretty, aren't you?" she asked.

Those apparently weren't the words he needed to hear.

Her tone was strained. If she'd only pull him in and hug him, rock him the way Dillon had on that first day…

"He's still tired," Dillon said angrily, and he started to move forward.

Colleen looked into his eyes. *Stop. Not yet,* she wanted to say.

Her expression must have told him something. He stopped.

"I probably shouldn't have been so…so insistent that you wake him from his nap," Lisa said. "But I was so eager to see him. I've missed him so much. We'll…he and I will get to know each other better when he's rested. I'll come back another day. I guarantee it. I so want to be a family with him." She said all of this to Dillon. She widened her eyes; she softened her voice. And all the time she was doing this, Toby had gotten louder and louder.

That could have been because Colleen was looking at him and standing just out of reach. Maybe. He sounded so pitiful. His tears were breaking Colleen's heart. *I'm so sorry, sweet-heart,* she wanted to say. And she was.

The louder he got, the stiffer Lisa became. Whether she realized it or not, she was inching him farther away from her body.

"Mommy will be back when you're not so sleepy, bunny-kins," she told Toby. And then without even looking at Colleen, she held him out.

Colleen whisked him into the next room.

"Just a few more seconds," she whispered to Toby, listening as Lisa's voice continued to murmur something to Dillon. It wasn't until Colleen heard the sound of the door clicking shut that Colleen pulled Toby to her.

"I'm never doing that to you again," she promised, rocking him and cuddling him. "Waking you up from a sound sleep— not even giving you a chance to adjust or get a dry diaper. I would never want to hurt you."

She kissed him again, she swayed with him and murmured to him.

His tears began to stop and she quickly got him out of the wet diaper and into a dry one, then cuddled him close again. When she turned, Dillon was standing in the doorway, staring at her.

"I'm sorry," she said, "but I was afraid that with both of us questioning and criticizing her, she might do something drastic, so I had to make sure of her true feelings for Toby. After all, she's his *mother*. I know it was wrong to make her look bad to her baby."

Dillon was shaking his head. "Genetics doesn't make a person a parent. I know that all too well. My parents were totally ill-prepared to love a child."

"She might get better at it."

"I'm sure she could, if she wants to. In spite of the fact that I hated her coming in here and just assuming I would turn him over to her after she's ignored him for months, I'll make a place for her in his life if she really wants to try."

Colleen nodded. "That's only right. I probably should have warmed him up for her a bit."

He gave her a funny smile. "She didn't warm him up for you a bit when she thrust him into your life. Somehow I doubt you complained or ran out the door, saying that you'd be back later when he was behaving more pleasantly."

"That's because…"

I loved him from the start, she started to say, but that would just complicate things. Instead, Colleen merely shrugged.

Suddenly Toby laughed.

"Does that mean you're ready to go see the town?" Dillon asked.

And as always, Toby looked at his father as if totally entranced by his voice. As usual, he gurgled and cooed in response to the sound.

"All right, then, let's show Colleen what Chi-town's all about."

They dressed Toby and put him in his stroller and went out into the city. Dillon showed his son and Colleen the sights he had already mentioned, and she discovered that he had a genuine affection for the city that couldn't be faked.

"You love it here."

"It's busy and bustling. A city that works and lives and breathes, night and day. It's the heartland. Chicago was built and then burned to the ground, and its citizens put their heads down and built it again. People work hard here and they play hard. It has grit and beauty all rolled into one."

"And a lake," she added.

"A magnificent lake," he agreed. "I'll show you that tomorrow."

And he did. For the next few days, when Dillon wasn't consulting with his assistants on projects they had in the works, when he wasn't visiting job sites and getting back into the swing of the city, he took Colleen and Toby everywhere, or as much as he could in a city this size.

And Lisa didn't call.

But they both knew she would, eventually. Dillon began to hear rumors, delivered by friends, that Lisa was embracing the prospect of motherhood. She was buying baby clothes and toys.

Maybe she really did want to be Toby's mother.

Colleen fretted and worried and hoped that whatever Lisa wanted, her wishes wouldn't hurt Toby and Dillon. She tried to hope that Lisa meant what she was saying, because that would be good for Toby.

Even though her heart felt heavy at the prospect, her heart couldn't matter. She wasn't the important person here.

Then, three days after they arrived, Dillon came to her. "I have a dinner tonight." He was staring directly into her eyes, looking apologetic.

"Don't worry. I'll be fine here with Toby," she told him.

"Colleen, I want you to come with me. I need you to."

"But Toby…"

He cleared his throat. "Taken care of. Millie is on her way here right now. Her plane lands in ten minutes. I have a limo picking her up. Toby will have a loving babysitter."

Colleen blinked. She didn't know what to say, to think. "You could have asked me."

"I know we discussed the reasons you might need to play dress-up back in Montana, but I also know that while the real scary stuff in life doesn't faze you, big social events make you tremble a little. I was afraid you'd make some silly excuse about how you wouldn't fit in with my business associates and friends at a formal party."

"Formal?"

"A bit."

Since she had been on the verge of trying to make an excuse about how she wouldn't fit in *before* she heard about the formal part, she was doubly nervous now.

"Dillon…"

"Colleen, all my friends want to meet you. They've been waiting. Begging me. They're almost as bad as Harve was about the Ferrari. They're dying to meet this paragon I've been talking about."

"Me? A paragon?"

"And an Amazon. And a woman who made my child feel loved the first few months of his life. Jace, my assistant, especially wants to meet you. He hopes you'll wear your red cowgirl boots."

"He did *not* say that."

"Cross my heart. And he's going to be terribly disappointed if you don't show up."

"I can't believe you called Millie and that she and the girls kept this a secret."

"We all know how you are. You would have found some way to wriggle out of it."

"Are you saying that I would back down from a challenge?"

Dillon grinned. "I would *never* say that. I know that you once kicked a man in the shins. You're one tough cowgirl."

"Yes," she said, "I am. And I would appreciate it if, in the future, you trust me enough to come to me and ask me if I want to do something before you go off and take control of things." Although she felt a little guilty at that comment. She still felt bad about panicking and taking over with Toby that day Lisa had showed up.

"Let's agree to discuss things first in the future," he told her.

She nodded. But, of course, there wasn't going to be a future. Surely the business with Lisa was going to come to a head soon. Either Lisa wanted Toby or she didn't. And if she did, there would have to be a showdown and some ground rules set. There might be attorneys and judges involved. But it would have to happen soon or Lisa's failure to act would put her out of the picture. Public opinion wouldn't favor her. She would do something soon.

But not tonight, Colleen told herself as she went to get ready. *Tonight I'm going to a dinner with Dillon. As his date.*

Which wasn't exactly what he had said.

But Colleen needed to dream a little, to pretend a little. Soon enough all pretending would be done. But tonight was hers.

CHAPTER THIRTEEN

COLLEEN received a video call a few minutes later. Harve Enson came on the screen. "Hi, Colleen, the girls hooked me up so I could talk to you. I just wanted to tell you that even though Millie's on her way to Chicago, you don't have a single thing to worry about. The women are expert ranchers, of course, but I hear they can't cook worth squat and with you gone, there's too much work for two, so if it's all right with you, me and some of the other people in town want to help out at the Applegate. All of us here in Bright Creek are aware of how much you've done for the girls and we know we've been insensitive, unfeeling snots in the past. We want to make up for all that. So, if it's all right with you, we'll make sure that the fishermen pay their fees, we'll get people to cook and we'll help out in any other ways the ladies need us to."

Colleen was sure that her mouth was hanging open. Insensitive, unfeeling snots?

"Harve, I don't quite understand. I certainly appreciate your offer, but…this apology is unnecessary and…I mean… why now? You've known about the girls living with me for years."

Harve cleared his throat. Was his face a little red? Did he look embarrassed?

"I know all that, but when we were out riding around in the car the other day, Dillon explained things to us. He told us *all* the details. It's one thing to know something and another thing to know all the little things that make a man see a situation in a…a realistic light. I knew you hired Julie and Gretchen at a crucial time in their lives, but I always had the feeling that you were bent on teaching them to hate men. We all knew what your daddy and stepdaddy were, so we didn't exactly blame you for seeming mad all the time, but your anger made it easy to dismiss you. Then Dillon cleared things up for us. He told us how you cared for that baby like your own and how you protected the girls and stood up to him to make sure he was a good father to Toby and…well, he reminded us that you had tried to protect him, too. That you weren't against men, just injustice. After that, it didn't feel right, knowing that we were part of the problem, the ones treating you like a man and going on about Lisa in front of your face and all. So…that's it, then. And you know I don't like feeling as if I owe someone something. I want to do my part."

Colleen blinked. Her throat felt too tight. She had spent years being "one of the guys" with Harve, and she couldn't really stop that now. At least not right away. It would embarrass him if she cried.

"Harve, I would be honored if you would help out."

She cleared her throat and turned to look at Dillon. He had taken care of Bill Winters for her; he had cleared things up with Harve and…who knew what other men had been in the car that day and who Harve had repeated this tale to?

Harve smiled and then laughed. "So the Applegate isn't no man's land anymore?"

She laughed, too. "Don't push it, Harve. The Applegate is still our sanctuary. But…thank you."

At that moment, the doorbell rang and she said goodbye

to Harve and went to greet Millie as Dillon opened the door. Millie gave the room an appreciative glance.

"Very nice," she said. "Now, where's my baby? I'm going to spoil him silly while you two are out tonight."

Dillon laughed. "Okay, but tomorrow I've got all kinds of things set up for you," Dillon told her. "You've got choices. I made sure I had tickets and entrance passes to a bunch of things, since I wasn't sure what you'd want to see and do."

Millie smiled and patted his cheek. "You're a good man," she said as he directed her toward Toby's room.

Colleen's eyes felt misty. If her throat closed up any tighter, she wouldn't be able to talk. Dillon…that man…he had known that Millie had never had this kind of treat before.

She turned to him to thank him, but he cut her off. "You'd better go get ready. My friends aren't quite sure that you're real. I've talked about you so much and so much time has passed that they're starting to think that I've made you up."

The funny thing was, Colleen thought later, as she stepped into the room where the dinner party was being held, that she was beginning to *feel* like a fictional character. The woman she'd seen in her mirror earlier wearing the off-the-shoulder cream-colored dress and the three-inch lacy heels looked nothing like the Montana cowgirl she had always been. It was difficult to know how to act.

But she was barely in the door when a man came up to her and introduced himself. "I'm Jace, Dillon's assistant, and you have to be Colleen, the woman who makes those wonderful sculptures."

Colleen blinked. "Did Dillon ask you to say that?"

He laughed. "No, he just showed me your Web site and I saw the ones in his yard when they were first installed. I've ordered one for my rooftop apartment."

"I…thank you," she said.

"And I really loved the red boots in the photo I saw. You left them at home?"

"Waiting for my next race," she said with a smile.

"My first cowgirl. I'm honored to have met you. You *are* an original," he said. Which was a much nicer way of saying she was odd or different than Colleen had ever heard.

In no time a crowd had gathered around Colleen.

"Dillon gets all the gorgeous women," one man complained, and for a second Colleen didn't realize that he was talking about her. "Do you allow guests at your ranch?"

"Hardly ever, Tom." Dillon's voice sounded from Colleen's right and he slipped his hand around her waist. Her heart picked up the pace.

"You must be the babysitter, right?" a bejeweled woman asked.

"That's far too anemic and limited a term for what Colleen does," Dillon said. "Colleen takes care of people, both babies and adults. She creates art, she runs a ranch and she's a barrel racing champion."

"Barrel racing? I'd love to see footage of that."

"So would I," Dillon admitted. "Don't you have any video of that?" he asked her.

"No, but Gretchen loves to take pictures and videos. The next race I'm in I'll have her tape it and send it to you," she told him.

Because she wouldn't be seeing him anymore. But she wouldn't think of that right now.

But the question about barrel racing had spurred other questions, and Colleen tried to explain what it was like to live on a ranch, how big the sky and land were, how small she was in comparison and yet how the feeling of being small was…right.

"You love it, don't you?" a woman asked.

"It's who I am and it's what I know."

"You're a fascinating woman," one man in his thirties told

her. "A rancher, and yet you seem perfectly in your element in this high-rise apartment surrounded by city dwellers."

"Well, we're not completely rustic. There are plenty of cowboy poets in Montana, and some urban dwellers who have relocated from more cosmopolitan areas. And even though Montana's miles from here, the Internet brings a lot of the world into everyone's lives, doesn't it? I'm sure we must share a *few* things."

"A love of art, for one," someone suggested and another person went looking for their hostess's computer, calling everyone to come look at Colleen's Web site.

The whole time they'd been talking, Dillon had been by her side as if he was guarding her. The darn man was supposed to be having a good time with the people he hadn't had a chance to see in a long time, not watching over her. So, when the group moved away, she stood on her toes and whispered in his ear. "You don't have to babysit me, you know. Your friends seem nice."

"They like you. And all the men want your phone number."

She gave him an incredulous look. "I don't believe you."

"Believe me. See that man off to the right looking daggers at me?"

She looked. There *was* a man staring at them.

"He specifically asked me if he could ask you out."

"What did you tell him?"

"I told him that he wasn't good enough for you."

Colleen opened her eyes wide. "What's wrong with him?"

But Dillon was prevented from answering by the ringing of the doorbell. The hostess frowned. "I wasn't expecting anyone else."

When she went to answer the door, Lisa swept into the room. "Nancy!" she said, giving the woman a hug and a kiss. "It's so good to see you. I love that red dress. You always look so fantastic in red."

A visibly startled and embarrassed Nancy stuttered and stammered and finally thanked Lisa, who gave her a glowing smile.

"I know. I'm sorry to just drop in on you unannounced," Lisa said, "but I've been meaning to call on you ever since I got back in town and…"

She looked around. "Oh. Look at this. What a dunce I am. You're having company. I'm sorry. I'm so, so sorry." A look of distress came over her face. "I hope you'll all forgive me for barging in like this. I didn't know. Nancy, don't worry, I'll come back another day. We'll talk."

"Lisa, don't be silly. Don't go," Nancy was saying, smoothing her palms over the red dress. "Come in. You know almost everyone here, anyway. I would have invited you, except I thought…maybe…"

She looked at Dillon.

"Oh, that," Lisa said. "Don't worry. Dillon and I still talk. We share a child. Our lives will always be entwined." As if to emphasize that, she moved over to Dillon and put her hand on his arm. Now he was flanked by both Colleen and Lisa.

Immediately, Colleen started to pull free. Dillon didn't let go.

"Lisa," he said, nodding his head. "Colleen and I were just going to discuss some details about the ranch with Jace. You'll excuse us?" It was a command, not a question, but Lisa seemed unfazed. She looked, Colleen thought, like a princess, dressed all in white with her dark hair perfectly coifed and just the right touch of red on her lips and nails. And when she walked, her gait in heels was much smoother than Colleen's had been.

"Colleen, you look so out of place here in the city. I almost didn't recognize you without your old work jeans."

I almost didn't recognize you without your tiara, Colleen wanted to say. But she didn't. Making that kind of catty comment would only cost Dillon in the end.

Besides, the fact that she had instantly wanted to strike out and defend herself by criticizing Lisa stunned her for an instant. She had never been averse to defending *others*, and she would physically fight when taunted by a bully, but despite the fact that she'd known Lisa was a phony in many ways, Colleen had never confronted her in that way. At all. Instinctively, she'd known that Lisa possessed attributes she herself never would. A fight with Lisa wouldn't be a physical one, like kicking Rob in the shins, and it wouldn't be a fair one, either.

So, Colleen had always lain low and stayed clear of Lisa's territory. There had never been any reason for conflict between them because the two of them posed no threat to the other one. Had that happened, Lisa would have won. Colleen had no feminine wiles, no tools like the ones Lisa possessed, and her confidence in herself was limited to the narrow sphere of horses and ranching. She hadn't even seen her art as an accomplishment but as therapy. It was being sold only because Julie had claimed they needed space.

But Dillon had changed all that. He had given her a confidence in herself as a woman that she had lacked earlier. A sense that she could demand things for herself when she needed to.

So, what did she need?

She needed to know that Dillon and Toby were safe. Happy. Secure. Not being manipulated or used. But…how to accomplish that? Her usual, mulish methods of putting her head down and butting at the offender wouldn't work with someone like Lisa. If she did that, in the end, Dillon and Toby would pay the price. Especially given the fact that she was physically larger than Lisa, she'd look like a bully and Lisa would look like a fragile, wounded woman, a part she knew how to play well. Public opinion would, once again, be in Lisa's favor.

Colleen suddenly realized that everyone was staring at Lisa

because of the "ranch jeans" comment she had made. And maybe because she still hadn't responded to Lisa's comment.

"Not that there's anything wrong with dirty ranch jeans, exactly," Lisa had dropped into the conversation somewhere while Colleen had been panicking.

"Except when there's a vulnerable little baby around who might be subject to all those germs," Lisa added when the room remained quiet, apparently stunned at her rude comment. "Do you realize how many horrible diseases ranch animals carry?" she added. "It's probably silly and ridiculous of me to worry, but…a mother worries about these seemingly insignificant things."

Now, some of the women and even some of the men were shifting their feet and murmuring. They clearly didn't want to insult Colleen but some of them had to be parents. Few of them would have any experience of ranching. Lisa's argument was beginning to sound sane, as if Colleen would unwittingly or uncaringly subject Toby to infection.

From the corner of her eye, Colleen could see that Dillon was nearing tornado stage. His brow was furrowed, his fists were clenched. He was going to wade into the fray and…and do what?

He's going to defend me. She knew that, just as she knew that anything he said here would be remembered, replayed in people's minds. Possibly used against him later. She held out her hand to stop him.

"I can assure you," he said, his voice steel, his eyes ice, "that Colleen would have moved heaven and earth to protect Toby. She subjected him to nothing that would have harmed him. And if you're implying that she did, then you never really knew her very well at all. Even though you dropped a newborn baby on her and walked away for months."

A collective gasp went through the group. Colleen felt her

own heart pounding hard. Would this be all it took? The crowd would surely remember this fact. Not that it had been a secret, but…phrased this way in these circumstances, Lisa's abandonment of Toby seemed exceptionally bad and unfeeling. Would this be what helped Dillon to win?

"You're right. You're so right," Lisa said, her face crumpling, "but as a totally inexperienced mother…I was scared. I didn't know how to be a parent at all. I went to Europe. I took parenting classes. I worked on my confidence. Now, I'm…I'm ready to be a mother, finally." Her lip quivered. With her pale, pretty face she looked fragile, vulnerable, repentant.

Colleen could see that at least some of the people here forgave Lisa instantly with that speech. And what could anyone say to that?

Everyone was staring at Dillon, waiting for a response. Colleen wanted to help him, but anything she could say right now would be taken as interference by his friends, she was sure.

His jaw was taut, but he tilted his head as if digesting Lisa's words. "Every child should have a loving and attentive mother," he said quietly. "A woman who cares enough to go the extra mile."

Lisa smiled. She glowed. She practically smirked as she looked at Colleen.

"Of course, not every child gets that attentive mom. And Toby is used to the very best," Dillon said, looking at Colleen with that fierce blue gaze of his that did her in every time.

Colleen's throat practically closed up. She couldn't have spoken if she'd been able to think of anything to say. She wished she was alone with Dillon, but of course, that would have been rude to his friends.

So for the next hour, Colleen smiled and laughed and talked. She tried to pretend that Lisa wasn't in the room. She tried not to look at Dillon for fear that anyone watching would see the naked longing in her eyes. She'd learned early on in life that she couldn't have everything she wanted, and she couldn't have Dillon.

She didn't even know all that she said, who she talked to. Men, women, that man Dillon had warned her about. She feigned animation and a carefree attitude. And she must have done all right, because everyone smiled and laughed right back and no one seemed to be acting as if anything was wrong. They couldn't begin to imagine the rush of feelings that was going through her mind.

Lisa was going to challenge Dillon for the right to Toby. Somehow she was going to hurt him. Colleen couldn't let that happen. But she couldn't stop it.

So, despite the fact that Colleen liked Dillon's friends, the dinner seemed interminable. Finally, though, everyone rose from the table and Dillon moved to her side. "I'm afraid Colleen and I have to leave."

"It's still so early," their hostess said, but Dillon shook his head. He took Colleen's hand and led her outside.

"We need to talk," he said.

CHAPTER FOURTEEN

THE house was quiet when they got home, but Dillon's mind was a whirlwind of activity. Colleen had been the princess of the evening tonight. Men had fawned over her; women had wanted to emulate her. She'd been beautiful and funny and witty and…Colleen, the woman he couldn't have. And Lisa had tried to insult her, hurt her.

Lisa was going to be a major problem. He was going to have to bring out the big guns. He hadn't wanted to go that route, but he would.

Later. Right now, he was consumed by the woman at his side. His beautiful, giving ranch woman, whom he couldn't hurt and couldn't have. When she'd spoken of her ranch tonight, it had been clearer than ever just how much she belonged there. And she'd been appalled about Nick, the man who had set his sights on her. Letting Harve help with the ranch while she had no option was one thing. Letting a man into her heart was another. And it was a sure thing that if she ever did go that route, it would be with someone linked to the land. Like Rob, Harve's son and a man who'd grown up with ranching, not a Chicago businessman.

But Dillon had been watching Colleen all night, breathing her in all night. When Lisa had insulted her, he'd wanted to insult Lisa right back, and it wasn't his way to beat up on a woman. When Nick had drooled over her, he'd wanted to warn the man away.

He was in over his head. He was falling for another woman he couldn't keep and he was going to lose her any day now. Already Jace had given them a list of nannies to interview. And Jace had great instincts. It wouldn't take long to settle on one. She was going to ride right out of his world.

"Everyone's asleep," Colleen whispered quietly, but the sound went right through Dillon's body.

"We're not," he said.

She gave a low, sexy laugh. "Don't try to be cute, Farraday. You knew what I meant. We were out partying, so we're excused for still being awake."

"You were a big hit," he said. "A Montana marvel."

"Your friends were being very nice."

He didn't answer right away. When he did he couldn't keep the anger from his voice. "I'm sorry Lisa tried to insult you. You shouldn't have been subjected to that when her battle is clearly with me."

She shook her head and the silk of her hair brushed the underside of his jaw. He breathed in the scent of her shampoo. "I can handle a little insult from Lisa."

"I don't want you to have to. I'm not letting her get away with it again."

She looked up, the dim light from the moon outside casting part of her face in shadow, part in milky light. "You can't battle her, Dillon. She knows how to get her way. I saw how it was the day she came here and again tonight. She plants doubts in people's minds and wins them over. She uses half-truths that are difficult to disprove. I've seen it."

He had, too, but he'd had Jace and the rest of his crew on

the job. Lisa wouldn't get her way this time. And he didn't want Colleen taking a hit for him.

"I'm not letting it happen again," he said firmly. "You're not a pincushion or someone's punching bag."

"I'm not fragile," she argued, clearly a bit miffed.

Now it was his turn to smile. "No, not fragile but…Colleen, when this is over I don't want you to have regrets."

He pulled her against him.

"If you mean you don't want me to miss the two of you, it's too late for that. I will." She raised her arms. Her fingers brushed across his jaw.

He groaned. And then he pulled her closer. He kissed her deeply. "You make me do things I know I shouldn't do. I don't want to hurt you."

As if he'd pushed some sort of button he'd been unaware of, she pulled closer. "Only I decide who can hurt me. You can't hurt me. Touch me."

He snaked his arm around her and pulled her up against him. She was part of him, and he drank from her lips. He breathed in her scent. He wanted more.

"Colleen?"

"Your room," she whispered.

Together they somehow made their way up the stairs to the back of his house, where his room took up half the second floor. The door closed behind them. Colleen stepped forward, grabbed the lapels of his jacket and jerked down the sleeves. "I've been wanting to do that all night," she said.

He slid the strap of her dress down and kissed her bare shoulder. "Not as much as I've been wanting to do this."

"That's what you think." She pushed him down on the bed. He let her. Then he reached out and she slid right into his arms, right up against his heart. She lay on top of him and they tangled themselves around each other. He kissed her long and deep, again and again.

"You're very good at this, aren't you?" she asked, just before she kissed him back.

He laughed against her lips.

"What?" she demanded.

"It's a strange question to ask a man, to comment on his own prowess as a lover."

"Well, I don't really know what a woman is supposed to ask, since I've never actually done this before."

Dillon stopped laughing. He stopped kissing her. His heart was still slamming around in his body. He still wanted her as much as ever, but his mind was issuing warnings left and right.

"Colleen, you've never done this before and this…us, here, together…how much wine did you have tonight?"

She lifted her head and stared into his eyes. "I didn't have more than a sip and this…us…it's not the wine talking. Are you saying that you don't want to do this with me?"

The doubt in her voice broke him. "Colleen, I've been dying to do this with you for weeks."

"Then…"

"You've never done this."

"Are you afraid I won't be any good at it?"

He groaned and rested his forehead against hers, cursing himself.

"Because *I'm* a little afraid that I'll suck at it," she told him. "If I'd had some practice I'm sure I'd be better." As she was talking, still lying against him, every word echoed from her body to his, driving his temperature higher. The slightest movement she made brought her flesh sliding against his skin.

He couldn't stop himself. He kissed her hard, fiercely, possessively. "I don't need you to be better at it. You're already driving me crazy. But, Colleen, if this is your first, if this is your only… For now, anyway, I have to make it good for you. If it's not, if *I'm* not, it's all on me, not you. You understand?"

"Yes. I understand that you're trying to do one of those male domination things. Taking all the blame. But you know that's not my way. I'm a full participant. I just wanted you to know that I might be awkward and clueless and—"

"Don't say another word, Colleen," Dillon said, pulling her against him. Jace was right. Colleen was unique. What other woman would apologize in advance for being clueless when she was so clearly burning him up? His lips captured hers. He rolled with her so that she was beneath him now. "I'm going to tell you what I'm doing," he told her as he began to peel her dress away. "Just in case you're worried about being clueless. Right now I'm revealing all the parts of you that I've been dying to see for so long."

He kissed his way down her body as he drew her dress away from her.

"And I'm kissing all the parts of you that I've been wanting to kiss," he told her as his lips brushed her curves, her soft skin, as her breath—and his—came quicker.

"And I'm—"

"Ripping your shirt off. Undressing you, too," she said, awkwardly but forcefully doing exactly as she said. Why had he ever thought that Colleen would be a recipient and not a participant?

"I'm kissing you the way I've been wanting to for a long time," she said, wrapping herself around him so that his breath hung in his throat.

He groaned, tangled his fingers in her hair and held her still as he kissed her, as he ran one hand down her body.

Their bodies tangled, they traded kisses. The fire grew hotter. Their whispers grew more feverish.

"Dillon, what—what are you doing now?" she asked.

"Driving myself crazy. Touching you…everywhere."

"Do that," she said. "Yes. Tonight. Just…tonight…do that with me."

Which only made this more pressing, more poignant, because yes, tonight would be their only night.

He placed his hands on hers, palm to palm. He kissed her lips, her throat. Lower, then lower still and then he rose up. "Are you ready? Are you sure, Colleen?"

Her answer was to meet him, to join with him. Together they tumbled through dark and light, thunder and lightning, sunrise and sunset, falling, falling, all control gone as they fell into bliss.

Dillon whispered her name hoarsely, collapsing and rolling with her, keeping her by his side.

But in the morning, she wasn't there.

Tonight, he remembered her saying. *I love her,* he thought, but he had agreed to her terms. One time, one night. Their days together were ending. He wanted to hold on, but that wasn't what she wanted.

Just one night. He had to free her in such a way that she could be happy, even without Toby. If there was a way, he would find it.

Colleen was a mess. A total mess. What had led her to sleep with Dillon when she'd already known that she was falling in love with him? Now, after a night in his arms, after an experience that still had the power to make her breath stop with wonder just thinking about it, she was lost. Completely and utterly lost.

I'm fine, she tried to tell herself over and over again, but the truth was that she was anything but fine. How was she going to survive this need to be with him, this desire to just hear his voice or see his smile or…more? What was she going to do? What if he discovered that she loved him?

Then she would be pathetic. He knew he'd been her first, her only, and he'd been concerned. Probably about this. That she'd make too much of it, get in too deep. He'd hated hearing Lisa try to insult her—how much more would he beat up on himself if he suspected that he was about to break her heart?

I'm not letting that happen, she told herself. Firmly. She had made a point of never letting others suffer when she could stop it. She had always been a woman of action, and action was called for now. She had come here to help Dillon set up his house, find a great nanny and make sure that Lisa didn't try to abuse her title as mother to manipulate and blackmail Dillon the way she had manipulated others in the past.

"Well, let's do those things," Colleen whispered. She was capable. She could do all of them, except…Lisa had never lost. At least as far as Colleen knew of. What to do? How to manage? If she just concentrated on this, she couldn't allow her hurting heart to sideline her.

She thought of all she knew about Lisa. About the "mother lessons" Lisa had mentioned the night before and about how Dillon had not had a relationship with his parents and would want Toby to know his mother if Lisa was genuinely interested in her child.

Maybe this *would* work out for Dillon and Toby. Maybe Lisa *was* changing. If that was so, they might all become a family, which would be good for Dillon and Toby.

But how could anyone read a person who had always made herself unreadable, a woman like Lisa who had been born playing whatever part was expedient?

Maybe you gave that person an audition, Colleen reasoned. There might be a way to find out some small bits of information…but she would need help, planning and a lot of luck. Colleen took a deep breath and went in search of the one person she knew would help her give Dillon the gift of truth. She tried not to think about what she planned to do next. Instead, she just plunged in.

When Dillon woke up and made his appearance an hour later, Colleen was in her bathrobe. "I'm sorry. I'm not feeling myself," Colleen said, trying not to look directly at Dillon.

His look of concern drove an arrow right through her heart. She knew he had to be thinking that she was experiencing buyer's remorse and regretting that she had slept with him, but what could she say?

"You won't mind showing me a bit of the town, will you?" Millie asked. "I promised Gretchen and Julie I'd buy some souvenirs and give them a report."

"Jace—" Dillon began, but Colleen drove herself to give him a wounded look, to appear appalled that he would send a substitute. Guilt trickled through her.

"I'd be delighted," he said, even though he looked worried. Colleen's heart was breaking just looking at him, but she tried to tell herself that this was necessary. As soon as they were out the door, she threw off her robe, revealing that she was fully dressed.

Forgive me, she silently told Dillon. *I have to do this. I have to at least try to help.* She had invited Lisa over, and the woman would be here soon. She hoped against hope that she was doing the right thing, because if she wasn't…if she was wrong…Colleen's stomach began to churn. If she handled this wrong, the fallout would be unthinkable.

So, by the time the doorbell rang a short time later, Colleen's heart was in her throat. She had to coach herself to go slowly, to make Lisa wait a normal amount of time. She had to pretend that everything was normal. As if anything could be, given this whole horrid situation.

Colleen only knew that the truth was important. To Dillon

and to Toby. They deserved truth, love, everything. Not being blackmailed or threatened. So, if there was any way to cut through this game Lisa was playing, if there was any warmth in Lisa's heart at all, Colleen had to find it. And if there was no warmth or love within the woman…

She'll have to go through me to hurt the people I love. That was Colleen's last thought before she went to the door.

"Lisa, I'm glad you agreed to come by. Come on in the kitchen. It's sunniest there."

Lisa looked around as if expecting to see Dillon.

"I'm sorry. He's not here," Colleen told her. "I wanted to talk to you alone about last night."

"No hard feelings, I assume, Colleen? If you're referring to the ranch clothes line, I was just being friendly."

Colleen shook her head. "I meant the mother lessons. It must have been hard for you without Toby and now you're still separated from him, so today while it's just you and me, I thought you could have some quiet time to get to know him."

Lisa blinked. "I…yes. That would be great."

"I'll go get him out of his bed."

Lisa's eyes widened. "He won't be screaming like last time, will he?"

"No, he's been awake for a while." Colleen left the room and returned with Toby. "Sit right there. It's a good chair with enough room for you and the baby." She handed Toby over to Lisa as soon as the woman sat down. Then she prepared a bottle and handed it to Lisa, who was awkwardly holding the baby. Toby was listing slightly to one side.

"He'll be hungry," Colleen assured her.

"Hungry. Yes." Lisa poked the bottle at Toby. Fortunately for her, he knew what the bottle was about and latched on to it, drinking it quickly. When he had finished, Lisa looked up, triumphant.

Maybe the woman really did want to be a mother, Colleen thought, even though she was holding Toby away from her body as if he might explode at any minute. For Toby's sake, she hoped that was true.

"You'll probably want to burp him now," Colleen said. "I usually do."

"Of course. I know what I'm doing," Lisa said. She started to bring her hand back.

Colleen's eyes widened. "Softly!" she said, just in time.

Lisa's hand slowed. She began an ineffectual series of movements, barely making contact. "Takes a long time, doesn't it?" she asked, gritting her teeth. "What's that smell?"

"Baby," Colleen offered. "Most people like it."

"Yes. Very nice." Lisa smiled.

Just then, Toby did what he did so well. He spit up all over Lisa's hand, the curdled mess dropping onto her black dress.

"Uck! My dress!" Lisa yelled. "Here! Here! Take him. Give me a wet cloth! This is a Versace. Colleen, help me."

Colleen frowned, but she took Toby and cuddled him to her. She gave Lisa a damp cloth and watched as Lisa rubbed at the milk stain.

"In the future, you'll probably want to wear something less fragile when you're with Toby. These things happen."

Lisa frowned. There was a damp spot on her dress.

"Here, take this," Colleen told her, handing her an apron.

"Excuse me?"

"To protect your dress. Now that he's spit up all over himself, he needs a bath. Here, we keep the tub on the counter. Just…prepare the water and we'll get him all clean."

"Maybe you should prepare the water."

Good idea. Lisa might make it too hot or too cold. "All right. You hold Toby."

Lisa let out a long sigh. "*I'll* do the water."

Colleen let her, but she nudged Lisa aside and adjusted the temperature before she would let her fill the tub. "You must have forgotten about making sure it's not too hot," she said.

"Yeah, I forgot," Lisa said. But she took Toby when the water was ready and made a rather ineffectual attempt to clean him, holding him at arm's length. When she was done, Colleen handed her a diaper and gave her a pad to lay Toby on to change him. Lisa studied the diaper as if it were a puzzle. She started to put it under Toby. Colleen turned it around so that the diaper wouldn't be backward.

"I knew that," Lisa said. She tried to put the diaper on without touching Toby and managed to get it fastened, albeit with gaps at his legs.

Toby was getting impatient and starting to kick his legs around. He was starting to whimper. Up until now he had been relatively calm, willing to put up with the lady who had given him a bottle, but now his diaper was crooked and probably uncomfortable. He had managed not to gift his mother with the ultimate insult, but Lisa had barely gotten his diaper on and sat down with Toby when Colleen noticed that his diaper was already wet.

"At least he waited until he was wearing a diaper," she pointed out, but Lisa was holding him even farther away from her body than she had been before.

"You change him," she told Colleen. "I'll have a nurse to do all this stuff, anyway."

To Colleen's chagrin, Lisa looked as if she might cry. "Lisa," she said gently, as she took the baby, quickly changed him and turned to face the other woman. "*Why* are you doing this? You obviously don't really want to…to…" Be a mom, she had started to say, but that almost seemed too cruel. Even though she had no doubt that Lisa wouldn't have hesitated to say the same thing to *her*.

"I'm a year older than you. A year closer to thirty," Lisa said. "I don't even know who my father was, but my mother…we had no money. All those dresses I wore came from a thrift store fifty miles away. And I promised myself that I would have nice things when I grew up. But Dillon was so into his work that he didn't even look when I bought a nice purse or nice shoes. And he didn't care about parties. He was so boring, so into working and going off to save the world and…and boring. Still, when I divorced him, my unlimited supply of funds was limited. I need nice things, Colleen. I don't want to be my mother."

Despite the petulant, spoiled sound of all that, there was something so sad about it. "Nice clothes won't bring back the father you never knew, Lisa. You know that. They won't buy you the attention you want."

"I get plenty of attention."

"And just look at this baby, Lisa. You helped make him. He's wonderful."

Lisa looked at Toby. "He *is* pretty," she said.

"He's very pretty," Colleen agreed. "And he deserves to have…everything a child wants and needs."

Lisa froze. She looked at Colleen with cool, beautiful eyes. "And you think I can't give him that, don't you?"

Suddenly, Colleen began to wonder at her own audacity in testing Lisa to see if she had a trace of loving mother buried inside. She had lied to Dillon to set this up, she had taken control from his hands and now…

"I don't know if you can, Lisa. You don't really seem as if you want to take on the role of mother. And if this is just about money…if that's all you're after…"

"Then what would you do, Colleen? You know me. I go after what I want and I get it."

"Not this time."

Lisa smiled sadly. "He *is* a pretty baby, but I told you, I need things, and Dillon has money."

"Toby and Dillon aren't just tickets to pretty dresses."

Lisa shook her head. "I'm sorry, Colleen. I really am sorry it's come to this between you and me, because this is a contest you're going to lose. I never had anything against you when we were growing up."

"Maybe not, but you hurt people I liked. I'm not letting it happen again."

"So…all that stuff…the bath and the bottle was just a test to trip me up?"

"I'd hoped you'd pass it."

"And I hope you know better than to cross me." Lisa's expression was cold. Her pretty eyes weren't very pretty.

Colleen felt a trickle of fear slip in, but she refused to give in to it. "I know better than to cross you. I've seen how you fight, but I'll still stop you." Colleen heard the door open, but she didn't drop her gaze from Lisa. "I'll do whatever it takes. You're not going to ruin their lives for money."

"Of course I'll win, Colleen. I have all the cards," Lisa said, even though her voice sounded less certain than before.

Slowly, Colleen shook her head. She stared straight into Lisa's eyes. "You have powerful weapons, Lisa. They've helped you cheat and win for most of your life, but not this time. I have something better."

Lisa frowned as Dillon and Millie and Jace came through the door. "What do you have?" she demanded.

Colleen was extremely aware of Dillon's presence, but she couldn't allow herself to be distracted. "I have friends in Bright Creek. So does Dillon. And I also have a good memory. I know everyone you hurt. If I have to, I'll get down on my knees and beg them to tell their stories before a judge. I don't want to hurt you, but I'll do everything I can to keep you from harming Dillon and Toby. I promise you that."

"You'll lose."

For half a second, Colleen felt paralyzed remembering who she was and who Lisa was. Lisa had always been the best, the prize, the winner. Then, Colleen hazarded a glance at Dillon, who was studying her closely. But he wasn't interfering. He was trusting her. She couldn't fail him now. She raised her chin. "I might fail, but I don't think so."

"Why not?"

"Because you have so much more to gain by not fighting and lying. If this goes to court, at least some people will see the less attractive side of you. I'll force you to fight, and that won't be pretty."

"It won't be pretty for you, either."

"But that's why I'll win. Not being thought of as pretty doesn't scare me a bit. I don't need it."

Lisa paled just a bit. She tilted her head. "I never saw this side of you, Colleen."

"You never pushed me before."

"This…you said I had a lot to gain by…I assume by letting Dillon have Toby. What would I win?"

Colleen felt Dillon's eyes on her. She turned to look at him. His expression was indecipherable, but he hadn't taken his eyes off of her. She sensed the tension in him and she knew he wanted to take over, but he was still letting her have her say.

"Toby *is* a pretty baby," Colleen reminded Lisa. "And Dillon is a good and loving father who'll be fair in all ways. And if you don't drag Toby through the mud, you'll get to keep your untarnished image as the queen of the Lupine Festival. I won't try to make you look ugly in the eyes of the citizens of Bright Creek."

Lisa shook her head. She frowned.

"Don't underestimate her, Lisa," Dillon said. "You chose well when you chose her to care for Toby."

"I know that. At least give me credit for knowing that," Lisa said.

"I do," he told her.

"And just for the record," Lisa said, "I know there's been speculation about whether or not you're really Toby's father. You are. I was faithful until weeks after you went to war. He's yours."

"He was always mine," Dillon said, "but thank you for saying that."

And suddenly Colleen felt like an intruder. Her part here was over. Had she helped or harmed the situation? Dillon had complimented her, but would he, ultimately, end up regretting this day?

Colleen turned to face him. Her skin felt tight, her spirits low. Maybe she'd just made a mess of everything. "I'll just let you and Lisa talk now. I'm sorry that I lied to you about feeling sick. And that I didn't tell you I was going to do this when I know we agreed to be up front about our plans."

He still hadn't spoken, so she faced Lisa again. "What's between you and Dillon and Toby is between the three of you, but he's a wonderful little boy. You'll miss a lot by underestimating the joy of being with him."

Lisa shook her head. "Not everyone can be a mother, Colleen."

As Colleen knew all too well. "Maybe not. I happen to believe that people can change their lives…if they want to. I believe in leaving doors open."

Lisa studied her for long seconds. "I never really knew you at all. You're more interesting than I thought. And maybe a little more dangerous. I could almost like you if I wasn't starting to hate you." But her voice held no antipathy.

Colleen shrugged. She started to leave.

"Colleen." Dillon's voice stopped her. "We have to talk."

"I know. When you and Lisa are done, I'll be upstairs."

She went upstairs and took out her suitcase and piled things in it. Millie had never unpacked. "I promise you," she told Millie, "that someday I'll make sure you get a trip where you get to see more, but…I can't stay here now."

Millie slowly nodded. "You love him?"

"I have to go home."

"But—"

"I really have to leave," she told Millie, zipping her bag shut. The shadow in the doorway told her that Dillon was here.

"Toby's in his bed, Millie," he said.

Millie didn't even ask what he meant. She just left the room.

Dillon stared at the suitcase. "You're leaving."

"I don't have any reason to stay any longer. I've talked to Jace and told him that I'm not sending his sculpture until he helps you choose the very best, most caring nanny in the world." Her throat was closing up. Getting the words out was so difficult.

"You did all that downstairs for me and Toby."

"I had to be sure she really didn't want him and that she knew it wouldn't be as easy as it's always been for her before."

"You didn't need to do this. Jace and my other employees and I had enough information about her actions in Europe to keep her from being able to threaten to take him from me. She's giving up. We reached a compromise."

Somewhere Colleen found a small smile. "Good. I'm glad. but this way…I'm hoping that she can claim that giving him up was her own choice. Even if I threatened her, I hope she knows I'll let her keep all the gold stars if she does the right thing. And maybe if the door stays open, she'll find a part of her heart for him. She's…I think she's still avoiding issues left over from her childhood, and I just didn't want her to be able to blackmail you. I had hoped that there was something maternal buried deep inside her. There isn't…yet, but maybe someday there will be."

He ran his palm over her jaw. "I know what this must have cost you. You're not a person who goes looking for trouble or controversy. And you've told me that you never mixed it up with Lisa the way other people did. To pit yourself against her…I…"

He kissed her. It seared her soul. She fought tears.

"I needed to do it," she said, "and look. Everything is great now. You and Toby have a wonderful house and a wonderful life and I've got to get home and start working on my sculptures again and make sure Harve hasn't run my ranch into the ground. It's been…it's been nice. It's been a pleasure getting to know you, Dillon."

How was she maintaining that calm, friendly atmosphere? Colleen had no idea.

"You could stay longer."

She shook her head. "No, I don't…I just…can't." She rose on her toes slightly and kissed him, then turned toward the door.

"I'll drive you to the airport."

"No, that's okay. We'll take a cab."

"Dammit, Colleen, at least let me get you home. At least let me send you in a limo and in my airplane."

And because she was wild now just to be away before she broke down, she said yes. Somehow she would keep from doing anything that his employees could report back to him.

She surged from the room. Millie was waiting with Toby in her arms. Colleen took Toby from her and kissed him.

Darn those tears. She looked through them at Dillon as she handed over the little boy.

Love him, she wanted to say, but she knew he would. Love *me,* she wanted to say, but she knew he couldn't.

"Goodbye, Dillon," she whispered. "Thank you for sharing your child for a while." Then she stumbled out of the house.

Hours later, she was back on the ranch. It had been her sanctuary for years, the place that had protected her and insulated her from all the bad things in the world.

This ranch was still her home, it was where she was needed, but…she didn't need it to insulate her anymore. Dillon had pulled her out of herself. She'd thought things and said things and done things that wouldn't have been possible weeks earlier. She no longer needed the crutch of a place to hide away from the world. What she needed was the man she loved.

But his life was full, even more full than it had been when he had married Lisa. He had a major company to run that took up most of his time, a child to raise, social engagements. And those women in Chicago he'd meet weren't just novelty items. Some of them would know how to help him with his company. They would be more than convenient caretakers of his son. And they didn't have obligations in a state many miles away, Colleen thought, as she rubbed Mr. Peepers down, said hello to the rest of her animals and prepared to throw herself into running the ranch again.

This place and these tasks had always brought her forgetfulness before. Now, she hoped the ranch could help her get some perspective on Dillon and turn him into simply an unexpectedly nice memory.

But for the first time in her life, the ranch felt hollow. And there were no answers or comfort to be had here.

CHAPTER FIFTEEN

HE HAD let her go. Why had he let her go? Dillon was still asking himself that question days later.

But he knew the answer. All of his life, whenever he started getting too close to people, they backed away. And Colleen had done more than back away from him. She had all but run from him.

"She's just a person who's nice to everyone, Toby," he told his son. "We don't have an exclusive right to her, you know."

Toby was fussing with his fingers, chewing on his fist, looking generally unhappy and whimpering. The doctor had said he might be teething a bit early, but Dillon was sure that he missed Colleen.

"I'm still amazed that she confronted Lisa to keep her from taking you from me," he said. "It was a desperation move that required multiple lies, and our Colleen is not a liar. No matter how tough she tries to be, how much she tries to conceal things, the truth shows through in her eyes. See?" he said, clicking through the photos of Colleen and him and Toby on the CD Millie had sent him with her thank-you note. "Look at her eyes when she's looking at you. She loves you, buddy, and I can't believe that Lisa didn't see that."

Toby started kicking and waving his arms when Colleen's

face came on the screen. Maybe it was wrong to show him these pictures. He might think Colleen was really here.

But Dillon couldn't tear his eyes away. And when a photo of him and Colleen together appeared, when he saw the expression in Colleen's eyes as she turned to him…Dillon clicked through the photos again.

And again. And again, always coming back to that one. He looked into Colleen's pretty eyes. His heart began to pound. Then he turned to his child. "I know you're too young to understand, but you need to know this about your father. Every major decision I've ever made in my life since I've been an adult was based on logic. And only logic. I—I'm ashamed to say this, but I married your mother because I thought she'd make a good CEO's wife, I went overseas because I knew I could do some good, I went looking for you when I didn't even know if you were really mine, because…all right, that might not have been logic, but it didn't concern a woman, either. I don't lose my heart to women, Toby, and if I did, I'd ignore it. Logic tells me that following my heart ends up burning me every time. And being burned by Colleen would be much, much worse than being burned by any other woman. But…

"I just don't care much about logic right now. I'm running on total emotion. Feel free to throw this up in my face some day, son, but we're going to Montana. She might not want to see me. She might have taken up with that cowboy she kicked in the shins, the one who was falling all over her that night at Yvonne's. She might want me to leave, but…I have to risk it. This time I don't want to do the logical thing. I know she can't leave there. I know my business is here. But…heck, I don't know…at the very least we're going to see her one more time. No, I'm going to do more than that. Even if she asks me to leave, I'm going to do one thing. One totally illogical and crazy thing I've been thinking about.

"And yeah, I'm doing this eyes open. The truth is that I can feel heartbreak headed my way already, but I can't seem to back away. Let's lay the groundwork. And then, let's go find our cowgirl."

Colleen had just finished brushing the coat of Arianne, a pretty little black pony. She was washing the dust and dirt off herself when Harve drove up in his big Suburban with two other trucks following him.

Confused, Colleen tilted her head. Then, the passenger door opened, and her heart became a bass drum, thundering through her entire body. *Careful. Careful,* she told herself.

"Dillon, why on earth are you here?" she asked. "And Harve?"

"I'm just delivering him and the kid and all this stuff," Harve said, taking the baby from the big SUV and heading up to the house. The men from the other trucks started unloading lumber.

The two strangers didn't have to ask where it went. They already knew. Two weeks ago they had shown up, given Colleen a note from Dillon saying that by way of thanks he was building her bunkhouse for the ranch camp. And no, she didn't have any choice in the matter. He needed to do this.

She'd been grateful, but even sadder. Seeing something he was building for her and knowing she'd never see him again had sent her spirits plummeting.

But here he was. And she could barely breathe. "Dillon…" she began, but she didn't get any further. He pulled her right into his arms and kissed her. Hard. Then he kissed her again. Slowly.

"That will have to keep me satisfied for now," he said. "Even though it's not nearly enough."

"Are you…not staying?"

He stared at her, long and hard, his blue eyes bluer than

water, bluer than her bluest bit of glass. And hotter than…something so hot she couldn't think of a word. She just plain old couldn't think at all with him looking at her that way.

"I'm staying," he said. "All the forces of nature couldn't keep me from staying. Only you could make me leave. If you didn't want me here, I…"

"I want you here," she said, afraid of what he would say.

"I was prepared to beg."

Tears started to fill her eyes. She blinked them away. "Dillon…"

He shook his head. "I have something to do before I can talk."

Then he kissed her again and marched toward the lumber. He put on a tool belt, took his tools and began to construct a wall. He didn't look at her. He just worked, swinging his hammer, cutting the lumber, pounding the nails. He began to build her dream for her.

But hours later when he was still out there, she couldn't take it anymore. "Millie, give me some iced tea. The man is building my dream. The least I can do is bring him something to drink."

"Absolutely the least. Right, pumpkin?" Millie asked Toby, who was in his glory, surrounded and pampered by the women of the Applegate.

But for once Colleen didn't stop to listen to Toby. With glass in hand, she marched out to where Dillon worked. She moved right up next to him. He was shirtless. He was sweaty. She had never seen anything she wanted so much.

When she moved, he saw her there. "You shouldn't stand so close," he said, and she instantly felt chagrined. He wasn't feeling what she was feeling. "I didn't hear you coming. I might have accidentally hurt you, and that would kill me, Colleen."

"I was careful," she said, watching as he took his T-shirt and dried himself off. It was all she could do to keep from asking him if he would kiss her again. Her heart…hurt to be here with him, because the building seemed to be going up quickly. That comment about staying? He'd meant staying to build the bunkhouse, she knew. Soon, he would be gone again. How was she going to handle losing him twice?

She wasn't. She was going to be a total wreck, but he was doing this wonderful thing for her, and she hadn't even said one nice thing about it, hadn't even paid that much attention to the structure he was building with his own hands. And all for her. Colleen kicked herself for her insensitivity.

She handed him the tea. "May I look?" she asked, stepping up onto what would eventually become the threshold of the doorway.

He held up his hand and said, "Wait," but she had spotted something, and nothing was going to stop her now. She moved into the still roofless structure. The room was all golden wood, the scent of raw pine filling her nostrils, but what had drawn her inward was the wood itself. Sturdy and strong, the walls rose before her, the studs straight and precise. And on every stud, on every flat panel of wood, there was a message: Dillon Farraday loves Colleen Applegate; Dillon adores Colleen; You're the woman of my heart and always will be; You're my soul; With love, to the very best woman in Bright Creek.

"You weren't supposed to see all of this until I was done. These were just rough scribbles. I was trying to find the right words."

"The right ones?" she asked, dazed, her heart so full she couldn't think straight.

"I wanted it to be perfect. You—everyone takes you for granted. No one does or says what they should be doing or saying. The people of this town, your parents, that jerk of a guy who didn't know what he had when he had you…even me…we take and take from you and no one gives the right things.

"And you…Colleen, you forgive us. You even were forgiving Lisa. I could see that you were, and…that cowboy who treated you mean…you let him off with barely an apology. As for me…I let you go. I let you go when every cell in my body was screaming at me to beg you not to. I let you go because I was a coward, because I was afraid that you wouldn't love me back, but that shouldn't have mattered. I should have at least told you how much you mean to me, because you deserve to at least know that—"

He never got to say the words. Colleen launched herself against his bare chest, right against his heart. "You amazing, wonderful man. Did you think I wouldn't love you? I had to bite back tears all the way home so your pilot wouldn't tell you that I cried."

Dillon swore. "I made you cry?"

She shook her head vehemently. "*I* made me cry by falling in love with a man I couldn't have. I love you so much, Dillon, and I have for a long time."

He plunged his fingers into her hair, kissed her lips. "I was being so darn logical," he told her. "Not telling you I cared because I knew you didn't want to fall in love and I knew you were only with me because of Toby. I knew you couldn't care and had to be here, not with me."

"And *I* knew you had to be in Chicago, not with me."

He smiled against her hair. "It's a big, mobile world today. I can do a lot of work from a distance."

"And I have enough people working here and other friends in town willing to help that I don't have to be here all the time. The ranch isn't the same without you here, and I don't need to hide here anymore, but I would like to be here some of the time."

"As much as you need."

She rose on her toes and kissed him again.

"And this building, we'll paint over the words, of course,"

he said. "I want it to be your perfect dream bunkhouse for those girls from the city you want to help."

Colleen smiled up at him. "I don't want you to paint over the words. Maybe I'll get you to build me another one and I'll keep this one as a haven for you and me. I've got a great bed we can put in here and a new sofa sleeper some wonderful man bought for me."

"It better not have been Rob," he teased.

"Oh, this man's much better than Rob," she promised. "I've heard via the grapevine that the man that I'm talking about got his ex-wife to sign over custody to him, but he promised her that she would have visiting rights and she's even thinking of getting to know her little boy a bit. A man like that who puts his child's needs ahead of his own is a good man."

"You know you'll always be his real mother."

A tear slipped down Colleen's cheek. Dillon kissed it away. He got down on one knee.

"Dillon, get up," she said, tugging at him.

"No. I want this to be special. I want you to remember this day and I want to remember it, too. Marry me, Colleen. Marry *us*, me and Toby. Be my wife. Be his mother. Be my love forever."

She took his carpenter's pencil and walked over to the wall. *I will,* she wrote. *I always will. I'll be your love forever. Be mine.*

"On this ranch, in the city, in the country, in a high-rise…everywhere. I'll love you always and everywhere." And he sealed his promise with another kiss.

"Even if I wear red cowgirl boots underneath my wedding dress?" she teased.

"Oh, I'm counting on that. I'm dreaming of it." He kissed her again and her heart turned to flame.

The sound of voices drifted to Colleen, and she and Dillon broke away and turned.

"What are you two doing?" Julie asked with a smile.

"I'm marrying Colleen," Dillon said.

"Harve, I know you've been around a lot lately, but now it's official," Colleen added. "The Applegate is no longer a no-men zone. Dillon changed all that."

"Good," Gretchen said, pulling out her camera. "Now if you two wouldn't mind kissing again, I want a picture to send out. Jace just e-mailed Millie. He and all your friends in Chicago want to know what's happening."

"What's happening is the best day of my life," Dillon said with a laugh.

"And much as we love all of you, Harve included, we'd like a little privacy right now," Colleen added. "No more pictures. And…close the door on your way out, will you?"

"We didn't see a thing," Millie said, closing an imaginary door. "You two just keep kissing."

So they did.

A sneaky peek at next month…

By Request

BACK BY POPULAR DEMAND!

My wish list for next month's titles…

In stores from 20th June 2014:

☐ Hot Bed of Scandal – Anne Oliver, Kate Hardy & Robyn Grady

☐ Taming the Rebel Tycoon – Lee Wilkinson, Ally Blake & Crystal Green

In stores from 4th July 2014:

☐ The Dante Legacy: Blackmail – Day Leclaire

☐ The Baby Surprise – Jessica Hart, Barbara McMahon & Jackie Braun

3 stories in each book – only £5.99!

Available at WHSmith, Tesco, Asda, Eason, Amazon and Apple

Just can't wait?

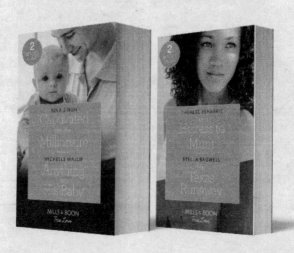

Liz Fielding was born with itchy feet. She made it to Zambia before her twenty-first birthday and, gathering her own special hero and a couple of children on the way, lived in Botswana, Kenya and Bahrain—with pauses for sightseeing pretty much everywhere in between. She finally came to a full stop in a tiny Welsh village cradled by misty hills, and these days mostly leaves her pen to do the travelling. When she's not sorting out the lives and loves of her characters she potters in the garden, reads her favourite authors, and spends a lot of time wondering 'What if…?' For news of upcoming books—and to sign up for her occasional newsletter—visit Liz's website at www.lizfielding.com.